Also by

RACHEL LYNN SOLOMON

Today Tonight Tomorrow
See You Yesterday
We Can't Keep Meeting Like This
Our Year of Maybe
You'll Miss Me When I'm Gone

Past

Present

Future

RACHEL LYNN SOLOMON

SIMON & SCHUSTER BFYR

New York   Amsterdam/Antwerp   London
Toronto   Sydney/Melbourne   New Delhi

SIMON & SCHUSTER BFYR

An imprint of Simon & Schuster Children's Publishing Division
1230 Avenue of the Americas, New York, New York 10020
For more than 100 years, Simon & Schuster has championed authors and the stories they create. By respecting the copyright of an author's intellectual property, you enable Simon & Schuster and the author to continue publishing exceptional books for years to come. We thank you for supporting the author's copyright by purchasing an authorized edition of this book.
No amount of this book may be reproduced or stored in any format, nor may it be uploaded to any website, database, language-learning model, or other repository, retrieval, or artificial intelligence system without express permission. All rights reserved. Inquiries may be directed to Simon & Schuster, 1230 Avenue of the Americas, New York, NY 10020 or permissions@simonandschuster.com.
This book is a work of fiction. Any references to historical events, real people, or real places are used fictitiously. Other names, characters, places, and events are products of the author's imagination, and any resemblance to actual events or places or persons, living or dead, is entirely coincidental.
Text © 2024 by Rachel Lynn Solomon
Cover illustration © 2024 by Laura Breiling
Cover design by Laura Eckes
All rights reserved, including the right of reproduction in whole or in part in any form.
SIMON & SCHUSTER BOOKS FOR YOUNG READERS and related marks are trademarks of Simon & Schuster, LLC.
For information about special discounts for bulk purchases, please contact Simon & Schuster Special Sales at 1-866-506-1949 or business@simonandschuster.com.
Simon & Schuster strongly believes in freedom of expression and stands against censorship in all its forms. For more information, visit BooksBelong.com.
The Simon & Schuster Speakers Bureau can bring authors to your live event. For more information or to book an event, contact the Simon & Schuster Speakers Bureau at 1-866-248-3049 or visit our website at www.simonspeakers.com.
Also available in a SIMON & SCHUSTER BFYR hardcover edition
The text for this book was set in Adobe Garamond Pro.
Manufactured in the United States of America
First SIMON & SCHUSTER BFYR paperback edition August 2025
10 9 8 7 6 5 4 3 2 1
The Library of Congress has cataloged the hardcover edition as follows:
Names: Solomon, Rachel Lynn, author.
Title: Past present future / Rachel Lynn Solomon.
Description: First edition. | New York : Simon & Schuster Books for Young Readers, 2024. | Series: Today tonight tomorrow ; book 2 | Audience: Ages 14 up. | Audience: Grades 10–12. | Summary: Rowan and Neil, in a committed long-distance relationship while attending different colleges in Boston and New York City, face the challenges of navigating the first months of college life and personal struggles as they strive to make their relationship last.
Identifiers: LCCN 2023028572 (print) | LCCN 2023028573 (ebook) | ISBN 9781665901956 (hardcover) | ISBN 9781665901963 (pbk) | ISBN 9781665901970 (ebook)
Subjects: CYAC: Dating—Fiction. | Long-distance relationships—Fiction. | Love—Fiction. | Universities and colleges—Fiction. | LCGFT: Novels.
Classification: LCC PZ7.1.S6695 Pas 2024 (print) |
LCC PZ7.1.S6695 (ebook) | DDC [Fic]—dc23
LC record available at https://lccn.loc.gov/2023028572
LC ebook record available at https://lccn.loc.gov/2023028573

For the readers
who asked if there was
more to the story

Uh-oh, made it through the winter
Uh-oh, summer too warm
I wouldn't live anywhere else but
Don't say you weren't warned!

—"I Love Seattle" by Tacocat

"I've never been the one. Not for anybody."
He closed the distance between them. "You'll get used to it." He tipped her face up to his, kissed her.
"Why? Why am I the one?"
"Because my life opened up, and it flooded with color when you walked back into it."

—*Vision in White* by Nora Roberts

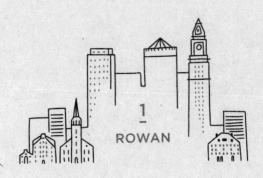

1
ROWAN

ROMANCE NOVELS DON'T talk about what happens when the heroine and hero go off to different colleges.

Of course, this is usually because both people are gainfully employed adults. Maybe they're lobbying for the same promotion, or one is an environmental activist trying to protect a park from a real estate developer—and its unfairly charming CEO. Or one is a governess to three wild rascals whose father is a grumpy, dashing rake with a hidden vulnerability at his core.

There aren't many rakes who attend small liberal arts schools on the East Coast.

"I can't believe I'm saying this," Neil starts, surveying my room with a grim expression, eyes narrowed behind his glasses, "but I think you might be bringing too many books."

I glance up from where I've been pleading with my suitcase's stubborn zipper. "If they're not close to me, how will I be inspired by them?"

Except he might be right, a statement I'd never have allowed to cross my mind until three months ago, because the suitcase is too small and too full and there are still too many things I can't take with me. In my defense, most of my stuff is already packed and waiting in the hall downstairs. This is my last suitcase. The one I've been dreading, because of everything it symbolizes.

When the zipper doesn't budge, I dig a hand inside and extricate two pastel Nora Roberts paperbacks, weighing them for a moment before putting one back on my bookshelf.

Neil lifts an eyebrow. His arms are crossed over his chest, giving him the appearance of a stern, extremely cute statue.

With a groan, I add the other one to the shelf too.

"You said you needed help," he reminds me. "In fact, 'I need you to be ruthless' were your exact words when you sent me that SOS text this morning."

"Yeah, but not about *Nora*." I return my attention to the suitcase, and after an initial stutter, the zipper slides shut. "You know, I think I've been demonstrating extraordinary restraint." I walk over to my closet, nudging aside a few dresses to reveal the stack of mass-market paperbacks that don't fit on my bookshelf, most of them collected from garage sales and thrift stores.

Neil doesn't even look surprised. "Ah, yes. That infamous Rowan Roth restraint. She never exaggerates. Never bends the truth. Never romanticizes anything."

I give him an intense side-eye, and his faux seriousness finally cracks, gaze softening and mouth tilting into a grin.

Late-August sun arrows through my window, illuminating the freckles on his skin and the lovely golden undertones in his auburn hair. This time of year, it doesn't get dark until after ten o'clock, and we've been taking advantage of those daylight hours as much as we can.

Most people seemed to think we wouldn't last the summer, but the past two and a half months have been the best of my life—and that's not an exaggeration at all. Some days Neil would hole up in the café where I work, sitting in a corner with an iced chai, busy with his own summer job—remote transcription for a local law office—and when Two Birds One Scone closed, we'd take unsold pastries to a park or sneak them into a movie theater. We'd bring his sister to the beach or skate park, double-date with Kirby and Mara, argue about *Star Wars* with his friends. A few days ago, we celebrated my nineteenth birthday with a ferry trip to Whidbey Island. We have eaten too much gelato and squinted too many times into the sun, picked out books for each other to read and mapped the entire city on foot. We've gotten great at pushing curfew, chasing sunsets, "just ten more minutes." And then fifteen more after that.

The whole time, what we've really excelled at is putting off talking about the inevitable: the fact that tomorrow, I fly to Boston while he boards a plane to New York.

I turn away from the closet. "You like telling me what to do," I say, placing the tip of my index finger on his sternum and slowly inching it upward. Teasing, which is still one of my favorite things to do to him.

He's already blushing, long lashes fluttering shut. At the

beginning of our relationship, I worried he might stop blushing altogether, and it's been the sweetest surprise that he hasn't, that he wears his emotions so plainly for me. "Only because there's no other circumstance under which you'd allow it."

The spark in my chest when I tug him closer by the collar of his T-shirt is a familiar little thrill. I intend for it to be a quick peck, but the moment my lips meet his, I dissolve.

His hands come up to my hair, deepening the kiss as I propel us backward, shoving at my suitcase to make room for us on the bed. Then I'm in his lap, his earthy scent altering my brain chemistry, each ragged exhale making me crave the next one. His fingertips on the waist of my shirtdress. My mouth on his throat.

There is something about this boy that undoes me every single time, and sometimes I still can't believe all of it is real.

As though perfectly attuned to what's going on behind it, there's a knock on my half-cracked door. Neil and I spring to our feet, smoothing our hair and pretending to be immersed in separate tasks: me, unzipping and rezipping the suitcase, Neil, examining the mug on my desk where I keep my pens and pencils, the one with a watercolor splash of the Seattle skyline.

We've gotten good at that, too, almost as good as my parents are at knowing exactly when we're about to cross the line into PG-13.

It's become something of a joke, albeit a frustrating one: the fact that it's nearly impossible to find some alone time. When we slept together for the first time on the last day of school—or I guess technically, the day after the last day of school, since it happened around four in the morning—neither of us had intended for the relationship to progress that far. I definitely hadn't woken up that day and imagined I'd be kissing my longtime rival Neil McNair, let alone sneaking him into my bedroom. But it had just felt *right*, the two of us being connected in that way. I had this new, persistent ache that I'd never be able to get enough of him; I wanted to have long, sometimes contentious conversations about the world just as much as I wanted to learn all the ways our bodies could fit together. Because even if we went from zero to one hundred in a single night, there's still plenty we haven't done, bases we've skipped that I've been hoping we can find our way back around to.

His sister just hit the age where their mom is comfortable leaving her home alone all day, and my parents work from their downstairs office. A few times, we tangled ourselves in the back seat of my Honda Accord, at least until a police officer banged on the window and it spooked us so much we haven't tried it since.

My dad steps inside my room and greets Neil with a wave before turning to me. "Ro-Ro?" he says, leaning against the doorframe. "You just about ready? We should leave soon if we want to get there by five."

Before answering him, I take a moment to gaze around the room. The bulletin board above my desk, where I've pinned photos of my friends and academic ribbons and a list Neil and I made on the last day of school: Rowan Roth's Guide to College Success . . .

and Beyond! My senior yearbook with his love confession in it, an item too precious to transport across the country because I'm not sure I could bear it if an airline lost it.

And Neil, standing there with an easy smile, one stubborn strand of hair refusing to lie flat.

Yes, and no.

Theoretically, I'm ready, but I'm also not sure how fearlessly I can let go.

"As I'll ever be," I say, and when I close the door, it somehow feels like I'm shutting away so much more.

My parents insisted on a send-off before I leave, a picnic at Green Lake with black-bean burgers and roasted corn. Kirby Taing and Mara Pompetti are already there, no doubt ready to gloat about their extra weeks of summer because the University of Washington doesn't start until the end of September.

Eager to have a job, my dad lights the grill while my mom passes out compostable plates. Neil's mom, Joelle, arrives with a Tupperware of cubed watermelon and a wide-brimmed sun hat. A family of redheads means a lot of SPF.

It's only mildly embarrassing for your parents to meet your boyfriend's mom, something I discovered last month when all five of us went out to dinner. It hadn't happened with my past boyfriends, felt too serious for those relationships. A strange kind of *So, how about our kids' raging hormones?* But they clicked instantly, bonding over their opinions about the new Seattle waterfront (mixed) and whether the Seahawks have a chance at the playoffs this year (no).

We take a few minutes to settle in, exchanging hugs and hellos. All around us, people are playing croquet and walking their dogs and Rollerblading, the latter two occasionally done at the same time, Seattleites soaking up what might be the last nice day of the season. Because in this city, you just never know.

"If someone doesn't promise me this isn't the end, I might cry," Mara says. Her wavy blond hair is in a loose bun, and a minidress emphasizes her calves, toned from years of dance.

With one eye, I watch Neil and my dad standing semi-awkwardly at the grill, as though they've decided that this is how they Bond as Men, though Joelle is the one to inform them that the burgers are starting to burn.

Next to Mara on the park bench, Kirby gives her shoulder a squeeze. "It'll be okay. Just think, only one hundred and twenty-two more days until we're all reunited."

"That's supposed to make me feel better? That's an eternity."

I reach for a passionfruit LaCroix and pop the tab. "Just think about all the times I've annoyed you over the years," I say. "You'll be too busy to miss me. How many credits are you taking again, Mara?"

"Only twenty-two," she says innocently. "I just want to get all my prereqs done as soon as I can." Kirby, long known for try-ing to get as much done with as little effort as possible, is taking the recommended fifteen credits for freshmen, unsure what she'll major in.

"And I still think you should have decided to take Anthropology of Ice Cream with me," Kirby says. "Although if we don't actually get to eat ice cream, I may riot."

Burgers and corn are passed around while we talk more about our fall schedules. My creative writing class is the one I can't wait for, taught by a darling of the literary fiction world whose books I devoured earlier this summer. In college, I will be entirely unashamed of my dream career, and Miranda Everett's class—undeniably full of other aspiring novelists—will be where I take the first step.

Mara bites into her burger. "If your roommate is cooler than we are, please don't tell us."

"Speak for yourself," Kirby says, miming putting on boxing gloves. "Personally, I think it's more advantageous to know your enemies."

"I'm not replacing either of you!"

Neil slides in next to me with his plate of food, our parents immersed in a conversation about the rising cost of textbooks. His knee nudges mine. "Neither am I. Who else could mercilessly torment us about our relationship like you, Kirby?"

It's true: Even though my friends knew how I felt about him before I did, they rarely hesitate to joke about our four-year rivalry and the game that made us realize what idiots we'd been. Lovingly, of course.

Kirby beams. "I try my best."

"Seattle's definitely going to feel smaller without both of you," Mara says as Kirby sinks her teeth into her ear of corn, the kernels blackened and buttered, and it's then that I realize something else: I've been so caught up in the logistics of packing, I've barely processed the fact that in twenty-four hours, I will no longer live here.

The place I've spent my whole life, the city that's just as much a part of me as my troublesome bangs or my affinity for vintage clothes. Case in point: the lavender floral shirtdress I'm wearing now, plucked from a rack at Red Light last month.

I wonder if thrift shopping will be as fun in Boston without my best friends.

Just as the black-bean burger starts to turn uncomfortably in my stomach, my mom calls out to get everyone's attention, lifting her can of seltzer in a toast. "Hear, hear," she says. "To Rowan and Neil, and all the adventures you're going to have next year on the other side of the country. We're all going to miss you, but we know you're going to do great things."

Joelle holds her own can high. "That's lovely, Ilana. To having new experiences and meeting new people, and then coming home and telling us all about it."

"To trying a slice of real New York pizza," Neil says.

"To exploring Boston's independent bookstores," I add, even as a lump forms in my throat. "And never being embarrassed to be caught in the romance section."

Everyone toasts. Sips. The fizz settles my stomach, and I try my best to banish my nerves for the rest of the evening. Because in a matter of hours, this—my life in Seattle—is really, truly ending. I thought I'd made peace with it, allowed myself to mourn while leaving space for all the excitement I'm taking with me to the East Coast. But now I'm just not sure.

Maybe that's how you're supposed to feel on the precipice of drastic change.

By the time the sun begins its descent in the sky, Joelle has to leave to pick up Neil's sister from a friend's house, and my parents, perpetual early risers, are starting to yawn, a fact we considered when we took separate cars. Kirby and Mara, realizing that Neil and I might want just a little more time to ourselves, hug us tight as I promise to text them the moment I land.

It's gotten chilly, but it's nothing that can't be solved by burrowing closer to Neil on the picnic blanket. I brought his heather-gray hoodie with me, the one I don't plan on ever giving back, but I left it in the car. His body heat is so much better.

"On a scale of one to ten, what do you think is the likelihood that our parents will become best friends while we're gone?" he asks, draping his arm across my shoulders and pulling me against his chest.

"At least a nine. It's cute, though. I don't want any of them to be lonely." When I let out a sigh, it sounds much more agonized than I'm anticipating. I'd hoped we could end the night without a therapy session, but apparently I was wrong.

"You're anxious. Do you want to talk about it?"

"Oh, just the usual fear of the unknown," I say. "I think the worst part is that I don't know *any* of what to expect. Every single part of it will be new. I can visualize the campus, but not my dorm room or my classrooms. I don't know what Boston's transit cards look like or if my professors will like me or where I'll sit when I'm calling you."

"Is it unhelpful if I remind you that you don't have to have it all planned out right now?"

"No, but it doesn't change the fact that I *want* to," I say with a small whine.

For a few thoughtful beats, he lets his fingertips play through my hair. A gentle rhythm. "Do you remember," he says, "sophomore year, when honors English went on that field trip to see a modern reimagining of *Macbeth* and we wound up sitting next to each other?"

"Shhh! The Scottish play," I quickly correct him. As if I don't remember all of it. Every moment of the last four years. "The one where all the characters worked in a McDonald's, and Lady Macbeth kept trying to scrub ketchup off her hands? Of course. I should probably apologize, huh. I think I tried to get Sean to switch seats with me."

His laugh drums against my cheek, that sound I love becoming something almost tangible. "You asked, once, if I remembered when I started having feelings for you. And I think that was it. The whole time we watched, I could hear everyone else making fun of it, but you were so quiet. You paid attention because it was school, and the fact that it was a field trip didn't change that. When you laughed, it was genuine. Sincere. The acting was terrible, but you took it seriously. And a couple times, you glanced over at me to see if I was laughing too."

"You were," I say, that seemingly trivial day coming back to me. A dark theater, my nemesis next to me. The pride that comes with getting the humor, obnoxious smart alecks that we were. Are. "At the same time, usually."

"Right. And it made me feel so connected to you, the fact that you were curious if I found the same things funny. Plus . . . you smelled really nice. I went home and thought to myself, 'This is it. This is the girl.' I was done for." His thumb travels down the length of my neck, and it would be so easy to close my eyes and fall asleep like this as the sky turns dark. Then he buries his nose in my hair, takes a deep inhale. "Still just as intoxicating."

I laugh-yelp as he does this, pretending to push him away.

"You've been important to me for years," he continues, as though he knows I need the reassurance, and I tuck those words right next to my heart. "The distance isn't going to change that."

We shift on the blanket, Neil sliding me on top of him while he kisses me, and it isn't long before I'm pressing myself more firmly against his jeans, grateful the park has emptied out. I've given a little thought to missing him like *this*, the abject neediness of his breaths and mine. The groan when my lips settle in the spot where his neck meets his shoulder. His hands on my hips and mine on his face, as though if we just cling tight enough, we can make those weeks go by that much faster.

I never expected to fall so hard, so quickly for someone right before our lives split in different directions. Even if my feelings had been dormant for most of high school, that night in June put the past four years in such sharp, renewed focus. A rose-tinted filter. While I also never thought I'd be starting college with a boyfriend, I can't imagine how I'd feel if we'd given ourselves an expiration date, the way some couples in our graduating class did, determined to go to school with zero attachments. A few times, I wondered if we'd break up before August and wouldn't have to worry about it.

But the thing is, dating Neil McNair isn't actually all that different from sparring with him. We just get to make out afterward.

Being with Neil, I realized a few weeks into our relationship, is *easy*. Which naturally makes me more convinced the universe was playing a trick on us this summer, two and a half months of bliss before catapulting us into a long-distance relationship.

All my years of planning and daydreaming, the times I swore I'd be different and live more in the moment, and the imminence of it takes me completely by surprise. It's nerves and uncertainty and a touch of nausea knotted up in one twisted ball.

It's the fear that once I drive away tonight, we will never again have what we had this summer.

Eventually we have to head back to my car, one of the last ones in the parking lot after we circled and circled to find a spot hours ago. His hair is wonderfully mussed, my body still buzzing with a desperate electricity. As though my bones and muscles cannot bear to let him go.

The drive is too short—we pull up to his house after several detours and "just five more minutes" that somehow last almost thirty. With more effort than it's ever taken, I shut off the engine and engage the parking brake, an ominous silence filling the car.

"We were too spoiled," I say, staring directly ahead because if I look at him, I might not be able to hold it together. "Seeing each other nearly every day for the past four years."

Neil shakes his head; I catch the motion out of the corner of my eye. "No, no, no. I was pining for most of those four years, absolutely tortured because the girl I liked couldn't stand me. You were simply going about your life, vaguely annoyed by some guy with too many freckles."

"Maaaaaybe. But before we got together, I couldn't imagine not seeing you every day. Did I ever tell you that?" I turn to him, and the look on his face tells me that I did not. "The few weeks leading up to graduation, I'd get your texts in the morning and feel a little sad that they were coming to an end."

A patented Neil McNair smirk. "And you, connoisseur of romance novels, didn't realize you were madly in love with me."

"Yeah, well. We all have our flaws."

When he reaches for my hand, there's no trace of humor in his expression. "I miss you already," he says as we thread our fingers together. "Is that weird?"

"We'll text and talk all the time. I already have my train ticket for the end of September."

"And then I'll be in Boston for Thanksgiving."

"Why does that feel so far away?"

Suddenly I'm worried we haven't discussed it enough, that we spent too much time living in the moment this summer when we should have mapped out call schedules with color-coded spreadsheets.

It's what High School Rowan might have done, but I guess that's not who I am anymore.

"We're going to be okay." His voice is solid, and his eyes on me will never not make me feel so wholly *seen*. "I can't wait to show you New York. Assuming, of course, that I know my way around after a month." A soft smile. "I love you, Artoo."

The nickname has its intended effect: to remind me that all our history cannot be undone just because we'll be in two different states.

"I love you too." I hold him close. Inhale deeply. One more kiss, and then another. "Fly safe and don't forget me."

"Impossible."

I try to stop the statistics about long-distance relationships racing through my mind as he opens the passenger door, kisses two fingers, and holds them to his heart. With a grit I honed over four years of trying to best him, I push aside the anxiety and replace it with a fierce resolve.

We're going to be the ones who make it.

After all, overachieving is kind of what we're known for.

Neil,

Hard to believe we're almost at the end of this.

I suppose in a way, I'll miss you, the same way you miss a pesky mosquito trapped between the window and the screen. You're not happy it's there, exactly, but when the buzzing stops, something just feels off.

I kid, I kid. You're much nicer than a mosquito, which is a strange thing to realize on the last day of school, but there it is. From elections to gym class contests, you've really kept me on my toes, too. Rude to find out that you're a decent human being underneath it all. Don't get a big head about this, but . . . I'm glad we teamed up today, even if we don't end up winning. (But how could we not?!)

Because I think, deep down, I might actually miss everything. Just a little.

Best of luck next year. HAGS! (Please know I mean that ironically.)

Rowan "Artoo" Roth

2
NEIL

"PLEASE STOW YOUR tray tables and return your seats to their upright positions," says a flight attendant over the intercom, and despite my grogginess, I'm quick to comply. An ardent rule-follower, even 2,415 miles away from home, according to the flight tracker on the screen in front of me.

Out the window, swaths of blue sky paint the horizon, barely a cloud in sight. I crane my neck to get a better view of the city taking shape beneath me, the island jutting into the East River—or is it the Hudson?—and buildings stacked like child's toys. A topographical map come to life.

"It's my first time in New York," I explain to the middle-aged woman sitting next to me when I accidentally jostle her armrest, if my eagerness hasn't already given me away. First time on a plane, too, but somehow that seems embarrassing to admit to a stranger. She just gives me a lift of her eyebrows and a mumbled "congratulations."

I try to imagine taking this flight so frequently that the views cease to impress. Even if I make this trip one hundred times, I am somehow certain I'll remain the overexcited passenger with his face pressed to the window, dying for a first glimpse of the destination.

Ever since I learned of its existence, I have dreamed of New York. My mom grew up outside Philadelphia and spent long weekends there in the summer as a teenager, and I've always wished we still had family on the East Coast so we'd have had a reason to visit. She talked about it like it was an amusement park, a one-of-a-kind sensory experience—the food and the energy and all the different languages she heard on the street, how you could never feel truly alone, no matter the time of day. I couldn't get enough of those stories. I pictured it the way it's shown in movies, with that famous, now-cliché shot of a New York City sidewalk: everyone in their own worlds as they bustle down the street to wherever they're going. Because everyone is always going *somewhere*, somewhere important, and I loved the idea of being caught in that tidal wave of determination. Of ambition.

Anytime I felt lonely, I simply reminded myself that one day I'd be swept up in that same tidal wave.

As I grew older, I set my sights specifically on NYU. We couldn't afford a visit, but that didn't matter—its top-tier linguistics program seemed a perfect match. I was certain I was meant to be there.

The only thing New York doesn't have going for it is the fact that Rowan Roth isn't in it.

Last night, I told her I missed her already, but the truth is that I have missed her all summer. Every moment she smiled, laughed, gazed at me in a way that made my heart swell—so, approximately 99 percent of the time we spent together—felt like something to stow in a secret pocket of my suitcase and take back out when we were deep in winter.

If we last that long, a tiny voice always reminded me, but it's been easy enough to ignore.

Now, as the plane's wheels strike the ground and we hurtle toward a stop, that voice is a little louder.

I text both Rowan and my mom that I've landed, adjusting my watch to Eastern time while waiting my turn to wrestle my carry-on down from the overhead bin. While I'm sure a digital watch would be more practical, this one belonged to my grandpa on my mom's side, who gave it to me as a sixteenth-birthday gift. The silver has dulled and the band is worn, but it ticks like a champ.

My sister Natalie's already sent me a picture of Lucy, our nine-year-old golden retriever, curled up on my bed. *Make sure she doesn't forget me*, I message Natalie, and she replies *on it*, with a photo of Lucy posed with one of our old family albums.

The flight was smoother than I imagined, my motion sickness kept at bay with some Dramamine tablets and a series adaptation of one of my favorite books, *War and Peace*, that I'd always meant to get around to watching and Rowan loved to tease me about.

"You're a nineteenth-century nobleman trapped in an eighteen-year-old's body," she said last month before giving me another one of those looks. Deep brown eyes, one side of her mouth curving upward, pure mischief. "Guess I have a thing for older guys."

I navigate JFK with my shoulders high, masquerading as a seasoned traveler as I follow the signs to baggage claim. My mom initially planned to help me move in, but Natalie falling off her skateboard and breaking her wrist earlier this summer necessitated a hospital bill we couldn't have budgeted for. Over and over, I assured her that it was okay, that I would be fine on my own, but I could see the guilt on her face as I packed my suitcases and then as she spent most of last night's picnic talking to Rowan's mom, who's probably getting off the plane in Boston with her right now.

I spot my bags right away, which instills in me a sense of false hope that the rest of this transition will be just as easy. It's only after I haul them off the belt that I realize traversing the New York City subway system for the first time with two massive suitcases and an overstuffed backpack may be a bit of a challenge.

My eyes snag on the signs for rideshares and taxis, and the mental calculations begin. I worked through high school, and combined with loans and work-study and a generous financial aid package, I should be able to get through freshman year comfortably enough, while allowing myself the occasional splurge on meals out and other activities. Plus, there's the prize money from winning Howl with Rowan—our school's senior class game that also happened to bring us together, although she insists I was the true winner because I happened to be the one who crossed the finish line—most of which I haven't touched. I already have alerts set to notify me of the lowest prices for my trip home in December.

Even so, all of it sits heavy on my chest, not unlike the pressure I lived with throughout high school. *Do more. Work harder. It'll all pay off soon.* I've been able to ignore it most of the summer, but now that I'm surrounded by the unfamiliar, it pushes against my lungs, winds its way up my throat.

I've only been in New York for forty-five minutes. If I'm already worrying about money, I'll barely last a week.

With a determined set of my jaw, I grab the handles of my suitcases and make my way toward the AirTrain to Jamaica Station. Once I get out, though, I'm expecting the subway to be right there—and it's not. I blink back and forth between the signs that lead back to JFK and the ones pointing toward the street, with symbols for the E, J, and Z trains. Still, I don't entirely trust Google Maps and want to make sure I'm going to the right place.

"Excuse me, is this the—"

The guy blazes past before I can even get the sentence out. Face flaming, I approach someone else. "Sorry, hi, does this train go to Washington Square Park?"

The woman yanks an earbud out of her ear. "What?" she asks, and I repeat the question. "You'll want to take the E to West Fourth and Washington Square. Can't miss it."

"Thank you so much."

Eventually I find the platform, huffing from the effort, my T-shirt pasted to my back. A few minutes to catch my breath.

Neil: *Is it dorky if I'm not even in the city yet and already taking photos of the subway station?*

Rowan's response is immediate.

yes, but the dorkiness is part of why I love you so much.

I still can't believe this is something we do, casual texting that isn't laced with barbs or taunts. When I confessed my feelings in her yearbook, I never anticipated she'd do anything but laugh in my face. Or maybe she'd pity me—that would have been worse. But school was over, I rationalized, and I'd only have to live with the humiliation for a short time. I could probably get over her by the end of the summer, especially if I wasn't seeing her every day.

Then we danced together in that darkened library. Fought with frosting at Two Birds One Scone. She wore my hoodie and read her writing at an open mic and met me at the Museum of Mysteries for Howl's final clue. We argued—because of course we did—before she kissed me for the first time, a kiss that may have permanently rerouted my neurons, tattooed ROWAN FUCKING ROTH all over my prefrontal cortex. And then a handful of other things for the first time, too.

Twenty-four hours, and our relationship had completely changed.

Her text is enough to soothe some of the remaining tension in my chest as the E train roars into the station, everyone on the platform seemingly unaffected by the noise. I drag my suitcases inside and claim an empty seat, my whole body still pulsing with adrenaline.

A sudden grin takes over my face, a broad and ridiculous thing I don't even try to contain. I'm on the subway going into

Manhattan, where I'll be a freshman at my dream school. New York has always meant freedom, and now here I am.

Then a guy stumbles into my car, flings out an arm to catch one of the poles, and promptly throws up on the seat next to me.

New York may be eager to humble me, but I manage to get into the city without any additional catastrophes.

My dorm is a magnificent brick building on the western edge of Washington Square Park, somehow both imposing and welcoming, though the latter may be due to the violet NYU flags waving in the breeze. One of the things I loved most about NYU from my research is that there is no actual campus, technically. There's no tree-lined quad like other schools have, no central square. The city is the campus, dozens of buildings spread across blocks and blocks, most of them here in Greenwich Village.

"You're going to get kicked out if anyone hears you saying 'Green-witch' instead of 'Gren-itch,'" my mom warned before I left, and I promised her I wouldn't dare. Besides, like any good aspiring lexicographer, I'd already looked up the etymology of it years ago, learning it had come from the Old English word *Grenevic* and had most likely never been pronounced "Green-witch."

Somehow I'm not sure this fun fact will make me any instant friends—but if it ever would, this is certainly the place.

After I check in and get my keys, I wait for the elevator to take me to the sixth floor. The dorm is a flurry of move-in commotion, most doors thrown wide open and the hallways crammed with more cardboard boxes than I've ever seen. And one detail I hadn't anticipated but probably should have: everyone is here with their parents.

Fighting off a too-early pang of homesickness, I make a vow to myself. Whatever it takes, I'm getting my mom back out here.

The hall is decorated with construction-paper cutouts of New York landmarks: the Statue of Liberty and the Empire State Building and the Brooklyn Bridge. And there's my name on the door to room 608: NEIL MCNAIR.

Over the summer, I'd made an appointment to legally change my last name but backed out before paying the fee. I hadn't been ready, even after I spent so long convincing myself I was. The idea of having a different last name from my sister when she'd been too young to remember everything that happened with our father—it held me back.

I told myself I could wait until I was truly certain, and even now, seeing my full name on the door, it doesn't seem strange to me. I thought I wanted to start college with no ties to the man who gave me that name, but I've been Neil McNair for eighteen years. It's on the academic awards and certificates of achievement and high school diploma. Yes, it's his name. But it's mine, too.

Before I see anyone in the room, I hear two male voices with thick New York accents having a loud but not angry conversation about either baseball or football, I'm not sure. I'm exhausted and sweaty and in desperate need of a shower, and my adrenaline has given way to anxiety. I'll be sleeping next to a complete stranger for the better part of a year, which is obviously a very normal part of the college experience and yet suddenly seems like a hell of a lot to leave up to chance.

Gingerly, I knock on the door, despite having a key. I don't want to interrupt anyone. When it opens, I'm faced with two broad-shouldered guys nearly the spitting image of each other: brown hair and blue eyes, casual in jeans and T-shirts, though one is five inches taller and probably thirty years younger.

Skyler Benedetti is a Staten Island native I messaged on NYU's roommate app over the summer. I sent a paragraph; he sent back *awesome man can't wait!!* ✌️

"Hi, I'm Neil," I say with an awkward wave. I point to my name on the door, as though needing it to back me up.

"Hey!" Skyler straightens to his full height, so tall that I'm unsure these beds can contain him, and gives me a half handshake, half high five. He's in a New York Yankees T-shirt and has the most symmetrical face I have ever seen. "Skyler. Good to meet you!"

"Sorry, I hope I'm not interrupting—"

"Nah, my dad and I were just saying that I could handle living with a Giants fan but probably not a Mets fan." His face turns serious. "Don't tell me you're a Mets fan."

"I, uh, don't follow sports."

I take a moment to glance around the room. The two sides mirror each other: beds and wooden bookshelf-desk combos and two tiny closets. Plain white walls, except for where Skyler's tacking up an NYU pennant. A plain blue comforter is draped haphazardly across one bed, a suitcase spilling open on top of it. I haul my largest suitcase onto the other bed.

"Probably the safest answer. You'll avoid a lifetime of disappointment that way," Skyler's dad says with a chuckle. He extends a hand. "Marc Benedetti. Your parents around here somewhere?"

I clear my throat. *Exhale.* This isn't a test. "I just flew in from Seattle. My mom wanted to come, but she couldn't get the time off work." It sounds better than *we couldn't afford it.*

"Lucky," Skyler says, so brazen even in front of his dad. Finished with the pennant, he extracts a sweatshirt from the duffel bag on top of his bed, STATEN ISLAND TECHNICAL HIGH SCHOOL blazoned across it, along with an image of a seagull. It doesn't escape my notice that his school's name is abbreviated as SITHS, which makes my inner *Star Wars* nerd—and probably outer *Star Wars* nerd, let's be honest—wildly jealous I didn't go there. "My dad's obsessed with reliving his glory years. He went here too."

"Those were some good times." Marc props an arm on Skyler's desk chair, his eyes lighting up. "Did I ever tell you about when my friends and I dared each other to go streaking through Washington Square Park at midnight?"

A groan from Skyler, indicating he's probably heard this story many, many times. "Unfortunately."

His dad holds a hand to his heart. "I met your mother that night. The most romantic night of my life."

"We can stop there," Skyler says. "Dad. Please don't scare my roommate away."

I can't help laughing at all of this as I unzip my suitcase, pulling out towels, pillowcases, extra-long twin sheets. For a moment I wonder about my dad's glory years, whatever they might have been. I don't allow myself to think of him often, but being confronted with the Benedettis right here in the space in which I'm going to live for the next nine months makes it inevitable.

I do know that for a while, my parents were happy. They met at work in their early twenties as cashiers at a home improvement megastore, but my dad had dreams of starting his own smaller shop one day, and my mom got pregnant with me after they'd been dating for a year. Although she had hoped to go back to school once she saved enough, she put that on hold, working nights while my dad worked days and her sister helped take care of me. Neither of them had big extended families—my mom's parents, who moved the family from Philly to Seattle when my mom was sixteen, had been only children, and though my dad was rooted in the Northwest, his parents were much older and he didn't have any siblings. They didn't have a lot of money, but from everything my mom has told me about that time in their lives, it didn't matter. They had each other, and they were building a family together.

Then there was the hardware store my dad opened that struggled to turn a profit. The drinking. The angry outbursts.

The night he caught a couple kids stealing when he was about to close up, and the moment he grabbed a bat from behind the counter and changed our lives forever.

The felony conviction when I was just eleven years old, a mouthful of words that even a child who loved words could barely understand.

Assault in the first degree.

A fifteen-year sentence.

Our lives, entirely warped.

Most of it, I've compartmentalized. I've shrunk it and hidden it away until it's nothing more than a speck. Infinitesimal, and yet somehow always there. Even when I try to put it behind bars.

Marc leaves to get something from their car while Skyler continues unpacking, hanging up a few button-downs and lazily folding some T-shirts. One thing I've learned from years of altering my own Goodwill suits: those shirts are definitely going to wrinkle. But Skyler seems unbothered, humming to himself and every so often swiping a hand through his artfully floppy hair.

"So, you're from here?" I ask as I stretch a sheet over my bed, though the answer seems obvious.

"Staten Island born and raised. And proud of it." He says this last part as though worried I might fight him on it, and I'm getting the feeling that New York as a state is a crucial part of his personality.

"So I know who to ask if I get lost."

He waves a hand, casual. Everything about Skyler seems casual:

the relaxed slope of his posture, the way he talks with his dad, how he decides to plug in his mini fridge instead of charging his laptop before I offer him one of the two surge protectors I packed. "New York's easy—most of Manhattan's on a grid. Avenues run north and south and streets run east and west. That'll help you out more than you might think."

He unfurls a piece of art designed like one of those old motivational posters, with a kitten poised on the edge of a table, trying to bat a fish out of its bowl. In lieu of something inspirational, HERE FOR A GOOD TIME, NOT A LONG TIME is printed across the top.

"I'm in the Gallatin school," Skyler says. "That's the one where you design your own concentration—they're really particular about not calling it a major. Pretty stoked about it, especially after I saw that someone last year graduated with a concentration in Orange. Literally just the color orange. What about you?"

"That's really cool." At NYU, you're admitted to a specific program; very few people start undecided. "I'm linguistics, which sounds a lot less thrilling than Orange."

"Oh shit. So I better watch my grammar around you, huh? Because if I'm being completely honest, I still have no idea when to use *lie* versus *lay*. Or *laid*." Then he lifts his eyebrows, his mouth forming a smirk. "Unless we're talking about very specific circumstances."

Here is the thing. I don't necessarily have low self-esteem, but there are some guys I can tell I'm going to have a difficult time bonding with, as though there is some kind of unspoken hierarchy and I am not exactly at the top. And it has nothing to do with the correct usage of "lie" and "lay." My closest friends from high school, Adrian Quinlan, Sean Yee, and Cyrus Grant-Hayes, are at UC Davis, UW, and Western. Last week, Sean sent a photo of his school's new computer lab to our group chat and we all geeked out over it. We were the presidents of the student council, chess club, robotics club, and Anime Appreciation Society. We even called ourselves "the Quad," short for quadrilateral, because—well, no big mystery, there were four of us. They're great guys, but none of us were under any delusions of popularity. We didn't talk about relationships and we very rarely made references to sex—largely because none of us were having it.

But even though Skyler Benedetti doesn't strike me as the kind of person who'd have seamlessly fit into my friend group back home, maybe here in New York, none of that matters.

"Getting late," Marc says when he returns with one last suitcase, peeking at his watch and then tapping the door. "You want to grab a bite with us, Neil?"

"I don't want to intrude." I glance at Skyler, waiting for some slight signal that maybe he wants this time with his dad to himself.

"Not intruding. By the end of the year, I'm sure we'll be like brothers."

I try to imagine myself integrating into this family of very tall, very confident men. I have no reason to say no, even if they're just being polite.

"Sure," I say after a beat. "Dinner sounds great." And then, worried about the kind of impression I might be making: "Do you mind if I hop in the shower first?"

After I've rinsed off the flight, we end up at a nearby pizza place, much to my delight, where Marc declares a little too loudly that it isn't as good as Staten Island pizza—though he and Skyler can't agree on which pizzeria is best. They argue and snip at each other in this practiced, loving way, and when Marc asks about my family, I mention only my mom and Natalie and Christopher, my mom's boyfriend, and no questions are asked about my dad. Marc even invites me to their house for Thanksgiving. I can't quite believe I'm having this conversation over pizza with two people who were strangers a few hours ago.

Four years of high school, and even earlier than that, I dreamed of going somewhere no one knew my past. A gorgeous city full of opportunity. A place I built up in my mind for so long that sometimes I worried it would never live up to the fantasy.

I have been enamored with words for much of my life, and yet no matter how deeply I root through my mental vocabulary, I cannot find the precise language to describe this feeling. So I settle for something simple:

Finally.

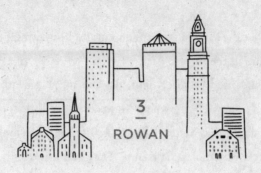

3
ROWAN

WHEN I UNLOCK the door, I'm convinced I have the wrong room. Because it already looks like two people—or maybe even a half dozen—live here, piles of clothes stacked on both beds, photos and fairy lights strung up on three fourths of the available wall space, notebooks and folders strewn across the desks.

The only thing missing is my actual roommate.

"Dios mío," my mom says under her breath, eyeing the walls with a particularly venomous glare. "That wasn't very considerate of her."

"Maybe she didn't think I'd be moving in today." I nudge aside an ironing board, almost impaling a stuffed penguin perched atop a tower of textbooks. "Or at all."

As gently as I can, I transfer a mound of sweaters from what I assume is my bed to the other. Despite what I reassured Kirby and Mara, I've kind of been hoping my roommate and I become lifelong friends. *I was Rowan's college roommate,* she'd say during her toast at my potential future wedding, *for better or for worse.* Then we'd share a wink because of all the mischief we got into back then. But Paulina Radowski from Sacramento never responded to my follow request on Instagram and remains as much of a mystery as the day her name popped into my email with the subject line *Successful Roommate Match!* Mostly I'm just impressed that she managed to do so much to the room in so little time.

My mom holds tightly to her purse, as though trying to protect it from the chaos. "It's . . . nice."

I roll my eyes, dropping my navy JanSport into a desk chair. "It's not supposed to be a luxury apartment. That's part of the experience."

Even though my mom and I are close, this trip is the most extended time we've spent alone together in . . . well, ever. Maybe because they work together, my parents have always functioned as a unit. They've always trusted me, either because I got good grades and stayed out of trouble or because I wanted to maintain that trust by continuing to get good grades and staying out of trouble. Sometimes they joked they barely had to parent me at all. I'm not sure what it must feel like for my mom, dropping off her only kid at college across the country.

She helps me unpack as much as possible before we make a list of everything we still need. I tell her we can figure out the public transportation, but she insists on renting a car, and I don't protest.

I applied to ten schools and picked Emerson because it seemed like the kind of place that valued creativity above all else. There's a heavy focus on the arts, and even walking through my dorm, I spot flyers for theater tryouts and comedy shows and all kinds of performance art. It was a bit of a gamble, given I'd never been there—a gamble Neil was taking too, since this is also his first time in New York. But as soon as I stepped onto campus, saw the towering brick buildings contrasted with the newer, more energy-efficient ones, I knew I'd made the right decision. I'd only ever pictured Boston as romantic and snow-dusted, didn't quite anticipate the blistering heat at the end of summer. But this is beautiful too, sprawling green lawns and the sun turning ancient pathways amber.

We stop at Target, and even on the opposite coast, the familiarity of a Target is oddly soothing. We left the bigger items for this shopping trip, figuring it would be easier. During the drive back to campus, we detour through Beacon Hill, and I can't stop myself from gazing out the window, trying to take in every detail of this new city. Uneven cobblestone streets. Row houses in shades of deep red. Gorgeous old streetlamps that threaten to pull me back in time. I love it all.

There's no sign of messy, mysterious Paulina Radowski when we get back.

"I swear, it wasn't this complicated when I was in college," my mom says as we struggle with a fitted sheet. She pauses to shove a dark curl out of her face, jostling her orange glasses. "Shower shoes? Since when do showers require a specific type of footwear?"

"Maybe they just didn't care about foot fungus back then," I mutter.

My RA stops by and introduces herself, a junior named Lexie who's majoring in comedic arts.

"You must be funny, then!" my mom says, and I have to fight a cringe.

Lexie gives her the kind of practiced smile that indicates she gets this question a lot. "Oh, sometimes. Would you believe that most comedy is born from tragedy?"

This might be the real tragedy: when Lexie leaves and my mom says, "She seemed nice. Maybe you two will end up becoming friends."

It's such standard mom behavior, and yet I can't explain why it irks me. "Pretty sure befriending your RA is like being the teacher's pet. Not sure if that's the reputation I want."

Both of us might be a little hangry, so we head to the dining hall, which I imagine will be some kind of sad buffet. But this— there's a sandwich bar, a pasta bar, a build-your-own burrito bar. Vegetarian options galore, everything marked with symbols for potential allergens.

"When can I move in?" my mom jokes as we get in line for burrito bowls. Then, when we take a seat: "You're not too embarrassed to be sitting with your mom?"

All around us, new freshmen are doing the same thing, some of them staring down at their plates while their parents talk, others on their phones. There are some sparse groups of students, but it's overall fairly calm.

"Of course not." This time, my smile is genuine, because I really do feel this way. "I'm glad you came. Thank you."

Because it's true that everything is new and different, but the undercurrent of excitement is stronger than the anxiety. I think I could really love it here, and not just because this burrito bowl is delicious.

We talk about my classes, about the books she and my dad are working on right now. Together they've written more than thirty children's books, my mom as the author and my dad as the illustrator. And yet more than my creative writing class, my mom is thrilled that I'm taking a 200-level Spanish course.

"I'm sure it'll be a lot of grammar," she says. "A lot of reading."

"Two things I love."

An easy smile. My mom was born in Mexico to a Mexican father and a Russian-Jewish mother, but I stopped taking Spanish junior year and haven't managed to become fluent. I used to hate that I wasn't, but maybe the silver lining is that I'm all the more eager to learn. To feel more connected to that piece of my culture.

"There's something I've wanted to talk to you about," she says. I motion with my compostable fork—maybe Boston and Seattle aren't that different after all—for her to continue. "It's about Neil."

I gesture to my phone, face up on the table. "He said he's out to dinner with his roommate and his roommate's dad, and I can't wait to hear *that* story."

"Good. That's good." Then she pokes at the brown rice in her bowl in this way that makes me certain something serious is coming. A little cough. "You know we love him, Ro—we have from the beginning. He's been nothing but kind to you and to us. And it's very sweet, how much he loves the Riley books."

We've talked about Neil before, of course. When I got home late one night back in July, she was still awake in her office, and emerged to ask if I was being safe. I said yes, but that I'd been thinking about it and I might want to get an IUD. She agreed that it was probably a good idea, so we made the appointment and she took me to have it implanted. Kept me company on the couch the rest of the day as I waited for the cramping to go away.

"But," my mom continues, a novel's worth of meaning in that single word, "you've only been together . . ."

"Almost three months," I supply, that length of time suddenly sounding so small. Three months doesn't account for all the time we spent trying to one-up each other at school, all the times I counted his freckles during class and later tried to rationalize that this did not mean my feelings for him were anything but simple curiosity.

Even at graduation, a mere forty-eight hours after we'd cemented our relationship, it felt like we'd been together for much longer. After I delivered my salutatorian speech and the two of us switched places, he squeezed my hand behind the podium so no one else could see. During his valedictorian speech, as he talked about what we'd accomplished as a class and what the future might hold, his eyes caught mine more than they probably should have. I was convinced I'd never seen anything more beautiful than that boy in a graduation gown, gazing at me with the purest admiration on his face. In every photo from that day, we are easy smiles and soft touches.

Now my mom has moved on to shredding a napkin. "This isn't easy for me to say, Ro. Your father and I talked about it before, and—"

"You two have been discussing my relationship?"

"Well—of course. You two became very serious, very quickly. You can understand how there was a little whiplash, hearing about this guy you despised and then suddenly you were bringing him home and telling us he was your boyfriend." At this, my face grows warm. "We're just wondering . . . if maybe now isn't the best time to be tying yourself down."

I pause with a forkful of plant-based al pastor halfway to my mouth. There's no way she's saying what I think she's saying, but I have to make sure. "I'm lost. Are you telling me to cheat on my boyfriend?"

Her eyes go wide behind her glasses. "No! My goodness. We would never—*no*," she affirms, brushing this off with a strained little laugh. "Just that you're going to be meeting so many new people here, people from all over, with all kinds of different backgrounds. I don't want you to feel like Neil is holding you back from any of it, and not just romantically. I want you to have the best four years here, and it might be tough if you're constantly running back to your dorm for a scheduled video call or using your weekends to go to New York instead of spending time with friends here."

I let those words sink in. Sure, in the back of my mind those fears have prodded at me, too. But I've always dismissed them. We were living in the moment this summer, which made those fears feel like wasted time.

"Being with Neil doesn't mean I can't have fun here at Emerson." There's an edge to my voice, a tone I'm not used to taking with either of my parents. A twinge of annoyance, a clench of my jaw. "I'm not going to be locked in my room the whole time on the phone with him. You should know I'm not the kind of person to let a relationship get in the way of school. I think I made that pretty clear in high school."

"I know that. You're a smart girl. But things are different now, with you being out here on your own," she says. "This is your education. Your future. It's the most important thing in the world, even if it doesn't feel that way."

Now that twinge deepens, an unfamiliar frustration tightening my chest. I can't believe we're having this conversation. "Mom. I know. Did I not demonstrate that for the past four years, even when I was dating other people?" My mom and I have never snipped at each other, not like this, and it makes me even more eager to end this conversation. Criticism from my parents has never felt quite this personal before. "I've worked too hard to get here. Neil doesn't change any of that."

"We just don't want you to get too in your head. You know— with all the books you read. You don't have to settle down quite yet. That's all we're saying."

It's a not-so-subtle jab at my genre of choice, something they've only recently become aware of. For years, I hid my love of romance novels, worried both friends and family would judge me. My parents have mostly been accepting, even taking a couple book recommendations, but every so often, I get the sense that they wish I loved something else.

If this really is all they're saying, then why do I feel like they might actually mean so much more?

My mom's staying in a hotel nearby and flies back tomorrow, and I don't want to end the trip on this note. But when she asks if I want to catch one of the move-in-week comedy shows, I lie and tell her I'm too tired, that I want to make sure I have all my energy for tomorrow's freshmen orientation.

The rest of the night, as I play Cards Against Humanity with some other freshmen in the eighth-floor lounge, Greta from Los Angeles and Minato from Tokyo and Ben from "just down the road in Quincy," as Paulina never shows up and I grow marginally worried about her and Neil texts me photos he's sneakily taken of his roommate's questionable taste in posters, I turn over my mom's words. And I make a promise to myself.

As much as I love him, I won't let having a boyfriend keep me from the full college experience. I don't want to put our relationship on a pedestal behind unbreakable glass, but there's a happy medium here. We're good together, and I'd be an idiot to give that up just because we don't live in the same city.

There's no reason I can't have both.

ROWAN

tell me again why I registered for a class that starts at 8 a.m.?

NEIL

Because you've wanted to study creative writing for years and you couldn't miss an opportunity to learn from this professor?

ROWAN

ughhhhh. past rowan was an absolute menace

NEIL

A cute menace.

ROWAN

are you trying to seduce me?

4
NEIL

THERE ARE FEW things I love more than the beginning of a school year, new binders and crisp notebooks and sharpened pencils all holding that promise of *possibility*.

In high school, September also meant Rowan Roth, the girl who tormented me all year and yet I inexplicably—and then all-too-explicably—missed during the summer break.

My family always bought school supplies at a dollar store or drugstore clearance aisle, though we reused as much as we could from year to year. But every August, my mom would bring us to the Office Depot in Ballard because she knew just how much I loved it.

"You can pick one thing," she'd say, while my dad grumbled about how it should be illegal to charge that much for a ballpoint pen. If he was even there—sometimes he'd complain he was too tired and stay in bed. My mom added the stipulation, "Anything you want, as long as it's under twenty dollars," after I tried to exploit the vagueness of "pick anything you want" to get an ergonomic office chair I definitely did not need when I was nine.

I approached this selection with as much logic as I could. I wouldn't pick anything too basic, no paper products or pencils. And why go for a tricolor set of slightly nicer highlighters when a twelve-pack would last me much longer?

Before I left for New York, I allowed myself to splurge on one thing with a portion of the Howl money: a new laptop to replace the aging Dell that coughed its way toward graduation, and I'm still not used to how the keys don't stick.

After a week of orientation activities that included a bus trip to Bed Bath & Beyond and a welcome seminar at a theater uptown, it's time for classes. While I've enjoyed this "the city is your campus!" introduction to NYU, I'm more than ready. That phrase has already been uttered an inordinate number of times, to the point where Skyler and I have started joking about it. *Have you been to the Statue of Liberty yet? It's technically part of our campus. That Olive Garden in Times Square? Campus.*

Along with the mandatory Writing the Essay class for all freshmen, I'm taking Psychology 101 and a linguistics prerequisite, which I'm most looking forward to for obvious reasons. In middle school, my affinity for words—and, unfortunately, my affinity for using big ones in daily conversation whenever I could—was enough to earn me raised eyebrows and annoyed glances. In high school, slightly less so, though every so often a teacher would circle a word I'd used in a paper and write, *English?* Just because there was a more interesting, more apt word in another language.

Years ago, I tried to memorize as many untranslatable words as I could, captivated by the way they connected to that language's culture. *Psithurism*, Greek for the sound of rustling leaves. *Gluggaveður*, Icelandic for when the weather looks pleasant but is best enjoyed from the inside.

Here, I have a feeling I'll find people just as passionate about words as I am.

I wake up much earlier than I need to and figure a morning walk will settle any residual nerves. This is part of the reason I'm here, after all—to explore. I wind up eating breakfast at an NYU dining hall near Union Square while consulting the map on my phone again. Linguistics is a bit of a trek from here, so I give myself plenty of time. There are a couple different downtown trains I could take—shouldn't be a problem.

Except when I get to the station at Union Square, there's a sign indicating both trains have been diverted.

"Fucking MTA," a guy in a suit mutters, a phone pressed to his ear as he turns to sprint in the other direction.

I check my phone again. The building is fewer than ten blocks away, and I've got fifteen minutes. I can make it.

This is when I learn that a New York City block is not the same as a Seattle block. I wasn't paying attention during my earlier walk, and now I'm full of regrets. As I'm dashing down University Place, dodging people with briefcases and suitcases and grocery bags, panic crawling up my throat, I can barely utter the word in my own mind. *Late.* I can't believe I'm about to be late for my first college class, on my favorite topic, the subject I've longed to study for years.

When I slow down in front of the building, I spend an agonizing half minute by the door, weighing my options. Go inside and risk humiliation? Or turn back and frantically email my counselor to switch classes and delay starting my linguistics courses until next semester?

But I've already been waiting so long.

The door gives a screech as I open it, prompting a full-body wince. The class inside goes silent, the professor frozen mid-sentence.

"Welcome, welcome, please find a seat," Dr. Liu says. "I know it can be tough for freshmen to find their way around on the first day."

This sparks some scattered laughs. My ears are burning, and I'm certain all my exposed skin has turned deep red.

The words themselves are kind, but the tone is flat. Condescending, even. The way he says "freshmen" makes me feel impossibly tiny. This is a class full of sophomores and juniors, and I was only eligible because I entered with so many credits from AP courses. It's a privilege to be here, and I've already fucked it up. Fifteen minutes into the start of the semester and I've branded myself a problem student.

As quickly and quietly as I can, I take the nearest seat and unzip my backpack slowly, tooth by tooth, to make as little sound as possible. I'll just have to wow him with my knowledge of semantics, show him how committed I am to my studies.

It's only when I take out a notebook and position it in front of me, pen poised on the first line, that I realize I am surrounded by laptops. No one is taking notes by hand, and the *click-click-click* of keyboards fills the room. I left my new laptop back in my dorm, worried about damaging it if I toted it all over the city. I hadn't imagined everyone would be taking notes this way, even though now it seems so painfully obvious. Personal laptops weren't allowed in classrooms back at Westview, but *of course* this is what people do here.

Because this isn't Westview. This is college.

And somehow, I get the feeling I've already failed some invisible test.

When I registered for the fall semester, the fact that three classes constituted a full course load seemed laughable. I wrote to a freshman adviser, asked if I could add another. She told me I'd better stick with three and reminded me not to go below fifteen credits, since my financial aid is dependent on it. Now, after seeing the linguistics syllabus and the one for my Psych 101 class in the afternoon, I can understand why. The amount of reading is no small task, which fills me with some of that first-day-of-school giddiness I've been missing today.

That's what I'm faced with when I get back to my dorm later: an evening of reading, and I'm already planning to get ahead a few chapters if I can. In high school, doing the bare minimum wasn't enough. That was average. "Meets expectations." I've always pushed myself beyond that—in part because Rowan was doing the same thing.

Rowan. I didn't realize just how much I looked forward to seeing her in class until I sat down in linguistics and she wasn't there. We said goodbye only a week ago, and yet I've already installed a countdown app on my phone, letting me know that she'll be in New York in twenty-two days. When I sent her a screenshot, she replied with an identical one.

"Good first day?" Skyler asks from his desk, glancing up from his laptop.

"Not bad." I drop my backpack into my chair. "How about you?"

"Didn't have to be in class until noon, so yeah, I'd say it was a pretty great day. My Writing the Essay prof seemed high as hell the whole class, so that'll probably be an easy one." It doesn't escape my notice that Skyler's given me much more detail than I have. I should want to share more—I wish I had some of his easy confidence. He rolls his chair toward me in the tiny room. "Dude. How is my side of the room already a hazmat risk and yours is spotless? Someone explain that to me."

I gaze around at the clothes piled on his bed, a laugh slipping out. "How *is* your side of the room this messy? It's only been, what, five days? I'm almost impressed."

"What can I say, it's an art. Or maybe I really did need my parents nagging at me to clean my room for all those years." Skyler tips his head toward the photo of Rowan and me in our graduation gowns pinned to the wall above my desk. Kirby captured us just as she was tugging off my cap and kissing my cheek. Rowan thought it was corny and groaned when I had it printed, but I loved how it captured her—so confident in showing her affection, even when we'd supposedly hated each other days before. "Girlfriend?"

I nod. "She's at school in Boston. Emerson College. She's a creative writing major, ridiculously talented."

"She's cute. Really cute."

"Are you seeing anyone?"

A shake of his head. "I'm single. Not planning to change that anytime soon," he says. "I abide by one rule, and one rule only. Three simple words."

"And those are?"

He grins, holding up three fingers. "Friends. With. Benefits. I don't know if I'm much of a serious-relationship guy." That makes sense—over the past week, I've seen him in the dining hall with a few different girls, and a couple days ago he texted that he'd be home in the morning and not to wait up. He followed it up with *working on the proper usage of lie/lay/laid*, plus a winking emoji.

"Ah. I guess—I guess we're pretty serious," I say, but even as the words leave my mouth, I'm unsure what "pretty serious" means. The fact that we've slept together, said "I love you," decided to do long distance? We never had a conversation about this being a Serious Relationship, something that suddenly sounds so, well, serious that it deserves capital letters. It's serious to me, and I'm fairly certain it is to her, too.

"That's great, man. I'm happy for you." And he does genuinely look it as he leaps out of his chair and starts lacing up his Nikes. "Gonna blow off some steam after class," he says, and I refrain from asking how much steam one can accumulate on a day that mainly involved the handing out of syllabi. "Ultimate Frisbee. Got a group together and we're going to go play in Washington Square Park. You should join."

I check my watch. "Oh . . . thanks, but I have a video chat scheduled with—" I nudge my head toward the photo on my wall. I've been dying to hear about her writing class.

"You sure? It's gonna be epic."

Even if Ultimate Frisbee doesn't sound like something I'd have a natural aptitude for, maybe I shouldn't pass up the invitation. From everything I've read about NYU, it's the kind of place where you need to chart your own path.

I was too shy to talk to anyone in linguistics, and Psych 101 is such a big lecture that I can't imagine finding a close friend in there, although there are smaller discussion groups that meet every other day. I should be saying yes more. That's what Skyler's doing, and even if his participation in the NYU hookup scene has reminded me that we are very different people, he's clearly putting himself out there.

"Well . . ." I glance at the photo again and make a decision. Rowan will understand—and she'd probably want me to go. "Just give me a moment," I say, thumbing out a text, asking her if we can reschedule.

My hunch is confirmed a minute later.

Rowan: *omg yes no problem, go bro it up. please send pics* 🙄

"Sure," I relent, wondering what the proper attire is for this game and if I have any of it in my closet. "I'm in."

College is about new experiences, and that is how I wind up on a grassy field in Washington Square Park with a half dozen strangers and a single bright red Frisbee.

When we first got here, after dodging pairs of older men playing chess and kids skateboarding and tourists taking photos of the famous arch—photos I'm not ashamed I've taken too, since it really is a stunning architectural icon—Skyler introduced me around. "It's great that so many of your high school friends went here too," I said.

He gave me an odd look. "I don't know any of these guys from high school. Akshay I met in the dining hall this morning, Donovan was in my essay class, and Thanh and Robbie are roommates on the other end of our floor."

I was both shocked and impressed that he'd not just met but befriended this many people in such a short period of time. Then he clapped me on the back and started explaining the rules.

In theory, the game is simple: Throw the Frisbee. Catch the Frisbee. It's advanced up and down the field like soccer, with an end zone on either side. I've lifted weights every morning for the past few years, something Rowan endlessly mocked when she found out about it, but I know secretly and sometimes not-so-secretly loves, given the way she ogles my arms when she thinks

I'm not looking. It's amazing, the number of things that girl thinks she can get away with because she's being sneaky when she has no poker face to speak of. She is terrible at hiding her ogling, and I adore that about her.

Still, I have little confidence in my athletic ability. I'm slightly below-average height with a not-insubstantial percentage of muscle, and yet my coordination leaves something to be desired. I'd be lying if I said part of the reason I bulked up a bit was because it was too fun to torment Rowan in gym class. If we could turn something into a competition, we would. But none of that is doing me any good out here.

I slide my glasses into the pocket of my gym shorts, even though I can barely see without them. But if I emerge from this with four new friends, it'll all be worth it.

We divide into two teams of three. I'm with Skyler and Donovan, and I hope with everything in me that I won't be dead weight.

"We've got this," Donovan says, bringing in his hand as we huddle. Each of his biceps is the size of my head. "Bobcats on three." NYU's mascot. "One, two—"

"Bobcats!" Skyler and I shout back, and maybe there is something inherently infectious about a huddle. Maybe it really is this easy, because sports are great! Sports foster camaraderie and teamwork and—uh . . . sportsmanship? And all those other good things I never experienced because there was no force strong enough to pull me away from my books.

I can do this. I can be a sports guy.

We spread out in our end zone, the other team having won the coin toss, aka Frisbee flip because none of us carry around coins. Skyler launches the Frisbee high in the air, Akshay catching it and making a quick pass to Robbie. I charge forward, attempting to block Thanh as he speeds toward our end zone. Robbie tosses the Frisbee his way. The interception fails. And they score.

"It's okay," Skyler says. "Still warming up!"

The game goes quickly, both teams easily racking up points. I make one beautiful pass to Skyler that he leaps for like a golden retriever, his body spiraling in a display of athleticism I'm not sure I've ever seen up close. I half expect him to catch it in his mouth. I even score a point, though Donovan is just a couple feet away when he throws me the Frisbee.

I won't attempt to count the number of times I miss the Frisbee completely, my nearsightedness doing me zero favors. Grass stains my knees and I'm sweatier than I've been in years, but this is fun. I'm having *fun* with these people I didn't know a week ago, and there is something wonderful about that.

"Watch out!" yells Donovan, and then it becomes clear I am not, in fact, a sports guy.

Because even without my glasses, there's one thing I can see with perfect clarity: the Frisbee hurtling right toward my face.

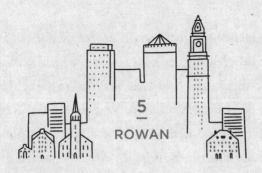

5
ROWAN

I DON'T KNOW where to sit, and right now that feels like the most important decision of my fledgling college career.

Yes, I'm being dramatic, but I'm also being realistic.

Humans are creatures of habit. I can't even count the number of times a teacher told a class we could sit wherever we wanted, and yet we picked the same spots every single day, irked when someone dared to switch things up, moving so they could be closer to a crush or farther from someone they weren't speaking to. So this arrangement of a dozen chairs in a circle, which gives the impression more of a kindergarten classroom than a college course, seems ripe for some classic Rowan Roth overthinking.

Half the chairs are already occupied, and when the door swishes shut behind me, a blond girl in an oversize chenille sweater turns to glance my way, her pen pausing in her notebook.

"Can I sit here?" I ask, gesturing to the empty seat next to her.

"Go ahead." She has a septum ring and sleek blunt bangs, the kind that I'm immediately envious of given how mine refuse to cooperate.

In fact, everyone in the room looks like they've put as much effort into their first-day outfits as possible, while also attempting to look like they barely gave them a second thought. There are jumpsuits and plaid blazers and meticulously applied eyeshadow, statement jewelry and fresh hair dye and even an artfully tilted bowler hat. I know this because it's exactly what I did when I got dressed this morning, plucking the lemon-patterned vintage dress with a flared skirt from a hanger in my tiny closet. A patent leather headband and a pair of tights and just enough makeup to look well rested.

I drop my backpack to the floor and slide into the chair. "Thanks." I haven't been faced with the prospect of making new friends since elementary school. I am the only Westview student at Emerson, and that means completely starting from scratch.

I've had a few conversations with people at orientation, attended a few group dinners, but either I have a sudden case of shyness or I haven't connected with anyone quite yet. This feels like my first true opportunity.

I had hoped my roommate would be an instant friend, but Paulina surfaced only with enough time to introduce herself and disappear again. She hasn't been at any of the getting-to-know-you events on our floor and wasn't there when I fell asleep last night, but this morning when I woke up, it clearly looked like someone had been there. I'm either amazed at my ability to sleep through it all or by hers to move about the room like she's conducting a jewel heist.

So I take a deep lungful of courage and turn back to the girl, aware I might be interrupting her writing. "Hey. I'm Rowan."

But to my surprise, she sets down her pen and gives me a smile. "Kait—K-A-I-T, because I was a pretentious little shit back in elementary school when there were four other Kates in my grade. Are you a freshman too?"

I nod. "I'm a bit nervous," I admit. "I have plenty of experience being a pretentious little shit, but I'm not sure what to expect."

When Kait laughs at this, I let myself relax.

A blue-haired girl two chairs away leans over, and I catch a too-strong whiff of perfume. "I've heard Professor Everett is *tough*, but if you get on her good side, it might make your whole career. She had a student years ago who's now one of her closest critique partners, apparently."

"Is that supposed to make us less anxious? Because now that I know what's on the line, I'm almost certain I'm going to mess something up," Kait says, and I decide I made the right choice by sitting next to her.

Two minutes before the start of class, Professor Everett enters the room, a tall mid-to-late-thirties white woman with curly dark hair in a loose bun, dressed in black trousers and a cream sweater-vest. A few simple chains are draped across her neck, and she wears clear glasses over kind eyes. She looks casual, cool, instantly at ease. Like she's about to start practicing yoga instead of lecturing twelve nervous college kids.

Miranda Everett has written two works of literary fiction: the first, *Thursday at Dawn*, was a finalist for the National Book Award. But her priority, she's said in interviews, will always be her teaching. When I registered for classes over the summer, this yearlong course was my first choice, and when I got in, I read both her books back-to-back. They were lyrical and modern—reviews called them "accessible lit fic for a millennial audience"—filled with the kind of deep character work that made me realize I could truly learn something from her.

"Good morning, good morning," she says in a warm, bright voice. "I'm Miranda and this is Introduction to Creative Writing. Glad you all made it out of bed and over here in one piece. Everyone seems to be at least halfway lucid—sometimes that can be a challenge on the first day." Some scattered laughter, as though people are wondering whether it's okay. Then she gives a roll of her shoulders and takes a deep breath. "I want you to be able to *breathe* in this class. It's my hope that it isn't too agonizing—writing is enough of that without throwing an asshole professor into the mix.

"That said—" She reaches into her shoulder bag and places a timer on the desk. "I'm setting this for ten minutes. I want you all to write anything you want. Anything at all. You can use a notebook or your laptop, whichever you prefer. The only rule is— no going backward. No editing. Anything that comes to mind, simply *write*."

She sets the timer and sits down at her desk, her serene expression unchanged.

All of us exchange glances. I have a dozen questions, namely: Is this going to be graded and what does the rubric look like and should it be double-spaced or—

But then, after the shock and confusion wear off, we start writing.

At least, the rest of the class does. Hands fly across keyboards and pens skate along paper, but my cursor blink-blink-blinks back at me.

I try my best not to focus on the vagueness of the assignment or how immersed everyone else seems. I drum my fingertips on the keyboard, waiting for inspiration to strike. Something. *Anything*.

When the timer goes off with a *ding* that startles a few people, I've only written a single sentence.

The classroom is small and sparsely decorated, but sitting here in a circle with other writers, one feels

Scratch that—half a sentence.

A boring, cliché observation about what's right in front of me. One is clearly a bit of an idiot and should have had more of one's coffee this morning.

"So? How did that feel?" Professor Everett asks.

"Stressful," one guy calls out, which is met with laughter.

"I like to begin every class this way to jog our creativity, to loosen ourselves up. I've found that nothing opens up the mind like ignoring craft for a moment and giving yourself space to play, and there are far too many assignments with a concrete goal. It can be easy to lose the reason for *why* we write. The pure joy of it. These freewrites aren't going to be turned in unless you decide to expand upon them for any of our assignments. They're just for you."

A murmur of excitement spreads through the room, all of us arriving at the same conclusion at the same time: Miranda Everett is the real deal, and we're lucky to have her.

I urge my too-stiff shoulders to soften. This is why I'm here: to learn from the best. To grow into the kind of person who won't be intimidated by a freewrite.

Professor Everett talks about the structure of the class, which is unique in that it runs both semesters here at Emerson. A third of our grade will be based on participation, and she wants us to grow more and more confident with sharing our work over the course of the year.

"Let's go around and have everyone introduce themselves with their name, their pronouns, their year, and why they decided on creative writing."

A wave from the student she gestures to first. "I'm Tegan, they/them. Sophomore. And, well"—they break off, blushing—"I swear I'm not sucking up, but I really loved *Thursday at Dawn*."

Though Professor Everett has surely heard this hundreds of times, she looks genuinely touched. "Thank you so much, Tegan. I'm thrilled to hear that." Then she gives them a wink. "And might I say, you're well on your way to a 4.0?"

After Sierra, Felix, and Noor, it's my turn. "Rowan, she/her," I say. "I'm a freshman, and even though I've been writing for years, I only just recently started sharing it with other people and admitting that I, um, want to be a writer." Even this admission in a classroom of other writers makes me a little fidgety. I drag a hand through my bangs, blow out a breath. "See? Still getting used to it."

"Welcome," Professor Everett says. "Talking about your writing, putting out into the world that you want to be a writer—those are *huge* steps. I hope you're proud of yourself."

And just from the way she says it, I really am.

"Kait, she/her, freshman," Kait continues next to me. "And I write . . . because it's cheaper than therapy?"

For the rest of class, Professor Everett explains Emerson's creative writing major and discusses the different paths we might take, the ways we might use this education in our future careers, whether we're novelists or essayists or reviewers or marketers. Or something else entirely, since creative writing can open up plenty of doors.

"For our next meeting on Thursday, I'd like to get to know you better through a somewhat open-ended piece of writing. I want you to tell me what brought you to this classroom today in the form of a personal narrative. No more than a thousand words."

I write this down in one of my new notebooks. I love that she gives us a maximum but not a minimum, because these aren't the kind of people who are going to write a scant paragraph and turn it in expecting full credit because she didn't define the parameters, like some kids might have done in high school.

Despite my performance anxiety during the freewrite, I'm

eager to get back to my room and open up Word again, a new kind of adrenaline running through my veins. At first I'd been worried Professor Everett would be a cold, no-nonsense literary type, but she couldn't be further from it. And everyone in class is so engaged, which wasn't always the case in high school.

Next to me, Kait is sliding her laptop into her bag. "That was . . , wow."

"I know. Nothing like I expected, but everything I wanted."

Kait nods vigorously, the room's fluorescent light glinting off her septum ring. "Miranda Everett is an icon."

Then I see an opportunity. "Not to be, um, too forward or anything, but would you maybe want to grab some coffee or lunch after this?"

"I have another class at noon."

"Oh. Sure. Sorry."

"But I'm free after that," she says. "How about two thirty? Coffee at the Lion's Den?"

I grin back at her. "Sounds perfect."

I have never had writer friends.

I think I might love it here.

The Lion's Den is one of the campus cafés, and I make my way there after Spanish, which I was pleased to find was largely conversation-based, although much more fast-paced than any of my high school classes. Over the past week, I've been grappling with the sudden sense of freedom here. Example: I can get coffee with someone in the middle of the day without telling anyone where I'm going.

"I might be a snob," I warn Kait as we sit down with our mugs at one of the only open tables. Twinkle lights crisscross the ceiling, an abstract mural on the wall behind us. "I worked part-time at a café in Seattle, and we are very serious about coffee."

"Seattle kind of has that reputation, doesn't it?" She brings the mug to her lips. "Coffee, music . . ."

"Weather, microbrews, apples—"

"Apples?"

"Yes!" I say. "Washington State takes a lot of pride in their apples."

I learn that Kait Donnelly is from Hartford, Connecticut—"where we're snobby about our seafood"—and that we're in the same dorm, with her on the third floor and me on the eighth.

"And you're a creative writing major too?" I ask, sipping my hazelnut latte. Not as good as Two Birds One Scone, but perfectly acceptable.

"Destined to be a tortured literary soul for the rest of my existence, yes," she says. "Not that we need to suffer for our art or anything. Just that sometimes I do, and I've made my peace with it."

I laugh at this, even though writing has never been that way for me. At least, not until earlier today. "What do you write that tortures you that much?"

"A lot of fanfic," she says. "Do you read any? Or write it? I *have* to know who your ships are."

I shake my head. "No, but I'm open to recommendations." With what I hope is nonchalance, I readjust my headband, which has been slowly digging its way into my skull. "I . . . read and write romance."

The words come out with only a tiny bit of hesitation. This thing I kept hidden for so long, worried people would judge me for it.

"That's really cool. So you get that people can be shitty about it."

"So shitty! Even though, of course, most of those people have never read it."

"Some of my friends think I just want to write about hot people banging."

I let out a small cough. "I can relate."

"Which, to be fair, sometimes I do," Kait continues, "but I like a good fluff fic as much as the next person." She twirls a short blond strand around one finger. "My boyfriend doesn't get it. He thinks it's a complete waste of time, since none of it can be published as is, even when I remind him that plenty of successful books started out as fanfic."

"Does your boyfriend go here?" I feel an immediate rush of affection for Neil, who not only understands my love for romance—after an admittedly rocky start at the beginning of high school—but has now read my favorite Nora Roberts, along with a handful of others.

"He's back home. UConn."

"I'm in a long-distance relationship too," I say, and it's nice to have this in common. "He's at NYU."

She swipes around on her phone before showing me a photo of the two of them . . . in front of the Colosseum in Rome. Gabriel has thick dark hair, a kind smile, and a stud through one eyebrow. Pretty sure anyone would look great with that backdrop, though, the ancient ruins and bluest sky.

"Sorry, not to vacation-flex," she says, a touch of pink on her cheeks. "We backpacked around Europe over the summer. Best month of my life."

"I wouldn't even mind the flex. That sounds *incredible.*" I motion for her to show me more photos: Kait and Gabriel rolling pasta dough, wandering the Louvre, cannonballing into the Mediterranean Sea. "You just . . . went to Europe? Just the two of you?"

"Took a little time to convince our parents, but yep. We started dating sophomore year, so everyone pretty much assumes we'll get married someday." She says this casually, and I'm not sure if it's because she believes it or because she finds it to be such a ridiculous statement that it isn't worth taking seriously. "But I don't feel like I really *knew* him until this trip."

"Wow." It's about all I can say, because it's impossible not to imagine doing something like that someday with Neil.

Because what if that someday could be next summer?

We'll be reunited in Seattle, sure, but that's not the same as traveling together with so many days of uninterrupted time. Picturing him in Europe, completely in his element with his love of languages as we explore places we've only ever read about—the vision is such pure bliss, it makes my heart ache.

Then Kait gestures to my phone, and I have to blink myself back to reality. Boston. September. I don't have to search very long to find one of my favorite photos of Neil, taken at Two Birds One Scone a few weeks ago. He's reading a book, an afternoon sunbeam slanting through the window and illuminating his red hair. Peak Neil—so entranced by Bukowski that the rest of the world doesn't exist.

"How long have you guys been together?" she asks.

"Oh—um, since June." My face heats, as though I don't have a right to a long-distance relationship because we haven't been together that long. "We sort of had this rivalry throughout most of high school, and then on the last day, I realized that I'd had feelings for him for a while."

"Enemies to lovers," Kait says with a knowing smile. Because of course a fellow writer would understand the value of a good trope. "You truly love to see it."

We talk more about Professor Everett's book—Kait loved *Thursday at Dawn*, while I preferred her second book, *Helvetica*. *Thursday* had a large ensemble cast, omniscient POV, while *Helvetica* was a more intimate character study. Two aimless twentysomethings on opposite ends of the world, a friendship they sustained through letters as they struggled with relationships and careers and the loss of their adolescent innocence. It absolutely crushed me, and even though I adored it, it reminded me why I prefer romance: because even if your heart gets broken along the way, the author always promises to repair it by the end.

However, I didn't feel like hurling it across the room when I finished it, the way I might have a few years back. Is that . . . growth?

My mom was worried about my not taking advantage of everything college has to offer. But here I am, proving that it doesn't matter that my boyfriend is in another state. Well—it does, but it's not going to keep me from becoming a collegiate social butterfly.

We walk back to our dorm together, parting ways when Kait heads for a hall council meeting and it's almost time for my video chat with Neil.

Paulina's at her desk when I get to our room, stuffing textbooks into her backpack. "Hey," she says breezily, not even looking up. "Just about to head out."

And before I can even utter a response, she's gone. The indifference stings, leaving me racking my brain to wonder if I've somehow offended her. I did move one of her succulents in a penguin-shaped pot off the windowsill, but that was only so I could open the window. She moved it back the next day, but she can't possibly be upset about that, can she? Unless that was a classic passive-aggressive move.

Guess that lifelong friendship with my roommate isn't meant to be.

I toss my headband onto the bed because *God*, wearing that for a whole day was a special kind of torture. Then I settle in and open a fresh Word document, clamp headphones over my ears, and wait for my writing playlist to whisk me away. As the Smiths start playing, I tap my fingertips along the keys, focusing on Professor Everett's prompt. A simple one, surely, for our first assignment.

What brought you to this classroom today? I typed in class, as though there was a chance I might forget it.

A variety of images flash through my mind. The romance novels I found at garage sales. Reading them with my door closed. All throughout high school, I hid what I loved because I was terrified of not being good enough. Here I am, finally comfortable with it . . . and completely drawing a blank.

When I flick my eyes back to the painfully white page, the cursor keeps blinking. Mocking me. So I type:

What brought me here today was

Before realizing it sounds beyond juvenile, like I'm learning how to restate a question for the very first time.

I've loved romance novels since I was a kid and

Emerson's creative writing program seems like

Writing has never been difficult for me—it isn't arrogance; it's a simple fact. The words have just . . . *flowed*. I've written essays on the Civil War and *The Scarlet Letter* and cellular respiration. I even wrote thousands of words in a romance manuscript about two lawyers, despite knowing very little about the legal system that wasn't in AP US Government. I should be able to write about myself, the person I ostensibly know better than anyone.

I switch over to Spotify, deciding maybe I need to add some

new songs to my playlist. More new wave, naturally, plus some of Neil's favorite band, Free Puppies! Once I'm satisfied with it, I spend some time fiddling with my chair for a while before accepting that Emerson student life has simply saddled us with cheap uncomfortable chairs, and next time I'll go to the library or a café.

Then Neil asks to postpone our video chat because his roommate asked him to play Ultimate Frisbee. This is accompanied by only a sliver of disappointment, because he should absolutely be playing Ultimate Frisbee with his roommate—he and I can talk anytime. Besides, it's probably a good thing since I haven't managed a single sentence I don't hate.

There's no reason I should be struggling with something so basic, and yet this is the first assignment of the year. I want to impress Professor Everett.

An hour later, after I've brought dinner up to my room because maybe I can't write on an empty stomach, I get another text from Neil:

I may have sustained a minor ocular injury.

It's accompanied by a photo of him with a black eye. I drop my fork into the bowl of lo mein, holding a hand to my heart.

I don't think you're supposed to use your head in ultimate frisbee, I write back. *I'm so sorry. does it hurt?*

The pang of missing him is both sudden and sharp. If I were there, I'd hold an ice pack to his face, stroke his hair, tell him he could pick a movie to watch and I'd promise not to complain about it.

My trip to New York in two weeks can't come soon enough. A New York City fall, a Meg Ryan sweater, and a boy who looks at me like I am the sun.

No parents, no siblings, no interruptions. Just two and a half days of bliss.

A knock on my door makes me jolt in the uncomfortable chair.

"Game night in ten minutes, if you want to join," Lexie the RA says cheerily, and I save the document—pointless, there's nothing meaningful on it—close my laptop, and follow her into the hall.

Rowan—

I'm so happy to have you in this class. I love romance novels too, and I often feel they don't receive the proper attention in the literary world.

I will admit, though, that I was hoping to see more of <u>you</u> in this first piece of writing, and that it's feeling a little thin to me. I feel as though I'm reading from a distance, with a boundary placed between you and the reader. I'm not sure if that was your intention? Either way, what I encourage for your next piece is to let go of the reins a bit more. Let your natural voice out.

Looking forward to reading your next assignment.

—M.E.

6
NEIL

SHE'S AN AUTUMN fever dream of a girl: apricot corduroy jacket, striped turtleneck, short black boots. A denim skirt that accentuates her curves. Her long hair is wild and windswept, despite the fact that she's been sitting on a train for four hours, probably because she's been wrapping strands around her fingers, messing with her bangs in that adorable way she always does. A habit that imprinted on me long before I had the words for my feelings.

And the best part: her smile, broad and entirely unrestrained, dragging me like a magnet closer and closer.

I swallow back a sudden burst of nerves as people stream out of the train behind her, turning Penn Station into veritable chaos on a Friday afternoon. In my most anxious moments, I've been worried the distance will have turned us awkward, or if a month apart will have somehow changed us. We text almost constantly, with video calls every few days. But Rowan is not a girl meant for video calls—she is someone who needs to be perceived in vivid color. I'll take what I can get, of course, but 1080p can't capture her ambition or enduring optimism.

In an instant she's in front of me, throwing her arms around my neck while I pull her close, hugging her tight.

That scent, strawberry shampoo and sweetness and *home.*

"Welcome to New York," I say, mouth brushing her ear. I can feel her shiver as I do this, remembering how sensitive she is there. It's something I committed to memory the moment I discovered it, eager to make her shiver like that again and again.

"It's been waiting for me?"

"Well, *I* definitely have."

I'm not sure I can hold out much longer, so I kiss her, right there in the middle of the train station.

Instant bliss, a shot of warmth to every part of my body. She is every good thing I've missed. I've second-guessed myself too many times since I got off the plane before resolving that if she was out there doing her best in Boston, then I could sure as hell do the same thing here. My hands tangle in her hair, trailing down her back before settling at her hips, where the denim hugs her body. Her stunning sigh. Her urgency. How is it that she's even better than I remember?

Her fists are on the collar of my jean jacket, mouth parting against mine. I thought I'd overdressed for the upper-sixties weather—what locals are calling an unusually chilly week for September—but it's worth it for the way she clings to the lapels, drawing me closer.

Rowan Roth, here with me in New York City.

Someone walking by us lets out a catcall, and we muffle our laughter as we break apart.

Over the past couple weeks, I've settled in as much as a recent NYC transplant can settle. While I'm embarrassed by the number of times I've had to ask strangers for directions, no one else has vomited next to me on the subway—although I did witness an impromptu breakdancing competition on the A train last week—so I'm calling that a victory. Being out here has given me a strange new sense of independence, one I can't measure against anything else because nothing I've experienced comes close. I remember the first time I was allowed to watch Natalie on my own, the first time my mom let me take the bus by myself. Flashes of autonomy that felt monumental at the time.

It's overwhelming, too, just how many clubs and events are fighting for our attention at once, but I have to remain focused on academics over everything else. Classes, homework, video calls with Rowan, work-study—which consists of shelving books at NYU's Bobst Library three afternoons a week—and then more homework. That's my routine, and I can't afford to deviate from it.

At least, not until now.

Rowan gasps as she gets a look at my face. "I can't believe it. You look—"

"Devilishly handsome?"

The mottled purple bruise around my eye has been slow to fade, and Skyler's taken the opportunity to devise ridiculous explanations for it. "Five huge guys," he'll say when he's with me, usually at breakfast or dinner. Maybe Ultimate Frisbee bonded us. "Took them on all by himself."

Gently, Rowan brings her fingertip to trace the skin beneath my lash line. "Well, yes, always, but I was thinking more along the lines of, you got into a fight with a mob boss because you went on a date with his daughter."

"That sounds like the plot of a romance novel."

"About fifty, give or take. Does it still hurt?"

"Not anymore," I say. Especially not with her touching me like this. Maybe I should play Ultimate Frisbee more often. "Being a redhead is just the gift that keeps on giving—quick to bruise, slow to heal. I'd probably be among the first to die in a zombie apocalypse, huh."

"Oh, I'm much too weak to survive anything like that. Like, sometimes I don't eat the crust on sandwiches. We can die together as cowards."

I thread my fingers with hers as we offer up more of our softest traits, the ones that would make us completely useless in any kind of end-of-the-world scenario. Her inability to fall asleep unless she's drowning in blankets. My lack of hand-eye coordination. Her preference for scalding-hot showers.

By the time we drop off her luggage at my dorm, my nerves are gone.

Our first stop is a bagel shop a couple blocks away despite it being three in the afternoon, because her affinity for cream cheese is unrivaled and yet somehow, I have a feeling the metric ton of the stuff they put on their bagels won't be enough for her. My assumption is correct: once she finishes her bagel, she eyes the honey-walnut schmear on mine and asks if she can have a bite.

"This is deeply unfair. I'm going to be dreaming of these bagels until the next time I come back. Writing sonnets about these bagels." Her brow scrunches. "Figuring out how, exactly, one writes a sonnet."

"I'm sure they have a class about it at Emerson."

"You know what, I think they actually do."

From there, we make our way uptown, swinging by Levain Bakery and taking two of their massive cookies to Central Park. We make small talk that doesn't feel small—she tells me about the book her parents are working on, and I show her the Lucy photos Natalie has been regularly sending me. *Lucy expands her horizons*, posed with a book about learning Japanese. *Lucy uses the Force*, with my *Star Wars* poster in the background. *Lucy gets ripped*, her paws propped on my pair of dumbbells.

"New York suits you," Rowan says when we settle on a park bench amid a sea of tourists and street vendors selling everything from T-shirts and art prints to light-up key chains with miniature Statues of Liberty. "Maybe it was that casual way you swiped your MetroCard, but it's easy to see you here."

"Because you're literally seeing me here, at this very moment?"

She swats at my arm. "It's easy to see you *thriving*, I mean. I don't know anyone who loves learning more than you, and there is just *so much* here—you'll never get bored. You wanted to be here, and you fucking did it. You're just . . . exactly where you're supposed to be. Even as much as I miss you."

"That's the worst part of New York. The fact that you're in Boston."

We squint out into the late-afternoon sun, watching a trio of jugglers toss balls in the air while onlookers drop coins into a jar. Maybe I'll feel differently when the temperature dips below freezing, but there's a certain energy here that I don't always feel when I'm cooped up in my room studying.

"But you love it," she says, and I detect a note of concern in her voice. "Right?"

Rowan knows why New York is so important to me, what it represented throughout high school. Maybe the only reason it hasn't lived up to my vision of it is because *I* haven't—because I've slid right into a routine, the way I did all through high school.

I've been waiting for the excitement to overtake me the way it usually does at the beginning of the school year. It's there, of course, just buried underneath a few layers of stress and wrapped in a few more layers of trepidation.

"It's intimidating," I say after a long pause. "But amazing. Of course it's amazing. Any time of day, you can do just about anything. And there are always people out, even if I'm not one of them."

"What do you mean?"

"I've been pretty focused on classes and homework. I guess . . . I guess I haven't gone out and explored as much as I thought I would. Yet," I quickly add.

"You can do both," she says, and maybe it really can be that easy. Her dark eyes grow wide as she gives me this knowing look. "If people only went to college to study, there probably wouldn't be nearly as many of them. I know you worked hard for this, but it's okay to let yourself have fun too. We only get to do this once."

"Fun," I repeat, as though it's a foreign concept. "I can definitely try. I *want* to try."

"Good. I want a full report."

I polish off my cookie, making a vow that whatever Skyler asks to do next, I'll say yes. Even if it's bungee jumping off the Empire State Building. I'll pick a club to try out, too—something that'll get me out of my dorm and into the world.

Somehow, giving myself that permission is an instant comfort.

"How about Emerson? Is it everything you hoped it would be?"

"It's super artsy, which I love," she says. "Everyone's involved in a hundred clubs, and there's always someone making a student film outside my dorm. And I like what I've seen of Boston so far. Obviously nothing could ever top Seattle for me, but Boston is putting up a good fight." Her tongue darts out to sweep away a bit of chocolate. "And classes are good. My creative writing class . . . well, the professor's incredible. She gives us ten minutes to free-write at the beginning of each class, which I've never really done before, so that's been new. But I just—" And she breaks off, a hand fluttering through her bangs, not quite making eye contact.

I have only seen Rowan Roth nervous a handful of times.

Once when our class voted for freshman-class rep.

Then in AP Chem junior year, when our misguided partnership led to a lab station bursting into flames.

And finally, my personal favorite: right before she kissed me for the first time.

When it came to our rivalry, she always wore a mask of confidence. For so long, all I could see was her ambition—and her irritation with me when my ambitions matched hers. It's only recently that I've gotten to know the girl behind that mask, the one with vulnerabilities and fears she doesn't always show the world.

Whatever she's about to share, it must be serious.

"You can tell me," I say softly, trying to encourage without pressuring.

A nod, and then a deep breath. "My first assignment . . . didn't exactly go the way I planned." She reaches into her bag and takes out a couple folded sheets of paper stapled together. Passes them to me.

Rowan doesn't share her writing easily. Essays and projects, sure, but anything remotely personal—that's just for her. At least, it was until she let me read her fiction for the first time in June, the romance novel she's been working on for the past couple years. And then surprised us both when she read a portion of it out loud at an open mic.

The prompt for this assignment was a deceptively simple one that Rowan bolded at the top of the page: *What brought you to this classroom today?* I read her writing first and then the critique from her professor that I know must have felt terrible, no matter how kindly it was delivered. I feel the same kind of ache, a stomach-churning discomfort. When you're as conditioned for straight A's the way we've been, you can't focus on the positives. You see red marks on a sheet of paper and only the negatives matter. The rest of it might as well not exist.

"Artoo. I'm sorry," I say. "I know that's not what you wanted to see."

"You think the writing's bad?"

"No!" I place a hand on hers, meeting her eyes with mine. "Absolutely not. But I know how you write. And I don't know if it's up to your usual standards for *yourself*."

She chews her lower lip. "That's fair. And true. It's like, the nicest note, though. I don't know why I'm so upset about it."

"How did you feel when you turned it in?"

"Not great."

"Maybe you were putting too much pressure on yourself?" I say. "With it being the first assignment and wanting to impress your professor. Because I get it—I've been feeling the same way. Or maybe you were holding back because you don't know her well enough yet?"

"Probably some combination of the two. I must have been too in my head. Old Rowan is back with a vengeance," she says, and then groans. "Oh my God. Have we both been holding back in different ways? You with New York, me with writing? What is wrong with us?"

I can't help laughing at that because she might be right. "I don't know. It's just different now. We knew the rules at Westview. Small fish, meet big pond." To illustrate this, I wave a hand at the park surrounding us.

"It's not fair that we can't have everyone from high school here with us. To make the pond a little friendlier."

"You really want Brady Becker in your creative writing class?"

"Fine, not *everyone.*"

"If it makes you feel any better, I was late to linguistics my first day—"

"Neil McNair? *Late?*" She feigns a gasp as I nudge her, a half smile playing on her lips. "Let me write up a tardy slip."

"I've barely spoken in class since then. Which I suppose is mildly ironic." It's true, and I'm not proud of it. Of all my classes, Psych 101 has been the one keeping me up late with reading and only partially because there's just so much to read.

I picked it for a science requirement, and it's been a complete surprise. We began with the brain, because nothing else we learned would make sense if we didn't understand how our bodies' command center operated. I assumed the lecture would be huge and impersonal, without much engagement, but Professor Bayer is animated and passionate. The first few classes, I noticed some laptops open to social media or online shopping; now nearly everyone is immersed in their notes.

Though I took AP Chemistry and Biology in high school— fives on both, thank you very much—I've often felt more drawn to the humanities. And yet I realize I am curious about the human mind, too, those age-old questions about nature versus nurture, whether we're born innately good or innately evil. How we make decisions and how we tune our moral compass.

Questions that might help me understand my own family, if answers exist.

"You'll get there," Rowan says, and I wish I had her confidence in me. "It's strange, isn't it, to be somewhere no one knows you. To not have that history with anyone."

"To not have *you* there, urging me to be better."

Her eyes hold all the warmth and understanding I love so much. "I miss it," she says softly. Then she seems to brighten. "I had this idea," she continues, tapping my chest with her index finger. "Something that might make this year easier."

I lift my eyebrows, curiosity piqued.

"I've never been to Europe. You've never been to Europe. What if we did the whole broke college student backpacking thing this summer, as a way to cap off our freshman year? One of my friends went with her boyfriend and said it completely changed her. You can geek out about all the languages, and I can pretend to be annoyed with you when you order for us in flawless French but secretly I'll find it extremely hot."

A grin spreads across my face. I can picture it: sipping espresso in Italian cafés, exploring ancient castle ruins. Rowan there with me.

Unfortunately, I can also picture the enormous price tag.

"I love it," I say, even as that worry twists my stomach.

"Yeah?" Now she's grinning too, perched on the edge of the bench, one leg bouncing up and down excitedly. Her joy is infectious, and for a moment I think I'd say yes to anything if it meant getting to see her this way. "Because I know it's still not going to be cheap. We could take a flight with a hundred layovers and stay in hostels, of course. And it wouldn't be until summer, so that gives us enough time to save up."

"I think we can do it. I still have most of the Howl money, and—we can budget." If there ever was a perfect use for the Howl prize, this is it. I'd never have won without her.

All of high school, my life was full of no. If this is something Rowan wants for us—and the more I think about it, the more I want it, too—then I'll do everything I can to make it happen.

"I'll only eat croissants in Paris, if I really have to."

"And only chocolate in Belgium." I drop a hand to her knee, clutching it. "Or—oh! We could go to Basel, Switzerland. It's right near Switzerland's borders with France and Germany, and Switzerland has four national languages, which is really quite fascinating, and—" I pause. "I feel like I've never said *Switzerland* as many times as I just did."

"One, I love that you just know that off the top of your head. And two: that sounds amazing."

I've never given much thought to travel. It's always seemed as though I had too many other priorities to allow any space for wanderlust. But *God*, it's there, that desire to see the world. There's no way I could have studied those languages, often in my spare time, without it sitting beneath the surface.

The fact that she's looking ahead like this, making this plan for us . . . My heart is suddenly too big for my chest.

"And just so you know," she says, "you'll never be a small fish to me."

"Is that innuendo?"

She just gives an innocent shrug as I pull her toward me for another kiss.

This girl. She could take the gloomiest day and paint it brightest gold.

Eventually we make our way back downtown. Earlier this morning, I managed to grab rush tickets for a new musical adaptation of *Romeo and Juliet*, and when the lights dim and the curtain goes up, her hand in mine in a back row of the theater, I'm full of nothing but calm. We're sliding back into what we had before summer ended, the two of us fitting together the way we always have.

Only this time we have two new cities to learn. Apart, and then together.

And perhaps, this summer, so many more.

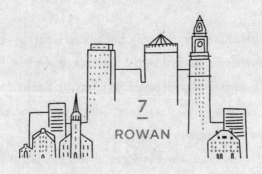

7
ROWAN

IT'S ALMOST ELEVEN o'clock when we get back to Neil's dorm room, after we've gone full AP Lit, analyzing the musical and all the ways it compared to the play.

"I'm sad I don't get to meet your roommate," I say as Neil shuts the door behind us and flicks on the lights. Skyler went home for the weekend, he informed me when I arrived earlier. "Although if it means we have the room to ourselves, maybe I'm not sad at all."

Five years ago, I was in New York with my parents for a book tour, but the reality of being here with Neil is almost too good. He navigated the streets with a tentative confidence, as though wanting to prove that he knew where he was going as he squinted down at Google Maps. It was adorable, the fact that he wanted to impress me. There was some envy, too—because I'm jealous of this entire city, these skyscrapers and streets and subway cars that get to wake up with him every day.

Part of me was worried he'd judge the note from Professor Everett, an imperfect record to begin my college career. We always kept pace with each other so evenly, but he's no longer my competition. I shouldn't be shocked by the feedback, given how I stared at that blank document until my retinas burned, finally dragging out sentence after agonizing sentence. She'd said no more than a thousand words. Mine was barely three hundred.

At first I wasn't sure why I brought it with me, but as he read it, I realized it was because I needed someone to process it with. Someone who understands me, who knows how out of character this kind of feedback is. And how much it might sting.

The joy on his face as he read my writing and then Professor Everett's note was so far from disappointment that I wasn't sure why I second-guessed it. He didn't tell me I was overreacting, or that I'd do better next time, or that her note wasn't really that bad. He knew exactly why it upset me so much.

Even better: the joy on his face when I mentioned Europe. Something we can look forward to later, when all of this feels too difficult.

Right now, though—right now he is all mine.

I unbutton my corduroy jacket and step out of my boots, the fact that we are truly *alone* for the first time slowly sinking in. Neil watches me. Swallows hard. As much as I love him in a denim jacket, I also love the way that jacket looks draped over the back of his desk chair, allowing me to take in the lines of his body for the first time all day. A simple black button-down, open at the throat. The freckles and features I've missed.

He is so lovely, especially with his messy hair in slight need of a haircut. When I slide my fingers into it, he lets out this low hum. His eyes fall shut for a moment, his hands settling at my waist on his exhale. Thumbs stroking along my skirt.

"I'd be lying if I said I hadn't been waiting all day for this," I say.

"Try all month." With a wicked, heavy-lidded look, he draws me even closer, one hand trailing up my back. "And the best part is, we can't be interrupted."

That rush of freedom turns everything more intimate. Slowly, I take off his thin oval glasses and place them on his desk before I kiss him, properly kiss him, for the first time in weeks.

It's slow, deep, the kind of kiss that tells the other person you have all the time in the world to keep kissing them like this. His tongue slips inside my mouth, teasing. A soft bite on my lower lip, and then a harder one, because this is something I've just recently learned I like and he's determined to make up for lost time. That sigh in his throat is one I feel deep in my bones, beautiful and satisfying and perfect.

The last time we had sex, a stolen afternoon in my room while my parents worked from a coffee shop, knowing we probably wouldn't have another opportunity for a while, he just stared at me for a long time, like he was trying to memorize every detail.

This time, we have a full weekend ahead of us.

Before we go any further, though, he pauses. He cradles my jaw, his thumb skating along my cheekbone. His eyes, blazing and intense, with always, always that underlying softness to his expression. "I love your face. Every part of it. It wasn't enough seeing you over video—I don't think there are enough pixels in the world to do you justice." A kiss lands on the tip of my nose, as though he knows it's something I used to be self-conscious about. He's never shy about his compliments, but this one feels different. Weightier. "You're a thousand times better in person."

After that, neither of us cares to slow down for very long. Our shirts land on the floor, my tights tangled with his jeans. Then I climb into his bed with bare legs, and he slides in next to me, lining his body up with mine.

"Small bed," I remark.

"I don't see anything wrong with that."

He traces his fingertips along the seams of my bra before removing it, and I arch my back into him as he kisses my neck, my chest. I stroke my hand along every cluster of freckles. His skin is so warm, as though every possible emotion is pulsing right beneath it. Lust. Sweetness. Admiration.

At the beginning of our relationship, he was shy and sometimes uncertain, and watching him gain confidence, even in the limited time we had together over the summer, has more than surprised me. But maybe it shouldn't—if there's something Neil McNair isn't instantly an expert at, he naturally wants to excel in it.

His breathing grows more ragged as I push my hips against his, his teeth landing on the soft skin of my shoulder, and this is one of my favorite things about him: how he begins in this undeniably wholesome way, until the sensation becomes too powerful and he gives in to the basest parts of himself. I cannot get enough of him like this, acting purely on instinct. On desire. Losing himself in me, simply *feeling*. Contrasted with the buttoned-up, glasses-wearing guy with the massive vocabulary—it's about the hottest thing I can imagine.

"Not yet," he says, and I can tell it's taking every ounce of self-control to utter those words. His hair is already wild, a flush spread across his cheeks and down the column of his neck. "We don't have to rush."

"I know, I know. I just missed you."

He readjusts on top of me, bending to kiss my waist, my stomach, my hips. "Could I . . . ?" he asks, and presses a kiss to the front of my underwear. Then another one, lower this time, the heat of his mouth finishing that silent question.

"I've never—" I start, because even though Neil wasn't my first, that's one thing I haven't done. Not with him, not with anyone. "Are you sure you want to?"

The look on his face makes me think I've asked the most obvious question in human existence. "Rowan. I wanted to all summer. I don't think . . . I don't think there's been a time I *haven't* wanted to."

"Then—yes," I breathe out, wondering if he can hear the longing in just those two words. Because suddenly it's all I can think about, and I am absolutely desperate for it. Even when a past boyfriend offered, I was never fully comfortable. I didn't want to be that exposed.

There's none of that self-consciousness now.

He hooks his thumbs around that last bit of fabric separating us and pulls it down my legs, and then, because he's Neil, folds it neatly on top of our tights-jeans pile. My breathing is already heavy as he settles himself between my legs.

The sensation is all warmth, a new kind of intimacy that tugs at something deep in my chest. I'm half sitting up on my elbows, watching him, but soon my muscles can't take it and I let myself sink into the mattress, head dropping to the pillow.

But after a few minutes, after the initial surprise of it wears off—and then longer than a few minutes, as he tries to find a rhythm—my mind starts to wander.

To my next creative writing assignment, and whether I'll be able to conquer the blank page.

To my train on Sunday, and what time I'll have to be at the station so I don't miss it.

I squeeze my eyes shut, willing myself to stay in the moment.

He keeps going, and while all of it feels *good*, none of it feels *amazing*, exactly. A new kind of frustration.

"Is it still okay?" he asks.

"Yeah. Yes. Just . . ." I'm unsure how to vocalize it. Even during our first time together I was able to guide his hand. For some reason, maybe because this is new territory for both of us, I'm now at a total loss.

"Oh," he says, that single syllable containing so much disappointment, his face beautifully flushed. Ever gentle, with the way his fingertips skim up my thighs, thumbs brushing my hips. "We could try something else?"

All summer, we were dying to be alone. And now that we are . . . what, we've got performance anxiety? I'm distracted in a way I hoped this trip would clear up. I want to be *here*, with him, and yet my mind is in a hundred other places.

Then, just as I'm reaching for his shoulders because he feels entirely too far away from me, a fire alarm goes off.

We bolt upright.

"Um," I start as the alarm blares, because the timing? Could not be worse.

Neil practically leaps off the bed, handing me my shirt before reaching for his own.

"It's got to be a drill," he says as he opens up his closet, tossing me a pair of sweatpants because I'm sure he knows putting my tights back on would require some serious acrobatics.

We have to take the stairs, six flights down with the rest of the dorm, some students in pajamas and some of them looking like they were mid–party prep. All of them looking pissed.

At almost midnight, New York is disorienting. A haze of noise and bright lights, cars honking and sirens in the distance, people laughing and shouting and pushing past us on the sidewalk. It takes me a few long moments to get my bearings.

I hug my jacket tighter around me, shivering, before Neil pulls me closer. It could be worse, though: there's a girl out here in only a robe and flip-flops, her hair soaking wet.

One of the RAs jogs over and addresses the group.

"Looks like someone burned popcorn in the microwave and set off the alarms," he says, which elicits a chorus of groans. "They'll let us back inside any minute."

It is, understandably, a challenge to get back in the mood when we return to his room twenty minutes later.

"I'm sorry," I say when he closes the door. "Not about the fire drill, about—before."

A little furrow appears between Neil's brows. "You have nothing to be sorry for. *I'm* sorry."

I shake my head, unsure why I couldn't have just been more present, a twinge of guilt settling low in my stomach. "It's fine. Really."

"I'm just happy to be spending time with you, whether we have clothes on or not." His arms come around me, mouth grazing my ear.

Because of course he's sweet about it.

"I love you," I say, having missed the way his features go soft when I say it in person.

"Adore you."

As nice as it is to fall asleep together and wake up in the same bed, the awkwardness of last night continues to weigh on me Saturday morning.

Last night, he tucked my body against his and we watched part of *The Force Awakens* because we've been making our way through the *Star Wars* franchise since the beginning of summer, when Neil was shocked to learn I'd never seen any of the movies.

The rest of the weekend, we play tourists at the Museum of Natural History and the Statue of Liberty, two things he's been saving so we could do them together. When we get back to his dorm that night, I tell him I'm exhausted and he agrees, which is true, but I'm also worried about what might happen if we try anything again.

Maybe that first time, with all its beautiful imperfections, was so lovely that nothing can measure up.

It's a thought I wish I could banish as soon as it enters my mind. We already had our big romantic moment on the last day of school, our epic love story that ended with both of us admitting our feelings for each other after years of animosity. We fulfilled the trope, in its most basic terms: we started out enemies and became lovers. We gave the speeches that characters deliver in all my romance novels. The declarations of love. Period, underlined, *THE END* in big bold letters.

What comes after that?

Sunday afternoon, when Neil drops me off at Penn Station after a farewell bagel, I find myself wondering, as the train pulls away, why I miss him more than I did three days ago.

KIRBY
so like
hypothetically
what would you do if your roommate left a piece of dining hall lasagna in the mini fridge two weeks ago and forgot to take it out?

ROWAN
kirby kunthea taing. are you the roommate in this scenario?

MARA
SHE IS, AND SHE SHOULD BE ASHAMED OF HERSELF

KIRBY

ROWAN
meanwhile my roommate continues to be a complete mystery
I *think* she still sleeps here, but I barely ever see her

KIRBY

wow. that is such a shame. i am so sorry, dear rowan, that you didn't instantly bond with your roommate and thus did not forge an everlasting friendship that would never have been as strong as the everlasting friendship forged with those two brilliant young women you knew from high school

KIRBY

who i hear are also super hot

MARA

What she means to say is I'm sorry, and maybe she's just having trouble adjusting? Maybe she'll pop back up when you least expect her.

ROWAN

I miss you both so much.

KIRBY

even my chaos?

MARA

Even Kirby's chaos?

ROWAN

especially that 🖤

8
NEIL

"I'M STARTING TO think you're my official activities director," I tell Skyler the following Saturday as we get off the F train at Second Avenue, in a neighborhood that's either Nolita or the Bowery. In fact, we spent five minutes arguing about it when he pulled it up on his phone, rotating and zooming in on the map until all it looked like was a series of colored lines and dots.

"It's Grandmaster of Merriment, thank you." Skyler swipes his MetroCard and breezes through the turnstile. "And it's a job I take *very* seriously."

"The last time I said yes to something with you, I wound up with this." I point to my eye.

"This is different. Just stay away from the beer pong table and you'll be injury free."

When Skyler asked if I'd been to any parties yet, I glanced up from a chapter on cognition in my psych textbook and simply blinked at him. "We have to change that," he said, clapping a determined hand on the back of my chair. "Tonight."

Admittedly, part of me worries he'll think I'm trying to cling to him when he knows other, more interesting people with better hand-eye coordination who have absolutely attended parties so far this year. He hasn't brought any of his casual hookups back to our dorm—at least, not that I'm aware of—but given his preference for them, it's clear he already has plenty of friends, both with and without benefits. I don't want him to think he has to be mine just by nature of proximity.

Then I remember that I vowed to get out and explore more, and the only reason it hasn't happened so far this week is because I've been studying for a test in linguistics.

It's okay to let yourself have fun.

And I'm going to try.

"You never told me how things went with your girlfriend," Skyler says as we climb the steps out onto the street. There's already a bite to the air, our mild September swept away by a chilly October.

"It was good." I jam my hands in my pockets, hoping this sounds casual. "Hard to see her leave, of course, but it was good having her here. Really good. Hopefully you can meet her next time."

This earns me a raised eyebrow. "You sure? Because you just said the word 'good' three times in a row, linguistics major."

Of course it was more than good—Rowan was there.

I've thought about it all week, and I can't shake what happened that first night, mostly because I'm not entirely sure *what* happened. It's clear my . . . ah, performance was lackluster, and I wanted so badly for her to enjoy it as much as I was—because oh, I *was*. I wasn't lying when I told her I'd been imagining it all summer, and the reality of her was so far beyond anything my primitive mind could have conjured. An out-of-body experience as she filled every single one of my senses.

Even though she insisted she had a great time, it's my fault it wasn't better.

Fortunately, I'm able to steer the conversation in a new direction by asking Skyler how the process of designing his own major is going, which he happily gabs about until we stop on Avenue B in front of a skinny brick building with an Ethiopian restaurant on the first floor. At least we can agree that the apartment is solidly in the East Village, and I don't doubt the monthly rent would terrify me.

He rings the doorbell, whistling a tune I don't recognize, and then we're buzzed up to the third floor.

The place is *tiny*, people crammed shoulder to shoulder and hip to hip, dancing and talking and drinking and laughing. If this is what New York real estate is like, then I'll gladly stay in my dorm until graduation. Bottles and snacks are spread on the kitchen counter, pop music on full blast, the room thick with the earthy scent of weed. It's all so heady that for a moment I get a contact high, my brain going pleasantly fuzzy and limbs loosening up. The closest thing I had to a party in high school was when I'd meet up with Adrian, Sean, and Cyrus at one of their houses and we'd game or watch movies, and they'd needle me about Rowan while I refused to admit my feelings for her. If we wanted to get really wild, we might even go bowling.

My dad was a heavy drinker, and as a result, I've never had much interest in alcohol. He seemed to self-medicate with it, and while sometimes it dulled his anger, other times it made him spit more vitriol. But when Skyler opens two beers with a bottle opener on his key chain, I graciously accept one. One will be okay, I tell myself, because I am not my father and I'll respect my limits. I don't hate the taste, cool and refreshing with an acidic tang. Plus, it gives me something to do with my hands.

Fortunately, Skyler's so tall that he's impossible to lose in the crowd. It isn't that I'm uncomfortable in large groups of people. I was copresident of student council senior year and have plenty of experience with public speaking. But Rowan was almost always next to me, baiting me, and long before we were together, that made it easier.

Skyler drapes his arm around a girl with medium-brown skin and dark curly hair parted down the middle. She's in denim cut-offs and a V-neck tank top, a vape pen dangling from one hand. "This is my friend Adhira. We went to high school together."

"A year apart," Adhira clarifies. She exhales a plume of blueberry smoke. A sophomore. That makes sense—most of the people at this party look a bit older. "Thanks for coming to our little shindig."

"This is your place?"

She nods, then turns sheepish. "Our parents help out with the rent," she stage-whispers. "And we are endlessly indebted to them." Adhira is objectively stunning, and I don't miss the way

Skyler can't take his eyes off her. I watch his face, wondering if there's something going on between the two of them. "My roommate and I—she's over there. Zoe!" she yells, and a petite blond girl hurries over. "Zoe, Skyler, and Skyler's roommate, Neil. Skyler and Neil, Zoe, best friend, queen of my life, killer of plants." To emphasize this, Adhira gestures toward a drooping fern in the corner of the kitchen.

"It's not my fault we barely get any natural light," Zoe says. Her gaze lingers on me for a moment. "How'd you get that bruise?" she asks. "Looks painful."

"By being absolute shit at Ultimate Frisbee," I say, just as Skyler says, "A tourist asked him how to get to Times Square."

Then Zoe turns to Adhira, nods toward Skyler. "This is the poor boy whose innocence you stole?"

Adhira grins and takes another pull from her vape. "There was nothing innocent about it."

"Didn't realize we were taking a stroll down memory lane," Skyler says, leaning closer to Adhira. Fluttering his lashes.

"A stroll, or a twisty path on a cliff's edge that gives you motion sickness?"

"They say you never forget your first." He takes her hand, brings it to his mouth, dropping a gentle kiss to her knuckles. "I haven't forgotten, my love."

If anyone else said this, it would sound painfully cheesy, but somehow it makes Adhira blush.

The puzzle pieces connect. "You two dated in high school?" I ask.

Adhira nods. "For three blissful weeks, until my family went out of town during spring break and our relationship couldn't survive the distance." She nudges Skyler. "Nice to see you finally made it out of Staten."

"Say what you will, but no one does bagels quite like Staten Island. Or pizza. Or pasta. It's a real culinary paradise."

"And no one stans Staten like you do."

"Honestly, I'm starting to think I picked the wrong school," I say. "Is it too late to transfer to somewhere on Staten?"

Skyler throws up his hands in mock frustration. "Look, one day you'll see Staten Island for yourself and you'll just *get it*."

Behind Skyler's back, Adhira mouths to me, *No, you won't*, and I have to muffle a laugh. "What's your major?" she asks. "I'm psychology."

"Linguistics. I'm actually in Psych 101 right now though," I say. "It probably seems basic to you, but it's kind of blowing my mind so far."

"No, I loved it! Professor Bayer?" she asks, and I nod. "Have you done the unknown psychologist project yet?"

"We just started," I say. The professor gave us several dozen names of lesser-known psychologists and challenged us to pick one we hadn't heard of for a semester-long project. After some preliminary googling, I selected Lawrence Kohlberg, an American psychologist with Jewish German roots whose research focused on moral development. Many of the people on the list were Jewish— something I've been eager to share with Rowan. "I have Lawrence

Kohlberg. He did a lot with morality that I'm still trying to understand. Do you know him?"

"Nope. I did Karen Horney—"

"A-plus name," Skyler interjects, which earns him a few eye rolls.

"—who was one of the first female psychiatrists. Her work was pretty groundbreaking for the time, and I'm kind of obsessed with her—like, the idea that women's psychology shouldn't be defined in terms of men. She had this *huge* beef with Freud, because his theories were so male-dominated and frankly disgusting." At this, she full-body shudders. "The deeper you get, the stronger your opinions on Freud. I for one would be elated if I never had to hear his name again."

"Oh—I'm not sure how far I'll go," I say, because as interesting as that sounds, my heart has always been with linguistics. "It's just for a science credit, really."

"Right." A shrug. "Well, if you need someone to vent with about Freud, you know where to find me."

This is followed by a lull in the conversation, during which Skyler gestures down the hall with his beer bottle. "So, are we gonna get a grand tour?"

"Obviously."

Adhira and Zoe show us around the apartment—modern, recently renovated, walls covered with vintage art deco posters—before Skyler spots their old yearbook in Adhira's room and begs to look through it. Zoe gives me a look before someone calls out to her and she disappears into the crowd.

I take a sip of my beer, heading back toward the living room. I don't hate the way it makes me less conscious of my body. Lighter. I wouldn't want much more than this, but the slight buzz I have going is enough to keep me from getting too in my head, letting me have a casual chat with a guy in my linguistics class and a conversation with a complete stranger about an upcoming *Star Wars* spin-off that we're cautiously excited about, which is generally the case with new *Star Wars* content.

About twenty minutes have passed before Skyler approaches me again, a different beer bottle in his hand this time. "Adhira just informed me that Zoe wanted to know if you're single."

I nearly start choking. "Zoe . . . *what*?"

A grin curls his lips. He clearly finds this amusing. "Don't worry, I told her you were taken and head over heels in love. But the news hasn't been broken to that girl over there, who's looking at you like she might cry if you don't ask her to dance."

I turn around, spotting the girl, who immediately breaks eye contact. "You're seeing things."

He holds his beer to his heart. "Swear to God. You could clean up here if you were single."

It takes a while for this to sink in, a swirl of surprise that mixes with the alcohol, jumbling my brain a bit. There is no question that I'm committed to Rowan, 100 percent. But my experience before her was minimal at best.

My previous girlfriend, Bailey—the relationship began because I overheard her talking with her friends about not wanting to go to prom alone, and because I had to admit I wanted to go to prom too, I asked her, which led to a few pre-prom dates where we never completely clicked. We turned out to be so awkward that we barely acknowledged each other at school, and I wasn't surprised when she broke up with me a few days after prom.

Rowan's reciprocated feelings took me entirely by surprise.

This conversation with Skyler sparks an immediate rush of guilt, even though Rowan and I talked about this. We knew it would be impossible to go through college without finding another human being attractive. I've just never been this flattered before, by complete strangers, and I'm half convinced it's all a joke.

"I don't get it," I say to Skyler. "Don't they realize I was a massive nerd in high school?"

"That's the thing. No one here knows what you were like in high school, and no one cares. You're nice, and good-looking, and—don't take this as an insult—you seem pretty nonthreatening. That's, like, catnip out in the real world."

Real world. And yet NYU feels like its own microcosm, not unlike Westview. Even if the city is our campus.

"Plus," he says, "that black eye is doing wonders for your street cred."

"I'm starting to think you're incapable of anything but ruthless positivity."

Adhira bounds up to us then, fortunately without Zoe. "Dance with me," she informs Skyler, not phrasing it as a question.

He gives his hair a flirtatious bat. "Because you've missed me?

Because you've been counting down the days until I moved to the city? Because you—"

"Because I don't know anyone else who likes the Mighty Mighty BossToneS unironically, and I put this on the playlist just for you," she says with a roll of her eyes. "Ska never should have been a thing. You inherited the worst taste in music from your brothers."

"They really are talented instrumentalists," I say. "At least, that's the impression that I get."

A beat, and then Skyler bursts out laughing, throwing an arm around my shoulder. "You just became my new favorite person."

Then he places his bottle on the counter and follows Adhira into the crush of bodies. "You're enabling him!" she calls to me. Skyler throws me a wink before he turns his full attention back to her.

I watch them for a few moments, this effortless way they sway together, his index finger hooked into the belt loop on the back of her shorts. Every so often, he says something that makes her laugh, and she grabs a fistful of his shirt and moves closer.

My phone buzzes in my hand.

Rowan: *I miss you. is it thanksgiving yet?*

That's our next visit: me in Boston for that holiday weekend. I wish we could do it sooner, but I bought this ticket early because prices would surely only skyrocket, and we'll be seeing each other back home in mid-December, too. Especially now that we have our hearts set on Europe, we want to save money.

The more I think about it, the more I love the vision of it so much, I almost don't want to think of the price tag. I've done some research—there are ways to do it cheaply. She'd lit up so completely while talking about it, and I'm not sure I could bear to disappoint her.

Neil: *Rudely, no. But countdown app says 44 and a half more days.*

We video chat and talk on the phone every few days, but the technology almost feels like it's mocking us. Here is the girl you love in full color, smiling and laughing at your terrible jokes, only you can't touch her. That's all I want right now: Rowan in my arms, pressed together on this crowded dance floor.

Rowan: *please know that I fully intend to lock you in my room and never let you out*

but not in a creepy way

Now I'm picturing something else. The two of us alone in her dorm room, her long hair tangled in my hands and my mouth on hers. A chance to prove that what happened in New York was a fluke.

Neil: *You got it. The rest of Boston can wait.*

As much as Skyler would probably love for me to join an intramural pickleball team with him and a dozen of his closest friends, I've found something even better: Linguistics League.

The club meets Wednesday nights in the Linguistics Building, and it's not a large gathering—about fifteen people with a few boxes of pizza, two-liter bottles of soda, and scattered cups and napkins. Surely this is what I need to fall back in love with linguistics, to gain some confidence to speak up in class. The free pizza is only a bonus.

I grab a slice, and I'm about to ask the person next to me if we simply sit around and discuss etymology when a long-haired guy at the front of the room calls out, "Hello, hello!" and the group quiets down.

"My dear friends and new faces, since this is our first meeting of the year, let's start with some introductions." He points to himself. "I'm Jay, the president of our small but mighty group, and next to me is your vice president, Chinara." The girl next to him waves, and I get a brief flashback to the student council meetings Rowan and I presided over.

"If you haven't been to one of our meetings before, you can expect some cheap food, excellent camaraderie, and a lot of good old-fashioned word nerdery," Jay continues, which gets a few laughs. "First things first—who the hell are we? Introduce yourself in any language of your choosing, your year, and where you're from. Let's see if we can get through the whole room without repeating any languages." A clearing of his throat, and then: "Soy Jay y nací en Miami, pero Nueva York es mi hogar."

Chinara goes next, introducing herself in what I believe is Danish. We go around the room, some students speaking in what might be their native tongues, others in learned languages. A guy named Tyler picks English and everyone laugh-groans, and then he says, "What, you didn't say English was off-limits!"

When it's my turn, I stumble for a moment. I took AP Spanish, French, and Latin in high school, much to my counselors' horror. The only language I know that hasn't been used yet is Italian, but I'm far from conversational in it. Still, if there were any time to give it a try, that would be now.

"Mi chiamo Neil, vengo da Seattle, e sono . . . un primo anno?" Imperfect, probably, but everyone seems to understand.

"Excelente!" Jay says. "Moving on. Last year, we got into a lot of arguments about language versus perception and which affects which—and no, Tyler, we're not bringing it up again yet. We don't want to scare the newbies away."

Tyler puts his hand back down.

Though I make a silent vow to participate as Jay leads a discussion about current events in the linguistics world, it's not as easy as I'd hoped. I'm the only new person, the interloper—it's clear they all know each other. I was foolish for assuming it would be an instant fit and hate that I'd rather be in my dorm with a book.

As everyone packs up, they chatter among themselves. I try to catch anyone's eye, offering up a smile, but it feels like intruding on a group of tight-knit friends.

"Do you have Mills for your senior capstone? He's supposed to be *the worst*."

"No, I have Kubiak, thank God."

These are the people I thought I would belong with, but when

I leave, I feel just as anonymous as before. Only in multiple languages.

It makes me wonder if there's something wrong with me, that in this massive school in this massive city, there isn't a space I've found yet that fits. I had a good enough time with Skyler at that party, even forced myself to mingle a bit before we stumbled home at two in the morning, but I'm not sure I could do that every weekend. As friendly as Skyler is, there's this inescapable thought that we are simply two very different people. As far as roommates go, I know I got lucky. Last week Cyrus texted about the guinea pig his roommate had sneaked in from home. *Do you know how much guinea pigs shit???* he'd asked. *IT IS ENDLESS. IT IS EVERYWHERE.*

Despite the heavy sense of exhaustion clinging to me, I'm not quite ready to head back to my room yet. Wandering New York City at night doesn't seem nearly as dangerous as I thought it might. Even on a Sunday evening, there are people everywhere, in pairs and in groups and some all alone, and I can't help wondering if any of them feel the same aimlessness I do. I have a linguistics paper due tomorrow that's only half-done, and though I'd regularly stay up late in high school, tonight I'm not sure I have it in me.

I debate calling Rowan before realizing she might already be asleep and try my mom instead, since she's three hours behind.

"Neil, baby?" she says, picking up on the first ring, and as much as the nickname usually embarrasses me, tonight I don't mind it at all. "It's good to hear your voice. How are you?"

"Fine, Mom." I dodge some garbage on the sidewalk and make my way over to a bench. "I'm just walking home and thought I'd see what you were up to."

"We just got back from dinner with Christopher." In the background, I can hear my sister's voice. "What about you? Late where you are."

"I was at a meeting for this linguistics club."

"Could that school be any more perfect for you?"

When I return her laugh, it's strangely hollow, and I desperately wish it weren't. I force a smile into my voice. "Yeah, it's really something."

Though the time surrounding my dad's arrest and trial is still a blur, something I viewed through childlike lenses later explained to me in great detail, what I know is this: his court-appointed lawyer tried to reduce the charges to second-degree assault, but given the fact that he had attacked a minor, that the minor had been in a coma for a month with a long way to go until full recovery, the first-degree charge had stuck.

The complicated feelings I have toward my dad are not because he is in prison. It's everything that happened beforehand—the terrifying display of violence toward that kid, and all the small, sharp ways he made it clear that I was not the son he wanted.

My mom was suddenly raising the two of us herself, a sixth grader and a kindergartener. Her parents and sister helped us out while she worked through a certificate program to become a paralegal. The divorce didn't happen right away. Two years into my dad's sentence, she filed for it, feeling it was what our family needed to move on, though we were still making semi-regular visits at that point. Several times a year—several times too many, it seemed to me.

I could have been angry at her that it had taken so long. But all I felt was a swell of sorrow mixed with hope for the future. My mom and I grew even closer, to the point where I must have told her too much about school because she recognized Rowan right away when she came to my house during Howl.

Christopher joins my mom on the phone. "Hey, hey, hey," he says in that easygoing way of his. It's his go-to greeting, one that made me cringe when I first met him because it sounded almost phony in its enthusiasm. But then I learned that's just Christopher: genuinely upbeat all the time. "I need your brain. *Blank slate*, ten letters, third one is a *B*."

He's a long-suffering crossword fan, and we've bonded over words. "Tabula rasa," I say after a moment. "You realize asking me is just as much cheating as looking up the answer online, right?"

"Yeeeeeah," he says, drawing out the syllable with a laugh. "But it doesn't *feel* that way."

Christopher's a few years younger than my mom, never married. Natalie and I were reluctant to let him in at first, but he's as opposite our dad as someone can possibly be. An accountant my mom met on a dating app her friends urged her to sign up for. Bright and sunny, just as happy to talk books with me as he is skateboarding with Natalie. They've been together for two years, and although it took a while for my mom to be comfortable with it, now he stays the night at our place most of the time. It's everything my mom deserves, and I couldn't be happier for her.

We talk more about school, about the weather in Seattle.

"A lot of overcast skies, if you can believe it," he says. "You're really missing out."

"Hold on," my mom says. "Nat wants to say hi." There's a shuffle, and then my sister takes the phone.

"I moved into your room," she declares. "I painted all the walls a toxic shade of green except for one, where there's a unicorn mural. And instead of a bed, there's just a giant beanbag, and you can only get to it with a skate ramp."

"Excellent. Unicorns are my favorite mythical creature."

A groan. "I miss you, you dork. Lucy does too."

"Back at both of you. You're not giving Mom too hard a time, are you?"

"I'm an angel. Being an only child is actually pretty nice. And I killed it as Squirrel Number Three in our class play. Everyone agreed that I was the best squirrel."

"I'm sorry I missed it. Send me the videos?"

"Okay, but Mom did something weird with her phone so it's all fuzzy."

For some reason, this fact of my mother not being great with technology hits me squarely in the heart. "Sounds like her."

A pause. A shuffling sound. "Christopher's getting out the Dominion expansion sets, and I might be able to stay up past my bedtime if I play my cards right. Literally. Gotta go."

A new kind of ache settles in my chest. My friends and I taught her how to play that game, and then Natalie and I taught our mom, and we all got a little too obsessed. I always vowed not to take my father's place as any kind of surrogate, but I've wanted to be there for my sister in all the ways a sibling could be.

Now I wonder if I've broken that silent promise by moving away.

"We miss you!" my mom says, and then to Natalie: "Don't think I didn't hear that."

"Bye, Neil! Don't study too hard!" Christopher calls in the background, and then the line goes quiet.

A CARE PACKAGE:

- *One shrink-wrapped bag of New York City bagels*
- *A mug with a map of Greenwich Village*
- *A gently used guide to backpacking Europe purchased from the Strand*
- *A gray-and-navy-striped scarf*
- *And a note, written in calligraphy:*

*A little piece of NYC
for my Seattle girl
in Boston.*

*Yours,
Neil*

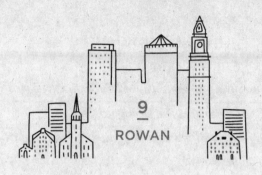

9
ROWAN

NEIL'S CARE PACKAGE gets there at the perfect time, right after I've gotten feedback on my next creative writing assignment and am in desperate need of a distraction. The best part: that the striped scarf, the one I've seen him wear on Seattle's coldest days back when my feelings were wrapped in animosity, still smells like *him*.

"Eventually you'll have a whole outfit and won't even need me," Neil says over video chat. We've been attempting to study together, but the amount of studying we've done so far is questionable, especially because he's wearing one of my favorite shirts: the black one with QUIDQUID LATINE DICTUM, ALTUM VIDETUR printed on it.

Also questionable: the way Paulina breezed out of the room once again when I said I was about to video chat with my boyfriend, as though interpreting it as me telling her to leave—which I wasn't. I'd be more offended if I had a sense of what I'd done wrong. I haven't touched her succulent again, and when I found one of her penguin-patterned socks under my bed, I put it in her hamper. I'm trying to be a decent roommate, but she's barely giving me anything to work with.

"Yes, I have all your clothes laid out on my bed and I cuddle with them whenever I'm lonely." I angle the camera toward my bed where, incidentally, I tossed Neil's hoodie earlier. And because the heat in here is garbage, I grab it and zip it up. It's the softest thing I semi-own, and I hope he's prepared to never get it back. "Seriously. Thank you. I swear the temperature dropped about thirty degrees in the past week—I've already been worrying that I might not survive the winter. Eighteen years in Seattle did not adequately prepare me for seasons."

"Our poor, weak Pacific Northwest bodies." Then he thinks for a moment, seems to type something. "*Friolero*—I knew there was a word for it. That's Spanish for someone who's very sensitive to the cold."

"Friolero. I love that. I am that. Or friolera, actually. Don't need my Spanish class for that, at least." I hug his hoodie tighter. "Almost as good as the real thing."

We go back to studying, Neil placing meticulous sticky notes in his linguistics book while I make Spanish vocab flash cards.

"Are you getting much done?" he asks after ten minutes.

"Tons. You?"

He gives me a hard, penetrating look I feel the weight of even through the camera. "Incredibly productive. Especially when you glance up at me every two minutes."

"How would you know unless you're also staring at me?"

"My peripheral vision is excellent," he says, though I can tell he's trying not to laugh. "Okay, okay. Let's go for twenty more minutes, no distractions."

Three minutes later, he glances up again. "You're still looking at me!"

"I'm sorry! You're very cute when you're concentrating!"

By mid-October, I've gotten two more assignments back from Professor Everett. Her critiques are all extremely kind, just as warm as she is, but I'm someone who thrived on straight A's and 4.0's in high school. Even if they're graded more on participation than content, it still feels like a pat on the head and a *sorry, you're not good enough*.

I'd love for you to dig a little deeper here.

Could we play with more sensory details?

I want to hear your <u>voice</u>, she wrote in her most recent feedback on a piece about a pivotal childhood memory. I wrote a solidly lackluster eight hundred words about watching a World War II documentary with my grandpa, hoping to turn that experience into a larger commentary about my own Holocaust education and how I can't recall the exact moment I learned about it.

Rereading it now, I can see it's heavy-handed, completely surface. Not what I wanted to communicate with it at all.

If Professor Everett were cruel or arrogant, then maybe I wouldn't want to impress her as much as I do. Surely, in four years at Westview, I turned in work that wasn't my best. But my teachers knew me, and they weren't about to judge based on one off assignment.

To Professor Everett, I am a blank page.

Our next piece of writing is focused on genre, combining one we're unfamiliar with and one we love. The goal is to demonstrate how so much writing cannot be confined to a single genre. My short story is science fiction about a lonely girl who falls in love with a boy via anonymous messages they send on the computers in their spaceship—only what she doesn't know is that he's actually her best friend.

I'm not taking any chances this time, approaching my creative block as logically as I can. Because it's not technically *writer's* block—I've been writing, just not *well*. So I'll simply rule out each element that isn't working until I isolate the problem.

Issue number one: my dorm room isn't exactly shimmering with inspiration, so I'm working in the campus library, headphones on, a soup bowl–size hazelnut latte with extra whipped cream in front of me (solving potential problem number two, no creativity on an empty stomach). I choose a seat near the window for prime natural lighting (potential problem number three), and I'm wearing the kind of chunky cable-knit sweater that I'm convinced was *made* for writers. Wardrobe isn't one of my potential problems, but dressing the part surely can't hurt.

The spaceship is

Shit. What does a spaceship look like?

Ten minutes of Google Image–searching later, I return to my Word document.

The spaceship is sleek and stark, its control panels emitting a soft blue glow.

No, no. I should start with character, not setting. Romance is all about the characters, and that's why I love it so much.

Unless I *should* start with setting because I'm writing outside my usual genre?

For Amara, the spaceship had always been home. She didn't know what most of the buttons or dials or levers could do, but

Wait. Is it anti-feminist of me if she doesn't know how to operate the spaceship?

Amara knew every button and dial and lever like she'd been operating the spaceship for years—because she had.

I yank off my headphones, because maybe I'm no longer someone who writes to music, but I overhear too many hushed conversations to keep focused. And despite my proximity to a window, the lighting isn't the best, so I switch tables. Then I switch floors, sloshing some of my soup-latte on my jeans and scrubbing at the stain for five minutes before giving up. It's not procrastination; I'm merely trying to eliminate distractions.

~~*Even in a galaxy of brilliant stars, Amara was lonely*~~

~~*Amara couldn't really open up to anyone except her best friend*~~

~~*Amara and everyone on board her fucking spaceship should die in a fiery explosion*~~

~~*Amara and her best friend arrrrrrrrasdfgladhfliasfasfharogrgirg*~~

I push my hands into my forehead, urging myself to take deep breaths. I've had bouts with perfectionism before, but this should be easy. My favorite thing about Professor Everett's class is that genre fiction is not only accepted but encouraged, which I know isn't the case in all writing programs. I've read several hundred romance novels and written my own. I'm in a relationship with someone I love. If anyone should be able to write romance right now, it should be me.

Unless.

A strange, uncomfortable revelation whispers at the back of my mind.

I've never written while in love.

Sure, I've been in relationships—but never *love*, the overwhelming, belly-swoop, stars-in-my-eyes feeling I have with Neil. It doesn't make sense that I wouldn't be able to write about it now that I know what it feels like. I should be more inspired, the words spilling out too quickly for me to catch them all. My hands should be tripping over themselves on the keyboard.

Yet at the end of an hour, I've somehow only written a single paragraph, and I detest Amara with every fiber of my being.

A shadow pauses in front of my table, an immediate relief washing over me.

"Hey! Rowan," says Kait, and when a few people shush her, a whispered: "Hey." She's in an almost identical sweater, which confirms my theory.

"Hey. I'm actually working on Professor Everett's short story right now."

"Ooh, I just finished. Need a reader?"

I shut my laptop a little too quickly, reluctant to admit how much it's putting me through the wringer. *Ugh.* Now I'm even thinking in clichés. "It's not ready yet."

"I get it. Some things need longer to cook than others."

"How's the class going for you so far?" I ask. "I loved what you read last week about collecting seashells in Maine." Sharing work in class: something else I don't have the courage for yet.

A blush tinges her cheeks. Kait doesn't often get embarrassed, but when she does, it's usually because someone's paying her a compliment. "Thanks. The class isn't as challenging as I thought it would be. Everett was a little intimidating at first, but I think she's a secret softie."

"I wish I could say the same." *Isn't as challenging as I thought.* I used to be that person. "I don't know if I'm exactly thriving."

"Well, if you let me *read* something of yours, maybe I could help you out."

I give her this grimace as I slurp the last of my latte.

"I hear you. Fan fiction probably made that part easier, even if I wasn't using my real name online," she says, sliding into the chair across from me.

"It's never a struggle for you?"

A shrug. "Sometimes."

"But . . . you like it. Right?"

"I like having written," she says. "No, no, I do love it. It's just not always one hundred percent love, right? There're some negative emotions in there too. The 'Is this actually good enough, or am I wasting my time?' or 'Am I kidding myself thinking I'll ever be published someday?'" Then she lets out a sigh and drops her head to the table, short blond hair fanning out across it. "Or maybe I'm just grouchy today. Gabriel was going to visit for Thanksgiving, but turns out he didn't book the flight when I asked him to. Now it's too expensive and the trains are completely sold out. So it's not happening."

"Oh no. I'm sorry," I say, meaning it.

She pulls herself back up, props her elbow on her chin. "It's fine. I mean, it's not fine, but it will be. We'll see each other in December anyway, but still. It's not easy."

"It's like everything the world told us about long-distance relationships was right."

"Hate it when that happens."

I glance down at my phone, realizing I don't know what Neil's up to tonight. Of course we can't know what the other is doing all the time, and it's not that I'm worried—I'm not. It's just that even after my trip, I can't always visualize how he's spending his time, and that makes him feel farther away.

"As thrilling as the library is on a Friday night," Kait says, "Tegan texted me that a bunch of them are going to meet up in the Common for a little . . . what did they call it?" She swipes at her phone. "Ah. 'A drunken trip down literary memory lane,' aka sharing some of our old writing. Sounds amazing and horrifying. I just don't know if I should bring the *Chronicles of Narnia* self-insert I very clearly plagiarized or the Sherlock slash fics. Ooh, or maybe the semi-satanic poetry?"

Kait has layers, I'm learning.

"Oh God, I have too much to choose from," I say. "All of it's way too embarrassing."

"That's the *point*," Kait says in a singsong voice, nudging the arm of my sweater with hers. "Laugh at ourselves. Blow off some steam." She lifts an eyebrow. "And maybe it'll help you get out of your head with what you're working on."

My shut laptop and that single paragraph aren't exactly beckoning me to continue.

"Count me in," I say, looping Neil's scarf around my neck and following her out of the library.

This time of night, Boston Common isn't empty, but it's pretty close. A handful of nighttime joggers, college kids probably on their way to parties. Tegan's text, which after checking my phone I realized I'd received too—I'd put it on do not disturb in an attempt to focus—instructed everyone to meet at the gazebo.

Seattle has some great parks, but the Common and Public Garden are on another level. Sweeping patches of green, autumn foliage out in full force, a symphony of brick red and tangerine and goldenrod. During the day, sometimes I have to pause and remind myself to properly take it all in. There's something special about being surrounded by these buildings and this history. *That obscure thing you learned about in APUSH? Here's where it happened.*

The gazebo is unlit, both of us using our phone screens and a few lighters to illuminate the path. It's a white domed structure, quaint during the day if not slightly creepy at ten o'clock at night. The kind of place where I could imagine someone proposing.

My romance-writer brain stutters over that thought. Is it corny or sweet? Romantic or cliché?

God, maybe I really am broken.

"Kait! Rowan!" Tegan whisper-shouts, beckoning us forward, and I'm shocked they can tell it's us in the dark. We hurry up the gazebo steps.

There are eight of us total, most of the class. This late at night, in the nearly deserted park, it feels like we're about to have a séance, not read the contents of our middle-school diaries. The fact that we're sitting in a circle only adds to it.

Sierra passes me a bottle of wine. "It's not very good, but it'll do the job," she says. Her writing is some of the most literary in class, to the point where I'm not sure I fully understand what it means. Like, I'm pretty sure it's beautiful, but I also never know what's going on.

"Can't say no to a little liquid courage." I pour some into a plastic cup and then hand the bottle to Kait, who does the same with a bit more generous of a pour.

She lifts the cup to the group. "Cheers."

Some of my old writing is stuffed in notebooks under my bed back home, but I have plenty of it on my computer, single chapters of books I abandoned when I got bored, lovesick poetry, lists of names I like.

Most of it, no one's ever read before.

That changes tonight. If I'm brave enough.

"Fellow Emersonians," Tegan says in a serious voice, and all the chattering stops. They're wearing a dark trench coat, the light from their phone illuminating both their nose ring and the determined gleam in their eyes. "We are gathered here tonight to indulge in a time-honored tradition, one perhaps just as storied as the Boston Tea Party or the midnight ride of Paul Revere: mocking our preteen ideas of literary genius."

We all bow our heads solemnly.

"It should go without saying, but I'll say it anyway—this is a safe space. What happens in the gazebo stays in the gazebo. Don't read something you wouldn't want someone else to laugh at, but also don't be an asshole, okay? We were all gentle souls with big dreams at one point," Tegan says. "Quiet applause after each piece only, please. We don't want to disturb anyone." They demonstrate this with a silent clapping of their hands. A devious grin. "Now. Who's our first victim?"

Kait's hand shoots up. "I feel God in this gazebo tonight," she says. "I'll go. And I'm going to preface this by saying that I was a very weird kid." Another sip of wine. "This is a poem called 'Toil and Trouble.'"

A few hoots. Kait swipes around on her phone and makes a dramatic show of clearing her throat.

> "Double, double, toil and trouble
> Yet I'm the one who's troubled
> Every time you look my way
>
> So I'll steal a lock of your hair
> And one of your toenails
> And your shirt from yesterday
>
> I know the spell
> Will make you fall
> When you sip my witch's brew
>
> I'll add some broth
> And stir the cauldron
> And feed it back to you."

The laughter comes easily, buoyed by the alcohol.

Kait slides her phone into her pocket and takes a little bow as we show our appreciation with a round of silent applause. "Thank you."

"You have a gift," Tegan declares.

"The gift of really freaking out my parents."

"I'm confused," I say. "Is it a love potion or poison?"

"Unclear."

"I wonder if there's some hidden meaning there," says Sierra, ever the literary analyst. "Why go for the toenail when a fingernail would ostensibly be much easier to acquire?"

Felix volunteers, sharing a heartfelt ode to his childhood dog that makes a few of us tear up. Then Owen, who wore the bowler hat on the first day of classes, pulls out a battered notebook and reads a snippet of a short story in which everyone is possessed by alien life-forms except for him.

"Who's next?" Tegan asks.

I chew on the inside of my cheek. Part of me wants to push myself, but I'm not sure I'm ready quite yet.

I think back to Bernadette's, the club in Seattle where I read a piece of my work during that open mic night in June. Romance author Delilah Park had been in the audience. Listened to me. Somehow, I'd gotten onstage on wobbly legs and the words had spilled out.

Of course—Neil was there. At the time, that had made it seem all the more frightening, but maybe the truth was that his presence was a unique kind of comfort.

One that I don't have here in Boston.

Unless I create it for myself.

So I lift my arm, a little shyly at first, and then stretch upward with more conviction. Maybe it's the cheap wine or maybe it's the literary camaraderie, but this is *fun*. "I'll read. For context, this is a story I never finished about a girl who finds a lamp with a hot genie inside and falls in love with him, naturally. This is a scene where they're arguing."

"What more do you want from me, Belinda?" Axel threw up his hands exasperatedly.

I felt myself blushing, whether out of rage or lust, I couldn't decide. What I said next was probably the most unpredictable thing I had ever said or ever would say.

"Damn it, Axel! I wish you would just kiss me."

Suddenly, his whole facial expression softened. I was more than a bit taken aback when he spoke. I thought maybe he'd get up and leave, or turn me into a toad or something. But what he did was as far from turning someone into a toad as you can get.

"You don't need to wish for that," he murmured, and then he leaned in.

It was so easy to write back then, wasn't it? Alone in my room, no pressure from anyone except myself—and that was barely pressure. I was writing purely for the love of it. Even if I can laugh at it, that girl was so carefree about it all. She kept it from people, sure, but when it was just her and the blank page . . . there was *magic*.

The night devolves into chaos, my head spinning delightfully and the laughter flowing more freely than the teen angst. We talk about the class, our pasts, our loftiest dreams for our writing.

"National Book Award or bust," Tegan says, and we cheers to that.

Felix: "*New York Times* or bust."

"I just want one person to tell me something I wrote made an impact on them," Noor says, and all of us murmur that yes, we'd love that too.

Suddenly a too-bright light sweeps across the gazebo, one that isn't coming from any of our phones.

"Hello? Who's out there?" a gruff voice calls.

"Shit. Cops." Sierra shoves the wine into a bag while Tegan rushes to collect the cups.

We've been caught.

"Because I'd really hate to find some alcohol in possession of anyone who isn't twenty-one," the voice continues.

A shriek, and then someone yells out, "*Run!*"

We thunderbolt into the night, feet pounding the grass and then the pavement, no pausing to catch our breaths. We don't stop running until we're safely in the lobby of our dorm, where all Kait and I have to do is look at each other before we burst into laughter.

If I was ever uncertain before, now I'm positive: this is where I belong.

NEIL

Are you alone right now?

ROWAN

my roommate is never here, so yes. starting to think she might be a 30-year-old masquerading as a student to bust an underground drug ring a la channing tatum in 21 jump street

(no, I haven't seen the original due to a distinct lack of channing tatum)

NEIL

I am too.

(alone, that is, not a 30-year-old etc etc)

I had this idea . . . that maybe you could describe your current wardrobe for me?

ROWAN

is that the Neil McNair version of "what are you wearing?"

NEIL

Am I that obvious?

ROWAN

maybe a little, but I kind of love it.
in fact . . . I could use a bit of a study
break 😏

10
NEIL

I'M ALREADY BLUSHING as I lean back against the pillow, phone lighting up in my hand. When I got back to my dorm after dinner and Skyler was out, I saw an opportunity. Territory other long-distance couples have surely charted many, many times before.

I've made sure the temperature in the room isn't too warm or too cold, double-checked the locked door, and tidied my desk. I am not sure how, precisely, one prepares for a sexting date with one's girlfriend, but this seems to be as good a place to start as any.

As though I need a reason to love her more, she's immediately on board with the idea.

Neil: *What if . . . you sent me a picture?*

Then I add, *Only if you want to*, still not entirely sure how to navigate this.

Rowan: *would this be . . . a sexy picture* 🌝

Neil: *Perhaps.*

When the image comes through, the laugh that slips out does little to dull my excitement.

It's a Microsoft Word screenshot, a snippet of the book she's been working on for the past couple years. The one about the two lawyers, Hannah and Hayden.

He reached for the hem of her dress, inching it up her thigh.

"Slowly," Hannah begged, a thread of desperation in her voice. "I want to savor this."

I love it, I type back. *You look extremely hot.*

Rowan: *in my pajamas and messy hair, no makeup?*

This time she does send a photo. She's lying on her bed, her wild dark hair splayed across the pillow. Her lashes at half-mast. The pout of her lower lip. The arch of her neck. And—*Jesus.* The T-shirt she's wearing dips just low enough to show a bit of cleavage. It instantly becomes my new favorite picture of her.

God, yes. Absolutely fucking stunning, all the time. Your face. Your body. Everything.

I hope she knows I'm being truthful here, that I have to hold myself back from adding "and your personality," which while true, somehow doesn't seem like it fits the moment.

Rowan: *what you can't see is that I'm not wearing underwear*

A groan slips out as I run my hand along the front of my jeans, already aching for her.

Neil: *What purpose does that serve, exactly?*

Rowan: *haha are you teasing me? I think you know.*

Of course I'm teasing her. Sparring with her is never not my favorite thing to do.

But we've never done this kind of teasing before, and she might be able to tell that it doesn't feel fully natural to me yet.

That doesn't mean I'm not eager to experiment.

On the last day of school, I type, *when we were about to break into the library to drop off your overdue books, and we somehow started talking about sex and you brought up masturbation. You were going on about double standards and I was just trying not to spontaneously combust. And I'd be the first human this ever happened to, and that would be very embarrassing.*

Rowan: *you wanted me.*

Neil: *So badly. And you have to believe me that I didn't think about you in *that* particular way all the time, but sometimes . . .*

I like that you did, she writes back, and all the blood in me rushes south. *this perfect gentleman in your suits, secretly horny for the girl you supposedly couldn't stand*

Before I can send anything back, another message appears.

what would you do if you were here right now?

My jeans are already unzipped, my hand reaching inside my boxers. I've been hard since the photo she sent, and there's at least one sad timeline in which this is over much too quickly. That's not the route I want to take.

With my other hand, I tap my fingers against the phone, debating how to translate the images in my head into coherent words.

Push you up against the door and kiss as much of you as I could.

I've read a handful of her romance novels and certainly had enough fantasies to get creative, but I'm unsure where the boundaries are. If we can truly say anything at all and if that's the beauty of this.

134

Maybe this is our chance to rewrite what happened when she was in New York.

I'd grab your hips so I could get closer to you and kiss you in that place you like, right in that dip of your shoulder against your neck. Then I'd drag you over to the bed.

Except in this version, our dorms have massive hotel room beds with giant headboards and the softest, fluffiest sheets you can imagine.

I stare down at the words, cringing. "Fluffiest" is not the sexiest word I could have picked.

But it doesn't seem to faze her.

Rowan: *amazing. so much space to spread out*

Neil: *But I don't want to spread out. I don't want any space between our bodies. I want to be beside you. On top of you. Beneath you. Wherever you want me.*

Rowan: *everywhere. I want to feel you everywhere*

Rowan: *you're really good at this, btw*

Neil: *Would you expect anything less?*

Neil: *The real question is, who's better?*

Rowan: *I think we can both win this time*

Rowan: *but I also think you're about to be very grateful for all the romance novels I've read* 😏

Neil: *Already am.*

Rowan: *let's get back to that bed. I'm on top, pinning you down, slowly taking off my clothes. it's agony, because you want me naked, but I think it's more fun to make you wait.*

Neil: *It's torture. That's what it is. Every moment my hands aren't on your skin: absolute torture.*

Rowan: *but we have so much time. we want to make the most of it.*

Rowan: *once we've both undressed, all I do is kiss you. your mouth. your neck. your shoulders. down your chest. all my favorite freckles.*

Neil: *You have favorite freckles?*

Rowan: *yes. it's a 7,000-way tie.*

Rowan: *finally . . . I wrap my hand around you and it's such a rush of relief, at least at first. but then you need more.*

I'm still going slowly. up and down. a little harder. a little faster. I love the way you feel, the way your eyes flutter shut as you grip the back of my neck, your hand fisting into my hair. all you can do is say my name, and then nothing at all.

then I let go.

but only so I can bend down and give you my mouth.

Fucking. Hell. My hand moves quicker, imagining her doing exactly that. The curves of her body, and how every single time I touch her, she somehow feels better than the time before. Her sweetness. The softest skin of her thighs. The way she tasted— *Jesus*, the way she tasted.

The way she might be touching herself right now, eyes closed and cheeks flushed, a mental picture that nearly makes me short-circuit.

Neil: *And I'd like all of that. So much.*

Neil: *But not nearly as much as I'll like trailing my hand up your thigh, waiting for that intake of breath that tells me how badly you want me to touch you. It's the sexiest sound in the world.*

Her next message is only two words.

Two perfect, fatal words.

Rowan: *so wet*

I almost lose it just at the sight of those words on the screen, a gnash of my teeth before I tighten my fist, forcing myself to slow down. They might as well be spelled out in neon on the ceiling for the way they send off alarms in the part of my brain that governs sexual activity. We learned about it in psychology, only I can't remember it now. Doesn't matter.

Light-headed, I yank myself back from the edge. I don't want this to be over just yet.

Neil: *Wish I could feel you.*

Rowan: *is that what you're picturing?*

Neil: *No.*

Neil: *I'm wondering what it would be like to watch you.*

I send that one off without a second thought, my breaths coming hard and heavy, focusing only on what this brave, empowered version of me would do. What I might be too shy to voice in real life. I don't overthink—I just let myself *feel*. In my imagination, we can be both filthy and sweet. Depraved and wholesome. I want her in every possible way.

Technology clearly gives us more courage. If we couldn't have this in person, this boldness, then at least we can have it now. Tonight is enough. Tonight is everything.

Rowan: *can you get on a train right now? it's only four hours*

When I laugh, it's followed by a pang of missing her.

Neil: *Not sure if I can last until then.*

Suddenly my phone starts vibrating in my hand, enough to jolt me into a sitting position. She's calling. Rowan is calling me.

At first I think it might be an accident, that she hit the button by mistake.

"Rowan?" I say when I pick up, breathless.

"Hey." Her voice is just as thrashed. Fucking gorgeous. "I just—I'm almost—and I wanted to hear you. And I thought . . . maybe you'd want to hear me too?"

Everything in my body tightens, a rubber band ready to snap. "Yes," I exhale, relief racing toward me faster and faster.

She falls apart a moment before I do, her moan yanking me across the finish line. No holding back. No inhibitions. Her breathing is sharp and stunning right in my ear, somehow sounding closer than she's ever been, even when she's right next to me.

We listen to each other like that for a while, our slow sighs painted with satisfaction.

"That was . . . ," she says, breaking off with a laugh.

"Really, really good?"

"Yes. Ugh, I love you."

I love her. I love her so much in this moment—not just what we did together but this vulnerable version of her. It's never not a novelty that I'm the one she opens up to like this, and I'm not sure I could verbalize it if I tried.

"Next time," she says, her tone all too innocent, "we'll have to do it on video."

The weeks leading up to Thanksgiving are a blur of exams and reading and rescheduled calls because one or both of us has to study. I go to one more meeting of the Linguistics League before realizing it's something of an impenetrable fortress. After that night on our phones, I feel more connected to Rowan than ever, which is enough to keep me going when we can't talk as much as we did earlier in the fall.

Then she texts two days before the holiday with about a hundred crying emojis, saying she's sick and that she doesn't think I should come tomorrow. I tell her maybe that's exactly why I should: to take care of her.

Rowan: *no no no, no one should have to see me like this. I'm a bit heartbroken, but I don't want to make you sick*

As much as the reality of it stings, as much as I like the idea of taking care of her, I get it. The frustration and disappointment swirl together in my stomach, but I can't be upset with her—it isn't her fault. Winter break is just two weeks away. We can make it, even if this news makes the disappointment hang low in my stomach the rest of the day.

When Skyler hears, he invites me to his house for Thanksgiving again. I thought it had been a joke when his dad brought it up during move-in, but the guy is relentless.

"It's really no problem, having one extra mouth to feed," he says. He has two older brothers and two younger sisters.

The idea of being around a dining table with a huge loving family . . . I'm not sure I'm in the right headspace for it.

"I should probably study for finals," I say, and I think we both know it's a terrible excuse.

Except when he leaves and I'm alone in the empty dorm room, I can't help wondering if it's too late to tell him that I changed my mind.

Thanksgiving morning I spend with Lawrence Kohlberg and his stages of moral development, which my textbook explains with an example called the Heinz dilemma.

In this story, Heinz is a middle-aged man with a wife on her deathbed. The only drug that can save her costs two thousand dollars, but it only costs twenty dollars to make. Heinz tries his best to collect enough money but can only pull together one thousand dollars—which the drug seller refuses to take.

There are three options to solve the dilemma:

Heinz doesn't steal the drug because stealing is illegal.

Heinz steals the drug, but he should be punished by the law.

Heinz steals the drug, and he shouldn't be punished by the law.

The third option is the most developed set of morals, the realization that right and wrong aren't rigid concepts. Heinz's wife's life is more important than the money is to the store and more important than whatever consequences await him for breaking the law.

While all of it is intriguing, it's not a particularly easy read. Because of course I can't help seeing parallels to my dad, although no matter how many times I read through the dilemma, I don't find any rationalization for what he did. There is no explanation for his drastic mood swings when I was little, how sometimes he couldn't get out of bed and I'd secretly be glad, because once he did, he'd find too many things to be angry at.

"Dad's just really tired today," my mom would say, and I assumed all adults were like this. That their grown-up jobs and lives were so stressful that sometimes they needed to sleep half the day to make up for it.

I still cannot fathom that kind of violence from someone I share half my genes with. It's something that used to terrify me most late at night, when trees threw shadows on the walls of my bedroom and I grew desperate for answers where there weren't any. So I remade my identity at school, turned myself into the stoic overachiever. I couldn't let it define me, didn't want anyone to assume what kind of person it made me. As though his crime was some kind of reflection on my own morals, which of course it wasn't—but my younger self couldn't have known that yet.

There is no universe in which he would have sought therapy or medication. He was a man who believed in sharp boundaries between genders, and "talking about feelings" was something he often scoffed at for being too feminine. None of my interests matched any of his—not the dance classes my mom had me take to help with my coordination after I started wearing glasses, not my books, not academics. He couldn't even fake that he cared about them, the way I imagine most parents do when they proudly display their kids' finger-painting art on their fridge. For Lyle McNair, there was only *you're still doing that girly stuff?* and *fucking* look me in the eye *when I'm speaking to you*, and a hundred other things too painful to repeat. Things that even now make me squeeze my eyes shut against the memories.

But I can't stop myself from flicking through the DSM, attempting to diagnose him.

A futile task. The therapist I saw for a few years talked about the dangers of that, how it wouldn't do me any good to try to rationalize my father's behavior. I know there is nothing in this book that could excuse or explain what he did—what landed him in jail, but also how he treated us growing up. *No son of mine* when he caught me rehearsing for dance class or picked apart the secondhand books on my shelf. And his tempers, so unpredictable that my mom would try to get my sister and me out of the house when he started to raise his voice. He never lifted a fist to any of us, or at least, not that I know of.

But he didn't have to break skin to break our hearts.

I close my textbook, wondering how it's possible to be trapped between a desire for understanding and the simple wish for all of it to go away.

On Friday I sleep in much too late, which I never do, after an evening of dining hall turkey and stuffing and a phone call from my mom at my grandparents' place in Bend, Oregon. I'm groggy all through the afternoon, which I fill with more reading.

After a few sluggish hours, my gaze drifts from my linguistics book toward the window. Fuck it. There has to be something going on out there better than this. It's a Friday night in New York, after all.

It's . . . Shabbat.

Of course. I'd wanted to get involved with the Jewish community at NYU, but I've been so preoccupied that it hasn't been top of mind. There's even a flyer on the bulletin board on my floor, one I pass at least three times a day.

NYU REFORM SHABBAT AND FREE DINNER! it says, bold letters on bright yellow paper. JOIN US AT HILLEL! DID WE MENTION IT'S FREE? They certainly know how to catch the attention of broke college kids.

New York has many more Jews than Seattle, and I feel both a sense of belonging and otherness when I pass Hasidim on the street, men with shtreimel hats and long black coats and sidelocks called pe'ot. We are similar, but we are different in that similarity. My family hasn't regularly observed Shabbat since Natalie and I were younger, but the Roths do it every week, and I'd often join them during the summer. Of all the things I've loved doing with Rowan, that one is near the top of the list.

The Bronfman Center for Jewish Student Life is only five minutes away, and yet I find myself speed-walking.

"Shabbat shalom," says the girl at the entrance with a warm smile.

"Shabbat shalom," I return, my heart lifting in my chest as I grab a kippah. I already feel like however Jewish I am, whatever my level of observance, it will be welcomed here.

The sanctuary is small, four rows of chairs with slim prayer books on the seats. When I was younger, I used to go to synagogue with my mom all the time, though we've gone less frequently over the past few years. There was always a test to study for or an extra shift for my mom to pick up that felt more important. My dad isn't Jewish and never had any interest in religion, but it was one thing he never judged us for. A small freedom.

Ridiculous, too, to view it as a freedom—something he allowed us to do without getting angry about it later.

There I go, thinking about him again.

Throughout high school, I distracted myself so much that sometimes I could move through an entire school day without him crossing my mind. Then I'd go to work at the library and maybe he'd float to the surface if something reminded me of him, but for the most part, he stayed buried.

At home, he was impossible to forget. We were never big on family photos, but he was in the hutch he built for the TV, the plaster covered over where he punched a hole through the wall when I was nine. I saw that every morning, every evening.

But at school, I didn't have to think about any of it. School was *mine*.

Or at least, it used to be.

Just as I'm flipping to the right page for the evening service, grateful the book contains the English transliterations, I spot a familiar face, a girl with a blond ponytail unwinding her scarf and taking a seat in the back row.

Zoe. Adhira's roommate, the girl from the party who asked Skyler if I was single.

I glance away quickly, hoping she hasn't seen me.

144

The service begins. "Lecha Dodi" has always been my favorite and has a different melody than the one I'm used to, but it's easy to pick up. By the end, I decide I might prefer this new tune. That's the thing about Hebrew prayers. There are so many versions, and yet they all mean the same thing. Sometimes I'll even find myself humming one, unable to figure out what the tune is . . . and then I'll realize it's "Hashkiveinu" or "Ahavat Olam."

It hits me that I don't know which version of these prayers Rowan grew up with, and I'm suddenly desperate to ask her the next time I see her.

After the service, I follow the parade of college students to the free food, a room with a half dozen round tables, a covered loaf of challah in the middle of each of them. A small buffet with a dairy meal tonight.

I take a seat at one of the tables, saying "Shabbat shalom" to the couple who have already claimed some chairs.

Zoe approaches a moment later with an awkward wave. "Hey," she says. "I thought that was you. Neil, right?"

I nod.

"Zoe," she says, as though my silence is because I don't remember her name. "Cool if I sit here?"

"Sure—of course."

The rabbi leads us in the kiddush, and then invites anyone for whom it's part of their practice to wash their hands at the stations set up around the room. After the hamotzi, the challah is passed around, everyone tearing off a chunk.

When Zoe hands me the loaf, she must be able to sense my unease when I struggle to make eye contact. "Oh. About that party," she says with a grimace. "I'm guessing Skyler told you what I asked Adhira. I hope I didn't make you uncomfortable. Honestly, I just meet a lot of fuckboys, and you seemed . . . sweet."

"Would Skyler fall into that category?"

"Skyler is his own category."

"And that's the way he'd want it."

The rest of our table heads for the buffet, but I get the feeling Zoe has more to say.

"The stories I've heard from Adhira . . ." She trails off, toying with a piece of challah. "I swear, I don't want to make anything weird between you and your girlfriend. When I first saw you here, I got really nervous. I didn't want you to think I was stalking you or anything."

"I swear I didn't think that."

Her expression turns serious. "I was cheated on last year, and it was really shitty. I would never, ever want anyone to think I was flirting with their boyfriend, or anything like that."

There's an immediate sense of relief—not that she was cheated on, of course, but that this can simply become a friendship.

Because I'm starting to think I could use a couple more friends out here.

"I'm sorry that happened to you," I say.

When she attempts to shrug it off, I can tell she's still bothered by it. "Yeah. Thanks. I guess he was under the assumption that what happens on study abroad stays at study abroad." A forceful bite of challah. "But nope, if you're monogamous, turns out cheating's still cheating whether it happens here or in Prague." She gestures to the buffet, where there's no longer a line. "Shall we?"

We get up, fill our plates, make some small talk. When we return to the table, I realize I've taken more food than anyone else. A meal I don't have to pay for—I am probably about to become extremely devout.

Because Zoe's already been vulnerable, I can't help sharing too. "I wouldn't mind having a Jewish friend to go to things like this with," I say. "I haven't met anyone else here yet."

"That actually sounds pretty nice," she says, seeming more visibly relaxed. "Maybe Adhira and I could throw a Purim party!"

We spend the rest of dinner chatting with the others at our table—Chaim, a history major from Orange County; Marnie, a business major from Toronto. I learn that Zoe's from upstate New York and met Adhira during orientation week last year. She's majoring in biochemistry—"which makes it even sadder that I can't keep a plant alive," she remarks. I tell her more about Rowan, about Seattle, about the first time I had Shabbat dinner with her family and acted starstruck around her author parents.

By the end of it, when we all exchange numbers, I finally feel like this school and city are exactly where I'm supposed to be.

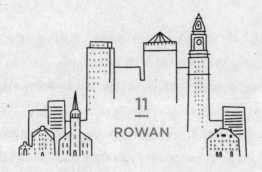

11
ROWAN

"YOU LOOK DIFFERENT."

I roll my eyes. "I look the same, Kirby."

Mara leaps off Kirby's bed, where she's been paging through an old magazine, and draws me in for a tight hug. Then she pulls back to look at me. "She's right. You do look different. And we missed you."

"Fine. I trimmed my own bangs and it went terribly and you'd really think I'd have learned my lesson by now. Thank you for noticing."

If anyone looks different, it's the two of them. Nothing in their physical appearance, at least not obviously so—maybe it's just the fact that I haven't seen them for months. And yet it hits me that this, the two of them in Kirby's room, is entirely normal. The way it used to be for all of us. Clothespinned above her desk is the collage of photos we helped her arrange a few years ago because she saw it online and wanted to re-create it. In a place of honor on her bookshelf is a small figurine of Angkor Wat she got on one of her trips to Cambodia with her family, along with a few awards from dance, though she doesn't dance anymore. A dried corsage from prom, one that I know lives in Mara's room, too.

I plop down onto the bed, picking up the discarded magazine. "What's this?"

Kirby laughs. "You know how my parents have been asking me to clean out my closet for, um, the past three years? Well, I decided now's the time, and look at this absolute *relic*."

"'Fifteen tips to drive him wild in bed,'" I read off the cover, beneath an airbrushed photo of an actress who used to be on some werewolf show we all watched. "'You won't believe number seven!' Wait, what's number seven?" I flip through it. "'Make eye contact'? Seriously? No wonder print journalism is failing."

"And there's more where that came from." With concerted effort, Kirby shoves the door of her closet, where stacks of magazines and clothes and even a pair of skis threaten to topple over.

"If you can believe it, it was worse three hours ago," Mara says.

"I can, in fact." Kirby has always been a predictable kind of chaos, and I've missed it. "Almost as much as I can believe that Kirby's about to put me to work less than five minutes after I got here."

Kirby swings her desk chair over to the bed, nudging me with her foot. "Yes, but first I want to hear everything about Emerson! Tell, tell."

So I do—or I try to. I tell them about my mostly nonexistent roommate, and about Professor Everett's class, and about how much I love Boston.

"But Seattle will always have my heart," I assure them.

I got home late last night and passed out, and this morning I allowed myself to sleep in until ten o'clock, which was still just seven a.m. Pacific time. Neil got home a couple days ago, but I had to see Kirby and Mara first.

Three weeks until I go back to school, and I plan to make the most of it.

"And how's our favorite former nemesis?" Mara asks.

I consider this for a moment—not whether our relationship is going well, but how much I want to tell them. They know we slept together on the last day of school, made suggestive eyebrows at me all through graduation. But what happened in New York felt too complicated to text. Besides, both of us are back in Seattle for the next three weeks, and with that comes an instant sense of comfort.

Neil and I know how to be together in Seattle.

"He's good. We're good," I say. "The distance isn't always easy, but we've been texting . . . creatively."

The two of them start squealing, and Kirby tosses a pillow at me. "Oh my God, you *icon*." Kirby tells me about her classes— "Anthropology of Ice Cream has forever altered the way I view mint-chocolate chip"—and Mara mentions a performance she did with a modern dance troupe on campus.

"I think it went okay," she says shyly, braiding a strand of her blond hair.

"She's being modest," Kirby says. "She was the *only* freshman in the show, and she rocked it."

Mara blushes, gives Kirby a tender look.

If they've heard too much about these things from the other person, they don't give any indication of it. From the very beginning, they have just been *good* together, Kirby's sharper side balanced by Mara's gentleness, and a mutual respect and compassion that's easy to admire. I love that they haven't changed, that Kirby is still a mess and Mara won't stop teasing her about it.

I love my best friends separately, but I really love them together, too.

Most of winter break is quiet, and that's exactly what I want it to be. Neil and I spend plenty of time together, sometimes with Kirby and Mara, sometimes with his friends. We spot some of our high school classmates around town, trade stories about our first few months of college. We stand in the rain to get burgers at Dick's—fries and a chocolate milkshake for me, one of my favorite Seattle meals. Afterward, when we're eating in my car, Mara announces, "I got Dick's sauce all over my arm," as someone inevitably says while eating at Dick's, and we can't stop laughing for a solid five minutes.

And of course, there's the time I spend with my parents, too, and some stilted Spanish with my mom. She speaks slower with me than she does when she talks to my grandparents, uses more basic words, but I don't mind. Most of all, my parents are curious about Professor Everett's class—her grading process, her methods, her teaching style—and whether they agree with it.

"That's interesting," my dad says when I tell them about the freewrites. "A little like journaling?"

"Yeah, I guess so."

They didn't go to school for writing. My dad, who illustrates their picture and chapter books, studied art and my mom studied European history.

"We just want to make sure she isn't leading you astray," my mom says with a wink.

I can't bear to tell them the whole truth: that I'm ashamed of the work I've turned in so far, despite the creativity buzzing through campus. Seems like everyone's been bitten by that bug except for me, though I've been holding out hope that returning somewhere familiar will get the words flowing again.

Neil comes over to celebrate Hanukkah with us on the second night. My parents are always especially affectionate with each other around the holidays, and this one is no exception. At one point my dad notices a smudge of latke batter on my mom's glasses, leans down to wipe it off with a damp cloth. She grins at him, giving him a quick peck when she thinks I'm not looking.

Their recipe for vegan latkes is one I dream about in the weeks leading up to Hanukkah, and I've been eager for Neil to try it. It feels so radically normal, spending a holiday with him. My parents are almost as obsessed with him as I am—or at least, I thought they were before my mom's warning during move-in. It probably helps that he loves their books, and so does his sister, Natalie, though she didn't grow up with them the way he did. The way we both did, technically.

152

But my mom hasn't mentioned that fraught conversation during any of our phone calls, and tonight there's only comfort and ease as my parents ask him how school's going, how he likes New York. Maybe my mom truly heard what I said and changed her mind.

"We're hoping our publisher brings us out there in the spring," she's saying, spooning applesauce onto a latke. "We're just waiting to finalize a few more details for the tour."

"I'll be in the front row."

"And make all the little kids sit behind you? Evil," I say between bites of latke.

"None of those kids know what it was like to have to wait for each book to come out," he says. "Now they can just go to the library and get them all at once."

"Kids these days," I deadpan.

"What's the Jewish community at NYU like?" my mom asks.

"It's great," he says. "I've been to services a couple times and met a few other Jewish friends."

My dad eyes the last latke on the plate, and while all of us encourage him to go for it, he splits it with his fork and gives half to my mom. "They must have something like that at Emerson."

"I haven't gone yet," I admit. Back in high school, I'd never met an extracurricular I didn't like. Student council, quiz bowl, yearbook. I guess I haven't gotten involved in many activities at Emerson yet; I've been too preoccupied with my writing. "I've wanted to—it's just been busy."

"Completely understandable," my mom says. "Your focus should be on your studies, anyway."

The comment rubs me the wrong way, reminding me what she said about our relationship.

"She can do both," my dad says. "College isn't just about academics."

Then a look appears on my mom's face that I swear I've never seen before, an almost tenderness. "That's true. I suppose it's where we met, after all." On top of the table, she covers his hand with hers.

They were twenty when they started dating. How can she judge me about Neil when she was only two years older when she met my dad?

"Actually—" I glance over at Neil, giving him a grin. "We were talking about maybe going backpacking in Europe this summer."

I swear I see my mom's hand tighten on my dad's.

"Backpacking," he says with a low whistle. "That would certainly be an experience. We must have some old Rick Steves guidebooks around here somewhere. . . ." As any good Pacific Northwesterner with a hint of wanderlust, my dad worships at the altar of travel icon Rick Steves.

My mom turns serious again. "Just the two of you?"

Beneath the table, I slide my foot over to Neil's ankle, letting it linger there. "Yes."

"We haven't decided on any countries yet," Neil says, and turns to my dad. "I'd love to check out those books."

154

My dad leaps up from the table, eager for a task, and starts perusing our bookshelf, muttering, "I know they're in here somewhere."

Meanwhile, my mom goes silent. Neil could personally deliver them a national award for children's literature and she'd still have doubts about us. Thankfully, she doesn't say anything else about it.

After dinner, Neil and I get overly competitive with dreidel. He wins a game and then I win a game before we decide it's probably too dangerous to continue. Then when it's time for Hanukkah gifts, he gives me a knitted beanie—"to complete your outfit"— and a pastel-covered notebook from a local stationery shop, because he understands that for a writer, a notebook is not a lazy gift. I give him an NYU sweatshirt, because I have a feeling it's something he'd consider too much of a luxury to buy for himself when he has other sweatshirts.

"Thank you," he says, holding it close after he unwraps it.

We stay awake after my parents go to bed, watching *The Last Jedi* on the couch in the living room. We're half paying attention, half simply enjoying being this close to each other. There are two mugs of hot chocolate on the coffee table in front of us, mostly empty, while outside, a light dusting of snow covers our lawn. My parents told us he could stay over if the weather gets bad enough, since he doesn't drive. *On the couch,* my mom emphasized.

Right now, at least, the couch feels pretty perfect. He's lying behind me, head resting on top of mine, our legs intertwined. A blanket on top of us.

I will the creative part of my brain to use this as inspiration, to capture this feeling and put words to it later. *Look, here's your romance. Write about this.*

"This is the good part," he murmurs into my ear. His body is so warm that I think I could fall asleep like this, dozing off while his thumb gently strokes my knuckles. My elbow. My hip bone.

"You've said that at least five times."

"And I meant it every time."

Even though he can't see me, I roll my eyes, then watch as Kylo Ren, with Rey in front of him pleading for her life, uses the Force to turn Luke's lightsaber on Snoke instead—which, he's right, is a fantastic moment. But what I love the most is the anxious hitch of his breath, even though he's probably seen this a dozen times. I could watch Neil watching *Star Wars* for hours and never get bored.

There's a novelty to the fact that we get to see each other again tomorrow, and next week. That night in New York was a blip—I'm sure of it now. If we haven't been physical since then, it's only because we haven't had the opportunity.

"What's it like being home?" I ask as his hand slides into my hair. I catch it just in time to plant a kiss on his palm.

"Mmm. Good. Weird."

"Neil McNair, monosyllabic? Who *are* you?"

He tugs gently at my hair. "It's hard to describe. All of it is familiar, of course, but it also feels a bit like being a guest in someone else's home. Little differences you wouldn't usually notice, like a new brand of toilet paper, or the way the house smells. Not *bad*, but then you wonder if it's always smelled that way, or if you just got used to it."

"I had some of that too. My parents made the bed in my room nicer than I've ever made it, and they had all these towels set out already, but not the towels I used to use. The *guest* towels." I nestle more deeply into him. "It's probably going to be a little more different each time we come back, huh."

As he nods, my heart twinges slightly. Change is never easy, and I knew I'd be opening myself up to so much of it by going to school across the country. I am already a different person than I was in September, than I'll be on my flight back home in June.

"But you're here, Artoo," he says. "And that makes it so much better."

"I can't believe I used to think that name was an insult."

"Nope, just my way of secretly pining for you."

"Tonight was really great." I slide my foot between his ankles, letting his weight anchor me. "Best Hanukkah I've had in years."

"Your parents are still so in love," Neil says. "You can tell."

It's true, despite my lingering annoyance over my mom's reaction to our backpacking idea. I'm not sure if it's the holidays or I'm only just now seeing it through his eyes, but they've never been shy about their affection for one another. Working together the way they do could so easily be a disaster, and yet it isn't.

"Yeah," I say. "I guess they are."

"Do you think that'll be us someday?"

I pause the movie as the characters are gearing up for a third-act battle on the salt-covered planet Crait. I already know we'll have to rewind and watch it again later.

Slowly, I wriggle around to face him. His glasses are off, and there's such a sweet sleepiness on his face that I wish I could take a photo of him, just like this, though I'm not sure any camera could capture my favorite details. The sweep of freckles along his cheeks, his long lashes. The soft mess of his auburn hair.

In any other relationship, a question like this might be terrifying. Too much, too soon.

We're only eighteen and nineteen, I might say. *We've only been together six months.*

And yet with Neil, everything felt serious right away. Maybe it was because we were on the precipice of graduation, knowing that anything we started would be tested in the fall. We were already thinking about the future. Or because we'd both had our hearts broken, and we respected each other too much not to jump in with both feet. Eyes open.

That was how it was supposed to feel—I'd been so certain of it all summer. We were serious about everything in our lives: school, our futures, each other. We were giving this everything we had or nothing at all. There was no in-between.

"Going to bed early while our kid stays up to make out with their boyfriend?"

He laughs a little, but then: "You know what I mean."

Neil McNair is a deeply sentimental person, and it's one of the things I like most about him. After all, he was the one who said "I love you" first—or wrote it, technically.

I allow myself to really, truly consider it, that kind of future with him. Picking a city to live in. Decorating an apartment together, bickering over what to put on the walls. Coming home from work, cooking together in the kitchen.

Falling asleep together every night.

I don't know yet if that future includes kids, if that's something I want, and I don't know what I'll be doing.

But even as I try to resist painting some idealized portrait of the future, Neil is there. He's at the front door, in the kitchen, beneath the sheets of a bed we probably found cheap on Craigslist.

My eyes fall shut, that vision suddenly seeming so real.

All I know is that I want this, *him*, as long as I can.

So I burrow closer to him, because *this* is the good part, the two of us cocooned on the couch while snow falls outside, and say with complete sincerity: "I hope so."

ADRIAN

The Quad is BACK, baby, and ready to
wreak havoc* upon Seattle!

*meet up for a casual dinner or
something

CYRUS

Equal parts embarrassed and excited.

NEIL

That one HURTS. Where's the loyalty?!

SEAN

Don't say you've outgrown us!

ADRIAN

What do we think, Hilltop Bowl? For old
times' sake?

SEAN

I could destroy at least two whole
baskets of their nachos.

NEIL

I'm in, minus the nachos. Cheese isn't
supposed to be that color, Sean.

CYRUS

That's because I don't think it's really cheese.

ADRIAN

Quad liiiiiiife! 🐷

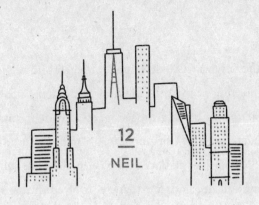

12
NEIL

EVEN ON WINTER break, even back in my own bed, I am incapable of sleeping in. It's a marginal amount of relief—back in New York, those cold, darkness-shortened days between Thanksgiving and winter break somehow managed to feel eternal. Here, the fog of exhaustion I felt on the East Coast lifts, replaced by a soothing sense of comfort.

Home. I never imagined I'd be so happy to be here, surrounded by the familiar.

We keep the house a bit cooler to save on energy costs, but this winter I don't mind it, not when I'm essentially living in Rowan's violet NYU sweatshirt. The weather taunts us, that light layer of snow turning to slush right away, and then it's just gloom and gray onward through the end of December. I'm surprised to miss Skyler, but the worries I had in New York don't seem to exist here when I'm able to see Rowan almost every day.

That night with her on the couch, those three whispered words that sounded like a promise.

I hope so.

162

And the only way I could respond, the truthful way: *Me too.*

The morning of the fifth night of Hanukkah, a Saturday, all of us are home for breakfast together. A rarity, with my mom not having much time off. Christopher's just stepped out to run a few errands. He's not Jewish, but he loves celebrating the holidays with our family, and he's gotten extremely involved in the whole one-present-each-night component of Hanukkah, despite the fact that we've never really done it and it's mostly for kids. Still, it doesn't stop him from surprising my mom with something small each night: a candle, a new kettle, a toy for Lucy.

Natalie is at the kitchen table next to me, attacking the wax buildup on our menorah. "How is there *so much* in here," she mutters.

"That's part of its charm." My mom takes a bite of yogurt. She's in athletic wear, her red hair tied in a ponytail. Recently she stopped dyeing out the grays, informing us that she'd made her peace with the aging process. "All the wax from all the years we were too lazy to scrape off."

"It's art," I agree.

Lucy finishes her kibble and wanders over to the dining table, nudging at my leg until I let her drop her head into my lap. She must realize I'm the easiest target, and she's right because I sneak her a few Cheerios when no one is looking. Though she's slowly losing her vision, her sense of smell is as strong as ever.

My mom stirs yogurt around, glancing up at me and then back down, as though working up to something. I have a feeling some kind of serious discussion is coming. "Nat? Do you mind if I talk to your brother alone for a minute?"

"Fine, fine," she says, bouncing up from the table and toting the menorah down the hall to her room.

There's only sugary milk left in my bowl, but I wait at the table while my mom stands, opens a drawer beneath the coffeemaker, and pulls out an envelope.

"This came for you," she says, and I know without looking at it exactly what kind of letter it is and who it's from. "Last month, even though I've asked him to stop writing. I didn't want to tell you and have it be hanging over you, and then I wanted you to be able to enjoy Hanukkah with the Roths, and well . . . there's probably no good time to get these letters, is there? I hope that was okay."

"Yes. Of course. I wouldn't have wanted that either." I reach down to scratch behind Lucy's ears, as though this sweet dog will keep me from falling apart. Maybe she will.

My mom passes the envelope to me, and the Cheerios in my stomach threaten to crawl back up my throat. Each letter is formed so carefully that for a moment I worry I inherited my love of calligraphy from this man, too, before I realize that he probably had endless amounts of time to write this.

The previous letter I received, a week before graduation, is fresh enough that it's still rattling around in my brain. *Hope to see you before you go to your fancy New York school.*

This letter is long. Too long. And it's nothing I haven't read before—how much he misses us, how he's doing, how he fills his days.

And then, at the end:

Really hoping to see you soon. Maybe when you're home for Christmas?

Dad

The casual way he signs it, just "Dad"—that's the part that gets me. And the notion of being home for Christmas when my sister and I have always identified as Jewish, when he must know that "winter break" is how I'd prefer this vacation be acknowledged.

The smallest movement of his wrist to twist the tiniest of knives.

I fold the sheet of paper back up.

"So he's going the emotional manipulation route," I say dryly, as Lucy glances up at me with those soulful brown eyes to wonder why I've stopped petting her. I slide a hand back into her fur, trying to keep my voice even. "Please don't tell me that even though he's done some horrible things, he's still my father. We both know the kind of person he was before."

"I wouldn't," she says, walking around to my side of the table and draping a hand over my shoulder. "I can never apologize enough times."

"And I can never tell you enough times that you have nothing to apologize for."

We talked about it in family therapy. The guilt she felt over not leaving him when the Moods started, and the ensuing guilt over having those thoughts when he so clearly needed help. Help he refused to get.

We were all victims, our therapist said, and though it broke my heart to imagine my mom that way, she was right.

"I wish you didn't have to deal with this at all. You have no idea. When you're in New York, even though I miss you, I'm so, so happy for you. So proud of you. You know that, right?"

Slowly, I nod. She's never made it much of a mystery, the fact that she wanted me to do something big.

"Whatever role you want him to have in your life—or not—that is entirely your decision," she says. Another thing she's told me multiple times. "You have my full support."

The last time I saw him, I was sixteen. The three of us made the journey to Walla Walla together, four and a half hours in the car that felt like forty.

"I know that. Mom—I love you."

A hug. "You too. Always."

I rinse out my bowl and place it in the dishwasher while my mom heads out for a morning jog. Lucy trots behind me down the hall. This dog has always been so attuned to our moods, ready to give (or request) love when we're at our lowest. In fact, she wasn't even a cuddly dog until after my dad went to prison. Then she started sleeping with me or with Natalie when she used to prefer her own bed. Like she knew we needed it.

"I could hear you guys," Natalie says after I knock on her door. She's at her desk, still working on the menorah. "The walls in this house aren't very thick." And then, before I can decide what to say: "He sends them to me too, you know. The letters. Sometimes I don't read them."

I did know, but the letters to Natalie are more infrequent. She was so young when he left. So young now, too—too young to have to deal with this unfairness. Every time there's space between them, I hold out hope that they've stopped.

But then my overactive brain wonders the opposite. If they stopped, would it mean he no longer cared about us? Which would be worse: to be loved by a monster or not loved at all?

"I'm sorry." I lean against the doorway as Lucy leaps onto Natalie's bed, turning in two and a half circles before lying down. "It's not fair to you. It's . . . more complicated than it needs to be."

"I wish he'd just stop." Natalie's ponytail quivers just the tiniest bit. A hunk of wax lands on her neon-yellow nightgown, and she brushes it off. On paper, we couldn't be more different—her, with her love for adventure sports and bright colors, me with my preference for the indoors. This has eternally tied us together. She was five when he was arrested, and I used to envy her, if only a little, because she'd spent less of her life with him. But as I grew older, I realized that maybe I had it backward. Worse, I think, to have known the man only as he is now. I have never felt such a fierce protectiveness as I do over my sister—a desire not just to keep her safe from the world, but from our family.

Maybe the age gap prevented us from fighting with each other, or we figured our parents had enough to deal with. Whatever the reason, we've never had a disagreement that lasted longer than a few minutes.

She scrapes at the wax with renewed gusto, a small rainbow pile on her desk. "All Christopher has to do is the bare minimum, and he's already a million times better as a dad. Even if he's not our actual dad."

"He's pretty great," I agree, because we both know he does far more than the bare minimum. "Do you want to talk about any of it?"

She tries to shrug this off, but I don't miss the quiver of her chin. As tough as my sister wants us to think she is, she's still a kid. "It's bad enough that I barely remember him. I definitely don't remember anything *good* about him." She looks up at me, misty-eyed and curious. "Was there ever anything good?"

There was. Of course there was.

It's just that the *anything good* is trapped beneath a layer of impenetrable *bad*.

There were the times he'd take us to the park with puppy Lucy and we'd just let her run, and he'd marvel at how fast she was. When our whole family snuggled up to watch a movie, not caring the couch was threadbare or the TV was shitty or the fact that everyone else had already seen it in theaters when it came out.

When I was ten and my sister was four, we went to Ocean Shores on vacation. Wet sand and saltwater taffy. My dad chasing us into the water, even as we shrieked that it was too cold.

The last happy memory of all of us together.

Before the Moods and the ever-present exhaustion. Before the anger, before the night he changed all our lives.

"Some," I say finally.

He's invaded my brain too much lately. An unwelcome visitor, taking up space that doesn't belong to him.

The way this has affected my sister—the teasing at school, the fight she was in last year. I had plenty of it when I was in middle school. People would make jokes about my dad, try to pick fights with me to see how I'd react. Never with violence. I wish I could shield her from all of it, even though I know that's impossible.

All I can do is be there for her when she needs me.

"I've been practicing my tail drop," she says, already content to change the subject. "I almost have it."

"Yeah? You'll have to show me when the weather improves."

"Or we can beg Mom to take us to the indoor skate park next week," she says, making her eyes wide.

I laugh. "Of course. But you are *not* getting me on a board."

Natalie flings her arms wide, putting on a dramatic pout. "If you just let me teach you a few tricks—"

"Because it went so well last time?" I ask, rubbing a phantom bruise on my elbow.

"Not my fault that your center of gravity is all the way in like, Iowa."

"I missed you. Have I said that already?" I hug her tightly.

"Why did New York turn you into such a sap?" she says with a groan, even as she hugs me back.

"I've always been a sap. And I'm really glad you didn't actually turn my room into a unicorn skate park."

None of us have ever been very good at bowling, and yet that's where the Quad ends up when all our family obligations are over.

"Another gutter ball," Sean says with a good-natured sigh. "How many is that?"

"Five," Adrian and I reply in unison. On-screen, an animated ball drops off a cliff while "*G-G-G-GUTTER BALL!*" sounds through the speakers.

"Is there a way to turn that off?" Sean asks, sinking back onto the bank of chairs and taking a sip of soda. "I feel like it's getting louder."

I pretend to check the keypad. "Nope. None."

The whole afternoon has been tinged with nostalgia. The last time I was here, I bowled another imperfect game with my friends and discovered Rowan spying on our classmates, who were plotting to take us down during Howl. Tonight Rowan's out with Kirby and Mara, but we have plans to meet up for New Year's Eve tomorrow.

So many places in Seattle hold those memories.

I wonder if the East Coast will ever feel that way.

Adrian drapes an arm across the back of the empty chair next to him. "So we all know you and Rowan are madly in love. I am tragically single, despite my elite bowling skills compared to the rest of you." He lifts his eyebrows at Sean and Cyrus. "Anyone else?"

Sean says he's been indulging in the hookup scene at UW. "Zero regrets," he says.

"Maybe not from you, but from them. Once they see your bowling score," Adrian says, and Sean rolls his eyes.

"There's . . . this guy in my sociology class," Cyrus says, not quite making eye contact, as though worried how we'll react. He didn't date at all in high school, never talked much about anyone of any gender.

"That's awesome, Cy," Sean says.

I sit down next to him. "Tell us about him?"

And he gets this wild grin on his face. "We've hung out a few times, just gotten food or met up to study. He's a really great artist, and he's drawn a bunch of scenes from my favorite anime. . . ." At that, he pulls out his phone to show us, and we nod and whistle appreciatively.

Quad life, indeed.

When we take a break for terrible nachos in between games, my mind wanders back to the letter. I haven't mentioned it to Rowan yet, and there are only seven more days until we go back.

When I told her about my dad in June, it wasn't because I was hoping for sympathy. I hadn't planned to tell her at all, of course, but once I let her into my house, into my room, it was as if all the fences I'd worked so hard to build around myself started to lower.

Even deep in my unrequited feelings for her, I never imagined opening up in that particular way.

Yet I did. And even if I told her I didn't want her pity, I don't know how to guarantee she won't feel it this time, now that we're dating. Probably because I can't. For weeks afterward, I wondered if I'd told her too much. I didn't regret it, exactly, but I also couldn't take it back. Couldn't go back to the Neil McNair I'd been before June 12, although for obvious reasons, I didn't want to. She knew the basics, and she loved me. It could be as simple as that, couldn't it? We didn't need to analyze every ugly piece of history.

Maybe she thinks I've moved on—that single confession, and no mentions of it since then, only in passing. "My parents used to drive a Honda Accord too," or "my dad built that shed in the back."

And maybe it's better for her to believe that. For both of us.

I'm still thinking about it later that night in my room, propped in bed with a textbook. Even though fall semester is over, NYU has something called January term sandwiched between the fall and spring semesters. Along with a couple other core requirements, I picked another psych class for spring—Adhira will be thrilled—and a linguistics seminar for January, and I want to get a head start on my reading for both. But my mind is drifting. Unfocused, although academics have always managed to hold my attention. Then my eyes start drooping, and—

A commotion at the front door jolts me awake. I spring out of bed, abandoning my textbook as I stumble down the hall, Natalie following behind me. My mom and Christopher have just come in from the cold, their hair windblown and cheeks stained red. They're in matching puffy coats they got from Costco last year. They're both grinning, *glowing*, and I think my mom might even be giggling. "Mom?" I ask, though it's such a sweet and unexpected sound. "Is everything okay? I thought you were going to be out for a while."

"We had to come back and tell you two." Christopher's arms are around my mom's waist, holding on to her like he can't bear a single second he isn't touching her. In an instant, I understand what's happened. "Joelle?"

My mom presents her left hand to a shrieking Natalie. "We're engaged!"

My sister catapults herself into our mother's arms as my mouth drops open. And then I can't stop smiling. I'd wondered about this, of course—impossible not to when they'd been dating for a couple years. Sometimes I even hoped for it.

"Mazel tov! That's incredible," I say, hugging my mom and then Christopher.

"I feel like the luckiest guy alive. I was so nervous." He swipes a hand across his bald head, as though reliving the anxiety. "I'd arranged with the restaurant for the ring to be carried out on one of these decadent slices of chocolate cake—"

"—but I said I was too full from dinner," my mom finishes, laughing. "And he looked *so* worried."

"I didn't know what I was going to do," he says. "So I said that I'd have the cake myself, but then the waiter brought it to the wrong table!"

"He had to politely ask them if he could have their piece of cake. I was so embarrassed."

"Until the cake finally found its way to the person it was meant for." Christopher shakes his head. "Not exactly the romantic engagement I had in mind."

"That only made it all the more charming," my mom says, and the two of them embrace again.

It's then that I make a decision with full conviction: I cannot tell Rowan about the letter. I don't want her to associate us only with sorrow, and I never want her to look at me with pity.

It doesn't have to be a secret. It can simply be *nothing*, the way I spent so many years acting like it was.

Besides, I'll have this much better news to tell her instead.

Christopher rummages in the kitchen for sparkling cider and finds none, so we all toast with orange juice instead. I try my best to soak it all in, the four of us sipping juice from wineglasses while Natalie begs for a full play-by-play of the evening.

One perfect happy moment for a family that hasn't had nearly enough of them.

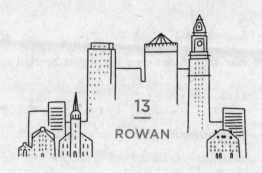

13

ROWAN

THERE WAS A great uncoupling over the holidays, relationships that couldn't withstand the distance or crumbled when it was time to face reality again. Plenty of the breakups were mutual, cordial, while some soured with rumors of cheating. I saw a few announcements on social media, including my first boyfriend, Luke Barrows, and his girlfriend, Anna Ocampo, and heard about others from Kirby and Mara.

My own goodbye with Neil, while obviously not permanent, was somehow both harder and easier than it was in August. Harder because I'd just gotten used to seeing him regularly again, and easier because we did this for four months and we know we can do it again.

Then there's Kait, who informs me of her breakup during our first creative writing class back.

"We knew it wasn't working," she says, unzipping her jacket. "We just weren't happy anymore."

The heat hasn't kicked on inside the classroom yet, and I'm still shivering in my coat and Neil's scarf. Seattle's year-round mild climate has truly made me incapable of weathering extremes.

I remember what Kait said about their Europe trip, how it brought them even closer, and the romantic in me is devastated for her.

But she doesn't look heartbroken, even though I'm ready to offer up any evening this week for a movie marathon or junk food run or however she handles a breakup. "It's for the best," she continues. "I was flirting with this girl in my film class yesterday, and now I'm completely unattached."

While I'm happy for her, I'm also a little surprised by how easy it is for her to move on. Granted, I've never had a relationship last that long, but I can only imagine a breakup like that would render me useless for at least a week. Maybe that was a sign for her that it was really over—the fact that it didn't leave her gutted.

During the freewrite, I try to summon all those inspiration-bright feelings from Gazebo Night, which is what we're calling it, with plans for another one next semester, once it's warmed up a bit.

I've been trying not to stress myself out about this class, and yet it seems to be the thing that always keeps my creativity locked up. I don't like the way the words look on the page when I'm struggling like this, when I can't get any of the sentences to sound the way I want them to.

I tried writing over winter break, but I couldn't tear myself away from Neil or my friends or my parents. And maybe that was for the best. Maybe I needed to give myself space to refill the creative well.

Today, though, I try something different. I take out the note-book Neil gave me for Hanukkah. If I'm writing by hand, maybe I won't be as focused on getting it exactly right. No red or green squiggles in Microsoft Word, no blinking cursor. The romantic link might also untangle the parts of my brain that are still tied in knots.

It seems like such an easy hack that I'll be both astonished and a little mad if it works, if switching to a notebook somehow unclutters my mind.

And it does.

For about five minutes.

Distraction comes in the form of a sharp sting in my abdomen, one that began over winter break and I dismissed because it was only ever a dull ribbon of pain.

This pain, though: definitely not dull.

Since I had the IUD implanted, my periods have been a little unpredictable. Lighter, too, which has been a great benefit. But now what's happening down there doesn't feel entirely normal.

I grit my teeth and try to focus. The pain reaches a crescendo when Professor Everett passes back an assignment we turned in before the break that earned her typical critical feedback in that kind way she's so good at. She loved the creativity, she said, but she worried the writing was a bit rushed.

Rereading my work—a short piece giving a fictionalized his-tory of any building on campus—I can see it's full of clichés. I'd picked the Lion's Den, coming up with a fake backstory about a lion tamer who fell in love with the founder of Emerson. Then I sputtered out, realized I didn't know anything about lions, and spent an hour watching videos about them reuniting with their owners after years apart. I have a particularly emotional paragraph describing hugging a lion, but the rest of the piece doesn't come close to the epic romance I pictured when I first sat down to write.

She had to get back on the road, for there were many more lions to tame and few of them lived in Boston.

Hmm, I guess I don't hate that sentence.

In her honor, he made the school mascot the lion. He wouldn't forget her. Couldn't forget her. The mascot was a symbol of that.

Professor Everett wrote, *slight repetition? And maybe a connection here between how lions remember their humans, as mentioned above?* Of course—that should have been obvious.

And my final sentences, which induce the highest level of cringe, alternating between an Emerson brochure and trying too hard to sound smart.

Now the Lion's Den is a popular spot on campus for anyone looking for a caffeine fix. Boston may be historically associated with tea, but here at the Lion's Den, it's all about the coffee. Students have come and gone, but the one thing that's remained constant is the mighty lion, its den, and all the coffee consumed therein.

Therein. Thousands of words in the English language, and I couldn't have picked a better one to end it on. And *it's all about the coffee.* Just throw me into the Boston Harbor.

It's been a slow revelation, but maybe what Professor Everett is trying to say is that her class isn't the right place for me. That it's better to cut my losses and try something new than make her suffer through another mediocre piece of writing.

My mind is too jumbled to analyze it now, so I shove the assignment into my JanSport and flee the room the moment she dismisses us.

I make an appointment at the campus health center that afternoon.

"I had an IUD put in over the summer," I tell the gynecologist. "And I haven't had any problems with it, but over the past couple weeks I've had some abdominal pain. Cramping."

"Occasionally there's some movement during the first few months, which would cause what you're describing," she says. "It's rare, but it does happen. Even if you're a little past that, we should make sure it's where it's supposed to be. Let's take a look."

I have always felt in control of my body, comfortable in my skin—my pear-shaped curves and my ability to tell my boyfriend what I like. Although apparently that's changing, too. So it's with a new kind of anxiety that I undress behind a curtain before draping myself with a paper gown and positioning myself in the exam chair, feet in the stirrups and legs still clamped together.

I'm still not entirely used to this, but the doctor is as gentle as she can be as she conducts the examination, letting me know that the IUD slipped and she'll try to put it back in its proper position as quickly as she can. I close my eyes, take a few deep breaths, and then it's over.

"It's a good thing you came in," she says after I get dressed.

"Let us know if the cramping hasn't gone away in a few days or if anything else seems out of the ordinary."

Back in my dorm bed with a heating pad, I discover there aren't enough emotional lion videos to lift my current mood. Paulina and I said a quick hello when I got back to campus and she was on her way out, but otherwise she seems just as mysterious this semester as she was the last. Suddenly I feel unmoored out here in Boston, the ground shaky beneath my feet. Everything over winter break was easy. Cozy. Now I've been tossed out into the unknown again, only it's colder and less hospitable than ever.

Even though vaginal health is not a topic Neil and I have ever broached, I send him a text about it, my thumb only wavering for a moment before I hit send. Because I want this to be something we can talk about, the same way we would books or academics. Well—probably not with the same frequency, but hopefully with the same comfort level.

And because he is Neil, his response doesn't disappoint.

Neil: *I'm so sorry—that sounds miserable.*

Neil: *I wish I were there. I'd keep you company and bring you soup.*

Rowan: *haha I don't think it's soup-level serious, but thank you for the virtual minestrone*

Neil: *That's your soup of choice? You have every soup available in your imagination, and you go with minestrone?*

Rowan: *I'm a simple minestrone-loving gal!!!*

I can't deny that it sounds so nice, imagining being taken care of like that. There's not a doubt in my mind that Neil would drop everything to bring me soup.

The vision comes with a terrible ache, one that weighs down my limbs and makes me drop my phone to the nightstand. I miss, the phone smacking the sliver of linoleum floor not covered by a rug, and I don't have the energy to pick it up. Because no one's bringing anyone soup, not anytime soon, unless one of us gets sick during a break from school. And who wants soup in July, anyway?

Then I'm spiraling about soup, and because my brain is a hell-hole right now, suddenly I'm thinking of all the couples that broke up over winter break. The romantic in me had been sad, but now I wonder if they rationalized that the temporary heartbreak would hurt less than the distance. Tonight, the finish line feels so far away.

Three and a half more years of this, I realize when I finally trudge downstairs for dinner, devastated to learn they've just run out of chickenless chicken noodle, the soup of the day.

Of him not being here when I wish he would.

January turns out to be the fucking worst.

An intense bout of homesickness has me googling things like "Seattle in the summer" and "Space Needle at night."

My writing continues to stagnate.

And despite having hugged him goodbye at the airport at the beginning of the month, I miss Neil with an urgent new feroc-ity. We try to hook up over video, but his roommate barges in (thankfully) before either of us has removed too much clothing. When we slept together over the break, I still couldn't get there. I was home, in my own bed, the place where I should feel the most comfortable—and yet I couldn't turn off my mind. We should be tearing each other's clothes off every time we see each other, given that time is so limited. I don't know why it doesn't feel that way.

I'll scroll through his Instagram when I'm supposed to be studying, liking the photos he's posted with his NYU friends. I want to be evolved and mature, and yet there's a twinge of jealousy when other girls are in them, even though I trust him completely. It's more the sense of being left out, of him having this whole other life there that I can't be part of.

Maybe it's all the recent breakups or my own ever-present anxiety, but I can't help reading into the spaces in between our texts and phone calls, wondering if he's having doubts about us. Ever since winter break, I've sensed a strange new distance from him. The biggest change I can think of is that his mom got engaged over the holidays, but he's never seemed anything but thrilled when he's talked about it. The wedding will be this summer because they don't want to wait.

The worst part of long distance, along with all the other worst parts, is that I can't simply call him up to get that reassurance. Even if he's not in class, talking on the phone or even on video just isn't the same as talking face-to-face. When he's next to me, I can read his expressions. With two screens and hundreds of miles between us, he might as well be on another planet.

He was in love with me for years, and now he has me. Is there a chance the excitement is just . . . gone?

No. I won't allow myself to think that way.

But instead of going back to my creative writing assignment, I open a new browser window and type in *transferring to NYU.*

My stomach squeezes even as I hit enter, every feminist urge in me expressing deep and thorough disapproval. *You don't understand*, I tell those urges. *I really fucking miss him.*

Maybe it's not just my writing that's stalled right now. Maybe what's wrong with me is that I'm in the wrong city. I skim the page, *official transcripts* and *letters of recommendation* and *highly competitive.* Essentially a lighter version of a regular college application, a process I'm not exactly eager to repeat.

My document blinks back at me. Taunting me.

There has to be an easier solution.

The door bursts open. Only then do I glance at the clock on my laptop—it's past one a.m. and I'm still at my desk.

Paulina Radowski is flushed and out of breath, holding a hand to her heart to steady herself. She yanks her AirPods out of her ears, tosses them on her bed.

It isn't as though we don't speak. It's just that the time we spend together is usually limited to when we're both semiconscious.

"Did you just run up the stairs to get here?" I ask.

"Yes, but that's not important right now." She takes a few gulps of air. Her long red hair is in a messy braid, one of her shoes untied. "Okay, so. I was studying in the library and then they shut down for the night, and as I was on my way here, I realized something."

I close my laptop screen, intrigued mainly because it's the first time I've had Paulina's full attention. "I'm listening."

"I've been in Boston for nearly five months, and I've yet to experience what I'm sure is the life-changing magic of Boston cream pie." Her blue eyes go wide with a desperate sense of urgency as she white-knuckles her desk chair. "I can't let another day go by without it."

"It's one thirty in the morning," I say, laughing, even as my stomach growls. I've never had it either, and it does sound delicious. . . .

She just blinks at me, as if to say, *so?*

"It's a Saturday night," she says. "There's got to be somewhere in the city that has some."

There's none of her earlier indifference. This is a new Paulina, and that must be the explanation for what I say next.

"Then let's go find some."

As soon as the words leave my mouth, I realize this is precisely what I need to do. I've been cooped up all month, marinating in my anxiety. And even though I can barely keep my eyes open, I could use the break. A quest with someone who isn't connected to the writing program, who I may not have anything in common with except for the randomness of Emerson's roommate match.

If Paulina wants Boston cream pie, we're going to scour the city until we find it.

Our plan is only slightly foiled by the weather, powerful gusts of wind and freezing rain that make us consider turning back for a split second.

"Just think how amazing it's going to taste when we finally get it," I say, and so we soldier on.

The first place, a diner that's known for serving up some of the best, doesn't have its hours posted online, and when we show up, it's closed. But we refuse to let Paulina's dream die, even though her phone does and we have to rely on my 20 percent battery to navigate the city.

"This might be a stupid question," I say, clutching Neil's scarf tightly to my throat as we head down Tremont Street, "but what exactly is in Boston cream pie?"

"Well, you have the cream. Obviously."

"Obviously."

"And then it has all that chocolate on top." She considers something for a second. "You know, I think it might be more of a cake than a pie." Then she spots an open door up ahead and breaks into a run, almost slipping on a patch of black ice. "Excuse me!" she calls.

A guy in an apron pauses as he reaches to take in the restaurant's sign.

"Do you have any Boston cream pie?" she asks. "I know you're closing up, but whatever you usually charge—I'll pay double. Triple, even."

He shakes his head. "Ran out hours ago."

"Thanks anyway." I give him a wave as he hauls the sign inside. "Have a good night!"

The next few places are all closed too, for the evening or for the weather.

"We might have to call it," Paulina says, dejected as I continue to frantically Google Map the dessert, clutching my coat tighter against the wind.

"No no no—there should be a place right around here. . . ." Then I blink down at my phone. "Except it might actually be a—"

I break off, the sight in front of us stealing my words. We stare up at the neon pink-and-orange logo I've seen around the city only a thousand times since arriving here in August.

It's a Dunkin' Donuts.

And it's beautiful.

Paulina and I glance at each other before bursting out laughing, then hustle inside and out of the cold, ordering two Boston Kreme donuts and cups of hot chocolate to warm up. Then we wait in a dingy booth with a few other college kids, taking refuge from the cold in one of America's most cherished institutions.

"Cheers," she says, tapping her chocolate-glazed donut to mine, and together we bite into creamy, chocolaty, doughy goodness.

"Mmm—oh my God," I say with a mouthful of vanilla custard. "Incredible. Amazing. Showstopping. Spectacular."

"After all this, we could have just gone to any of the five Dunkin's across the street." Paulina marvels at the intricate pattern of frosting on the donuts. "But there's something special about this one, isn't there?"

Even if Dunkin' is like Starbucks in its ubiquity, there aren't any in Washington State, and it's still something of a novelty for two West Coasters.

"We have them in California," Paulina explains. "But they're nowhere near as popular. And Dunkin' was founded here, so technically we're supporting a local business."

"True." I take another bite, unable to sit with the awkwardness much longer. "Okay, this might sound weird, but . . . I've been convinced that you hate me?"

Paulina's eyes go wide. "What? No! Why would you think that?"

"You barely spend any time in our room."

For a few moments, she doesn't say anything, just chews silently. "I guess I've been really busy with school," she finally explains, a bit of a mask settling over her features. "A lot of homework. A lot of study groups."

While I get the feeling there's more to the story, at least I'm fairly certain now that it's not about me. A difficult thing for an anxious, overthinking perfectionist to admit, but college is supposed to be a place for maturity and growth.

She tells me more about her major—she's studying business of creative enterprises and wants to work in music management.

"I love music and want to be near it all the time," she says, taking the last bite of her donut. "But I can't play anything to save my life."

"Favorite bands?" I ask, and this leads us into a ten-minute conversation during which she names at least a dozen I've never heard of.

"Perfect," she says when I tell her about creative writing. "My bands can play the soundtrack for your future movie adaptation."

"It's a deal."

As we re-layer ourselves to make the trek back to campus, the idea of transferring seems as ridiculous as it would have a few months ago. How could one person not feel indebted to the other? Maybe I just needed to remember why I picked Boston to begin with.

All it took was a single night. A single adventure.

Maybe that's what I need to do with Neil, too.

HOWL, EAST COAST EDITION

- ☽ An embarrassingly over-the-top tourist
- ☽ A spot tourists don't know about
- ☽ A local delicacy
- ☽ A street that shares a name with one in Seattle (numbered ones don't count!)
- ☽ Your favorite place in the city
- ☽ Wildlife in action
- ☽ Street art that really ~moves you~
- ☽ Something that reminds you of me

14
NEIL

WHEN I MENTION the scavenger hunt to Skyler, he immediately wants in. I should have known—Skyler's never met a game he didn't like. He turns laundry into basketball, dinner into rounds of "Would You Rather." I'm still reeling from last week's revelation that he'd rather speak to animals than speak every language in the world. "Just think what we could learn from them," he said, sounding awed.

Now his gaze flicks over Rowan's list one more time before he passes back my phone. "This is excellent. Do you want help? I could ask Adhira if she wants to come too—she loves this kind of stuff. Hopeless romantic," he adds with a roll of his eyes.

I'm surprised to discover that I don't hate the idea of having other people to do this with, and when I ask Rowan if my roommate and his friends can join, she agrees that we can enlist the help of others. During Howl, she and I were together almost the whole time. That was what made it great.

Right away, she established that it was a competition. The prize: bragging rights and free rein to pick our next movie without the other person exercising veto power. We'll take photos of each item on the list, text them to the other person for vetting. We are who we are—people who love parameters and guidelines, even in something of our own creation.

We set aside the same Saturday in late January, and I may have a slight ulterior motive for suggesting it: because it's NYU's freshman family weekend.

They do this a couple times a year, once in the fall and once when flights and hotels are cheaper. Aka now. At first I couldn't decide whether I wanted to tell my mom or not. I knew she'd feel guilty because she and Natalie wouldn't be able to come, and ultimately that's what made my choice. Christopher is well off but not wildly so, and especially with the wedding coming up, I'm sure they'd rather save the money.

At breakfast with Skyler, as he debates whether he'd rather be able to fly or turn invisible—"Flying's the obvious choice, I mean, who among us hasn't wanted to fly? But with invisibility, you could get away with so much. . . ."—I can't help noticing how much more crowded the dining hall is. Of course I'm familiar with Tolstoy's *Anna Karenina* principle: "All happy families are alike; each unhappy family is unhappy in its own way." And yet this morning, even the seemingly unhappy families look alike—all of them, something I cannot have.

"You're taking *what* class this semester?" one father asks at the table next to us, aghast.

"The Science and Psychology of Marijuana?" his son replies in a tiny voice.

"Thousands of dollars in tuition, and this is what he wants to study." The mother shakes her head, stabbing her stack of dining-hall pancakes.

There must be something wrong with me that even listening to these people argue makes my shoulders tighten, my heart swell. I want so badly to replace that mental image of "family" with one that includes Christopher.

I think about that letter I left at home, recycled and hopefully halfway to becoming a math test or dog-walking flyer. Something significantly more useful than what it was. I was so close to telling Sean and Cyrus and Adrian about it over winter break, and even now, I've stopped short of messaging them, the medium feeling too casual. They're living their best collegiate lives, and I don't want them to worry about me—because they don't have to. If they don't know and Rowan doesn't know, it's easier to act as though I don't, either.

I spent so many years pretending that part of my life didn't exist, and it's wholly unsettling that he's come to haunt me when I'm hundreds of miles away from home. I practiced how to be someone who didn't have a mess of anxiety and resentment attached to his father. I *studied*, that thing I have always been so good at.

I should be long past the worst of it.

"No family weekend for you guys?" Zoe asks when we meet her and Adhira in front of our building, and for some reason my brain interprets it as a no family weekend—a weekend with no family.

Fortunately, Skyler speaks first, waving this off. "My family's been here a hundred times."

"My mom couldn't get the time off work," I say, wondering if this is the same thing I told Skyler when I moved in. Given the way one of his eyebrows lifts, I think it might be.

"On a weekend? Capitalism is the fucking worst." Adhira sucks on her vape, then passes it to Skyler.

Zoe peers up at the sky before sliding a giant pair of sunglasses onto her face. The day is freezing, with rare sunshine peeking through, but competing with Rowan always puts a fire in my veins. "What does she do?"

I shouldn't be shocked by this question. NYU is a place where people flaunt labels, where who you are and more importantly, who your parents are, matter. The school comes with a price tag, not just tuition but the cost of living. Adhira's parents are surgeons, and Zoe's dad has the kind of finance job that keeps him at the office so much she rarely sees him when she goes home to visit. There's a guy on my floor whose mom is a senator and a girl in my psych class who was a child actress.

And this is the only reasonable explanation for why I tell them "lawyer," a single word I wish I could swallow back.

The lie is sour on my tongue. I don't want to be ashamed of where I come from. And yet once it's out there, I can't take it back. Can't say, "just kidding, she's a paralegal"—even though a paralegal is a more than respectable career, that she works so hard, that this job is the only reason we were able to gain some semblance of financial independence after my dad went to prison.

"My mom too!" Zoe says. "What kind of law?"

Skyler, seeming to notice my discomfort, lets out a dramatic groan. "As much as I love talking about our parents, are we gonna do this thing or what?"

"We're not just going to do it; we're going to win it," Adhira corrects, then turns to me. "What's the first clue?"

The heaviness is slower to lift than I'd like, but by the time we've grabbed *street art that really -moves you-* (three sparse lines of poetry stickered to a telephone pole) and *a street that shares a name with one in Seattle* (Broadway, which seemed so obvious that Rowan sent back a dozen eye roll emojis), my laughter is more fluid, my limbs looser. It's my first time hanging out with all three of them, and Adhira and Zoe get extremely invested in the game, helping me stage more artistic shots.

We get cupcakes at the world-famous Magnolia Bakery, because I admitted I hadn't been there yet. Adhira leans in and snaps a photo of me with a vanilla cupcake. "An embarrassingly over-the-top tourist," she says, and I groan and try to swipe it from her.

"Uncalled for. This is delicious."

"Yeah, but it's just so *basic*."

"Gotta agree with Adhira on this one," Zoe says. "They have much better cupcakes at Billy's."

Skyler polishes off his cupcake in two bites. "That's only because you haven't tried—"

Adhira gives him a death glare. "If you're about to mention a cupcake shop in Staten Island, I swear to God—"

This leads us on a quest to Billy's Bakery in Chelsea for a taste test, because it's only fair.

"This *is* better than the Staten Island Cakery," Skyler whispers to me, and I try my hardest not to laugh. "But don't tell Adhira."

Rowan sends back a Dunkin' Donuts for *local delicacy*, and I send a picture of a halal food cart. Pigeons fighting over a sliver of hot dog for *wildlife in action*.

Zoe points out the High Line, an elevated park built on a former strip of railroad. "My favorite place in the city," she says. "Maybe it'll be yours, too?"

The park is a mix of greenery and public art with stunning views of the city and Hudson River. With a burst of pride, I realize I'm starting to identify more and more pieces of New York geography.

"So I want to know more about this girl," Adhira says as we weave our way around locals and tourists taking advantage of the sunshine, posing for photos, asking each other, *Hey, what's that building over there?* "She must be really special to have made this for you. And you guys are still together in January of freshman year? That's impressive."

I lower my phone, examining the picture I just took of a building that looks as though it's been folded like an accordion. I have to take Rowan to this park the next time she visits.

"Well . . ." I trail off, because while I've talked about Rowan, I haven't exactly told our whole story. I'm not sure if anything could do her justice, but I'll give it my best. "We were rivals in high school. Always the top two, obnoxiously competitive with each other. I'd sort of had feelings for her for a while, but I thought she absolutely despised me. Until the last day of school."

Zoe lets out a squeal. "You're kidding. That's adorable."

"And hot," Adhira adds. "You thought you hated each other and then turns out, you love each other?" Then she shakes her head, black curls sliding off her shoulder. "God, I feel so single."

I give them an abbreviated version of what happened on the last day of senior year, explaining Howl, the scavenger hunt-slash-Assassin game we played, and how we teamed up when we overheard other students plotting to take us down. A familiar warmth blooms in my chest, the awkwardness from earlier nearly gone.

"And you had her name the whole time?" Skyler says. They're all rapt, Zoe's chin propped in her hands, Adhira barely blinking. We've managed to snag a spot on some benches that overlook car traffic below. "She was your target? That could have blown up in your face so hard."

"I thought it would be my undoing too. We had this huge fight about it, but then we met up for the last clue . . . and the rest is history."

"That is so fucking romantic, I can't stand it," Zoe says. "The most effort my ex ever put in was when he bought me a box of chocolates for my birthday. And he ate half of them before giving them to me because he was, and I quote, 'really hungry.'"

"I feel like I need higher standards after hearing this." Adhira glances at Skyler, gives him a nudge with her elbow. "Why didn't you ever do that for me?"

"Because I was sixteen and an idiot?" he says, and though they both laugh at this, I don't miss the way his gaze lingers on her after she's looked away.

"I went on a date with a guy I met on Hinge last night," Zoe says. "He was really sweet. Not a fuckboy." She nods toward my phone. "Maybe I should send him this as inspiration."

I save the last clue for the end, not broadcasting it to the rest of the group because I like the idea of keeping this one close. *Something that reminds me of you.* A bookstore window with a Valentine's Day display, stacks of romance novels.

Rowan: *you win, but that picture melted my heart so much that I don't even mind* 🩶

Neil: *Video chat tonight?*

Rowan: *please. I miss your face.*

"You guys really didn't have to spend your whole Saturday doing this," I say, inordinately touched. "Thank you. Truly."

"It was fun," Adhira says. "We'll have to do it again sometime."

Zoe grins. "I'll bring Steve!"

As we part ways, Adhira and Zoe off to an East Village nursery for a new plant Zoe promises not to kill, while Skyler and I head back home to Greenwich, I realize two things:

One, that I can tell which direction is uptown and which is downtown without looking at a map.

And two, that I'd asked Rowan if "my roommate and his friends" could help—maybe they're becoming my friends, too.

"You didn't have to cover for me," I tell Skyler. Despite the cold, the sun was too difficult to resist, so we're sitting in Washington Square Park. "When they were asking about my parents earlier."

"Yeah. No problem." He stretches out his long legs. "I could tell there was maybe something else going on there?"

I know I don't owe him an explanation, and I don't want to bring it back up and risk sinking myself underwater. That letter has to remain firmly back in Seattle—it's my only hope of staying afloat. Still, I find myself wanting to give him a fragment of the truth, just enough to keep him from asking any additional questions. "We . . . don't have as much money as some other people here. As a lot of people here, I don't think."

Skyler nods. "You don't have to hide that if you don't want to. You know they don't *really* care what your parents do, right?"

"What my mom does. It's just her."

"I'm sorry," he says in this tone I've never heard. "I'm sorry it got weird. Family shit can be complicated."

And if that isn't the most succinct way of summing it up, in pure Skyler fashion.

I paste on a smile, trying to push away the swirl of feelings that this conversation has dragged to the surface. My chest won't tighten if I don't let it. My breathing can remain calm. Not thinking about him, not going there, not now. *I am in control.*

"It can indeed. It's a wonder all of us are so normal and well adjusted."

Then Skyler gives me this goofy grin. "Is it weird to say I missed you over the holidays?"

And that's when I finally break. I have to know the truth. "You really like hanging out? With me?"

Skyler just blinks at me. "Did we not just spend the whole day hanging out?"

I can't help laughing at that, because maybe I really am an idiot. My smile is unforced now. Easier. "No, we did—I'm just . . . I guess I've just wondered if maybe you felt obligated because we live together. The whole making friends thing—it's something I'm still trying to figure out on this coast, I guess."

"You have to put yourself out there."

"But it seems to come easy to you. That day when you put together that game of Ultimate Frisbee, you'd just met all those guys and they were immediately on board with playing. That doesn't happen in Seattle."

"I don't think it's regional," Skyler says, tossing a wink to a girl giving him a very clear once-over. "But if we're being real, I haven't seen any of those guys since then. I mean, I've seen them around campus, but I haven't spent quality time with them. Maybe I know a lot of people, maybe I have a lot of friends, but they're not the kind of people I can really be myself with, I guess. The kind of people I can open up to." It's to his credit that he's able to follow up the casual arrogance of "Maybe I have a lot of friends" with something truly genuine. "You know how you had, uh, a certain reputation in high school?"

"I was a nerd. You can say it."

He laughs, swipes a hand through his floppy hair. "Well . . .

I was a bit of a partier. I was the guy with the older siblings who could get alcohol, the guy with the parents who didn't care if anyone came over and drank or smoked. People came to me for a good time, but that was pretty much it."

None of this is too surprising, and yet—

"That's not what you wanted?"

"Back then, maybe. I liked the attention. The status. But now that I'm here . . . no, I don't think it's what I want. Not all the time, at least." He gestures between the two of us. "I don't think I've had a meaningful conversation with anyone not related to me in a long time. Being around Adhira again is making me realize just how much of an ass I was in high school. I was trying so hard to prove myself to people, to be the life of the party . . . and it's only recently that I've decided I don't really care what anyone else thinks about me. I don't have to try so fucking hard."

Even if he and I had significantly different levels of popularity, I can relate to that: the trying so fucking hard. The fatigue that accompanies that kind of effort.

"I think I might want those deep-level friendships? Like, I still want to have fun, but I'm pretty sure I can have both," Skyler continues. "And you're nonjudgmental. I feel relaxed around you, like I could tell you anything and you'd still think I'm a decent human being."

I am so touched by this, I'm not sure I could put it into words. At the beginning of the year, I thought Skyler was so surface level that we'd have nothing in common. I assumed he wouldn't want to be friends with me, so I created space between us, when all this time he's wanted a close friendship just as much as I have.

"Of course. Of course you can."

"I'm not hanging out with you because of obligation," he emphasizes, and then turns the question on me. "Are you?"

I shake my head. "At first I thought I'd have dinner with you and your dad and then we'd be polite to each other, but we'd eventually have completely separate lives. But being here is more overwhelming than I thought it would be, and I think you might be helping me get out of my shell. And convincing me that Staten Island is a hidden gem of the tristate area."

Skyler laughs, but I can tell he's touched, too. "We're really bonding, huh," he says with a nudge of my arm.

"I think we are." I can feel my own body relaxing as I stretch out my much shorter legs, shoulders finally settling against the back of the bench.

"Speaking of putting yourself out there. I have something I should probably tell you." For the very first time in the nearly six months I've known him, Skyler looks *nervous*. It's a bit like seeing a golden retriever refuse to play fetch. "I, uh, might have feelings for Adhira?"

I have to bite back a smile—it's far from a surprise. "I've been wondering about that."

He lets out a long whoosh of breath. "Shit. It's obvious, isn't it?"

"Actually, no. Both of you flirt, but that's also just a *you* thing. I've seen you do it with the janitorial staff and the people who work in the dining hall, and—"

"It's a gift and a curse," Skyler says glumly, hanging his head. "I can't help being charming."

"And the security guards—"

"Okay, okay!" He holds up his hands, laughing, but then turns serious again. "She was my first real girlfriend, and I think she might have ruined me for anyone else. No one's ever measured up to her. That might be why I don't do relationships," he admits. "Because some part of me is waiting for her to decide that she still has feelings for me. And if she does, well . . . I'm not that immature kid from high school anymore."

Despite all the flirting, I realize I haven't seen him with any other girls in a while. I have to choose my words carefully, because I can't quite believe I'm about to give Skyler relationship advice.

"She clearly likes you," I say. "I'm not sure if I can tell whether it goes beyond friendship, but there's *something* there."

He buries his head in his hands. "It's not just like for me," he says with a little heartsick moan. "I think I really love her. I'm not sure if she'd ever take me seriously, but we were kids back then. Sixteen and seventeen. And now . . . I feel like if there's any chance we're on the same page, we could give it a real shot." He thumps a hand to his heart. "I know sometimes I act like this happy-go-lucky guy, but I'm tortured, man. Pining for someone, having no idea if they feel the same way . . ."

"I think I know a little something about that."

"It's fucking brutal, isn't it?"

"Is it too obvious to say to tell her how you feel? Without

pushing her, of course—you don't want her to feel any pressure to respond a certain way," I say. "But without sounding too cliché . . . honesty can go a long way. Especially if it's earnest. Adhira's used to you joking around, not being too serious. Show her that you can be. That this isn't a joke to you, and that you want to be serious when it comes to her."

"Serious. Yes. I can do serious." As though to prove it, he schools his face into a properly stoic expression, though I catch one eyebrow twitching, unable to keep up the ruse. "Is that how you did it? Did you both just come out and say it?"

"Sort of," I say. "I actually wrote it in her yearbook first, earlier that day. But I told her not to read it until the game was over and then proceeded to silently panic for the next few hours." I'd been so nervous, terrified she'd glance at it during the day and then laugh in my face.

"Oh shit. That's romantic as hell. You guys are really making it work," he says. "It's still going well? I assume so, what with the whole scavenger hunt and all."

"It's . . ." I catch myself before "good" or "great" spills out of my mouth. With Skyler opening up, and especially after our earlier conversation, I can't help wanting to unpack some of my own baggage too. "If I'm being honest . . . we've had some challenges."

He spreads his arms wide across the back of the bench. "Well. Lay it on me."

It takes me a while to work up to it. I've never had conversations like this with friends that go beyond the theoretical, and certainly not in public, though no one's paying us much attention. Sean, Cyrus, and Adrian know Rowan and I have slept together, mainly because when they asked, I immediately turned bright red, but that's it. When we talked about dating over winter break, a bowling alley didn't seem like the place to bring it up.

This seems to be a pattern with me: never having the right words or the right setting to have any kind of conversation that matters.

If I can't have it with my friends from high school, then maybe I can have it with Skyler.

"Things aren't as good . . . physically . . . as they used to be," I finally manage, keeping my voice low. I run my anxious palms over the thighs of my jeans. "That isn't—that's not something you'd have any experience with, is it?"

Instantly I regret it, half expecting him to make a joke.

"Not unusual for a long-distance relationship, I'm guessing," he says, sounding sincere, and that gives me more courage.

"It's almost like there's more pressure when we're together, and we don't get much alone time when we're at home. But lately I've been wondering if I'm just bad at this."

"And you guys have talked about it?"

"Well, not *exactly* . . ."

He crosses his arms over his chest, as though there is a truly simple solution here. "How are you going to know how to make it better if you don't talk about it?"

Excellent question.

I bury my head in my hands, letting out a low groan. "Oh my God. I am an idiot."

Skyler claps me on the back. "You're not! You're just still figuring it out. Hell, we all are. It's not the easiest thing to talk about. But believe me, it's much easier to talk when you're not caught up in the moment."

Of all people, Skyler giving me advice about communicating in the bedroom is not at all what I expected and yet so deeply appreciated. Skyler Benedetti: feminist icon?

"Have you ever used lube?" he asks.

My cheeks grow warm as I shake my head, mentally kicking myself for never thinking of it. Maybe that's the problem: our first time was so special that everything else seemed like it would fall into place without effort.

But with Rowan, there's nothing I want more than to make that effort.

"You should. It's incredible. And not just for her," he adds. "You can ask her what she wants. What she likes. It's a lot easier than trying to read minds." A grin. "Communication is probably fifty percent of the whole thing. Maybe more."

This sexual enlightenment is making my mind spin. "Thank you," I say, meaning it. "If my face ever returns to its regular shade of pale, then I'll put all of this to good use."

"Thank *you*. I've got to start brainstorming how to tell Adhira I'm a lovesick idiot."

To prepare for my next trip to Boston, I buy three different brands of lube from an adult shop in the West Village, each one promising to completely transform my sex life. I only blush a little when the cashier tells me to have fun.

We fully intend to, I think to myself, and that confidence buoys me for the rest of the week.

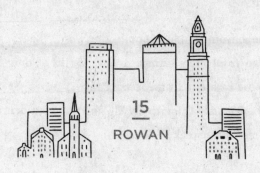

15
ROWAN

"SO WE'VE NARROWED our list of countries down to—" I set the phone on speaker while I count. "Fifteen. From twenty."

"Seventy-five percent. Not bad."

I laugh, blowing on my nails. "We'd need months to do that many. My feet are aching just thinking about it."

As much as I love video chats, there's something great about being able to talk to Neil like this too. The old-fashioned way, as it were. I'm in an ancient, gigantic T-shirt with a hole in the armpit and mismatched socks, hair haphazardly piled on top of my head. Sheet mask on, Crest Whitestrips pressed to my teeth, an open bottle of nail polish on the desk in front of me. Full self-care mode.

January was a low point for me, but now that campus has started to thaw, my optimism is back. We're making this work. Spring break is at the end of next month, and even summer doesn't seem as far away as it used to. It helps that we've gotten creative with the distance lately. Last week, we watched a movie at the same time—Neil's choice, since he won East Coast Howl, although I'm pretty sure he picked *You've Got Mail* just for me. And a few nights ago, we went on a date to an Italian "restaurant," aka the pasta bar from both our dining halls, then ate together while listening to Dean Martin. I even lit a candle in my dorm room that I immediately extinguished upon realizing it could set off the fire alarm. We waxed poetic about what it'll be like to eat pasta together *in* Italy, a country that remains near the top of our list.

A lot of our relationship may be happening at this desk, but we're doing the best we can.

"We should probably book our first flight soon," I say. "Before it gets too expensive."

"We will. As soon as I get my next paycheck."

There are some shuffling sounds in the background. Neil was drinking a cup of tea, and I imagine him fishing out the bag, saving it for the school's compost bin. I reach to my mouth before realizing—whoops, probably shouldn't have painted my nails while whitening my teeth.

"Oh! I wanted to tell you. This might be a bit cart before horse, but . . . I found a Spanish copy of *Vision in White* online." I'm in 202 this semester, along with a first-year seminar called American Popular Culture that I can't believe counts for school credit. "I figure I already know it so well, and I can work my way up to reading it. And it's slightly more interesting than what we're reading in class. Just slightly."

"Yeah? That's fantastic. I hope it's just as romantic in Spanish."

"Probably even more so," I say, because none of our calls are complete without some discussion of academics. "Did you ever go back to that linguistics club?"

Neil's quiet for a moment. "Just once . . . but I don't know if it's really for me. I've actually been working on this project in psych about the links between Judaism and psychology."

"Do tell."

"Well, I noticed that the majority of psychologists we were studying were Jewish—Sigmund Freud, Alfred Adler, Erich Fromm, Abraham Maslow. . . ."

"Of Maslow's hierarchy of needs?"

"The very one," Neil confirms. I can hear the spark of excitement in his voice—I've always loved that. "Some of them were influenced directly by religion. The concept of self-actualization, for example, has roots in Jewish thought. I think there's also an argument to be made that Jewish tragedy drove people to seek out ways to better understand human nature and ultimately find ways to heal."

"Wow," I say, impressed. "You're not thinking of changing your major or anything, are you?"

It's mostly a joke—obviously I'd support him changing his major if he decided that was what he wanted to do. But it's so out of character that I can't wrap my mind around it. Neil and words go together like . . . well, like me and words.

Or the way we used to.

"No, no, of course not," he says quickly. Then, when we realize how late it's gotten: "See you next Friday?"

He'll be in Boston for the first time, coinciding with his birthday, and I'm already deep in planning mode. "Next Friday. Can't wait."

At any given time, there is a limit-does-not-exist number of student films in production at Emerson. Flyers and online notices are always asking for extras, and that's how I end up in an old warehouse in Charlestown one Saturday afternoon, clad in a yellow unitard with aluminum scales pasted to my back, green paint covering my face.

"*Planet Dread*, take twenty-seven," calls out Leilani, a freshman with long braids and red cat-eye glasses. She settles into a makeshift director's chair, a threadbare love seat probably destined for the dump. "And . . . *action*."

My fellow snakes and I lie flat on the ground, arms clasped above our heads. We're supposed to be slithering, which sounds a lot easier in theory than it is in practice. More than once, Leilani had to call "cut" because someone was crawling instead of slithering, so she got down on her belly to show us how we could scoot ourselves around on our toes and forearms. The flyer for this particular film failed to mention it would involve a killer core workout—my abs are already protesting.

Kait emerges from behind a tower of cardboard boxes, motioning for someone else to follow behind her. Then, in a grave voice, she says, "I don't think we're in the right place."

Another actor enters the frame, stroking a fake beard and looking deeply concerned. "That's the thing," he says, gazing around the warehouse. "It's the right place, but the snakes have made it uninhabitable for humans. Twenty years ago, this was a city. A civilization. And now—"

We hiss.

"And now it belongs to them." Kait reaches into her holster, pulling out a prop axe, which she brandishes like a baseball bat. "And they're not going to let us take it back without a fight."

"Cut!" Leilani says from behind the camera, and the dozen of us on the ground heave a collective, pained sigh of relief. "Amazing job," she says, giving Kait a sweet smile. "Space snakes, great slithering."

We break for some water while Leilani and a couple of her friends reset the scene. I've already made the mistake of referring to Leilani as Kait's girlfriend. *We're just hanging out,* Kait said when I asked. *I'm not eager to get into another relationship right away.*

Maybe the best part about this film is that it's reminded me of all the creativity on campus that exists outside my major. Actors and directors and painters and comedians and musicians and designers, all of us yearning to make art out of nothing. There is something about seeing others so immersed in their art that makes me want to get lost in mine, that undeniable contagious spark. The reason I was drawn to Emerson in the first place. When you have that desire deep in your bones, you can't simply shut it off.

Even during a drought, it's always *there*, waiting to seize inspiration and weave it into something beautiful.

Maybe I never had to be tortured—just inspired. Because even if this movie, a snake-based sci-fi epic meant to be a parable for climate change, isn't going to win any awards, it's been a ridiculous amount of fun. Leilani is no-nonsense and knows exactly what she wants, a trait that's easy to admire, and the costume-design majors glued scales to our snake outfits with utmost care.

Sure, it's not high art, but none of these people are giving it any less than their full attention and love. And that makes it feel that way.

Leilani asks for one more take, promising "I think we really got it that time!" before we do it three more times.

When I get back to my dorm, stomach muscles aching, I don't rush to scrub off all the green paint. Not yet. My mind is whirring, fingertips itching to create. I peel off my unitard, flexing my hands before sitting in my desk chair. Microsoft Word will not send me into a panic spiral this time. Somehow, I'm sure of it.

The first few sentences are buttery smooth, just as lovely on the page as they are in my head. An auspicious start. For this assignment, Professor Everett brought a sack of mystery objects to class and asked us each to pick one. "Your character cries when they see this," she said. "Why?" My object: a bright purple finger trap.

Paulina's gone, so it's just me and my laptop and the soft hum of the radiator. While I assumed our Dunkin' adventure would bring us closer, that hasn't happened yet. We exchange pleasant small talk when we're in the room, but she still seems perpetually frazzled, always on her way out the door. I use that as inspiration, crafting a character who never stays put long enough to build strong connections with anyone.

One night she meets a charming guy at a carnival, both of them having been ditched by their friends, and she's so miserable at every game that all she manages to win is a cheap finger trap. The two of them gamely stick their index fingers inside, joke that now they're bound forever. After a magical night together, she fears he's getting too close and pulls away. Deletes his number. Ten years later, she runs into him the night before she's about to be married to someone she doesn't truly love—and because he's been hoping he'll see her again one day, he still has the finger trap. Cue tears.

I tinker. I nudge. I search for the right words, massaging my phrasing until the prose reads exactly the way I want it to, soft and romantic and threaded with nostalgia.

I don't break until my phone pings with a text from Kait, reminding me that we had plans to crash an MIT party later and asking if I want to get ready together. I give my work a quick reread, save, and send it off to Professor Everett.

Then I allow myself to smile, drawing in the first deep breath I've taken in the past hour.

It takes far too long to scrub off all the green paint, even with Kait's help. In the eighth-floor bathroom, we apply eyeliner and mascara, try on a couple outfits before landing on the right one. We'll meet Leilani there, along with a few other kids from the shoot.

All of it brings me back to getting ready for high school dances with Kirby and Mara. Watching them sneak glances before they knew they liked each other, Mara seeming to go catatonic while Kirby lined her lips with a deep red. Mara asking us to pause in the middle of pinning up our hair so she could get a photo that looked candid, the two of us dramatically moving our hands in slow motion. I'm hit with a pang of homesickness and longing— because I never realized, back then, that those kinds of experiences were finite. I just assumed I had all the time in the world to get ready for school dances, that the hour we spent huddled around the mirror was only a precursor to something grander when it was usually much better than the dance itself.

"A picture for your boyfriend?" Kait asks now, holding out her hand. "Because you look *gorge*."

"It's just because I'm not space-snake chic anymore," I say, but I finger-comb my dark waves one more time before she snaps a photo. One for Neil, and then one of the two of us together.

It's not the same as it was in high school, but it's not terrible, either.

The Emerson party scene mostly consists of partying at Boston's other, bigger schools—Harvard, BU, MIT. MIT is a few stops on the red line away in Cambridge, its campus spread along the Charles River, and the frat house is a quaint brick building a block from the water. Having spent the past four years as an AP kid, I already know that nerds can go hard, and that's exactly how it appears when we step inside.

The lights are dimmed, music blasting, floor littered with SOLO cups. Kait makes herself at home in the kitchen, pouring us each a shot of vodka. Deciding not to overthink it, I toss it back.

"Ughhhhh, that's *awful*."

"Welcome to college," Kait says with a wince. "No one can afford the good stuff."

Leilani comes up behind us, throwing an arm around Kait's shoulder. "Now the debauchery can really begin." She nods to me. "Thanks again for being one of my snakes. Hopefully I wasn't too much of a dictator?"

"Just the right amount," I tell her. "I can't wait to see the finished product."

"It'll take a *lot* of editing to get it there." Leilani grins at Kait as she passes her a cup. "But it'll be worth it."

And if that doesn't sound familiar.

We head toward the living room, where the couches have been pushed aside to make room for people to dance. I don't have the greatest sense of rhythm—Neil could more than attest to that—but dancing in this house of strangers feels like freedom, a blast of heat after an endless winter.

At one point, a guy in an oversize polo shirt attempts to shimmy up to me, but I give him such a vicious glare that he immediately backs away, after which Kait and Leilani dissolve into laughter. It feels good, this night.

A couple hours and too many EDM remixes later, I'm waiting in line for the bathroom when my phone buzzes in my pocket. I pull it out expecting to see a message from Neil, so I'm surprised to find an email instead. From Professor Everett. Who . . . was apparently working on a Friday night. Considering how I spent many a Friday night in high school, I'm not one to judge.

Then I read it, and everything changes.

Rowan,
I just finished your finger trap story. Do you think we could speak after class next week?
M.E.

My stomach sinks all the way to my toes, the floor swaying beneath me. I'd felt *so great* about that piece, better than I've felt about anything I've turned in so far this year. I thought I was finally writing what she wanted. I'd layered in all that backstory, labored over every word until each one felt right.

"You going in?" a girl behind me asks, motioning to the open door. Numbly, I shake my head no, and she pushes past me into the bathroom.

I read the email again and again, as though there could possibly be a hidden meaning in those two sentences. Turns out the only hidden meaning is someone I deeply admire telling me *you're not good enough.*

"Rowan? You okay?"

Kait's next to me, and my head is pounding and the music's too loud and this dress I borrowed from her is too tight. I dig a hand into my bangs, pressing my palm to my forehead as I wordlessly pass my phone to her.

"Shit," she says when she finishes reading, her brow scrunched with concern. "That's not good."

Yeah. I know.

Her assessment comes with a twinge of annoyance, and then a surge of unease. Because in any other scenario, Neil would have been the first person to see this email. Maybe that's another thing they don't tell you about long-distance relationships—that the first person you confide in may not be the person who means everything to you. He would have tried to reassure me, prevented me from assuming the worst. *Maybe she wants to talk to you about something positive*, he'd say, and I'd raise my eyebrows and joke, *When has a teacher ever wanted to see a student after class for something positive?* Maybe he'd be right and maybe he wouldn't, but it would have made me feel lighter.

Kait's comment makes me feel just this side of doomed.

This time when my gaze drifts back toward the living room, all I see are intertwined couples, the ones who might be in love and the ones who might be hooking up and the ones who might be somewhere in between. That could be us, swaying together in a stranger's house. No matter how many phone calls and video chats we have, it doesn't change the fact that Neil isn't here.

There's that worry at the back of my mind again, only this time it's louder.

Maybe I'm too settled in my relationship to properly write about love, disconnected from the yearning that defines all my favorite books. I'd fought my way to optimism, but reality was waiting to push me right back. Because what if I haven't just romanticized romance—what if I've romanticized writing itself?

I tighten my fist around my phone, shoving it back into my pocket.

Then I make my way into the kitchen and down two more shots. Then another. By that third one, I can no longer remember what my story was about.

By the sixth one, I can't feel anything.

I throw my hair back, dancing with Kait and Leilani, screaming the lyrics to songs I'm not sure I've ever liked but have invaded my subconscious anyway. Another shot, because it's starting to taste so much better.

This is still fun. I'm having a fucking blast.

At least until later, with my face stuck in a toilet and my hair sweat-pasted to my forehead, when I decide I'm never doing this again.

NEIL'S RECENT SEARCH HISTORY

Q how to maintain intimacy long distance relationship

Q how to sext

Q how to sext for beginners

Q nyu grading scale

Q judaism and psychology

Q attribution theory

Q transactional analysis

Q greenwich village adult shops unintimidating

Q moma student discount

16
NEIL

ON THE TRAIN to Boston, I listen to the Smiths, her favorite band. I once teased her that they were too melancholy, but today they sound defiantly full of *life*. Every song is joy and sunshine, optimism and blue skies.

Maybe it's the long winter, but I've been fighting with my alarms in New York, snoozing them for much longer than I usually do. When I finally peel myself out of bed, I'm groggy during my classes, a strange kind of brain fog preventing me from raising my hand. If I'm able to focus, it's only during psych, which is raising questions I'm not sure how to answer.

Being here will silence all those questions. For two days, I get to focus only on her.

I could take in the buildings and the scenery and the splendor of a new city. But right now, all I see is Rowan waiting for me at the station, eyes lit up and mouth curved into my favorite smile. The entire trip to Emerson, I place my hand on her knee and then on her thigh. Every so often, she glances down, runs a thumb along my knuckles. I can tell exactly what she's thinking, because I'm thinking the same thing.

As soon as we get to her dorm, I drop my bags and reach for her, hands in her hair as I push her back against the door. Just like I told her I'd do in those texts on that night that now seems like it happened ages ago. Her mouth meets mine, frantic and sweet and perfect.

"Missed you," she says, breathless, tugging my hips to hers. *God*, she feels good.

"Missed you more." I drag down her hoodie zipper. "Am I ever getting this hoodie back?"

"Nope. It's mine now."

Seeing her in it would have been enough to send my heart into overdrive if it weren't already halfway there. I never thought I was someone who'd feel such a primal surge of desire over a girl wearing my clothing, but I suppose I'm learning new things about myself all the time.

It's enough to make me wonder what she might look like in one of my button-ups.

And nothing else.

"You know what, I prefer it on you," I say, pulling her closer by the drawstrings.

But then I get a flash of us back in my dorm at NYU, and over winter break in her room, and just as she reaches for my belt, I pause.

"Wait, wait, wait." It takes all my willpower to put some space between us. Strength I did not, until this moment, know I possessed. "I want to talk first."

Her face is beautifully flushed. "Okay."

My body needs a few extra moments to respond, and then I follow her over to her bed, sitting down next to her. Her side of the room is similar to mine—photos of her friends, Seattle, the two of us—while her roommate's is covered with various penguin paraphernalia.

This doesn't have to be scary. It *shouldn't* be scary, not with her. I think back to that conversation with Skyler, knowing this talk is probably long overdue.

"I've been realizing," I start, "that I may still have some insecurities about this."

Her brow furrows. "About us?"

"*No*. Never about us. About . . . this." I wave my hand at the bed, summoning the confidence to use real words, not euphemisms. "About sex. And, well, I don't think we've ever really discussed it since that first time."

A deepening of her blush, even though this is something she is usually so confident talking about. It was one of the things I admired about her during that endless night in Seattle.

The difference, I realize, is that this time it's about *us*.

I want to talk about this without shame or fear, forcing every ellipsis and shaky word out of my voice. "Because I came into this without much experience. Because you haven't had an orgasm the last couple times, and I've worried that maybe I'm not experienced enough for you, or not good enough for you."

"Neil." Her eyes fill with emotion as she tucks her knees up underneath her, nudges her body closer to mine. Just that hint of contact, of pressure, is enough to remind me that everything will be okay. "I have never thought that. Ever."

"You're sure?"

She is so solid here next to me, something I miss so desperately when we talk on the phone. "Don't get me wrong—I'm glad we're talking about it. I've probably been . . . a little distracted." She brushes her bangs to one side of her forehead and then the other, never able to figure out what she wants to do with them. "With school, there's just been a lot on our minds, for both of us."

"And that's okay," I rush to say. "Perfectly okay and understandable."

"What we do in here, the actual physical component—that doesn't matter to me as much as just being with you. Even if we sat here staring at each other for five hours, I'd still love every minute of it."

"That's extremely nice to hear." The relief is immediate. I reach for her knee, tapping a rhythm on her leggings. "If it ever seems like I don't know what I'm doing . . . well, sometimes I don't. But I want to learn. I really do."

A flicker of a smile. "Here's the thing. Whatever experience we had before we started dating, now we're doing it together. And that makes everything feel new to me. *Everything*," she repeats for emphasis. "Even if it's not fireworks right away, the fact that it's *you* . . ." She trails off, shaking her head, leaning forward to place a hand on my chest. My heart lifts to meet her touch. "I don't think you fully realize the effect you have on me."

The laugh that slips out is a small, disbelieving thing. I cover her hand, turning it over and tracing circles on her palm. I want to create fireworks for this girl every fucking time. "Trust me, I'm still trying to wrap my head around it."

We sit there like that for a few moments, me drawing a fingertip along her wrist, her seeming deep in thought.

"We could probably both be better at communicating," she says after a while. "I want to think reading all those books has made it easier for me, and it has, in a way. But I'm still learning too, what it's like to talk about this with someone who means as much to me as you do. If you're not comfortable—"

"I am." I say it solidly, steadily. The truth. "With you, I am. When we were texting . . . *God.* I want to be able to have that in real life." I can feel her press even closer, her free hand landing on my thigh. "I want to be open with you in every possible way. You just . . . you make me feel like I don't have to be ashamed of anything."

Rowan just gazes at me for a few long moments with this soft, awed expression, so beautiful she should be at MoMA next to *The Starry Night.* "I really, really love you," she says before her arms come up around my neck.

"So just to be clear," I say, "you *don't* want to sit here staring at each other for five hours?"

She laughs and pushes me down on the bed. My hands go to the small of her back, molding her body to mine. I will never not love the feeling of her on top of me. "I have a few other things in mind. If we're getting better at communicating"—a kiss to my cheek, my chin, a sly smile—"what if you told me what you want to do right now?"

"I'd . . . really like to go down on you again." This time, finding the right words is easy. "I haven't been able to stop thinking about it."

Her eyes are heavy-lidded, her mouth still swollen from the way we kissed when we first got here. I drag my fingertips up her spine, beneath her shirt. Slowly, slowly, one corner of her mouth kicks upward. I don't know how the effect I have on her can be any fraction of what she does to me, these simple expressions able to completely unstitch me.

"Without any pressure," I add. "Whatever happens or doesn't happen—it's okay. More than okay. I just loved feeling that close to you."

"I'd like that. But if it takes a long time, I don't want you to get bored or feel like you're doing anything wrong. . . ."

I'm not sure how to tell her that it would be rather impossible for me to get bored with my face between her legs, how I've imagined it every night I've had my dorm room to myself. No amount of her could ever be enough.

"That's not going to happen. I can promise you that." Then, remembering, I shift to grab my backpack from off the floor. "I also, uh, bought a few things? Just in case." I show her my haul from the adult shop, and her mouth drops open.

"Neil McNair," she says, leaning forward so she can take off my glasses. "You are the very best surprise."

We return to kissing, deeper and harder this time as I help her shed the hoodie and she reaches for the hem of my shirt. The rest of her clothes, I take off as slowly as I can bear, trying to draw out the anticipation. Make this as enjoyable for her as possible.

When I finally touch her with my mouth, she lets out the loveliest sigh, one that I feel all the way down to my toes. Another thing I'm not ashamed of: the fact that I did a little research on what, specifically, I'm supposed to do down here. Last time, I was so overwhelmed by those new feelings that I could barely keep myself steady. This time, I want to spell the alphabet against her skin and learn everything she likes.

"What is it?" she asks when I pause for a moment, a note of concern in her voice.

I channel the confidence from that night we texted each other with such heady abandon. "I just—I love the way you taste." It's the filthiest thing I've ever said, and I'm instantly obsessed with how she reacts, a breathy little whimper that leaves me desperate for more. I could probably come just like this, without her even touching me.

She throws her head back against the pillow, exposing the arch of her neck. "You're perfect."

The words only embolden me as I return my tongue to her and slide into a rhythm. The gasp she lets out is a gorgeous, decadent thing. I can feel her pressing closer, a hand in my hair, nails digging into my scalp.

If I died tomorrow, I'd be certain I spent my last night on earth doing exactly what I was meant to do.

"There." That syllable is a sliver of sound. A wisp of lace. "God . . . that feels so good."

I exhale against her, unable to catch my breath but hardly caring. "All I ever want is to make you feel good."

It feels more intimate than anything we've ever done, possibly the most intimate thing I've ever experienced. Everything I have ever done in a bed suddenly seems like a ridiculous waste of time when *this* exists. The way she surrenders herself—there is not a single word in any language that describes how wonderfully wrecked my senses are.

Then her legs are trembling, her whole body seeming to tighten before she lets go, shuddering out an "oh my God" and "Neil" and "please." She shatters around me, breaths loud and chest heaving. Her hands in my hair and my name on her lips.

All of the anxiety and overthinking are worth it if I get to see her like this, sexy and uninhibited and *alive*.

"Good?" I say.

"Might have to do it a few more times to know for sure," she manages, her voice hoarse. With my last shred of consciousness, I realize it's the same thing I said to her the morning after we slept together for the first time.

Then she's reaching for my waist. My hips. A kiss to the fabric of my boxers and then lower, lower.

"Are you sure?" I ask, sucking in a breath. "Because you don't have to if—"

"I know." Another kiss. "And I am very, very sure."

When she closes her mouth around me, the sensation is absolutely unreal. Warmth and longing. Ecstasy and trust. All my awareness dims to only the places where she is touching me.

"What do you think?" she asks. "Any notes?"

"N-no. None whatsoever."

And she gives this lovely laugh before her mouth renders me useless.

I might last two more seconds or two more hours. Time no longer has meaning when she's hovering over me like this, rewiring my brain. I pull away at the last moment, not wanting to finish in her mouth if she doesn't want me to, but a silent exchange seems to pass between us.

I want this if you do, her wild, determined eyes tell me.

Yes.

Then she takes me back in.

The way I fall apart is a brilliant burst of neon behind my eyelids as pleasure crashes through me. She holds tightly to my hips, anchoring me to the bed.

To her.

Later that night, after a round two and a silent blessing that her roommate seems to be permanently MIA, we order a pizza because we can't bear to leave this room. Tomorrow I'll finally see Boston, but right now is just for the two of us, laughing and joking and teasing the way we usually do. And yet tonight it feels different. A new kind of closeness.

With a grimace, she tells me about her first hangover, and I tell her about Skyler and Adhira, and she squeals and makes me promise to send her updates as soon as they happen.

"You have to understand, this is total catnip to my romance novelist heart," she says. "I'm already so invested."

When we're here, the family weekend where my family wasn't present doesn't matter. The letter from my dad doesn't exist. I am wholly *myself* in a way I've never known, comfortable in my skin and radically fearless. My boldly independent, aspiring romance novelist girlfriend who makes me aspire to absolutely everything. She always has.

Here with her, there is none of that darkness, not even when the sun sinks below the horizon and the sky turns black.

She is the brightest light in any room.

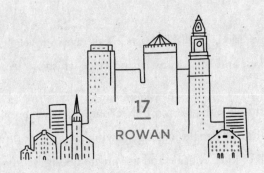

17
ROWAN

THE REST OF the weekend is the New England winter of my dreams, the two of us wrapped in scarves with hats pulled down low over our heads, traversing the city on foot and by train, admiring its history.

We celebrate Neil's birthday in the middle of the night, eyes still closed as we reach for each other, and then again early this morning. The fact that we've now spent one of each of our birthdays together feels like some kind of milestone. I've never paid much attention to astrology, but I have to admit that during the summer, I looked up Aquarius and Virgo for compatibility. An unusual match, most of the sites said, but an intriguing one with the potential for long-term compatibility. Aquarius and Virgo even motivate each other in their intellectual pursuits.

And I just stared, wondering if the planets had always known something I didn't.

Neil's birthday breakfast is a dining-hall feast with Kait and a few others from creative writing, though we can't stay long because I have a full day of touristing planned.

"The mysterious Neil! He exists," Kait says over veggie bacon and pancakes, and then leans in and stage-whispers, "And even cuter in person."

Our first stop is the Boston Public Garden, which even in this weather is full of people jogging, playing lawn games, pushing strollers full of kids. A bride and groom are taking wedding photos, a trio of bridesmaids following close behind to keep the dress from trailing along on the damp ground. I show him the *Make Way for Ducklings* sculpture, the bronze ducks dressed for the cold in tiny hats. I don't even care how dorky it is; I'm not sure I've ever been more in love with Neil than I am right now, and not just because of what happened last night—but because we were able to be open with each other in a new and freeing way for us.

We go ice-skating in the Common, and I'm not shocked to learn Neil has a little more grace than I do, probably because of those dance lessons he took as a kid. I'm glued to the wall until he holds out his hand and beckons me toward him.

"Not too far," I warn. "I'm really attached to this wall."

"We'll go slow. I promise," he says, and true to his word, we do.

His gloved hand squeezes mine as we glide along the ice, the rink a blur of brightly colored coats and scarves, blades carving delicate designs beneath our feet. When I wobble, he holds me tighter.

"I have to admit," he says on our third or fourth lap, "I've always kind of wanted to do this." The rosy tint to his cheeks deepens. "Go ice-skating with a cute girl."

Somehow, even after last night, this is enough to make me blush, too. "Who would've guessed that'd be me?"

Little kids spin circles around us, and I fall an embarrassing number of times, but none of that matters when Neil is the one helping me up. It doesn't matter when I take such an uncoordinated tumble that he plummets to the ice with me, laughing harder than we should for how sore we're going to be tomorrow. He's not frustrated or annoyed—he just seems content.

I missed him *so much*, but he's here and I'm here and we are making all of this work.

This should be the kind of scene that inspires me. I want to hold tight to this feeling and take it back out during my next writing session, convince myself that being in love has only made me a better writer. As much as I'd been fully *in it* during my finger trap piece, maybe what Professor Everett wants to tell me is that it all sounded false. Inauthentic. Lacking the kind of emotion she'd expect from a creative writing major.

Or she's already decided I'm a complete hack.

Neil wrote in my yearbook that I had a "shimmering optimism," one he wished he could borrow for himself, and when it comes to this class, I'm starting to think I've run out of it. Because no matter how hard I try, I can't force writing out of my head completely. And as much as I'd love his advice, I'm not about to bring it up on a day we're supposed to be celebrating him.

"I have so much skating-related trauma from my childhood," I say instead. "Do you remember that old skate rink in Northgate that closed down last year?"

"The one by the mall? I didn't know it had closed."

"Yep. And probably for the best, because I don't think whatever they were spraying in those skates to clean them was environmentally friendly."

"I haven't thought about that place in forever," Neil says, steering us out of the way of another couple, avoiding a collision. "It always smelled like burned pepperoni pizza, even though—"

"—they didn't actually sell pizza? Yeah. Anyway, I swear, like, everyone had their birthday parties there when we were kids, and inevitably the DJ would always make us do one of those snowball skates. Where everyone has to find a partner."

Neil groans. "I remember that. I think I'd blocked it out."

"In hindsight, it seems pretty problematic to force a group of twelve-year-olds to pair up," I say, gripping his hand tighter. "But this more than makes up for it."

It's interesting to have this shared memory of our hometown, something we didn't experience together but have the same language for nonetheless. I hope we never stop discovering things like that—metaphorically reliving the burned-pizza smell of our childhoods.

When we can't feel our toes anymore, a constellation of bruises blooming on both my knees, we return the skates and warm up with hot cocoa during the quick walk to our next destination.

A museum had to be part of Neil's birthday celebration, and from the moment I discovered it, I knew the Boston Athenæum would be perfect. In addition to being a stunning library, it's also a museum with thousands of rare books and sculptures and other historical artifacts.

"Happy birthday," I say, unable to bite back a grin as he gazes around in wonder, head tipped toward the ceiling. This look on his face, the awe so vibrantly painted across it—I'm not sure how I resisted it for four years. There's such a wholesome sexiness in Neil's love for learning, for knowledge.

He shakes his head. "'Happy' doesn't even begin to describe it. Joyous birthday. Jubilant birthday. Euphoric birthday—that one might be it." With a wave of his hand, he gestures for me to pose for a photo with him, holding out his arm to capture us. "Thank you," he says, pressing a kiss to my cheek while he snaps another photo. "I love it."

With high domed ceilings and chandeliers, long wooden tables, spiral staircases, sky-high shelves of books, it really is the platonic ideal of a library.

"I should start studying in here," I say as we wander down an aisle marked with a bust of Alexander Hamilton. "Maybe that would finally jog my writer's block."

"The words still aren't flowing?"

Shit. There goes keeping it in. "I mean, I'm writing, but am I writing anything good? Who's to say." A sharp laugh slips out before I can stop it. "Actually, I can say, and I'm not. Writing anything good, that is. But we really don't have to talk about it on your birthday!"

He must be able to sense my anxiety in those words, because he frowns, auburn brows pinching together. "Why wouldn't we talk about it? It doesn't matter what day it is—I always want to know what's going on with you."

I close my eyes for a moment, wishing I hadn't brought it up. But he has a point, and ever since the email landed in my inbox, that's all I've wanted. His reassurance, sure, but more than that—I've never been able to talk about writing the way I do with him. Even if our tastes are different, he was the first person I told about my romance novel, and he's only ever seemed awed by it.

"I guess we *are* good communicators now, huh." A flicker of something I can't quite interpret passes over his face, so brief that I'm certain I imagined it. "My professor emailed after my last assignment saying she wanted to talk to me after class, and I just . . . haven't?" I reach for my phone, showing him the message. "I told her I had to meet with my adviser and then that I had a doctor's appointment, and now I'm not sure what to do when I see her next. I'm running out of excuses."

Two girls in matching winter coats start to turn down our aisle, but then, sensing we're having a moment, head for the opposite one instead.

Neil's hand lands on my back, making a slow trail from one shoulder blade to the other. "Why are you afraid of seeing your professor?" he asks gently.

The possibilities run through my head. Because she's going to tell me I'm not good enough. That I'm a fraud. Because she's going to kick me out of the class.

None of them are realistic, of course, but that doesn't make me any less convinced one of them is going to happen.

"I guess . . . I've just kind of lived in this bubble where I write something, and then she gives me feedback, and none of it's spoken aloud. Once we start talking about it, that means I have to acknowledge what's going on. That I can't fucking *write*." I take a few steps forward, shaking my head as tears threaten behind my eyes. I will not allow myself to cry on my boyfriend's birthday, not inside this beautiful library. "Am I fooling myself, thinking I can turn this into a career someday when I can't even turn in an assignment I don't hate? And the one time I managed to— *that's* the time she decides she needs to talk to me? Because I feel like such a failure. Or maybe I shouldn't even be thinking that far ahead if I'm struggling this much in an intro class. Like, I'm already at the lowest level. I can't go backward from here. I don't know where I'd even go—"

I break off, pressing a hand to my heart as my breaths come out in sharp bursts. Even when I'm trying to be quiet, the library only amplifies the sound, creating a dull echo.

"I don't know who I am without writing," I say in a small voice. "And I don't know what to do if it turns out that I'm not very good at it."

"Hey," he says, the single word more soothing than it has any right to be. His arms come around my shoulders, and he holds me tight to his chest in this aisle of antique books. "Hey. Artoo. This one class doesn't determine your future." A soft brush of his fingers through my hair. "And you *are* a good writer. Maybe you're going through a rough patch, but you don't just lose that overnight. You are a fantastic. Fucking. Writer."

I want so badly to believe him. "You're biased," I whisper instead. "You're sleeping with me."

"And I've known you were talented since long before that. And"—he lowers his voice, speaks right against my ear—"now I have the privilege of saying that your talent extends to other arenas, too." His attempt at humor has its intended effect: I feel my cheeks heat as I reach for the lapels of his peacoat to keep him close. "Do you remember what you told me in June? When we were in a library significantly less grandiose than this one?"

"First of all, what a dig at the Westview High School library," I say, sniffing. "Second . . . vaguely?"

"That as soon as you told people you were a writer, you thought you'd have something to prove. That writing made you feel lonely. But then you told me. You showed me your words, and you read them on a stage in front of one of your literary idols. You have come *so fucking far.*" He pulls my shoulders back so we can face each other, his eyes both serious and sweet behind his glasses. "You're not a failure—you're just still figuring it all out. You're turning your brain inside out for other people to see, and that takes a wild amount of bravery."

Now I'm crying for an entirely different reason. "Why can't I be anywhere near as nice to myself as you are?"

This makes him laugh as he hugs me again, his familiar warmth and earthy scent, a comfort I'm not sure I could describe in words even if I had an entire year to put them on paper.

It makes me feel even worse about the one part of my anxiety that I haven't mentioned.

The fear that because I'm in love, I can't write about it.

I'm not sure I could tell him that.

"Why are libraries basically like therapy for us?" I say, swiping under my eyes for mascara stains. Because this is far from the first heart-to-heart we've had inside one. "This place could get us to tell her all our secrets if she really wanted to."

"Maybe there's something to that. So many people have sought comfort here, so many stories and worlds contained in this single building. It's hard to conceptualize the amount of imagination in this space. Letters that were meant to reach people but never did . . . portraits made by artists who revered their subjects, or hated their subjects, or were in love with their subjects and only able to express their emotion through paint. All those centuries of heartbreak and hope."

"I love that you love words just as much as I do, because that's one of the most beautiful things I've ever heard."

For some reason, this makes his expression go flat. He's a fidgeter when he's nervous, and when he starts tugging at the sleeves of his coat, jamming his hands in his pockets only to draw them right back out again, I can tell he's unsettled. No longer quite at ease.

"Neil? Something on your mind?"

"Actually . . . yes. There's something I've been wanting to tell you. Needing to tell you."

"You can tell me anything."

"I—I know that." Then another wave of uncertainty passes over his face, and I'm frustrated I can't immediately recognize it. "While we're talking academics, I guess I've been . . . a little unsure of my major lately."

"You don't want to study linguistics?"

"I don't know. It sounds ridiculous, doesn't it? It's what I've been working toward for years. The language books, the AP classes, all the dictionaries . . ."

"But—you've always loved words," I say dumbly. Neil was going to be a lexicographer one day, a person who compiles dictionaries—that was what he told me on the last day of school, and I was absolutely enchanted by it.

Maybe words have betrayed both of us.

"I still do," he says. "I just . . . might like other things too."

Then I collect myself. "That's perfectly okay. Isn't the whole point of college to figure that out? It's okay if it's not linguistics. It's okay if you change your mind a dozen times."

"I don't know if my scholarships will quite cover that," he says with a half smile. "I told you how much I loved my psych 101 class. The one I'm taking this semester is even better. We're studying personality theory, and I suppose I never thought there might be researched, psychological theories to explain why we act the way we do. And that there would be so many different ones, to the point where even one major theory can't cover every facet of personality. It almost feels *limitless*, the language we have to describe how our brains work." The way he lights up while talking about it, his words almost tripping over each other—how could I have missed this joy, this new passion he has? "You know how much I love school. I've never felt this way about a class before. Not even linguistics."

"Psychology," I say, the pieces clicking together. "I can see it."

"Yeah?"

"It makes sense that you'd want to understand . . . well, because of your dad."

All at once, the energy in the room shifts.

Your dad.

Your dad.

Your dad.

I might as well have shouted it, given the stricken look on his face, the way his shoulders go stiff like a statue. He blinks a few times. Swallows hard.

"I mean—" I try, but then I don't know how to finish that sentence. *Shit shit shit.* I've just made a colossal mistake.

Because we don't talk about his dad. We haven't, not since the afternoon of June 12, when we sat on his bed and he trusted me with a guarded piece of his history.

I'd always figured he'd tell me more when he was ready, but I wasn't going to pressure him. Obviously a single conversation couldn't account for all the trauma and heartbreak of his past, and

I hate that now I'm wondering if there's something wrong with *me* that he hasn't shared more of it.

"That's not—that's not the only reason," Neil finally says, not making eye contact.

"No, I know—"

"My dad—" He breaks off, and I'm struck with the realization that the way he says it is strangely foreign. A gap between those words, as though he's not used to putting them together. "I think I need to get some air."

I follow him down the stairs, gaze fixed on his back while my face flames. Wishing we could rewind to ten minutes ago. Hating that I brought it up. Every pound of my boots is a question: *Why? Why? Why?*

It takes an eternity to unwind ourselves from the Athenæum maze, weaving around tourists and tour guides and students. Once we're outside, his exhales puff white into the freezing air. He's breathing hard, the wind already turning his freckled cheeks pink and fighting with his hair. The collar of his peacoat is flipped upward, an extra barrier against the cold, his shoulders hunched up to his ears.

All I want in this moment is for him to let me in.

"Sorry—I'm not mad at you," he says, turning to face me. His dark eyes hold only concern. "I swear. I guess I was just . . . surprised to hear you make that connection. Wasn't expecting it."

I place a hand on his shoulder. "I shouldn't have mentioned it in such a cavalier way. *I'm* sorry." Maybe I didn't know there were limits when it comes to talking about Neil's family, because now it feels like he's shut the door to some secret vault. "If you don't want me to ever bring him up, just tell me. Okay?"

"No—you can. I'm fine. It's fine." He wraps me in a hug, leaving me more confused than ever. Because now I am definitely *not* going to bring him up again. "It's fine," he repeats, as though trying to convince us both.

I cling to him tighter than I usually do. "Maybe we were both due for a minor breakdown today," I offer, wishing it felt more like I hadn't just completely fucked up. He is my boyfriend, and I care about him more than I thought I could care about another human being, and whatever hurt he's dealing with—I want him to be able to confide in me.

As it turns out, maybe we can't talk about everything.

When he smiles, I can tell it's forced. "Are you hungry? I might be hungry. Let's go get something to eat."

The last day of the weekends we spend together is always the worst, a terrible mental countdown reminding me how many hours we have left. Five. Four. Three. Forty-five minutes. Fifteen. As amazing as it is when we're together, there's such a fierce ache in my chest the moment he leaves.

We're some of the lucky ones, really. We're in the same time zone. We're not all the way across the country, one of us in a small college town only accessible with a layover in between.

It shouldn't be this hard.

Just three and a half more years of painful goodbyes. Three and a half more years of trying to quash that fierce ache.

Three and a half more years of watching him walk away, wishing I'd said something different.

18
NEIL

"I'M STEVE," ZOE'S new boyfriend says when we meet him at a sushi restaurant uptown in mid-February. "And I am not a fuckboy."

"Why does he sound like he's introducing himself to a support group?" Adhira wants to know, hooking her thumb toward him.

"Because I want you guys to know that I'm making good relationship decisions now," Zoe says, and it seems to be true, because Steve is kind and attentive and slightly anxious, often double-checking his jokes with a look at Zoe, as though worried she may not find him funny.

We've become something of a group, Skyler and Adhira and Zoe and maybe now Steve, too. And yet ever since coming back from Boston last week, I haven't felt like myself. My body grows weary with an unfamiliar kind of exhaustion I don't entirely understand. I get in bed early most nights, unless I have plans with friends, and when I do, I force the smiles, worried that once people glance away and my features droop, they'll immediately know something's wrong. That I've been faking my excitement.

Boston was a fairy tale, this interlude of not quite real life. I'd felt so *good* with Rowan—until real life sneaked back in, sank its claws in me.

I should have told her. I should have told her about the letter, and about how I felt during family weekend, and the way I lied about my mom because I was too much of a coward to take off that mask it seems I wear for just as many people over here as I did at home.

And yet I can't let my burdens become hers, too. Especially with the distance between us, it would only create more anxiety for her when she's already stressed about her writing.

It's better this way—for both of us.

When the bill arrives, that heavy feeling drags me even deeper. Two hundred dollars.

Two hundred dollars for five people, and no one is batting an eye.

I have to work to keep the shock off my face because I have never been to a restaurant with a bill this large. I only ordered miso soup, the cheapest thing on the menu. I'd been surprised when the others ordered not just one but multiple rolls. "They're small," Adhira had explained.

"We can just split it five ways?" Zoe suggests, already reaching for her credit card.

"No, I got those dragon rolls—those were expensive." Skyler grabs the check. "I'll get it and everyone can Venmo me?"

We all take out our phones, and I send Skyler a silent thank-you.

I've always been so aware of money that I've wondered whether people who are more comfortable think about it as frequently. But NYU is the first place where that awareness turns into something physiological, capable of nesting in all my body's hollow places.

Perhaps that is the thing about money—the world never runs out of ways to remind you how little of it you have.

My life is lived in fragments, pieces of my heart in New York and Seattle and Boston. I am constantly wishing Rowan could hang out with us, and not just to prevent me from feeling like a fifth wheel, although nothing has officially happened with Skyler and Adhira yet. He tells me he's working up to it, trying to find the right words. And I can't fault him for that—it took me long enough to find mine.

Adhira and I wind up studying together a few times since we're in the same class this semester, though she spends a good portion of it asking questions about Skyler that make me certain she has feelings for him, too.

"You don't know if he's seeing anyone, do you? Like, is he bringing girls back to the room or anything?" Then she pauses, scrunches up her face. "Wait, I don't want to know."

"He's not seeing anyone," I say from across the table. Between work-study and study-study, Bobst Library has become something of a second home to me.

"Not that I care," she answers quickly, and then returns her attention to her laptop screen, where her notes are typed in organized, bullet-pointed sections. Karen Horney has made another appearance in this week's reading. "I fucking love this woman. Look, there's this bit where Freud called her 'able but malicious'—I need that on a T-shirt."

I push my jaw muscles into an impossible smile. I want to get as excited as she is about Karen Horney, about this course. But the words swim in front of my glasses, my vision blurred and unfocused. As much as I try to enjoy the time I spend in class and exploring the city with Skyler and Adhira and Zoe and Steve, I can't understand why it all feels like *so much*. As soon as I got back to New York, some dark cloud seemed to settle over me.

Adhira types away on her laptop while my thoughts spiral me backward. Those days my dad stayed in bed, none of us allowed to disturb him. Why is my brain so intent on bringing me to that place?

Maybe because it all comes back to him, no matter where I am. Always. Surely, that's the way he'd want it.

This is absurd. Rationally, I know that—two people being tired does not a pattern make. My dad battled fatigue, but he also drank too much and swore at his children. And yet I can't explain why this exhaustion comes with it such a sense of the familiar, the meaning beyond my grasp.

"Do you understand this bit about expectancy-value theory?" I ask Adhira, flipping a page in my textbook, trying to stay in the present. "I'm not sure I'm getting it."

And she launches into an explanation I only halfway follow.

The next week, before our first big test of the new semester, it happens again: I sleep through my alarm.

Or at least, that's what I tell myself happens.

What really happens is that my alarm goes off, and it goes off, and it goes off, and Skyler took an early class this semester so he's not there to groan at me, and then I switch it off because the idea of getting out of bed suddenly feels too difficult. I feel pinned to the mattress, my limbs aching and chest tight, as though there isn't enough room in there for my lungs. I'm not sick, I don't think, but I don't know how else to explain the symptoms.

I make it to class just as the last exam is being turned in, a horrible shame hitting me square in the chest. Adhira throws me a concerned look from the second row, and I purposefully glance away.

I have never missed a test, missed an assignment.

"I'm so sorry," I say to Dr. Serrano after the classroom has cleared out. Pleading my case. "I—I overslept. I don't know how. I swear I've never had anything like this happen before. I know there probably isn't a chance to retake it, but I really love this class, and if there's any way I could make up for it . . ."

I will him to believe this is firmly out of character. Fortunately, he must be able to tell that I'm panicking and takes pity on me.

"I don't know if I can give you a retake," he says, "since that might not be fair to the other students, and I don't have another version of the test." Right. I hadn't even considered the potential for cheating. "But I could use some help with data entry for my own research, if you're interested. Just a few hours a week. I could give you extra credit that would be enough to account for this zero as long as you get high marks on the rest of the exams."

Zero. A word that has never been associated with my own academics, except for: *there is a zero percent chance Neil McNair will fuck this up.* Until now.

Dr. Serrano lifts his eyebrows at me over his glasses. "*If* you can be on time," he adds. "This isn't a three-strike system. I'm giving you one chance, and I expect you to recognize it as the privilege it is."

"That's all I need. Thank you. Thank you so much."

Those few hours a week become a much-needed bright spot as the city veers toward spring. Gradually, Dr. Serrano starts to trust me, maybe because he can tell my interest in psychology is genuine. We meet in his office, a small room with messy bookshelves that demand reorganization, and while I bury myself in spreadsheets and he goes through emails or grades papers, we talk about what was discussed in class that week.

Just like my heart being rooted in two different places, I feel as though my mind is split too. I told Rowan I was uncertain about my major, but not the degree to which it's suddenly become a massive destabilizing force. I was so focused on linguistics before I got here, to the point where anyone who knew me would consider it a core piece of my identity, but now there's a new option: double-majoring in psychology, although right now the notion of even majoring in one thing sounds exhausting. Twice the credits, hours, assignments, exams. None of it has ever intimidated me before, but then again, I've never been so far from home.

Seeing Rowan in Boston . . . she seemed so natural there. She *fit*. I don't know why it's so difficult for me to do the same. I have always loved words, and maybe I've spent too many hours with dictionaries and language-learning guides, gone down too many *OED* rabbit holes. Psychology is new to me in a way linguistics hasn't been for quite some time.

Obviously I am far from a linguistics expert. But I'm even further from a psychology one, and something about that is immensely appealing. If I fully dedicated myself to this, if I really *understood*—then maybe I could rediscover that spark I've been searching for since I arrived in New York.

Everything feels like it might be okay until Dr. Serrano asks me to organize some news and journal clippings one afternoon.

The Role of Genetics in Predicting Severe Mental Illness, reads the title of one article, and I just stare while my heart plummets to my toes.

Because this is what Dr. Serrano's research is about—I've known that since my first day in his class.

"That was from a study we conducted last year," he says when he sees me frozen, the article clutched in my hand.

I blink myself back to my senses. "So it's very likely," I say, "that a parent's mental illness might be passed on to a child?"

The small office grows even smaller, my throat dry. I'm sure somewhere in my mind, I knew this was possible, but I've never imagined it in connection with my own family.

My father gave me his dark eyes and the shape of his nose. What else could he have given me?

Dr. Serrano takes a seat in his chair, spins to face me. "I'm not sure I'd say *very*, but there is more of a chance than if the parent didn't have a mental illness, yes. Some disorders are likelier than others to have a genetic link: bipolar disorder, schizophrenia, major depression, ADHD. We were specifically studying bipolar and schizophrenia. But of course, mental illness is caused by a variety of factors, not all of them genetic. Environmental factors, life history, substance abuse, various social issues."

"Right. Nature versus nurture," I say stupidly, but he nods.

"It's not a foregone conclusion that a child will develop a parent's illness," he says. "Depending on the disorder, sometimes it could be a one percent chance compared to a ten percent chance. Those aren't exact numbers, but just to give you a ballpark." Then he gives me a warm smile. "I could get you notes from the whole study if you'd like to read them."

"Yes." My response is immediate. "Please."

"There's an undergrad psych club that meets here on Thursdays you might be interested in too," he adds, and for that, I can only give a maybe.

Even if his notes can't give me precise answers, they might lead me to a place I've been silently scared of ever since that horrible night eight years ago, and so many nights since.

They could mean whatever my dad has—if there is indeed something undiagnosed there—I am more likely to develop it, simply because of the DNA we share.

That Natalie is, too.

Back in our room, Skyler's at his desk, squinting at his laptop and tossing a foam football up and down.

"Hey," he says, greeting me with a nod. "Were you studying for psych? Did Adhira say anything about me?"

And maybe it's Dr. Serrano's research burning a hole in my inbox. Maybe it's my lack of confidence in the major I used to be certain about. Maybe it's the fact that my eyelids are drooping and it's only six o'clock but my bed is the only place I want to be right now.

But for whatever reason, Skyler's question pinches the wrong nerve, like skin rubbed hard against sandpaper. Against a fucking cactus.

"It's not my job to memorize every single thing Adhira says," I snap, shutting the door a little too loud behind me.

The words are all steel, rough on my tongue, and at first I don't even recognize them coming out of my mouth. I don't talk like this. Even when my sister and I squabbled, rare dumb arguments about nothing in particular, I never had such—such *malice* in my voice.

Skyler catches the football. Holds it. "Whoa whoa whoa. It was just a question."

A few deep breaths, and then I can respond like myself.

"No—I'm sorry." I bite down hard on the inside of my cheek, the regret sinking in. Skyler has only ever been kind and generous toward me. It's the least I can do to help him out with Adhira. "I was working on some research with a professor. I didn't see her today."

"Don't worry about it. Sorry I asked." But Skyler's voice has turned chilly. Then he nods toward my desk. "Checked the mail earlier. That letter came for you today."

I pick up the nondescript white envelope. Turn it over.

The return address blurs everything else around me, bending the room until I'm no longer certain where I am.

Washington State Penitentiary.

No. It's just not possible.

Somehow, I move toward the desk, my backpack sliding to the floor with a soft thud as I close a fist around the envelope. My heart is in my throat and my stomach is at my feet and my lungs are in another fucking country. Maybe it's something else—a request for a donation. An update about a renovation. Junk mail.

Ridiculous, every option.

"Neil?" Skyler's saying, at least I think he is. "You okay?"

"Yeah. Fine. Must have been the wrong address. I should . . . go sort that out with the RA."

I stumble out of the room, the letter trembling in my hand.

He found my address. How the hell did he find my address?

When I get a good look at the letter, I realize it's not addressed to my specific room—just Neil McNair, and NYU's address. My room number is handwritten, as though it was sorted by someone at the residence hall. So he doesn't know exactly where I live, but the universe was more than happy to intervene and help him out.

Breathe. Just keep breathing, I urge myself, because suddenly I'm unsure whether it's something I've ever been able to do naturally.

I don't read it until I'm outside, until I can gulp in lungfuls of midwinter air while unassuming New Yorkers stream by me.

Dear Neil,

I've been working on my penmanship. can you see a difference? It made me think of you, how you loved those expensive pens and all that calligraphy stuff. I remember seeing you bent over the kitchen table, spending all that time making each letter look perfect. Seemed like a waste of time back then—when would you use something like that in real life? But maybe I'm starting to see the value.

Haven't heard from you, so school must have you pretty busy. But that was always the case, wasn't it? Guess I really thought you might surprise me at christmas.

What I'm trying to say is . . . it's been lonely in here.

Miss you, buddy.

Dad

If his goal was emotional manipulation, then congratulations to him, because I'm feeling manipulated as fuck.

I hate that it hurts for a moment, the idea of him being lonely. I hate that split second of sympathy immediately followed by the crushing feeling that I don't know what to do about this.

I have always had the answers. Always had a *plan*. But there is no set of rules for this, no formula I can follow that generates a perfect answer. He hasn't listened to my mom. If I wrote back, telling him to stop? I'd be on edge every time I opened that mailbox. The simple presence of an envelope would make me break out in a cold sweat.

All this time, I've wanted to deal with it without dealing with it. Ignore it, and it would go away.

Well, it isn't going away.

Because even if those letters stopped, he'd still be in my head, taking up far too much space and pressing on old bruises. *No son of mine is taking a dance class*, he spat at my mom one night so many years ago. I'd been in bed, but sound carried easily through the thin walls. *You've spent his whole life babying him—what's he going to be like when he's older? He'll barely be able to take care of himself.*

I'm not babying him, she responded. *This is what he wants.*

And who put that idea in his head in the first place?

Then a loud noise. A muffled, foreign sound.

Hair straightener was too hot, my mom said the next morning, when I pointed to the red mark on her wrist, her voice shaking. *Clumsy me.*

The weight of it nearly knocks me over—I have to dodge a cyclist at the last minute. A memory warped by time and by force.

I'd somehow convinced myself—self-preservation?—that he'd never become physical with us. Suddenly I'm no longer sure what truly happened, what my mind conjured to protect me.

The way I snapped at Skyler when he asked about Adhira. How many times did my dad snap at us like that?

How many times did he leave a mark?

Now it feels overwhelming that the whole city is the campus, this intangible thing for an intangible feeling. Too many sidewalks, too many people. But it's slightly better than the claustrophobia of that room, with a roommate who might know my darkest secret.

I should love it here. I should be grateful for every minute. I'm in college in one of the greatest cities in the world, and I would dare to not have fun? What a fucking asshole.

Yet all I feel is a bone-deep weariness mixed with unease, as though I've been put in a blender along with every uncomfortable thought I've tried to keep from coming to the surface. Pureed and panicked.

I go all the way across the country, and he's still here in my head. He's next to me in the dining hall at breakfast and in my classes and on the subway platform. His voice, as clear as it was when I was sixteen, when I was eleven. Mocking me.

Miss you, buddy.

Buddy.

As though the two of us have a relationship where that word makes any kind of sense. There were times I doubted whether he loved me at all—I was certainly never his *buddy*. Because it didn't seem right, that he could love me while telling me in a hundred different ways that I was too soft. Too weak.

I fold up the letter and shove it deep in my pocket.

It crosses my mind that I could explain all of this to Skyler. But opening up about our relationships and friendships—that was easy. I'd be starting from scratch with this, and I wouldn't even know where to begin or how he'd feel about me afterward. I'm not ready for that kind of judgment.

In my pocket, my phone vibrates. A text from Zoe, asking where I am, if I got held up somewhere, because tonight we were going to Shabbat again with a few others.

Then Rowan calls.

It aches to send her to voice mail, but I can't talk to her when I'm like this.

Of course, after our conversation about communication, this has me feeling even worse. The letter is a reminder of an ugly past, one I've been trying to move on from for so long. Telling her would risk changing how she feels about me, and that's not a risk I'm willing to take.

The gray sky rumbles with the threat of rain, and more than anything, I wish I could be home right now.

No, not home—on the couch in the Roths' living room on the second night of Hanukkah. That instantly becomes my new happy place. The memory I'll return to whenever I need to escape.

Two weeks. In two weeks, she'll be here in New York for her parents' book tour.

I have to get myself under control before then. I'll let myself spiral now, and by the time she gets here, I'll be the person she fell in love with again.

Because I don't have anywhere to be, I just wander. Apparently New York is the kind of place where you can openly have a breakdown on a city sidewalk and no one pays you much attention. All around me, the city is abuzz with nighttime activity, people dressed up and going out or dressed down and bringing takeout back to their apartments. Everyone has somewhere to be, a fact that once comforted me and now just makes me feel lost.

I'm not sure how it's possible to be this lonely in a city of eight million people. Somehow that only makes the loneliness heavier, as though I am the only one stumbling around on unsteady feet with the weight of the past on my back, trying to outrun the darkness.

ROWAN

hey, never heard from you after I called last night. just want to make sure everything is okay?

NEIL

Completely fine, sorry. Fell asleep in the middle of my textbook and it was too late to call when I woke up. Didn't want to bother you.

ROWAN

you're never bothering me.

well, except for grades 9-12, but you've more than made up for it 😊

free to video chat tonight?

NEIL

I wish . . . too much studying to do, I'm sorry.

Tomorrow?

ROWAN

I have a creative writing thing at my professor's house. saturday?

NEIL

Skyler and everyone wanted to go to
Coney Island. But I could cancel . . . I
probably should, I'm way behind in psych.

ROWAN

no no, don't cancel

we'll figure it out!

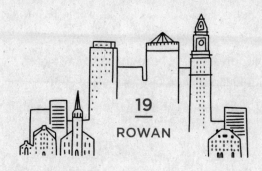

19
ROWAN

PROFESSOR MIRANDA EVERETT lives in Brookline, a picturesque town less than thirty minutes from Emerson on the green line—although calling something in Boston picturesque is a bit like calling romance novels romantic.

"Welcome, welcome," she says with an easy smile, beckoning Kait and me inside. Professor Everett is chic in a patterned wrap dress and suede heels, hair glossy. "Get out of the cold; take a seat wherever you like."

A few other classmates are already here, spread across the living room. An accent wall is painted a deep teal, a gallery wall arranged above a lush velvet sectional, where Owen, once again clad in his bowler hat, is showing Sierra something in his notebook. Soft jazz plays from some hidden sound system so modern that it remains the same volume no matter where you are in the room. Then there's Professor Everett's framed National Book Award over the mantel of a real wood-burning fireplace. Coziness personified.

"I want to live here," I whisper to Kait as we take off our coats, handing Professor Everett the Trader Joe's snacks we brought.

She adds them to the growing pile on the coffee table.

Kait unwinds her scarf and fluffs out her hair. "Already planning to get 'lost' later just so I can explore the rest of it."

Professor Everett does this a few times a year: invites the creative writing cohort over for a potluck and a night of literary games. As close as I was with my teachers in high school, I definitely never went to any of their homes, and while it wouldn't have sounded appealing back then, there's something about a professor's invitation that feels so incredibly *collegiate*. I even dressed up, a white collared blouse under a deep green sweaterdress, thick black tights, and vintage pumps.

We always feel like equals in Professor Everett's class, no patronizing, no arrogance. A fact that's cemented when someone addresses her and she laughs and says, "Okay, I get that it's very polite and all, but you really can just call me Miranda." She lifts her glass of wine—sparkling cider for the under-twenty-ones—in a toast. "I'm so glad you all could make it tonight. Keeping with the theme, I don't want this to be overly formal, either. Just a casual get-together of literary nerds."

Kait and I take seats on a pair of folding chairs near the fireplace while Professor Everett—Miranda—explains the first game. "I call it Chaos Story," she says. We'll each write a sentence inspired by a prompt and then pass our sheet of paper to the next person to write the next sentence. And so on, and so on, until the last person reads the piece out loud. Later we'll divide into groups for critique sessions and cap off the night with a freewrite.

"Naturally," Felix says from a goldenrod armchair, because we all know how attached she is to her freewrites.

I reach into my bag for Neil's notebook and a pen as Sierra passes me a carafe of spiced cider. This is the kind of dreamy writer gathering I've always imagined, and I want to soak up every detail.

Each round of Chaos Story, there are new rules: we can't use any words that begin with the letter *A*, or we can't use any adjectives or adverbs. Miranda plays too, adding herself to our haphazard circle and tipping over a vintage hourglass each time we pass our sheets of paper.

Next to me, Kait taps her pen on a legal pad. "Is 'always' an adverb?"

"Yes," says Tegan. "Because it describes *how* you do something."

"Are you sure?" Felix asks. This sparks a lively debate until we finally use our phones to look it up.

My phone buzzes with a text halfway through the next round. I'm about to turn it to silent when the name catches my attention. It's not someone who ever really texts me, except for when we traded numbers at the beginning of the summer before all of us met up at Golden Gardens one afternoon.

Sean Yee: *hey rowan, it's sean. have you heard from neil lately?*

I frown down at it, thumbing out a quick response.

I saw him four weeks ago and we texted just this morning.

Sean: *oh ok*

Sean: *so he's alive lol*

Rowan: *unless someone with annoyingly good grammar kidnapped him and stole his phone, yes.*

Sean: *he hasn't been replying to my texts. same with cy and adrian*

That's strange. Out of character for him. Sure, maybe his texts have seemed a little shorter than they usually are, but we've both been busy studying. That misstep I made, bringing up his dad—he hasn't mentioned it since.

I can go back to waiting, hoping that one day he'll decide he's ready. Even if the thought of him aching on his own is enough to crack my heart open.

I tell Sean I'm sorry, that maybe he's just been swamped, before putting my phone away and trying to push past any lingering worry. Surely it's just stress. I've gone a week without texting Kirby and Mara—at least, I'm fairly sure I have.

When we break out into critique groups to share snippets of our works in progress, I peek at my printed-out pages as others start reading aloud, flicking away lint on my sweaterdress. I decided to add a new chapter to my Hannah and Hayden story, the book I've been working on for the past couple years that never feels *done*. In it, they're on a company retreat and they've just discovered there's only one hotel room left—with only one bed, naturally. One of my favorite tropes, and I couldn't believe I hadn't found a way to use it in this book yet.

I should feel solid about it—I know these characters, Hannah's fierce ambition and Hayden's reserved-but-secretly-sweet nature. And yet as I reread, some of my sentences sound stilted. Awkward.

And worst of all: boring.

They looked at each other, and then at the single key dangling from the receptionist's hand.

I couldn't have picked a better word than "looked"?

Hannah's gaze held Hayden's, a silent question passing between them.

Okay, at least now they're gazing—

"We'll take it," she said, looking at the key and then back at Hayden, whose cheeks were starting to turn pink.

Jesus Christ, how many times can these idiots look at each other? Did I even read this back before I printed it out?

(Yes. And apparently I decided it was fine.)

Only right now it is solidly *not* fine, especially as I listen to everyone else read, feeling worse and worse about my only-one-bed scene. Kait's humor is unparalleled. Noor's sentences are sharp and choppy in the thriller she's working on. Sierra's literary fiction is *beautiful*, even if I still don't fully understand it.

Everyone has a *voice*, and apparently I left mine back in Seattle.

If I ever had one to begin with—something I'm seriously starting to doubt.

On Gazebo Night, I was so full of inspiration and optimism. I don't know why I can't have that all the time. Surely cheap wine isn't the answer.

Then there's the thing I haven't let myself think about that's been tapping away at the back of my brain. *You're in love but you can't write about it. Something's wrong with you.*

It's ridiculous—surely plenty of romance authors are deeply in love with their partners.

The group claps for Sierra before turning to me. *Fuck*, this is going to be brutal. Slowly, I unclench my fists around the pages as a half dozen eyes flick toward me. A thick swallow, my heart thumping in my throat.

It's starting to feel like I can't measure up to any of them. How can I truly feel like I belong if I can't do the one thing I came here specifically to do? Maybe I shouldn't be here, not in Professor Everett's beautiful home, not in this major, maybe not even on this campus.

"Sorry—I have to—" And I spring to my feet and escape.

I only make it as far as the kitchen before everything starts spinning and I have to press my back to the counter to keep from collapsing. My breaths are coming harder, faster. I guzzle down another cup of cider.

I should be able to do this. Why can't I fucking do this?

I half thought Kait might come after me—and half hoped she would—so I'm surprised when it's Miranda's voice I hear.

"Rowan?" she asks. "Is everything okay?"

I do my best to appear as though I haven't been having a mental breakdown and/or crisis of confidence. I lift a hand and give her a weak smile as she enters the kitchen.

"Just your standard why-is-everything-I-write-garbage kind of breakdown," I say, trying to sound light and breezy.

"Ah. I see." She gestures for me to sit down at the sleek marble kitchen counter, so I tuck my dress underneath me and hop up onto a wooden stool. Bowls of overflow snacks cover the countertop, but my stomach isn't having it. In the other room, everyone is sharing, laughing. "Is this maybe why you've been busy every day after class?"

"I'm sorry." The guilt underscores the way my pulse pounds, *not good enough, not good enough, not good enough.* "About this, too. I don't want to disrupt the night for you or for anyone else."

Miranda fills a glass of water, placing it in front of me before taking the seat across from me. "You have nothing to be sorry for. Unless you're the one who made those oatmeal raisin cookies, because—" At that, she screws up her nose, and we both laugh. There was definitely an overly doughy consistency to them. "I feel I've gotten to know you a little through your work and during class, even if you tend to be a bit quiet."

I have to wince at that. In high school, "Rowan Roth" and "quiet" would never have been uttered in the same sentence, unless that sentence was "Be quiet, Rowan Roth and Neil McNair are about to get into it."

"I've just been . . . a little blocked." A gulp of water. "I've never felt this way before. I've written for myself even after long days when I was working on an essay for class. I'd open up my work in progress and the words were just *there.* I didn't have to fight nearly as hard for them. I haven't been fully happy with anything I've turned in, if I'm being honest. And I'm starting to wonder if I'm even supposed to be in this class."

"That's what I wanted to talk to you about," she says, and when my eyes widen in horror, she's quick to correct herself: "*Not* if you're supposed to be in this class, because I firmly believe you are. I'm not concerned about the quality of your writing, but I can see some of the pressure you're putting on yourself—even right now. Writing for yourself is very different from writing for an audience. I had a similar experience with my second book."

"I loved your second book. More than your first," I tell her. "All those reviewers who said the themes didn't seem as universal as the first, or that the characters weren't likable . . . Not every character needs to be likable for a book to be good. I mean—" I break off, realizing too late that maybe she didn't read the reviews or doesn't want to know what critics thought.

But she just says, "You know what, I think I prefer that one too."

At the opposite end of the kitchen, the backyard door swings open. A tall, bearded man dashes in, carrying two jugs of cider.

Upon seeing me, his expression morphs into alarm. "Sorry! I'm not here!"

Miranda laughs. "Thanks, Jon."

"No problem." Her boyfriend, husband—whoever he is— holds a finger to his lips before he disappears outside. "You never saw me."

I expect Miranda to explain him in some way, but she seems thoroughly immersed in our conversation. "And you've always wanted to write romance?" she asks, stirring her drink.

"I've loved it since I was kid," I say. "I tried to write about it in that first assignment, but I know it sounded . . . a little flat."

"Not flat," she says gently. "Just not *you*."

"And I've had this worry—" I break off again, wondering if someone spiked the cider with truth serum and if there's a limit to just how many of my issues I'll spill to this poor woman tonight. "I'm in a long-distance relationship with someone really wonderful." Maybe it's a little personal to tell her about Neil, but I nearly started crying in her house, and writing is nothing if not personal. "He's at school in New York. Romance has always been the thing I want to read most. It's all I've ever wanted to write. And then as soon as I started dating someone I truly, deeply loved . . . it all dried up. Like, I don't know, I'm putting too much pressure on the writing to reflect that love."

Miranda considers this for a while as she reaches for a piece of white-cheddar popcorn. "Hmm."

"So I'm just wondering . . . is there something wrong with me that I can't write when I'm happy? Do I need to be in pain to be creative?" With a humorless laugh, I hold up my hands. "Are all writers tortured geniuses—not that I'm anything remotely close to a genius, I swear I don't think *quite* that highly of myself—and that's the secret? That I have to be tortured if I want to make anything worthwhile?"

"Wow. I'm not quite sure where to start." She tucks a lock of hair behind one ear, exposing a tiny book-shaped earring. If I weren't so distraught, I'd ask where she got it. "First of all, I want to give you an adamant *no* that you don't have to be unhappy in order to create art. That's bullshit. Maybe there is something of a history of tortured geniuses, people in pain making beautiful things. Maybe we as a culture have even romanticized it."

I nod, thinking about how Neil, with his love of Hemingway and Fitzgerald, would know all about that.

"Every writer is different, of course. Are all writers perfectly well-adjusted human beings? Well, no. None of us are. But that doesn't mean we're all miserable, either. I wrote *Thursday at Dawn* when I was going through a rough patch, and it's a very sad book. Then I wrote *Helvetica* when everything started to stabilize—and that's the one you and I like the most. And I'm inclined to believe we're right—I think it's the better book. I was happier, I was healthier, I was taking care of myself, and I think it shows," she says, and I wonder how that must feel for her rough-patch book to be the one beloved by critics. Complicated, I imagine. "Inspiration takes form in many different ways. Sometimes even I don't understand it, but I've grown to trust the process."

"What is it, then?" I ask. "Why am I so stuck? Why I am incapable of getting a decent grade on one of these assignments?"

As soon as the words leave my mouth, I realize that's part of what I've been craving: the validation, the way it feels to see an A circled in red on top of a paper.

"Rowan. You should know by now that the assignments aren't graded. Not on any kind of scale that you're used to, at least."

"But—but all the red," I say. "You always scribble all over them. I feel like that wouldn't be the case if I were actually getting an A."

"I write that much on *everyone*'s assignments," she says. "There's a reason I emphasize participation in my class, and that can mean any number of things. I find that freshmen sometimes have a hard time letting go of perfection, this notion that whatever they put on the page needs to be instantly brilliant. Especially the ones who were high achievers in high school. There might be a bit of academic burnout there, and the last thing I want to do is add more stress."

"Okay, fine," I say. "But it doesn't change the fact that everything I write comes out like absolute shit."

Miranda's voice is warm as ever but with a new firmness. "Nah," she says. "I would love to see you write absolute shit, but you're not there yet."

I half laugh at this. "Are you making fun of me?"

She shakes her head. "It's advice I've been given at a few stages of my own career. Sometimes we can get so in our heads that we think everything needs to be beautiful the moment it hits the page. I'll build up a book for so long that once I start writing, I'm furious with myself that it doesn't match the vision I have in my head."

"Yes," I say, nodding vigorously. "That's exactly it. How do I get it to match that vision?"

"You don't." She says it flatly. Of all the encouraging things I thought she might say, I definitely never thought she'd agree with me. "You embrace the absolute shit. That's why I do the free-writes. To get all of you out of your heads, to realize that writing is revising. Writing is rewriting. Nothing comes out beautifully the first time, except for maybe a handful of very unusual writers. Who we hate, naturally."

"Naturally."

"Most of the students in my classes are used to being told by their teachers that they're good writers. They're used to getting top grades. And I'm not here to drag you down or tank your GPA, but I want you to think about writing differently than you have in the past. You might have that compounded because of your relationship—the fact that you're in love, so you should be able to write about love."

"Write what you know," I mutter.

"But that's so much pressure," she says. "Not to mention most of you are going through considerable emotional upheaval— leaving behind your homes, your safety, your comfort. Starting over in a new place."

It would be so easy for her to sound patronizing, and yet all I feel is the deep compassion she has for teaching, for her students. Because that's undeniably part of it, the onslaught of newness, ever-shifting beneath my feet.

"So how are we ever supposed to write something good?"

"Let go of it," she says, "by doing the exact opposite. I'd rather read bad writing that's full of heart than good writing that's devoid of emotion." And then she gives me a smile as she pats her chest. "Because if it has that heart, how bad can it really be?"

I'm still struggling to wrap my mind around this. Then again, nothing I've tried so far has worked, so maybe it's not the most ridiculous idea.

I let out a deep breath, trying to relax into it.

"Write badly, Rowan," she urges, holding out a bowl for me to take a handful of chips. "Give yourself permission."

I go back out into the living room for the final freewrite, where Kait gives me a cheery smile and asks where I wandered off to.

"Bathroom," I tell her.

And even though I don't write another word the rest of the night, somewhere deep in my bones, I sense myself start to change.

It doesn't happen right away, the writing badly.

But a couple nights later, Paulina's out and Kait's with Leilani and I'm caught up on all my reading. Gingerly, as though it's a small animal I might spook if I go too fast, I reach for my laptop.

Give yourself permission.

So I do.

I write the worst trash I've ever written. Objectively speaking— this time, I'm not being hard on myself.

It's a surprise, how bizarrely fun it is, to let myself go like this. My writing has always been so restrained, so calculated, but when I switch off my inner editor, let the words trip into each other, it's a mess—a little sandbox of words I've created to play with.

I put all my heart into that terrible piece of writing. There's a turn of phrase I like here and there, but as a whole, it's not very good at all. I repeat words, I end sentences with prepositions, I use too many question marks and exclamation points. It's ugly and unpolished and downright *bad*.

And when I finish, I'm so fucking proud of it.

Meet **Jared Roth** and **Ilana García Roth**, bestselling authors of
THE EXCAVATED SERIES!

A new chapter book about
ROXY RODRIGUEZ,
everyone's favorite little sister,
and her quest to become

the world's youngest
pastry chef.

BONUS RECIPES INCLUDED IN THE BACK!

Saturday, March 1, at 6:30 p.m.
BOOKS OF WONDER
42 West 17th Street
New York, NY 10011

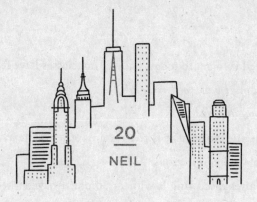

20
NEIL

"YOU LOOK... HOLY shit," I say when she opens the door to her parents' hotel room. Then I crane my neck to see around her, waving to Ilana and Jared. "In fact, I'm not sure I should finish that sentence with your parents in the room."

Rowan grins her lovely, magnetic grin. Nudges my arm. "You are amazing for my self-esteem."

A familiar warmth spreads all the way down to my toes, that full-body glow I can never get enough of when she's around. She's in a vintage black dress that seems tailor-made for her curves, with a tight bodice and flared skirt, lace sleeves, and a hint of shimmer. With her wavy hair pinned to one side and a swipe of red across her lips, she could be a 1940s starlet on her way to a movie premiere. Rowan has made me speechless a fair number of times in my life. I used to lament the fact that we were never able to attend any high school dances as a couple, but it was probably for the best: I wouldn't have been able to keep my jaw off the floor. The past week has been a study in patience. That mix of exhaustion and dread has followed me around, trailed me like a shadow. All

I've wanted is to get to today, and yet my classes have felt endless.

School must have you pretty busy.

Miss you, buddy.

Maybe the worst of it is that in any other context, his words would be wholly innocuous.

Even after discussing it with my mom, I haven't been able to get the letter off my mind. Skyler hasn't said anything about it; in fact, he and I have exchanged only pleasantries lately. I can't tell if he's tiptoeing around me or if we've both made a silent agreement not to acknowledge it. Again and again, I've told myself that everything will be okay the next time Rowan and I see each other.

It has to be.

She got to New York late last night and stayed at the hotel with her parents, and we planned a fancy date night before the book event. This rooftop Italian restaurant in Chelsea has spectacular views, city lights just starting to blink on at dusk, and it's early enough in the evening that we were able to snag a reservation. Although I don't have to force smiles with nearly as much effort as I do with everyone else, it feels like we're dining with an uninvited third guest. One Rowan can't see but is all too real to me.

As soon as we're seated, a blond girl passes our table—and then doubles back. "Hey!" she says. "I swear, this city really does feel like a small town sometimes."

"Hey," I say. "Rowan, Zoe. Zoe, this is my girlfriend, Rowan."

Zoe's face lights up as she bends to give Rowan a hug, lifting her eyebrows at first as though to ask if Rowan's a hugger. Rowan smiles, accepts the hug. "Rowan! I've heard so much about you. Amazing to meet you."

"You too," she says. "A little preview of tomorrow?"

Zoe laughs. We all had plans to hang out tomorrow so Rowan could meet everyone. "Guess so. Your scavenger hunt was a blast, by the way."

This makes Rowan beam. "I'm so glad. It's funny, I used to hate losing to him in high school, but I don't mind it as much anymore."

"Probably because I gloat a lot less?"

"It's true. He was so sneaky about that last photo, it took us a moment to realize the game was even over." Then Zoe gestures to a table with a few other girls I don't recognize. "I better get back before they finish all the burrata."

We exchange goodbyes as she hurries to her table.

And then, because I am a massive idiot, I say: "She has a boyfriend."

Rowan pauses while reaching for a slice of focaccia. "Okay," she says, drawing out the two syllables. "You're allowed to have friends who are single girls. I don't know why you needed to say that so quickly."

"Sorry." I fidget with the edge of a cloth napkin. *Idiot, idiot, idiot.* "It's just—this is stupid, really silly, and I should have told you when it happened. But back in the fall, I was at a party with Skyler, and she asked if I was single. Which . . . I'm obviously not. And then she started dating Steve, so. No big deal."

"Oh." She places the bread back in the basket. "Did any part of you . . . wish you were? Single?"

"*No*," I say emphatically. "Not once. I swear to you, that's never crossed my mind."

"Maybe we should talk about this. It's okay to admit that you find other people attractive. I'm not expecting you to go through your life with tunnel vision."

I shake my head, letting my shoe tap hers beneath the table while I wrap a fist around the napkin in my lap, my thumb warping the fabric. I've already screwed up my psych grade and my friendship with Skyler—I can't screw things up with her, which includes making her feel anything less than fully adored. I'm still kicking myself for how I reacted in Boston when she mentioned my dad. She shouldn't have ever had to see that mask slip.

"Artoo . . . I don't know how to say this in a way that doesn't make me sound completely lovesick, but I suppose that's what I am." A warmth creeps onto my cheeks as I lower my voice, reaching a hand across the table to link my fingers with hers. It nearly breaks me, imagining her feeling at all insecure when she looks this fucking radiant—as made up as she is tonight or as soft as she is first thing in the morning. "No one else has ever affected me the way you do."

"Even though you're in a city of eight million people?" She rubs her thumb along my index finger, a gentle brush that's all too easy to relax into. She's not upset. I should have told her about Zoe earlier, but she's not upset.

"They're all swamp hags."

"They're most definitely not," she says with a laugh, the sound loosening the pressure in my lungs, "but okay."

The food arrives, the slight disagreement forgotten as we lose ourselves in eggplant parmesan and delicate spinach gnocchi.

"I may have had a breakthrough in creative writing," she says between bites, and tells me about an epiphany sparked by her professor's advice to write badly. I just blink at her for a few moments after she says this. "Is your overachiever brain short-circuiting? Because mine did when she first mentioned it."

"A little, yes."

"I swear to you, it works. It might be the best worst thing I've ever written," she says. "But most importantly, I'm having fun with it."

I'm happy for her—of course I am. She deserves to be optimistic about her writing, for it to bring her joy.

At the same time, I can't deny there's a shred of envy at seeing her so settled. At Emerson, with her major, in Boston. Maybe it's a remnant from all our years of competition, or maybe it's something entirely new, but whatever it is, it feels vile and deeply unwelcome.

"You'll show me?" I ask, locking all of that in the box of things I cannot talk about, the one I wish had a tighter lid. The cloth napkin in my lap is a wrinkled wreck. "When you have something you're ready to share?"

"I may be enlightened, but not enlightened enough to show you this garbage. Yet." Still, she finds my hand again, brings it to her mouth to drop a kiss onto my knuckles. "Soon, though. Hopefully."

As I reach for the check, Rowan suggests splitting it.

"You don't have to be chivalrous," she says. "You know I don't care about that stuff."

"I know. I just—we never go on dates like this." I slide my credit card into the billfold, having prepared for this after what happened in the sushi restaurant. "I want to treat you."

"Fine, but I'm getting it next time."

The bookstore is a ten-minute walk away, and it's an unseasonably warm evening. With each step, my body loosens up a bit more. A magnificent relief—I only want to be my best self when I'm with her.

"Imagine if we lived here," I say, hand threaded with hers as we pass a quartet of musicians, a guy with a cello strapped to his back trailing three violinists. "If we could go back to our apartment at the end of the day and crawl into bed together. Not just once in a while like this, but every night."

The way that vision aches. The times we've talked about the future, it's always seemed so far away, with so many classes and exams and flights and train rides in between. But we've almost made it through this year. It's impossible not to think ahead in a long-distance relationship—to the time you'll finally be in the same place.

"Maybe we could. After graduation. Of course, the rent would be so astronomical that we'd never be able to afford a meal like this again." She turns her face toward mine. "Speaking of . . . we really need to book those tickets. Flying into London and out of Rome, right?" That was what we discussed during our last call about it.

Two weeks ago. Before the letter arrived.

"I know, I know." The anxiety starts its slow ascent up my spine again. "We will. Tomorrow."

Because here is what I've decided: I don't know if I can go on that trip.

I've saved up, and I still have a decent chunk of the Howl money. Truthfully, I can't imagine anything else I'd rather spend it on. But that's not the reason, even if it's the one she's likelier to understand.

Ever since that goddamn letter arrived, it's been impossible to imagine the two of us traipsing around Europe, a vacation that should be joyful and illuminating and wildly romantic. I'd be this storm cloud following her around, a heavy weight on her back.

I wish I could picture myself happy there with her, and I don't know what it means that I suddenly can't.

Though he went to prison long before I showed any real interest in girls, somehow my thoughts take on my father's voice.

What a fucking loser. Can't even keep your girlfriend satisfied.

He is always there, a ghoulish reminder of the family I once had, the pain my mom tried to hide from the rest of us. I must be doomed never to move on when it's what I want more than anything in the world.

"My parents looked through our itinerary," Rowan continues, and I will myself to remain in the moment. "They thought we should spend one less night in Dublin so we could spend more time on the coast, but that should be easy enough when we book the hotels."

"Right." The single syllable sounds so foreign, I'm not even sure my mouth is moving. I'm about to disappoint her. Ruin her summer.

The sleeves of my suit are too tight, the collar of my shirt too stiff. These clothes are choking me, and suddenly it all feels like too much. A swirl of confusion and worry, all trying to yank me back to that dark place where I couldn't get out of bed.

Another thought, entirely unbidden:

She deserves better.

I'm not sure if this one's in my dad's voice or mine.

She keeps talking about Europe but I can barely process any of it, which makes me feel even guiltier. There must be guys at Emerson who have money, guys who could take her out and not balk at the size of the bill. Guys without family baggage. Guys who don't have to try so hard to be happy when they should be having the time of their lives.

True, she chose me once. But that version of me seems more and more like a stranger, and there may come a time when I've changed too much, become too unfamiliar. Someone to be pitied—no longer an equal, the way we were through high school.

A sharp pain in my chest makes me stop abruptly on the

sidewalk. Suddenly I can't catch my breath, my lungs tightening and my throat closing up and—*no*. I have to stay in control.

"Hey, you okay?" Rowan's expression is unlike any I've seen before. This pure and genuine worry, one that she shouldn't have to feel.

I thought I could keep it away while she was here. Keep that monster hidden.

Because as soon as I acknowledge any sliver of it, I know it's all going to tumble out. The fear and insecurity and loneliness and loathing. Proof I am becoming a poor facsimile of the person she loved.

Everything is burning, sweat dripping down my back, and is this what a heart attack feels like? Have I been too dismissive of the signs, and this is what it was all barreling toward? My hands fly to my neck. This tie. Why did I wear a fucking tie?

"Of course. Sorry. Just, uh—too warm, I guess," I say, my thumbs stumbling over the knot at my throat.

She steps closer, lamplight casting her features in a delicate glow. "Let me?" she asks, leaning in so that she can undo the tie.

Instant relief—that's what it is. Her words are so steady. Calming. I cling to this feeling like a life preserver. Then she flicks open the top button of my shirt, kissing me lightly. I can finally drag in a full breath, my shoulders sinking back into place. I refocus on this gorgeous, clever girl who somehow chose *me*. The girl whose ambition I admired long before I could decipher my true feelings, the girl who challenges me in all the best ways.

I am so fucking lucky, and tonight I'm going to make sure she knows it.

I dip my head until my lips brush her ear. "What I wanted to say earlier was that you look incredibly hot in that dress. I've been having some very indecent thoughts."

"And you know how I feel about you in a tie."

"You might have to tell me a few more times."

"I will," she says. "All night, probably, while we act out your indecent thoughts." *God.* I may not make it until then. An innocent smile, and then she gives my collar a tug. "Now. Onward to make fools of ourselves in front of several dozen small children."

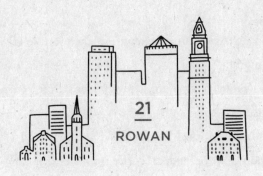

21

ROWAN

THE EVENT IS adorable in all the ways a chapter-book launch should be, with juice boxes galore and half the kids dressed up as their favorite characters. Which means, incidentally, because the books are somewhat based on my childhood, that a few of them are dressed as *me*—little buns coiled on top of their heads, striped leggings, bright T-shirts. Look through any Roth family photo album and that was my uniform from preschool to fifth grade.

And the best part: when my parents beckon me to the front of the room, introduce me as their daughter, and ask me to read a section of the book. I used to do this all the time, but it's been a few years, mainly sparked by embarrassment at my first period and bat mitzvah drama having made their way into earlier books. Tonight I wear being Jared Roth and Ilana García Roth's daughter with pride, and I'm surprised to revel in the attention of that many eight- to ten-year-olds.

Because then one of them asks if I write books like my mom and dad, and I meet Neil's gaze before announcing that yes, I'm a writer too. It comes out more confidently, more solidly than I thought it might.

"But you probably have to be a bit older before you read my books," I add.

After kids are whisked home to bed and Neil and I hug my parents goodbye, we order decaf coffee from a nearby café, sipping slowly as we wander through a park.

Boston already has half my heart, but I'm starting to think I could fall a little in love with this city too. My fatal flaw: I spend enough time anywhere, and I suddenly start making it part of my personality. The Greenwich Village mug back in my dorm that I've been using almost every day would have to agree.

There is something perfect about this, the two of us strolling through New York at night, the soothing pressure of his palm on my back.

At least, it would be perfect if Neil didn't seem slightly off.

When he thinks I'm not looking, his expression shifts, eyes appearing unfocused. Jaw muscles going slack. This boy has always been wound tight, but tonight I sense some tension simmering beneath the surface. Probably none of it would be noticeable if I didn't know him as well as I do.

After my misstep in Boston, I'm not sure how to bring it up. If whatever's going on in his head is off-limits the way talking about his dad was.

"I have a surprise for us," I say instead. If there's anything that will bring him back to me, hopefully it will be this. Neil gives me a lift of his eyebrows as I reach into my purse and pull out a room key. "Several blocks from my parents, so. Don't worry about that."

Conflicted emotions flicker across his face: excitement at first, and then concern. "That couldn't have been cheap."

"We're allowed to have something nice once in a while."

"Nice" doesn't even begin to describe it. The hotel is all gold and emerald decor and dripping chandeliers, his arm around my waist as we take the elevator up, up. When it reaches the seventeenth floor, it opens with a cheerful *ding*.

Inside the room, we both let out audible gasps. Even the bathroom is beautiful, with terrazzo countertops and a walk-in shower. I've never considered what it might be like to shower together, and yet the image appears in my mind with such a fierce determination I suddenly fear every fantasy with him has been utterly wasted. Slippery skin and slicked-back hair. Water pounding against our backs.

And the bed, huge and elegant, with a wrought iron headboard and brocaded duvet and at least eight different pillows.

"You like it?" I ask, and he just laughs.

I've missed that sound. Even over the phone, it's not the same—I don't get to see the way his eyes crinkle at the edges, the way his glasses slip down his nose and he has to push them back up. All these details I've sworn I could never forget, even if we were on opposite sides of the globe.

It feels so precious, this night together.

"That was amazing, seeing you up there with them. At the

bookstore." He moves closer, slipping down the sleeve of my dress so he can expose my bare shoulder.

My lashes flutter shut. "Please don't talk about my parents right now."

"No, I'm talking about you. How confident you looked when you talked about writing. Your whole face just lit up—I'd missed seeing that." His teeth flirt with the skin of my shoulder, and when I let out a sigh, he does it again. "I was so proud of you."

He delivers the compliments in between kisses along my neck, undoing the zipper of my dress only a few inches so that his mouth can dip lower.

"Oh God. I think I might have a praise kink." A soft bite at my collarbone. "File that under least surprising things about me."

"Good, because I could do this all night."

When our mouths finally collide, it's all urgency and heat. His hands on the sides of my face, diving into my hair. I reach for the tie I loosened earlier. Let it drop to the floor. In an instant, he has me pushed against the room's desk, our hips pinned together.

"How about those indecent thoughts?" I manage between kisses, loving the way this draws a laugh from his chest.

"Too many. Don't know where to start." A groan as I wrap a leg around his waist, urging him closer. His fingertips burning a path up my thigh.

I'm already dizzy with the scent of him, the one that's faded from his hoodie and scarf. I throw off his suit jacket and tug at his shirt where it's tucked in, freeing the white fabric. Without breaking the kiss, he reaches into his pants pocket for his phone. Tosses it onto the desk.

Just as it lands there, a message pops up. I don't mean to look—really, I don't—but the screen is bright and the room is dark.

Mom: I could call him. Or make a visit. This isn't fair to—

That's where the preview cuts off, but it's more than enough to set off sirens in my mind.

"What's that?" I ask.

"Hmm?"

I pull back for a moment. My breaths are still coming in hard bursts, my heart hammering for an entirely different reason. "Why is your mom texting you something about a visit?"

Neil's exhales start to slow down as he fumbles for the phone. ". . . Oh."

Even though everything in my body is begging me not to stop, I straighten my dress, the message a shock of cold water to my system. I still only have pieces of the story. Fragments of whatever he's been keeping from me.

"You weren't—I didn't want you to see that." He pushes a hand into his face, jostling his glasses.

"Neil. What's going on?"

He backs up, the sleeves of his shirt pushed to his forearms. His cheeks are scarlet and his jaw is tight, a thread of tension I'm not sure I've seen on his face before. "My dad sent me a letter," he tells the carpet, not meeting my eyes. "Two of them, actually. Including one here at school."

"How did he—"

"He just addressed it to 'Neil McNair, NYU.' Somehow it found its way to me." A wry, not-quite smile. "The mail room staff deserves a raise, evidently."

Two more letters.

I knew his dad had sent one before graduation. That Neil had considered visiting him over the summer, then told me on the only day we ever talked about it that he'd decided not to. "Let's sit down," I say gently, grazing his wrist with a few fingertips. "Let's talk about this?"

I phrase it as a question, because he didn't want to talk about his dad before and I want him to know, *need* him to know that I'm not pressuring him.

I have to stay calm. Give him the space to collect himself. So I get a glass of water from the bathroom and pass it to him with a shaky hand before realizing what I'm doing. Whenever I was upset about something as a kid, my mom would have me drink a glass of water, as though it was enough to clear my mind and help me refocus. Sometimes it was. It's what Miranda did, too, when I broke down in her kitchen.

Neil takes a sip and sets the glass on the nightstand, still not making eye contact. In my half-unzipped dress, I gesture for him to sit next to me on the bed with its brocaded duvet.

"When did you get the letters?" I ask.

He closes his eyes, grips my leg like a lifeline. "Winter break. And then a couple weeks ago."

Winter break. Two months ago, and he hasn't told me until now.

I quickly brush that off because this isn't about me. I can't center myself in this tragedy of his life. I didn't know him when his dad committed that crime. During his trial. When he was sent away. I didn't know him, and I cannot possibly know who he was back then, either, as much as I wish I could.

He has been alone in this, and I have arrived here so, so late.

"My mom almost never talks to him, but she's asked him to stop. And it doesn't do anything. Maybe if I could get on the phone or write back, but I can't bring myself to do it. I don't want him in my life—I've gotten so used to not having him here, and then these letters show up and they just drag me right back." A shake of his head, as though he's disappointed in himself. "I should be better. I should be stronger than this."

"You don't have to be anything. You feel the way you feel—you don't have to make excuses for it or pretend to be brave. This is me," I say softly, rubbing my hand along his knee. "I only want to know because I care about you. So much."

"Rowan." His eyes fly open, his expression pained, throat pulsing hard as he swallows. "I spent so long building myself up to be someone who wasn't defined by this. You know that. The whole reason I worked myself to the bone in high school was so no one would ever think of me as that kid with the dad in prison." Another moment of quiet. He shifts on the bed, the mattress squeaking beneath us. "Part of the reason I haven't told you . . . is because I don't want you to have to worry about me. You should be thriving," he says. "I thought if I told you before we came back to school, it would be weighing on you. It was already enough of a burden for me—I didn't want it to be a burden for you too."

My heart lurches in my chest. Should I have guessed at any of this? Asked more questions? Made it clear that I'd be a safe space for him to talk about his dad? Somehow I can't crush the feeling of thinking I should have done *more*.

"Definitely not a burden." There is no world in which my boyfriend going through a difficult time could be any kind of burden. "And I can do both. I can thrive in Boston and still support you. Isn't that what we're both doing?"

"Right. I guess so," he says, but there isn't as much conviction in those words as I'd like. "It felt wrong not to tell you, though, and I'm so sorry." Then, a massive exhale, as though he's gearing up for what's next. "And while I'm telling the truth about things, I should also say . . . I can't do Europe this summer. I've been terrified of bringing it up, especially when you've been asking about the tickets, but I just . . . I don't know if I can."

"It's expensive. I get it." Because of course, there is a tremendous amount of privilege that enabled me to go to Emerson, even with scholarships and financial aid. Those don't cover the cross-country flights, and I'll be taking a not-insignificant number of those over the next four years. "We can do it next summer. I think it'll still be there," I say, trying for a joke, but he doesn't crack a smile.

"That's it? Just 'okay' and we move on?"

"What do you want me to say? That I'm disappointed?" I immediately regret the ribbon of frustration in my voice. "Sure I am, but I understand."

"But that's the thing. I don't *want* you to understand."

Both of us startle at a sudden knock on the door, backing away from each other on the bed as though we've been caught doing something we shouldn't.

"Room service," calls a voice.

I grimace. "I, um. Ordered that earlier. In hindsight, maybe it wasn't the best idea."

Unfortunately, it happens to be the most beautiful dessert, a dark chocolate torte with fresh raspberries and cream, the plate drizzled with syrup. I thank the woman who delivers it about twelve times and tip her more than it cost because I can't think straight. Maybe Neil doesn't want me to understand because there's no way I can. There's this whole piece of his life I will never, ever understand. The fear and the anxiety and the pain, to the point where he wanted to be known only for his academics so no one would go digging into his personal life. And for four years, it worked.

"This isn't coming out right," he says once the door is shut again, the torte seeming to mock us. No one should be having a conversation like this in front of a dessert like that. "What I'm trying to say is that I don't want you to have to see me like this. This is all so nice, and it was probably so expensive, and I want to be the happy-go-lucky person you deserve right now, but I just . . ." He holds a hand to his face now, as though trying to shield himself from me, and it takes me a second to realize that he's started to cry. Slowly and almost silently, which is somehow all the more heartbreaking. "I—I'm sorry."

I wrap my arms around his trembling shoulders, each jolt of his chest making me desperately wish this were something I could fix. *God*, I cannot imagine what it's been like, keeping all of this locked tight.

"I've never wanted you to be some happy-go-lucky person," I say as I rub his back, everything in me aching for him. "Frankly, that kind of person sounds like a nightmare to be around. I just want *you*."

After a long moment, he pulls away and swipes a hand down his face. "I don't know what the hell is going on." His legs are tucked underneath him on the bed, an arm propping him up. He stares down at his fingers pressing into the brocade. "The letters were part of it, and all the newness of college, and being so far from home. I thought if I didn't say how I was feeling out loud, it would go away. Or it would get easier as the year went on, but it just—hasn't." A shuddery breath. "I feel like I never have any energy, even though I'm sleeping too much, probably. I have to force myself to be happy around my friends. Even my classes aren't as exciting as they should be. And I've been scared of telling you, telling anyone, because I should be having the time of my life." When he wrenches his gaze back to mine, his cheeks are reddened, eyes glassy. "That's why I can't imagine going to Europe with you. It's not fully about the money—I've been saving up. Because even though I'm happiest when I'm with you, I wouldn't be able to forgive myself if I was somehow miserable there. If I ruined the trip for you."

His words are a sharp physical pain. A slash to my chest.

This boy I love so much—he is not okay, and I feel absolutely helpless.

"You could never. *Neil.* I am so, so sorry." My mind tries to work out of the puzzle of *I never have any energy* and *I'm sleeping too much* and *I should be having the time of my life.* Maybe we can fix this together. I'm no expert, and fatigue could be linked to any number of different things, but based on everything he's said— "It sounds like . . . Could these maybe be symptoms of depression?"

The word comes out quiet, a timid little thing, and yet it slams down between us like it's made of concrete.

Depression.

Neil.

They don't seem like they should go together.

"I—I don't know," he admits. "I hadn't considered it, but now that you're saying it . . . maybe it doesn't sound completely off base."

"You saw someone before, right? A therapist?" I ask, and he nods.

"Years ago," he says. "But I don't even know what I'd say now. I'd be so self-conscious of them asking, what do you have to be depressed about? Because I'm so lucky to be here. I *want* to be here, but my brain has other ideas, I guess. And then I think about how my dad used to act the same way when I was little and I just fucking spiral."

It wasn't that I thought he'd moved on from his dad—if it's something anyone can move on from—but until now, maybe I didn't fully understand the scope of it. That of course he'd still be grieving.

Any advice I give is merely a guess as to what might help him when the reality is that I have no fucking clue. All the books I've read and the love for language we've shared, and I still don't know the right thing to say. How to support him through this.

I have never felt so out of my depth.

"Neil," I say with all the gentleness I can muster. My thumb rubs circles on his hand, his wrist, up his arm. None of it feels like enough. None of it can soothe how deeply he's hurting. "It's not fair that you have to go through this—I hate that you do."

"I don't want to seem like I need constant reassurance from you." These words come out in a whisper. "I thought I could look weak in front of you and it wouldn't matter, but—" He cuts himself off, shakes his head. "I don't want to be this burden. This depressed boyfriend in another state that you have to worry about all the time."

"You need to stop saying that word." Now there's more force in my voice because he shouldn't get to decide how I feel about it. "You couldn't be further from a burden. I *love* you, and I want to help however I can. Whatever you decide, you don't have to do it alone. I'm here."

"But most of the time, you're not," he says flatly, and I wish he weren't right. "It's not your fault. It's not anyone's fault. I just miss you so fucking much, it's like—it's like all I want is a really good book, but I've lost the ability to read. And sometimes I can't help wondering if we can really keep doing this for three and a half more years without losing our minds."

I'm struck speechless. My body suddenly feels limp, as though the bed is not enough to hold me up. I wait for him to take this back. To say he didn't really mean it.

But haven't I wondered the same thing? Even if I've pushed it down, the anxiety has still been there, waiting for its chance to pierce the surface.

I want to rewind thirty minutes, to when his mouth was on my shoulder and my hands were in his hair. When we were still naive. His posture is all wrong, shoulders bent at a defeated angle, neither of us having reached for one of the eight pillows that could have padded this conversation.

Because maybe we were always hurtling toward this conclusion, and we were stupid to think we'd be the couple to last.

Maybe he's the only one brave enough to say it.

"I'm just trying to be rational about it," he continues when I don't say anything. "I don't want to rely on you for my happiness. That's too much pressure to put on you." He swallows hard. "I'm sure there are plenty of great guys in Boston."

"What's that supposed to mean?"

"Maybe you'd be happier with one of them."

"Neil." I look him firmly in the eye, the room staring to blur at the edges. My pulse is threatening to leap right out of my skin, and I think I might actually pass out. "I've never seen you like this. You're scaring me."

He shoves his fists into his eyes and jumps to his feet. "I'm not trying to, I swear! It's fucked up that we're even having this conversation when we care about each other so much—I get that. But there's a pile of bricks on my chest all the fucking time, Rowan. All. The. Time. And even picking up the phone to make an appointment for some number of sessions that don't guarantee anything, even if the logical part of me knows all the benefits of therapy and medication, which I'm not even sure I can afford—every day, those bricks get heavier and heavier." Tears are streaming down his face now, so it shocks me when he says, "Please don't cry."

When I put a hand to my cheek, my fingertips come away wet. He's striding back toward the bed, reaching for my face. Thumbing away the tears with gentle, determined movements.

His voice is hoarse when he speaks again, still cradling my jaw. "I love you too much to put you through this. I can't let myself prevent you from having the college experience you deserve."

"What if you *are* my college experience?"

Somehow it feels like there's more distance between us right now than it does when I'm in Boston.

Maybe it's not about how much we love each other. Maybe it's about logistics and the specific pain of not getting to spend all the time you want with the person that you love.

"I just don't know," he says, and for how smart he is, I cannot stand in this moment that he doesn't have all the answers. "I'm going to hate myself for saying this, but I think—I think I might need some time to figure out what happiness looks like on my own. How I can be happy in New York knowing that you're happy in Boston."

He drops his hands, and just like that, I am rudderless.

A fish snatched out of water.

A plant without sunlight.

I want to ride out this darkness with him, whatever that looks like. I want to fight—but I am also so incredibly exhausted. Tired of missing him. Tired of uncertainty.

If he has to do it alone, then I might have to let him. Even if it kills me.

So I give him a slow, agonized nod that rips my heart in half. Leaves pieces of it scattered across Manhattan. "If that's what you need to do."

He gives me the same slow nod back.

We both go quiet for a while, just staring at each other, unsure what to do with our limbs. It's almost rhythmic, the way our chests still heave with the effort of it all. On another day, it might even be soothing. His suit is wrinkled, his hair wild, and while I must look similarly messy, I can't bring myself to care.

I don't know what happens now.

"Could I—could I still hold you?" I ask.

That's all it takes for the dam to break again. With new tears, he collects all of me in his arms, clumsy hands rushing over fabric and skin.

This cannot be the last time he touches me like this.

"Come here," he says between kisses that taste like salt, and even though I'm already there, I bury my face in his chest. Searching for his heartbeat.

"I'm sorry," he says over and over. "I'm so sorry."

Clothes start coming off; I'm not sure who reaches for what first. At the beginning of the night, I imagined slowly peeling away his suit and tie, how he'd react when he found the lace underwear I have on. Now I barely register any of it, too focused on getting my skin bare against his.

We arch and bend for each other like we are starving, wound tight, craving release. That release comes quickly for both of us, and when our bodies separate, even just for the minute it takes for him to dispose of the condom and for me to use the bathroom, I can't stop shivering.

Then he wraps around me like a shadow, one arm secured at my waist, my back against his chest. His mouth at the nape of my neck, his exhales traveling down my spine.

When I wake up the next morning, he's already gone.

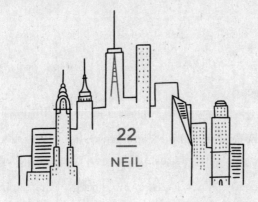

22

NEIL

IT'S POSSIBLE I'VE just made the single worst mistake of my life.

The next week is absolute hell.

The regret is an immediate, visceral thing—from what I said to the way I crept out of the hotel room. I justify it by telling myself it would have hurt too much to see her in the morning. I would have tried to take it all back. I would have let her remain my crutch, the way I have this entire year.

Maybe I should have, I wonder on the subway, though I quash the thought as quickly as it arrives as I slouch next to bleary-eyed partygoers and drunken night owls, all of us looking miserable in our own unique ways. The MTA: the great equalizer.

The ache in my chest doesn't go away. It only gets worse as I mumble excuses to Skyler and crawl into bed. As I cycle through what I could have said if I stayed.

My heart is breaking. There isn't an easy answer here, no matter how much I wish there would be. I already miss you more than I thought possible.

But I can't keep saying goodbye to her and feeling like she's taking a huge and vital piece of me with her when she leaves. It is too much expectation, too much pressure to heap onto the person I love so dearly. When I spell it out logically, I understand it completely. I made a rational decision, one that I thought was best for both of us.

This heart, I've realized, doesn't care much for logic.

NYU marches on without me, with one week left until spring break. I manage to email one professor that I'm sick but don't have the energy for the others. My bones pin me to the mattress, my body heavy with an unbearable weight. I get flashes of my dad doing the same thing, remembering those days he couldn't get up. If anything, that should motivate me to bolt to my feet and face the world, plaster a smile on my face.

All I can do is roll over and go back to sleep.

"Adhira brought over some psych handouts," Skyler says the next day, a softness in his voice I haven't heard before. A long pause. "If there's anything you need—just let me know, okay?"

I nod into the pillow, vowing to find a better way to express my gratitude once all of this is over.

I only wish I knew what *over* looked like, because any version of it without Rowan is too painful to contemplate.

I can sense Skyler's pity, our invisible third roommate, and it fills me with such intense shame.

I should be grateful.

I should be humble.

I should be better.

So on Wednesday, I grit my teeth and pull back the covers. Haul myself to the shower. Sleepwalk through my classes, fake my way through tests I can't afford to miss.

"We're all going to go to UCB tonight," Adhira says in psych. "If you want to join? It might help you feel better." Then she places a gentle hand on my shoulder. "I went through a terrible breakup last year—being away from home can make it especially brutal. I'm here if you want to talk."

Even though I haven't said anything, this is what they all assume. We were supposed to get together on Sunday, but I sent a quick cancelation text: *Change of plans, can't make it. So sorry.* The assumption is only partially true. What happened with Rowan feels more like a break*down* than anything else. Impermanent.

I wish I were capable of spending time with them in my current state.

"Thank you," I tell Adhira, "but I don't know if I'm there yet."

"I get it. Whenever you're ready."

Physically I'm in class, but my mind wanders, reckoning with Rowan's suggestion. Depression sounded sinister when she said it, something sunk so deep that it would take much more than therapy to climb out. But I've researched online and in my psych textbooks, and the more I think about it, the more I come close to diagnosing not just myself but my father, too.

Every time I've navigated to NYU's mental health counseling page, I've wavered. Wondered if I'd be taking a spot from someone with a case less hopeless than mine. If I'd just be wasting everyone's time.

I've never seen you like this, Rowan said.

What if this is simply how I am now? Because that's the other option, isn't it? I've hit adulthood and I'm doomed to life as a servant of the Moods, these unpredictable things that make me push away the people I love. My father had plenty of darkness, listlessness in between the bursts of anger. I haven't experienced that anger yet, not unless I count the time I snapped at Skyler—but what if it's on its way? What if there really is some hidden violent streak in me and I won't know until it's too late?

That night as I'm drifting off, it comes to me: a way I might begin that treacherous uphill climb.

It's terrifying.

And unsettling.

And it might also be my only option.

The flight home is a red-eye, a bumpy, near-constant tremble through the clouds that convinces me I am not used to air travel quite yet. I get precisely zero minutes of sleep.

I hadn't initially planned to go home for spring break because mine doesn't coincide with Rowan's. Fortunately, I was able to snag a cheap last-minute ticket, and my mom was overjoyed when I told her the news.

"It's so good to see you," she says when she picks me up at Sea-Tac at six o'clock in the morning. A hand comes to my cheek as I slide into the passenger seat. "You look exhausted, poor thing."

"Rough flight." I close the door, thank her for picking me up this early. "I hate to admit this, but there might be a slight ulterior motive for this visit." Then I let out a long breath, steeling myself for the confession. "I'm going to see Dad."

Her hands freeze on the steering wheel, her engagement ring catching the light of the early-morning sun. "You're sure?"

When I nod, I hope it comes across as confident instead of timid.

Though I know it won't be an instant salve, this is the closure I need, as much as the idea of coming face-to-face with him sends waves of panic through my body. When I was sixteen, I was awkward and uncertain, mumbled my way through our conversations. I didn't want my interests or personality to disappoint him, never mind the fact that he'd already disappointed me.

Three years later, I am more sure of myself than I've ever been, even if lately, I haven't felt very sure of anything.

"That letter he sent me at school . . . I haven't exactly handled it well. Maybe I'll be able to move on once I tell him to stop contacting me—and that this will be my last visit."

My mom is quiet for a few moments as she pulls onto the freeway.

It's then that I realize something.

Every time my mom has taken Natalie to see our dad, it's always been at Natalie's request. She has never pushed us, never pressured us to have any kind of relationship with him.

"You haven't wanted to see him either."

The sound of her sigh just about rattles my bones. "I go for Natalie, of course, though I know she's feeling similarly to you these days. But it took me a long, long time to be able to make my own peace with the situation. If you think this is what you need, I support you, one hundred percent."

"It is," I say. "And thank you. Thank you so much."

"If you want me to drive you, I could take the time off work. I wouldn't be able to go inside with you, I don't think—I'm not sure I'd be able to see him. But if you want me to be there with you, just say the word."

"I need to do this on my own," I tell her, half because it's true and half because I don't want her to take the time off, and I think she understands both my rationale and my unspoken gratitude.

The rest of the drive home, I assess my own moral compass. I believe in forgiveness, in growth and facing mistakes. But there are some things I don't believe people can ever come back from. Things that are unforgivable. Unforgettable. Has he ever truly put his kids first, or were we only accessories for him to mold? To impart his own views?

I want to have empathy for this person who was so clearly struggling—with his shop, with money, with his own brain. Human beings are too complex for any of us to be one-dimensional villains. But it has been so long since he was a proper father to me, and I cannot repair a relationship that's never been healthy—since long before he went to prison. And I cannot have the life I want with him hovering over me.

Even if he were still living with us . . . Well, that's a difficult path to go down. Unless something had drastically changed, I don't think I'd want that version of him in my life either. My family was small to begin with, but if I've learned anything in the past few years, it's that we have an interminable strength, too.

This weight I've been carrying around for nearly half my life—I thought I could ignore it, make myself into the poster child overachiever and everyone forgetting about it would help me do the same. I could outsmart it the same way I aced my exams.

As it turns out, and as I've been learning in psychology, that's not quite how the human mind operates.

Before we get out of the car, maybe it's the jet lag or the lack of sleep, but I ask my mom, "Do you think there's a chance of me turning out like him?"

Her gaze is steady. Unwavering. "I've been afraid of a lot of things over the past ten years," she says, placing a reassuring hand on my shoulder. "But I have *never* been afraid of that."

Four and a half hours on a Greyhound to Pasco, a small city in the southeast pocket of the state. Then two buses taking me deeper southeast, nearly to the Oregon border. I've spent the past couple days curled on the couch with Lucy, her head in my lap while I sketch patterns in her fur, and I'm already missing her comfort.

I'm cursed with a sensitive stomach, unable to read in a moving vehicle, so I stocked up on podcasts and listen to a few episodes of one about linguistics. Then, needing something lighter, I switch over to one about *Star Wars*. I draft and delete a dozen messages to Rowan, unable to come up with the right words.

Hopefully the next time I see her, I'll have a chance to try.

By the time I arrive in Walla Walla, I'm bleary-eyed and unfocused, every nerve in my body twisted in an anxious knot. I haven't eaten anything except a sad sandwich in Pasco. At four o'clock in the afternoon, there's only one hour left for visitation. I doubt I'll need that long.

Washington State Penitentiary looms ahead, tucked behind a white crisscrossed gate. The landscape out here is drier. Rural. Yet on the prison grounds, the grass is green and healthy, trees stretching past the power lines. As though all of it has been properly cared for, while the surrounding areas surrender to nature.

I wonder what he's going to say about my clothes. If he'll think my major, whether it's linguistics or psychology, is a waste of time or somehow not masculine enough. If he'll try to make me feel guilty for not coming sooner, for not responding to the letters.

Three years. Three years I haven't seen him, eight years since I lived with him down the hall, and I'm still wondering what he'll think of me.

I shove all of this out of my mind as best I can, square my shoulders. Head toward the entrance, up the concrete path, heart banging so viciously in my chest that I nearly grow dizzy from it.

The place hasn't changed at all. Stark beige walls, concrete floor, fluorescent lighting. Clean. The last time I was here, Natalie tried to get a bag of Skittles from that vending machine, but it jammed and got stuck. A janitor paused mopping the floor and walked over to give it a shove. "Happens all the time," he said as the candy dropped into the slot.

At the front desk, I present my ID to a security guard, who uses it to confirm that I'm on Lyle McNair's approved visitors' list.

"Backpack, belt, wallet, phone all go in here," she says, gesturing toward a plastic tub to the left of a metal detector, and I quickly comply.

I know there is so much wrong with the prison system in the United States. There are too many people locked up, many of them for crimes they didn't commit, disproportionately impacting people of color. We studied this in my civics class at Westview while I raised my hand far less than in any other unit, worried someone might draw a connection, and I've read plenty on my own. I believe that prisoners can be rehabilitated and reenter society—I support all of that.

At the same time, I also believe that the justice system did its job properly when it came to my father's crime.

I'm informed of the rules: I can only take one piece of ID into the room with me, and my backpack, keys, and wallet must be secured in a locker. A short hug or kiss is permitted at the beginning and end of the visit. Hands must remain on or above the table. The offender can end the visit at any time.

I nod politely. They don't have to worry. I want to spend as little time here as possible. Just enough to make sure I don't have to come back.

Then I am brought to the visitors' room, a similarly concrete-floored, beige-walled space, a pair of prison guards on each side. Two of the dozen tables are occupied—at one, a couple with their hands entwined, the two of them smiling. At the other, an older woman and a middle-aged man who bear a striking resemblance to one another, barely speaking.

And there he is at a table in the corner: the person who ended my childhood much too early.

My heart kicks back into that vicious rhythm, a rhythmic torment that reminds me I could turn around at any moment. Run out the door and never come back.

I don't.

The first thing that registers for me isn't his expression or his neon-orange jumpsuit. It's the way he's sitting.

I have seen that stance a thousand times before, forever imprinted in my memory. Shoulders back but head tipped slightly forward, a tribute to terrible posture. One leg bent, foot balanced on his other knee. Even if it's not something my dad has trade-marked, I've never allowed myself to sit this way.

Slowly, like a paint-by-number coming to life, I take in the details of the rest of him. The longer hair, not red like mine or my mom's or Natalie's but deepest brown, now shot through with gray. The depth to the wrinkles on his face. His smaller frame, thinner limbs.

Dark eyes that used to hold so much anger and that now hold an almost pleasant, cloying curiosity.

"Well, hey there," he says, the words casual enough to be uttered while picking me up after school or greeting me at the dinner table. "Neil. It's good to see you."

I'm expecting his voice to register like a record scratch. Instead it's rough gravel, less fluid than it used to be. As though he doesn't use it in here nearly as much as he used to.

I've been in his presence less than thirty seconds and it's already too surreal, to the point where I'm not sure I trust my legs to keep me standing for much longer.

Gingerly, I take the seat across from him. "Hi." I urge myself to remain solid. Firm.

"Haven't heard from you in a while. I was starting to think you'd forgotten about me."

Impossible.

When I can't come up with more words, he keeps going. "It's rough, you know. Never hearing your name called at mail call."

"I got the letters."

"Guess that school of yours keeps you busy," he says. "Everything you hoped it would be?"

I manage to nod. Every second I'm here, a new detail emerges. The gray-white stubble on his jaw. A scar on his left cheek that's either new or something I never noticed. "I love it."

The grin on his face looks so foreign. "I'm honored you made time to see your old man. A little surprised, though."

The small talk is too painful. I can't let him steer the conversation, make me forget why I'm here. If this is the last time I see him, I need answers. "Look . . ." I trail off because I realize I don't know how to address him. "Dad" reminds me of how he scrawled it on the letter, the too-familiar reverence that he doesn't deserve from me anymore. "I wanted to see you because—I have some questions."

He lifts an eyebrow. "Fire away. If this is about girls, then I'm glad you came to me. We should have had that conversation before, but you were too young—"

"It's not about girls." My jaw is set. He doesn't deserve to know about Rowan. "It's about . . . well, it's about you, I guess."

This piques his interest. "Really."

"It's for school," I lie, although maybe it's not a lie after all. "A genetics project. We're trying to put together a—a family tree." As though I'm twelve years old and crafting a literal family tree from poster board and puffy paint.

"You already know where my family's from," he says, and then attempts the worst British accent I have ever heard, clearly hoping for a laugh: "Jolly old England."

I don't give it to him. "Right. And I guess I was also wondering about our family's history . . . mentally. I know there were the anger issues. Obviously."

"I've been working on that. Never thought I'd end up in therapy, but here I am. Won't be in here forever, after all."

His voice is eerily calm, fingers linked together on the table. A portrait of stillness. In contrast, I'm a trembling mess—leg bouncing up and down, a hand alternating between darting through my hair and attacking my cuticles. I've always fidgeted when I'm nervous, and I have not been this nervous in a long, long time.

"That wasn't everything, though. There were other moods." This man is the only person who's ever made me unsure of myself. Even locked up, even allowed this brief time to talk to his son, he still intimidates me. I wish it weren't true, but there it is. "Did you ever feel . . . depressed?"

He just blinks at me. For a moment I'm convinced he's going to tell me his whole history of mental health, all the ways his brain has worked against him.

"I gotta be honest with you," he says instead. "This sounds a little too personal for a school project."

My face flames, stupid stupid skin giving me away as the bouncing of my leg reaches a breakneck tempo. My father may be cruel, but he's not an idiot. And I am completely transparent.

Then, slowly, a strange kind of smile takes over his face. "Ohhhh. I get it. You want to know . . . because you're going through it. What, you're worried you're going to turn out like me?"

At that, he lets out a full-belly laugh, so loud that a few other people turn their heads and a guard comes over to check on us.

"Everything okay here?" he asks.

"Fine, fine," my dad says, practically wiping away tears as he smacks at the table. But the guard is looking at me, and when I nod my head, he retreats, giving us space again.

When my dad finally collects himself, I speak again.

"I didn't realize it was such a hilarious question," I say quietly.

"You've got to understand," he says. "I tried so hard to see some of myself in you growing up. A natural bond between a father and son, right? I was proud of that hardware store. I wanted to work on the deck with you, show you how to safely use a power drill. But you were never interested. You wanted to read, or you took those silly dance classes, or whatever it was that your mother encouraged. And now you come to me, here in *prison*"—another break to chuckle—"because you're worried we might be *too alike*?" He dissolves into laughter again. "You're a smart kid. You can't not see the humor there."

Now I'm entirely too warm, something not unlike rage boiling inside me, and I shove my hands between my knees to keep from jumping out of my skin. And yet I keep my voice level. Maybe that's the difference between the two of us: I can control it. "Just answer the question. Please."

"Shit. Okay. He's serious now." He straightens in his seat, although years of bad posture won't let him keep his head from drooping. The whole performance is so patronizing. "Was I depressed? Sure. Hard not to be when you can barely keep your store afloat. When you can't take your family to the movies without calculating what meal you might need to skip the next week." He lets out a long sigh. "But I'm sure you don't have to worry about that, now that you're rubbing elbows with the who's who of society. Because you're better than the rest of us, right? You always were. You didn't care about anything I wanted to do with you, but if your mom suggested it, you were all ears."

That defensiveness, that ability to double down. Of course his concept of NYU is nothing like the reality. Of course he doesn't know about the multiple jobs I took in high school so I could save up for college, the loans and grants that made NYU a possibility. The constant worry that if I'm not careful, I might lose this life that I worked so hard to get.

This was a terrible idea. I shouldn't have come here, and all I want is to be back home, my mom and Christopher getting home from work and Natalie skateboarding in front of our house, Lucy lounging in her favorite spot on the couch. Sitting down to dinner together—as a family.

"Okay. Well. That's all extremely helpful."

"Neil. Hey. I'm sorry." He holds out a hand, realizing he's gone too far. I don't touch him. "I'll spend the next month kicking myself if I don't say a few things to you."

I steel myself, preparing for an apology or explanation that will arrive much too late.

There aren't enough words to undo what he did to us or to the other family. The boy who miraculously woke up from his coma but needed extensive rehabilitation. Every so often, I search his name online. Social media posts about his progress, a GoFundMe for his medical care. All of it heartbreaking.

"We've been talking a lot about forgiveness in here," he continues. "And I don't know when I'll have another chance to say this.

Obviously I'm hoping I don't have to wait three more years to see you again. But I'm not going to be in here forever. And when I'm out, I hope that we can start over, have a new relationship, even if your mom's moved on. I don't blame her," he says. "Neil. Can you ever forgive me?"

I stare hard into his eyes, which are so similar to mine, dark irises and lighter lashes. The resemblance between us used to make me proud, and then uneasy, and now it just makes me uncertain.

"Yes," I say finally, and the way this impacts him, the grin blooming across his face, doesn't bring me any amount of relief. "For what you did to me, and only that—I can forgive you."

"You have no idea how happy I am to hear that—"

"But I don't want to see you again. I can forgive, but nothing else."

I want to be the kind of person who can fix a relationship with an estranged parent. But deep down, I know that I can't. Not this relationship. Not this parent. He had my entire childhood to prove he was a decent father. The wounds are still too fresh, scarred over but never fully healed. Bruises that never faded.

This man has so many of his own demons, and I do feel a deep sympathy for him—that he didn't get help earlier, that apparently my mom and sister and I weren't enough of a reason. And I have to trust that I know what's best for me. If I have any hope of moving on, living my life without this darkness hanging over me, I need to sever this connection.

Part of me has always felt it would be wrong to remove my dad from my life. But I've been so focused on not being the son my dad wanted that I never considered maybe he is not the father I wanted.

"Now hold on," he says. "That seems a little drastic."

"Does it?" I say, my leg no longer bouncing, hands no longer shaking. "Or is it something I should have done a long time ago? Because that's what it seems like to me. You have *never* respected me, not when I was a kid and not now."

"Neil, that's just not—"

"*No*," I say, interrupting him because I have something important to say. He doesn't get to control this conversation. "I came here to tell you that I'm done. Please don't send me any more letters. If you do, I'll recycle them. I won't read them."

His face flashes with frustration. With hurt. "We're *blood*," he says. "It's not right. Families are supposed to stand by each other."

"That's what I thought, too." I swallow hard, gaining more conviction even as I strain to keep my voice at a level no one can overhear. "And yet my whole childhood, you made me feel like I was never good enough. How I spent my time, how I looked, how I acted. You made it so clear—*so clear*—that I wasn't the son you wanted." A few rapid blinks, wishing away the tears forming behind my eyes. Then I stop myself from trying. Let him see me cry. It's not a sign of weakness. "I wish you well. I really do. If it's true that you're getting help, then I'm very glad to hear that, and I hope you keep going. But I can't have you in my life anymore."

I'm breathing hard, as though I've just dashed up a flight of stairs. The words feel like they've been wrenched from my chest. There it is—everything I wanted to say to him but never could.

He's just staring at me, slack-jawed. "Well, well, well," he says. "Look who finally grew a spine."

As though, after all this time, he's finally *proud* of me.

"And don't you dare try to contact Natalie, either."

"Come on. She's only twelve. She was practically a baby when I left."

When I left.

As though he had complete control over the situation.

Maybe, in a way, he did.

"That's plenty old enough to decide that she doesn't want you in her life," I say calmly. "If she changes her mind at some point, she'll let you know. That's up to her—not you."

His lips purse tight enough to hold back all the fury I grew up with. I can tell he wants to say something else, but I'm not going to let him.

Even if whatever's going on in my brain is similar to what went on in his, I know for a fact that I will be an entirely different man.

I get to my feet, no longer making eye contact as I gesture to the guard.

Now I'm the one leaving.

ADHIRA

All of this is hurting my heart. Maybe we could do something nice for Neil when we're back from spring break? What does he like?

SKYLER

uhhhh . . . grammar? syntax?

SKYLER

we could get him a dictionary

ADHIRA

Would YOU want a dictionary if you and your girlfriend just broke up?

ZOE

Dear god, this is sad. Skyler, please do not ever give someone a gift without significant input from the rest of the group.

STEVE

I don't really know him, but maybe a gift card to the Olive Garden?

My parents give them out every year to our whole family. And who doesn't like the Olive Garden?

ZOE

Steve, sweetie, I think we might need to have a talk.

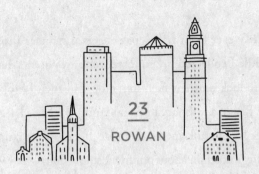

23
ROWAN

I WANT TO throw my romance novels into the Charles River. Drown my favorite couples. Watch the lies drip from waterlogged pages.

All those bookstores and garage sales, hundreds of paperbacks and special editions. Collections of tropes that brought me comfort and taught me what a relationship could look like. Yet not one single blueprint for what I'm supposed to do now, because those books are all about falling in love.

But staying in it? That's a different thing entirely. They don't give a fuck about that.

As I've learned over the past year, my life is not a romance novel. If it were, then I'd be able to see our HEA somewhere in the distance. Last June, when I realized Neil wasn't the perfect-on-paper romance hero I dreamed of and yet he was everything I wanted, I thought maybe I didn't need the kind of happily-ever-after in my favorite books.

Now I know that happily-ever-after is pure bullshit.

On the train back to Boston, I curl up in a window seat and

hide my puffy eyes from fellow passengers. I managed to keep it together while I collected my suitcase from my parents' hotel and wished them luck on their next tour stop, but then I broke down at a Duane Reade and bought several family packs of Kleenex.

I message Kait in full emergency mode. Because even if that party left me feeling uncertain about our friendship, I don't know who else to talk to. *Are you around?* I text, and when she doesn't respond right away, I figure she's just busy. Swamped with homework.

He said he needed time to figure out what happiness looks like on his own.

Maybe I do too—because I'm suddenly not sure I remember how it feels.

More than anything, that sadness inside Neil, the one that's been lurking there for longer than our relationship—it isn't anything I can fix. No amount of talking it out will ease that pain, even if I desperately wish it could.

Even if I want us to figure it out together, whatever this new version of life looks like for him, I have to respect that he wants some time to figure it out for himself first, no matter how much it hurts.

I video chat with Kirby and Mara the next day. Their voices, their faces are a welcome balm, but it's not the same as having them here in person.

"And then you had sad sex?" Kirby says. "My fucking heart. I'm too fragile for this! Neil being sad just doesn't compute."

"Right?" Mara props her chin on Kirby's shoulder. "He's just not Neil if he isn't baiting you or making bedroom eyes at you." Then she turns to Kirby. "Also, 'fragile' is not a word anyone would ever associate with you."

"When it comes to Rowan and Neil, it is."

"Whatever you need," Mara continues. "We're here for you. Just say the word, and we'll have a care package of Seattle chocolate and coffee in the mail tomorrow."

When we hang up, I lie back down on my bed and resume the ceiling staring that's kept me busy most of the day. I gaze at the penguin posters on Paulina's side of the room and then over at my bookshelves, where I've acquired a handful more romance novels since school started because Boston's indie bookstores are amazing. Now I'm craving their reassurance, desperately wishing I could be a heroine who owned a struggling bed-and-breakfast in a sleepy beach town, or a journalist forced to host a radio show with her ex, or even a high-powered lawyer in the big city. All that daydreaming is back with a vengeance.

"I didn't mean that thing about the Charles River," I whisper, reaching for a Nora Roberts book and then a Delilah Park. Every time a couple breaks up, it's so clear to me what they need to do to get back together. Sometimes it's a simple misunderstanding, and others it's a matter of proving they truly love each other. The common factor is that the other person always takes them back.

All this time, I thought Neil and I were the ones who were going to make it. I'd classified us as romance tropes, Neil the dashing rake with approximately zero rakelike qualities. We were enemies to lovers, rivals to lovers, forced proximity. Opposites attract, although I realized pretty quickly that we were never as opposite as I once thought. But there was one trope I never considered. Right person, wrong time—maybe that's us.

With everything I am, I hope that it isn't.

Despite how good it was to hear my best friends' voices, I can't shake the loneliness that keeps me curled up in bed. Kait still hasn't responded, and I've stopped checking my phone, my heart too damaged to care. So when the door to my room opens and Paulina Radowski steps inside, AirPods in her ears and rain boots dripping water, I've never been more excited to see her.

"Hey," she says in her breezy way as she hangs her jacket on the back of our door, until she spots me and then swiftly removes her headphones. "Rowan? Are you okay?"

I'm not sure what it is—the fact that she could instantly tell something was wrong or the urgency of needing a human being to talk to—but her question is all it takes for me to burst into tears.

"I—I'm sorry," I say around a hiccup, pressing my face into my hands. "You should—you probably have somewhere to be. I don't want to bother you."

Paulina shucks off her boots and pulls her chair up to my bed. She's been largely invisible since that late-night quest for Boston cream pie, but every so often, one of us will mention a food craving and the other will google whether Dunkin' makes it in donut form.

"I don't have anywhere to be." Her soothing voice—have I never noticed what a naturally soothing voice she has? I probably haven't heard it enough. "Do you want to talk about it?"

They're the best seven words in the English language.

Slowly, I nod, because even though I still barely know this girl, she is *here*, and she's listening, and those are apparently the only two qualifications for me to spill.

I only tell her parts of the story, unsure I can condense my history with Neil into a fifteen-minute conversation. She just listens. Asks if I've been hydrating and if I've eaten yet today.

When I shake my head, she disappears downstairs and comes back up with two plates and a bottle of water precariously balanced in her arms.

"This is—extremely nice of you," I say in between bites of pasta.

"You may have noticed . . . I'm not exactly here a lot," she says. "I went through a bad breakup in August. Right before I left for school. So I decided I'd be as busy as I could, and then the heartbreak wouldn't be able to find me. I joined a hundred clubs and took way too many credits, even tried a couple sports I was miserable at, and I refused to let myself have any free time."

Oh.

"Did it work?"

"For a bit," she says. "But I couldn't run from it forever."

"You could tell me about it. If you want."

She gives me this heavy smile. "Story for another day," she says. "But about you and Neil . . ." She trails off, spearing a hunk of manicotti. "I wish I had some kind of advice to give. All I know is that it sucks. It's a shitty situation, and it sucks, and I'm sorry."

"Honestly, just hearing that is making me feel a little better. Thank you so much."

Paulina has a Save the Penguins Club meeting she offers to cancel if I'd rather she stay here to watch movies or talk or just sit in silence with another person, but I wave this off, not wanting to take up more of her time and unsure how much longer I can keep talking.

"Oh—and I have a really excellent breakup playlist," she says before she leaves again. "If you want."

When she shares it with me and I hit play, I'm strangely comforted to hear the Smiths as the first song. "Heaven Knows I'm Miserable Now." Could not be more accurate.

On instinct, I reach for my phone. Neil and I didn't establish any rules for texting, but everything still feels too fresh. I let go, lying back on my bed and closing my eyes, letting Phoebe Bridgers and Kacey Musgraves and Olivia Rodrigo sit in the heartbreak with me.

I think back to that vision of the future again, the one I summoned that snowy night in Seattle, wondering if we can really wait that long to get to a place where we can be wholly independent, and how frightening that sounds, too.

What if all we have is our history, and the new memories we're making together are too few and far between to matter? I don't want our entire relationship to be defined by *remember whens*. Those will only sustain us for so long, and we can't spend these next three years living in the past.

There's no shortage of fascinating, beautiful women at NYU. In New York City. I'd hate for him to think he's still attached to the girl from his hometown just because our relationship is so tangled with high school. There is so much beyond our little bubble, and if he really wanted to, he could have *more*. Maybe that's what would make him happier.

He could have someone to grab a casual bite to eat with after class.

Someone he could run to Dunkin' with in the middle of the night.

Someone to sit next to during Shabbat services.

A gym buddy.

A coffee date.

And maybe . . . maybe that's what he deserves. Someone who's always there, the way I was throughout high school and now cannot possibly be. Maybe this was what my mom meant about not tying ourselves down. She didn't want our relationship to eclipse every new experience we'd have.

Because if I ever had to choose between Emerson and him, I'm not sure that's a decision I could make. It would have to be my education, the same way I know it would be for him.

The person who understands me like no one else ever has.

Phoebe and Kacey and Olivia keep me company while I turn these questions over and over. That day in June, I thought Neil might be my big wild love, but after all of this, what if it's merely a high school relationship? Are we the ones who make it to the happily-ever-after side of the LDR statistic, or the ones who wind up bitter and heartbroken?

I never imagined I'd find my person in high school, but what if I did? How are you supposed to know if it's worth clinging to with both hands and gritted teeth, heels dug into the dirt?

Or are you supposed to let it go, knowing you might regret it for the rest of your life?

In creative writing, Kait takes her usual seat next to me. She replied to my text late last night: *Hey sorry! I was wrapped up in some Planet Dread stuff. All good now?*

yep 👍 was all I sent back.

If she can tell something's off by my sweatshirt and leggings and messy bun, she doesn't say anything. Instead, the first thing she tells me is:

"I'm switching my major to film. I've been thinking about it a lot, and I think my brand of storytelling might work better in a visual medium. I just have to get Miranda's permission and then I can swap this for a film class."

"Oh," I say. "Wow. That's big."

She gives me a tight smile. "I'll really miss you, though! I'm sure we'll still see each other all the time."

I can't explain it, but somehow I'm not sure we will. I prepare myself for the loss—my first writing friend fading away after we bonded over so much, so quickly. But it doesn't come. There's a

329

small sting, but I'm happy for her if film is what she'd rather be doing.

Maybe Kait wasn't destined to be a lasting college friendship—just my first one. And maybe that's okay.

"Rowan?" Miranda asks at the end of class later in the week, after Kait has switched out. "Do you mind if I talk to you for a few minutes?"

I nod, and she lifts herself to sit on the desk next to mine. "Sorry," I say, drumming my fingertips on the cover of my notebook. "I know I've been kind of zoning out during the freewrites." If I ever doubted Miranda's assertion that I don't have to be tortured to write, here is my proof: I am miserable and have no desire to put sentences together.

"It isn't about that," she says. "But I've noticed you haven't seemed quite like yourself lately. So I wanted to check in with you."

"I haven't been doing great," I admit, plucking a wayward strand of hair out of my bun. I haven't washed it since I left for New York, and I'm a little afraid of what it looks like. "I told you about my long-distance relationship, back at the potluck?" Miranda nods. "We, um . . . we're taking some time to figure things out, I guess. Only I'm not sure how much time we're taking, or how we'll know when we've figured it out, or—" I break off, a pressure threatening behind my eyes, because I do *not* want to almost-cry in front of my professor. Again.

"That's really rough." There's no hint of condescension in her voice. "I was thinking, and only if you're comfortable—my partner is a fantastic cook, and I've found that a good home-cooked meal can do wonders for the heart."

I want to tell her that while I appreciate that offer, a home-cooked meal cannot possibility solve my relationship crisis, but I stop myself. Because maybe a home-cooked meal does sound kind of lovely.

"I'd love that," I say. "But I'm a vegetarian, and I'd hate for anyone to go out of their way. . . ."

She waves this off. "That's no problem at all. How about tomorrow night?"

When I show up the following evening, her partner answers the door wearing a wide smile and an apron that says BAHSTON TO ENGLISH TRANSLATIONS with a vocabulary list beneath it. PAHK = PARK. BEEAH = BEER. WISTAH = WORCESTER. I can't help thinking Neil would find it hilarious.

"Welcome! You must be Rowan," he says, holding out a hand. His beard has grown even bushier in the past month. "I recognize you from the party I was never at. I'm Jon, Miranda's lesser half."

Despite everything, I laugh. "Nice to meet you. Whatever you're cooking, it already smells incredible."

Miranda appears behind him, hanging up my corduroy jacket and offering me a drink—"water, seltzer, juice, whatever you want that's nonalcoholic"—looking more casual than I've ever seen her in wide-legged jeans and a white V-neck.

"Thank you so much for having me," I say as she leads me into the kitchen. The site of my breakdown. "Really. This means a lot."

"We love entertaining." Jon takes down bowls from the cabinet while Miranda lays out three sets of silverware. "When we were looking for a house, number one on my priorities list was a kitchen with an island and space for a massive dining table."

I get a flash of literary events that must have been hosted here, New England writers whose names I've seen on spines. *One day*, I think to myself.

Dinner is a white bean and kale soup, perfect for Boston's mid-spring cold snap, with a side of fresh sourdough from a local bakery. I must compliment the food a dozen times. Maybe the right soup on the right day really does have healing properties.

I thought this might be awkward—I'm not sure I've ever had a meal with two adults who aren't family—but Miranda and Jon are relaxed and easygoing, asking me about my life in Seattle, how I like Boston, what I've been reading lately. I learn that Jon is a carpenter who sells his work at a few local shops.

"He never brags about himself, so I have to." Miranda picks up the gorgeous wooden bowl that only has a couple hunks of bread left in it. "He made this, and pretty much everything we used for snacks during the party."

A little bashful, Jon gestures toward the backyard. "I have a studio out back," he says. "That's where I was hiding out. And you've been enjoying Mir's class? I have to assume she wouldn't invite one of her troublemakers over for dinner."

"Depends on who's cooking," Miranda says.

We all share a laugh at that.

"I have. Being able to let go of perfection and *write* has helped me enjoy the process so much more." I give Miranda a knowing lift of my eyebrows, and she grins and holds a hand to her heart. "I've even been freewriting a bit for myself lately."

"Then I think my work here is done," she says before turning serious. "Part of the reason I invited you here, Rowan, doesn't have to do with writing at all. And it's that Jon and I started dating when we were sixteen."

"And now you're—" I stop, face heating, because maybe you aren't supposed to ask your professor's age.

But Miranda waves this off. "We're thirty-eight."

"Been together more than half our lives," Jon says, casting her a look that I can tell, even after having officially met him only an hour ago, is bathed in the purest love.

The romance author in me aches at that look. Because despite all the meet-cutes and heart-fluttery moments that make me kick my feet when I'm reading, *that* is the true romance. The fact that that look is still this sweet after more than twenty years.

It's a realization that stuns me a little.

"It wasn't always easy," Miranda says. "We grew up in Southern California, and then I went to Boston University and Jon went to UCLA."

"I'm really putting that marine biology degree to good use."

"So you did long distance?" I ask. "All four years?"

"All four years," Miranda confirms. "And we didn't even have technology back then, so—"

Jon swats at her with his napkin. "We had phones! We had computers! We're not ancient. Yet."

Miranda pats his impressive beard. "Keep that in mind the next time we go to bed at nine thirty."

"How did you do it?" I reach for another piece of bread. "If that's okay to ask."

"Of course," Miranda says. "We found out pretty quickly that just because the other person wasn't there, it didn't mean we couldn't fully experience college. Having other friends in long-distance relationships helped too—or at least, people we could comfortably talk to, people who'd understand."

"Still working on that part," I admit.

"You'll get there." She has this uncanny ability to sound reassuring about everything. "We had to give each other space, I think, to grow into the people we were going to become. We weren't the same people at eighteen that we were at sixteen, and especially once we got to college, it seemed like everything started changing so rapidly. We couldn't be there for every single milestone."

"But we were there for the ones that mattered most," Jon says. "Racked up a *lot* of frequent-flier miles. Worked a lot of double shifts."

Miranda places her hand on top of Jon's. Ever so slowly, I catch his thumb stroking her palm. "I think what helped us the most, and maybe this is something that could help you—is realizing that we *are* going to grow, and that it doesn't mean that the relationship is doomed. It's a time of so much change, and you can change together. Those new versions of yourselves can be just as compatible as the old ones—maybe more so. We were fortunate that they were, but it doesn't mean that we didn't have to work at it."

I nod along with what she's saying, unsure I can put my gratitude into words. They've shared so much with me tonight with no expectation of anything in return. If that isn't true kindness, I don't know what is.

"My boyfriend . . . He's going through some difficult personal things." Most of it seems too private, but I can share that, at least. "And I've been feeling completely lost. Not because we're struggling—well, that's part of it—but mainly because *he's* struggling, and I haven't known how to help him."

Jon's expression of sympathy is nothing short of genuine. "I'm sorry to hear that."

"I just want to be there for him. However I can."

"The best you can do is make sure he knows that," Miranda says. "Sometimes that's *all* we can do."

Even if she's right, I still wish I could conjure some magic cure. I can understand why he hid those letters, given how long it took him to be vulnerable with me. It's painful to want to be let in so badly, to realize the other person's spent so many years dragging all kinds of heavy things to jam the door. Only natural, then, that it takes a tremendous effort to open it.

"This transition is already hard enough without relationship troubles on top of it," Miranda continues. "But if it means anything, Rowan, I really think you're going to be okay." A wink. "You've made it through the freewrites, after all."

When we finish dinner and Jon gives me a tour of his studio, I feel much lighter than when I arrived. Their advice isn't a quick fix, of course, but it's hard not to be ten times more optimistic than I was earlier today.

"Thank you so much for this," I tell Miranda and Jon as they walk me to the door, after we've polished off a heavenly blueberry tart. "I'm still trying to process it all, but seriously. This meant everything to me."

She gives me a hug. "I thought it might give you a bit of hope to see two people who managed to make it work. Even if we're ancient."

Jon drapes an arm around her shoulders as they wave me off, and a different kind of hope blooms in my chest. I head for the T station, digging my hands into the pockets of my corduroy jacket, fingers grazing a scrap of paper. Assuming it's a receipt or straw wrapper, I pull it out—and what's on it roots me to the sidewalk.

Forelsket (Norwegian): the euphoria you experience as you begin to fall in love; or, how I feel whenever I'm around you.

I swear time stops for a moment. Traffic freezes and birds pause mid-flight while I try to catch my breath, pressing the note to my heart.

I haven't worn this jacket since . . . I was in New York with Neil the first time. It was stuck in the back of my closet, impractical for a Boston winter. He must have slipped the note inside at some point before I left. Naturally, I can't not think about the time I found my name in the pocket of his hoodie during Howl, and I imagine he was thinking about it, too.

Even though this was from months ago, I wonder if I found it at exactly the right time.

I read it again and again, memorizing the word, my knees quivering and my pulse pounding like I'm thirteen years old and just learning a boy has a crush on me. Maybe everything I experienced tonight, from Miranda and Jon to the appearance of this note, isn't unlike what Neil observed between my parents during Hanukkah: couples who love each other in quiet and constant ways, where small gestures feel like the purest form of affection.

All this time, I have been surrounded by the kind of romance that most of my books never talk about. I've gotten so good at ignoring it—but now, with *forelsket* in my palm, I think I'm finally starting to get it.

ROWAN

hey . . . didn't know if it was okay to text you.

NEIL

Of course it is.

Hey.

ROWAN

hey.

just wanted to say that I'm thinking of you. and that I'm here whenever you're ready 🤍

NEIL

Thinking of you too.

Always 🤍

24

NEIL

DR. CLARK'S OFFICE is cheerily but sparsely decorated: plush couch, patterned rug, four succulents thriving on the windowsill. The first time I was here, my eyes snagged on the box of tissues in one corner, and I wondered how frequently she had to replace it. Whether psychologists have a budget for this kind of thing.

It took a couple false starts to get here, including one where I made it all the way and then doubled back because I couldn't fathom finding the right words for how I was feeling. But I finally made it, right words be damned. Our third session in two weeks, not because I'm determined to do this as quickly as possible—I understand that one cannot get straight A's in therapy—but because I have had a *lot* to say.

"Good to see you again," my therapist says after reminding me that I can call her Audrey.

"You too," I say. Meaning it.

Maybe there's some parallel here that my interest in psychology comes at the same time as my own mental health crisis. I want to understand my own brain better, and more than that, I want to arrive at a place of peace with it. Maybe that means more therapy and maybe that means medication, too—whatever it is, I'm keeping an open mind. Literally.

Unpacking my history in front of this stranger isn't easy, but I'm doing my best. During our first session, she told me to start wherever I wanted—"wherever feels right."

So I've told her about my parents. My dad. The ways he spoke to me and the rest of my family—and maybe even more than spoke. The trauma that I've been unable to excavate until now.

Everything I've repressed.

I've told her about school. About how I forced myself to become an overachiever because I thought it was the only way people would forget my background.

About Rowan.

About the depression that's been lurking beneath the surface this year, and most likely longer than that.

Then I took a deep breath and Audrey asked if I'd like some water or tea, because apparently I had been talking for thirty minutes straight.

What I've learned so far, and what I probably should have realized much sooner, is that my trouble opening up likely stems from the fact that I kept my home life hidden during high school.

And I don't want to do that anymore.

"How many people know about your dad?" Audrey asks today.

"A few friends from Seattle. And my girlfriend." Assuming, of course, that's still what she is the next time we talk.

"Right. Rowan." Audrey's memory is sharp—she rarely looks back at the notes she takes during sessions. "You haven't told anyone since you've been to college? It sounds like you have some close friends here."

"We're close, but . . ." I trail off, clutching at my knee to keep my leg from jiggling. "I don't know. There's never a right time to bring it up, is there?"

She nods, understanding. "Sometimes we have to create one."

"I haven't wanted to burden anyone, I guess? That was why I sort of ended things with Rowan, or took a break, or whatever it is that I did."

"You mentioned that last time," she says. "Neil. You simply being yourself—that is not a burden. Everyone brings baggage to a relationship. Some of it might be able to fit in an overhead compartment, but plenty of it needs to be checked with the airline. It's impossible to go through life without collecting any, and someone who loves you isn't going to consider you a burden."

This is what I'm trying to wrap my head around. All that time I didn't want to burden Rowan, I pushed her away because I didn't think she should have to deal with me like this. The shame sank me deeper and deeper. I thought I needed to handle this on my own, become well enough for her to love me.

When the whole time, she already did.

We've started texting again, mostly small talk and gentle check-ins, but I know that a proper reunion will have to happen face-to-face, not over the phone. Though everything in me aches to see her soft smile and intense eyes and bangs in their usual lovely state of disarray, I want to be certain I'm not relying on her as my sole source of joy.

Audrey and I schedule another session for next week, and on my way back to the dorm, I stop for shawarma at one of the hundreds of carts scattered across the city. They've always struck me as touristy, but they also always smell excellent.

Because here is a very simple source of joy: eating street food in Central Park on the warmest day of the year so far. New York in the spring more than makes up for New York in the winter, and the people-watching is sublime.

Gradually, I've gotten my psychology grade back up, which is vital if I want to change my major. I haven't yet been to the club Dr. Serrano suggested, but I plan to. Eventually.

I am okay with eventually.

By the time I get back to our dorm, it's early evening, Skyler holed up at his desk with his laptop and a sandwich. He swivels his head to greet me.

"Doing okay?" he asks.

I nod, sliding my backpack onto my desk chair. "Yeah. I, uh. Just got back from therapy, actually."

He closes his laptop and turns in his chair to face me. Suddenly I'm worried I've said too much, that this wasn't the kind of thing you bring up in casual conversation—

But he bursts into a grin. "Dude," he says, giving me a soft punch in the arm. "That's so great. I'm happy for you."

And this time, when Skyler asks if I want to go home with him for the weekend—"because no offense, you look like you could use a little fun"—I don't hesitate before telling him yes.

Skyler's dad is waiting at the ferry terminal to wrap his son in a hug, and while I'm surprised when he does the same to me, I also find that I don't hate it.

"Neil! Great to see you again," he says.

"You too, Mr. Benedetti."

"Please. Marc."

Skyler's room at home is exactly what I'm expecting: posters of sports teams, photos of his friends, a complete mess. He even blushes when my eyes land on a photo of a mostly nude *Maxim* model.

"Joke gift from one of my brothers a few years ago," he says, the tips of his ears turning bright red. "I kept it because of the, uh, artistic integrity. The composition. It's a really beautiful shot, just from a photography perspective."

In the kitchen, I meet his mom, who's petite and blond but with his same kind blue eyes. "I'm Maggie," she says after lassoing me for another hug, and I begin to wonder if Skyler told them I haven't been myself lately. Which might have actually been very thoughtful. "If you're thirsty, if you're hungry—feel free to grab anything you want. The rest of them certainly do," she says with a laugh, and though I thank her, I can't imagine being that comfortable in his house quite yet.

Meanwhile, Skyler's older brothers might as well be his triplets—tall, broad-shouldered former athletes with floppy brown hair and easy smiles. Luca is a banker in the city, and Emile is a high school math teacher. I also meet his ten-year-old twin sisters, Carlie and Kendra, and Carlie shyly asks if I'll sit next to her during dinner.

The meal is boisterous and delicious, everyone lovingly teasing each other. I can't believe I waited so long to take him up on this invitation.

Later, once we're full and the younger ones have gone to bed, Emile heads home and Maggie tells me she's made up his room for me. I'm running out of ways to tell this family thank you.

Skyler and I take bottles of hard cider out onto his back porch—he wasn't wrong about his parents not minding him drinking underage. "As long as they're doing it here, they're doing it safely," Marc explained during dinner.

The sun hangs low in the sky, casting the yard in a warm amber light. Branches of a cherry blossom tree sway softly in the breeze. There's a tire swing out here, a barbecue, a fire pit. I can picture the Benedettis spending hours upon hours out here, defying their bedtimes.

"Thanks so much for this," I tell him after we tap our bottles together in cheers. "I think I love your family."

"Don't tell them that. They'll adopt you."

I take a sip of cider, the tartness lingering on my tongue. I'm more relaxed than I've felt in ages, and I don't think it's just that

I've gotten away from the city. It's that Skyler is easy to be around, even when I've been a shit friend the past few weeks.

"I know I probably haven't been the greatest person to live with lately," I say.

"We're friends, man. I'm not going to cut you out just because you had a few bad weeks." He stretches his long legs out on the porch, bottle dangling loosely from one hand. "And I'm glad you're here, because I've been dying to tell you . . . I finally talked to Adhira."

My mouth drops open. "Way to bury the lede!" I say, nudging him. "What happened?"

"Well . . . I wanted to do it all romantic, right?" He's already blushing. "And I had this idea that I was going to spell it out with pizza toppings—'I LIKE YOU,' or something like that. Only I couldn't get my pepperoni letters to look like much of anything, and in the end, I just asked if she wanted to go for a walk. And I told her I'd been thinking about our past a lot lately, and that I wasn't sure if I ever stopped having feelings for her."

"And?"

"It wasn't the 'I've been in love with you all these years and it's been torture spending so much time with you when we're not together' I was hoping for," he says, "but she said she's been feeling something too, and she thought we should explore it." At that, his mouth splits into a grin.

"Skyler! I'm so thrilled for you," I say. "It sounds like a good start. Or restart, as the case may be."

Skyler tips his bottle to mine. "Hear, hear. And you? What's going on with Rowan? You never gave us the full story."

I hesitate, staring down at my bottle and scratching at the label with my thumbnail. "We sort of . . . took a break for a while."

"Shit. Did she say why?"

"It was my suggestion, actually."

His brows pull together in confusion. "Oh—I just assumed, because you were so . . ."

"Miserable?"

"Yeah."

I shake my head. "If I'm going to explain it, I have to tell you something about my family. Something I haven't shared with many people." A deep and calming breath of Staten Island air. The confidence that I can do this. "When I was eleven, my father was sent to prison."

Skyler doesn't interrupt. He doesn't have strong, outsize reactions. He listens, letting me unspool this tangled mess of story, and by the time I've given him the full tour through my family's scrapbook, I can't remember why I was so nervous to begin with.

"I'd wondered about that letter," he says, "but it seemed like you'd tell me when you were ready. If you were ready." Then he clasps my shoulder with his free hand. "Thank you for telling me. I mean that."

His reaction is both quiet and genuine, and it makes the pressure in my chest ease the tiniest bit.

It's a start.

"I'd look forward to my visits with Rowan as a way to pull me out of this funk that I'm now realizing was—is—depression," I say. "And none of that felt fair to her, so I told her we should take some space."

"Wow. That is like . . . really intense."

I blow out a laugh, because he's not wrong.

"But you still love her," he says.

"I'm not sure I'd know how to stop."

He gives me this solemn nod, as though he gets that on a deep level, and for a while we just gaze out at the sky. Silently understanding each other.

Before spring break ended, I sat down with my mom and Christopher, explained everything I'd been dealing with at school, and when my mom asked about therapy, I told her I'd already made an appointment.

Then I said, *I'd really like you to come for family weekend next year. I didn't tell you about it this year because I was worried about the money, but if it's possible . . . that would be pretty great.*

My mom held a hand to her heart. *I don't want you to feel like you have to keep anything from us,* she said. *If it's this important, we'll figure it out.*

Figuring it out seems to be a common theme in my life lately, and I think I'm beginning to embrace it.

"I guess I'm still learning how to be a whole person," I say to Skyler now, the sun dipping beneath the trees. "And that I can share all of that with people I trust without being this extra responsibility they never wanted."

Skyler shakes his head firmly, his hair remaining perfectly coiffed. "Nah. No way. If she really loves you—and it sounds like she does—then I'm guessing she loves you through all the shit you have going on."

It's not dissimilar to what Audrey said, and I'm finally starting to believe it. I think there might be a value in letting someone know all of you and realizing they won't let one single thing define you.

Because maybe I can have both. She can hold my baggage for a while, and I can hold hers. We can have these separate lives that beautifully intersect, and our time apart doesn't need to be any lesser because of it.

It's not dependence or reliance. It's the steady feeling I have when I'm with her. The safety and comfort, but also the thrill of continuing to learn about each other. The backbone that is our history and all our starry-eyed plans for the future.

As the sun sets over Staten Island, I'm filled with one solid, reassuring conviction:

We're not meant to end this way.

348

Dear Neil,

Once, you confessed your feelings when
you had no idea how I'd react, and I
never told you I thought it was the bravest
thing. I'm trying to be brave too.
    This isn't a love confession,
but a still-in-love confession.
    And I've fallen for you three times.
    The first time was a silly crush,
a passing infatuation that faded the
way most teenage crushes do: with
embarrassment and I can't believe I ever.
    The second time, over the wildest 24 hours
of my life. A perfect, unforgettable whirlwind.
    The third time, a slow burn in two different
states on the opposite coast. Odd, because
Seattle is in my blood the same way it's in
yours. But I think that just means we get to take
it with us wherever we go. We're lucky that way.
    And that third one isn't over—
I'm still in the middle of it.
    Sometimes I wonder about the what-
ifs. What if we hadn't teamed up that day,
if you hadn't found me when I overheard
that plan to take us both out. If you hadn't

had my name, and if I hadn't opened up my yearbook on the Ferris wheel. If we hadn't met up for that last clue. Would I have sulked through your graduation speech? Given you an awkward hug and wished you luck in the fall?

Slightly soul-crushing to imagine. You know I'm an optimist at heart—a romantic—so of course I'd like to believe that we'd have found our way to each other no matter what.

And I do. Believe it.

Because any kind of universe that brought us together in such a cosmically monumental way didn't do it by accident. Not a fucking chance.

If we were a romance novel . . . Do you know how many times I've tried to finish that sentence? Too many. And I don't think I've been doing it right. I've been too focused on what happens in the book itself, when lately, I've wondered more about what happens after it ends. We can guess. We can speculate. The author might drop some hints as they're tying things up with the neatest of bows.

But I'm not sure we're supposed to know.

Because I have a feeling everyone's been keeping a secret, a this-would-forever-change-the-romance-novel-world-if-it-got-out

Kind of secret—that the very best parts happen after the book is over.

And that's where we begin.

All my love,
Rowan

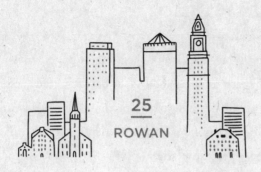

25
ROWAN

THE APPROACH OF finals week seems to wrap the entire city of Boston in a thick layer of anxiety. A twitchy energy swirls through campus, fueled by index cards and highlighters and practice tests. This time when we're staying out all night, we're partying at the library and guzzling energy drinks, waking up with John Locke's *The Second Treatise of Civil Government* tattooed on our cheeks.

I divide my time between Spanish flash cards and my final creative writing project, unable to process that this year is almost over. While I'm not exactly disappointed with what I've accomplished, it's a bit of a shock to realize there's plenty I've missed out on. Sure, Paulina and I finally tried real Boston cream pie, but I haven't joined a single club. I don't have the tight-knit group of friends I thought I might. And I haven't explored Emerson's Jewish community, even though it was one of the things I was looking forward to the most.

Next year, I decide.

I have time.

It's been seven weeks since that night in New York, six weeks of tentative texting and fragile hope. Living in the uncertainty has been less terrifying than I thought it might be, especially when I give myself space to write about it in between study sessions. As long as writing has been a part of my life, I've never written anything specifically *for* another person. And yet that's what I find myself doing—because all the words I've scribbled down aren't just about him. Without even meaning to, I've addressed this *to* him.

A few days before finals start, I slide those pages into an envelope, send them off to New York, and allow myself to exhale.

Back in my room, I settle in for a steamy night with the subjunctive tense. But just as I start quizzing myself, I hear the sound of a frantic key in the lock.

"Rowan?" Paulina's voice. "So . . . there was someone interesting in the elevator with me just now."

When I turn around in my chair, he is the last person I'm expecting to see. I even have to blink a few times to make sure he's real.

Neil McNair is in my dorm room.

He's standing next to my roommate, giving me a small wave, looking at once sheepish and sweet and maybe even slightly electric, like adrenaline took him all the way here instead of Amtrak. And maybe it did.

This is summer Neil, the one I grew so attached to last year, his hair windblown and brightened by the reappearance of the sun. He doesn't look anything like the boy I saw last time, the one with sunken half-moons beneath his eyes and a heavy slump to his posture. Now he's in an easy cardigan and T-shirt and jeans, his usual scuffed Adidas.

He is *here.*

I reach for my desk to shut the book I've been working out of, but I'm so distracted that my hand gropes air instead.

"How'd you get in?" I ask, and though that's nowhere near the top of my list of questions, it's what comes out first.

"Sneaked in with someone else," he says, cheeks turning pink in that way I love so much. "Possibly not the best security."

"I'm going to make myself scarce." Paulina grabs her laptop, tosses it into her penguin-shaped backpack. "Bye, have fun, tell me everything later!"

And then we're alone in my room.

There's a confident set to his shoulders I haven't seen in a while, since long before that night in New York. His spine, a little straighter. If I reached out and touched him, I wonder if he'd feel any different.

"So," he starts, just as I say the same thing. An awkward laugh passes between us.

"I wanted to surprise you," he says, ruffling a hand through his hair. Somehow even his nervous fidgeting makes my heart race.

"Consider me surprised. How . . . are you?" It's only when it leaves my lips that I realize it might be a bit of a loaded question, but Neil either doesn't pick up on it or doesn't mind.

"Good. Really good. Listen—I know finals are coming up, but if you have some time, I thought we could maybe go for a walk?"

Neil McNair came to Boston to ask if I wanted to go for a walk.

"Yes," I say, biting back a smile. "Of course. Yes."

This time, at least I manage to close my book properly.

I'm not sure which one of us is leading, but we end up in the Common, because it's impossible not to be drawn there when the late-April sun has turned it golden. We're not the only ones—people are laying out picnic blankets and setting up croquet and badminton. I'm already warm in ripped jeans and Neil's hoodie.

Once we're in the park, I can't help it—I start laughing.

"What's so funny?" Neil asks, looking mildly concerned.

"I just mailed you a letter." I shove up the sleeves of his hoodie. "And now you won't get it for a couple more days."

His mouth kicks into a smile as he reaches into his backpack. "I look forward to it," he says. "I have so much I want to say to you. But first . . ." He pulls out a sheet of paper adorned with calligraphy. I can already tell each letter is perfectly, beautifully formed. "I made this scavenger hunt for you. It's . . . a little unconventional, though."

I stare at him. "You want to do a scavenger hunt? Right now?"

"Just trust me," he says.

Despite everything that's happened, I do.

I think I always have.

"Is it okay if I show them to you as we go?" he asks, and I nod, still half-dazed by this whole interaction.

So he unfolds the sheet of paper, revealing the first clue and holding it out to me.

"'The place where I tell you what happened over spring break,'" I read, giving him a lift of my eyebrows, glancing around this entirely unremarkable portion of the park.

"I went to see my dad."

"Oh." The word somehow comes out with three syllables. It's all I can say at first, giving him the space to elaborate.

"It was something I needed to do. To get a sense of closure," he says. "He wasn't what I expected, and yet somehow exactly what I expected? I thought he'd take digs at my clothes, my school, my hobbies. He did some of that, I guess, and he seemed different in some ways—or at least, he wanted me to think he was. Now that I've had more time to process it . . ." He trails off, shaking his head. "After it happened, I wasn't able to be a kid anymore. It felt like my childhood was over in one fell swoop. And yet seeing him . . . I felt just like a little kid again. Part of me desperately wanted his approval, and the other was still so, so angry at him." His features are pinched, as though he's reliving every moment of it in his mind right now.

"It's okay to still be angry at him." We've paused beneath a tall tree, its branches giving us relative privacy. "I hate that you had to go through any of this."

"Thank you," he says quietly. "I told him to stop the letters, for both me and my sister, and that this was the last time I was seeing him."

"And you feel good about that?"

He nods. Firm. "I do. I've been worried that you'd think of me not wanting him in my life as some kind of personal failing."

We haven't broached the physical barrier yet, but suddenly I can't stand the fact that we're not touching. So I reach for his hand, sinking into the instant relief of his fingers wrapping around mine. I didn't think you could miss holding hands with someone the same way you might miss kissing them, but *God*, Neil gives good hand. Soft but strong, warm and familiar.

"*No.* Not at all. He was never the father you deserved," I say, squeezing his hand, rubbing my thumb along his. "He should have given you the absolute world."

"I can see that now." He squeezes back as he toes the sidewalk with his shoe. "I should have told you about the letters when I got them. I hated keeping something from you. But I wasn't used to having someone as close as you, and I spent so many years hiding. And that's the absolute last thing I want to do with you."

"I'm glad you could tell me now."

Then he holds out the sheet of paper again. "Ready for another clue?"

We venture deeper into the park, past the tennis courts, and this time he reads it: "'The spot where I tell you what happened with my major.'"

"Neil," I say, starting to understand the "unconventional" piece of this scavenger hunt. "I get it. You don't have to explain it—I understand that these things change."

"No, but I want to," he says. "Of all the things I was afraid of, telling you I may not want to study linguistics anymore just seemed cruel when we both love words so much, and how they've been this connection between us. I guess I thought that if we didn't have Seattle, maybe words were second best."

I shake my head. "One, we will *always* have Seattle. And two . . . things change. You told me almost a year ago, in the Westview Library, that I wasn't the same person at eighteen as I was at fourteen. We're all allowed to change our minds—many, many times. If you want to study psychology, then I can't wait to hear all about it."

"The more I go to therapy, the more I realize maybe that's something I'd want to do. Be on the other side of the couch, that is." He accompanies this with the softest smile, and suddenly I can see it so clearly. "I haven't fallen out of love with words. But if one day I could help someone who might be just as afraid of what's going on in their own brain . . . I think I'd really enjoy that."

This admission that he's gone to therapy makes me so fucking *proud* of him, I could cry. "I think you'd be *amazing*. Just please promise you'll still tell me the meanings of things even though I didn't ask for them?"

"Oh, of course. I can't stop being a pretentious asshole that easily."

At that, I reach to nudge him, but he catches my hand, holds it tightly against his chest. His heart taps against my palm. "I missed you," he says, eyes heavy on mine. An undeniable sweetness. "That's not part of the scavenger hunt, but I needed to say it."

"I did too. Every day."

"And look at that, we just so happen to be right here at our next clue."

The place where I apologize. Again. For everything.

"Rowan," he continues, taking both my hands now. I can see him grow lighter with each clue. "I am so sorry. For about a hundred things, but mainly for the way I handled that night in New York. I had a chance to let you in, and all I did was shut you out. I thought it was something I had to go through alone."

"I wish I could have been there for you," I say quietly. "That you would have let me. But I understand why you felt like you couldn't. I don't have this perfectly figured out, either. I love you, and—"

The way he reacts to *I love you* makes me pause, as though he's been quietly starving for it but afraid to admit it. A vulnerable arch to his brows, a slight wobble of his chin.

"I love you," I repeat, infusing those words with all the care they deserve, "and I want to be in your world with you. No matter what's happening in it." Then I shake my head. "God. I just feel so foolish now. All those times I complained about my stupid class when you were going through real shit . . ."

"It's not stupid. I know you don't believe that." He's right, of course. "Hey. I always want to hear what you're going through. If it's big to you, it's big to me."

I nod, wondering how he manages to keep impressing me. Surprising me. My heart is already at his feet.

"You're sure you still want me?" he asks, his voice breaking.

"Because I thought—I worried that being here at school might make you realize you had options, and you didn't have to settle for me. And maybe you'd want someone more whole."

"When you told me about your dad on the last day of school—I didn't run. And I'm not running now." With our hands still linked, I take a step closer until there are only a few inches between us. "You are the bravest fucking person I know—the only thing that's changed is that I'm one hundred percent certain of that. You are extremely whole to me. Exactly the way you are."

He swallows hard. Tips his head downward. I want so badly to cover his mouth with mine, but I have a bit more to say first.

I let go of his hands, because the feel of his skin on mine is much too distracting. "We can get through this," I continue. "I want to cheer for the good stuff and hold your hand through the bad stuff. Even if it has to happen over video chat." Then I gesture to the list. "Do you mind if I add one? Because beneath this tree is where I tell you the other major reason I was struggling to write this year." Even though I'm not afraid of this anymore, I draw in a deep breath. "For a while, I thought I couldn't write romance because I was in love—that I had to be in pain to write that kind of yearning. And it terrified me, so I was terrified of telling you. It made me question the two of us for a moment, too—because we already had our big romantic moment, and then it was just going to be . . ." I trail off, struggling to find the words.

"All downhill from there?" Neil supplies, and I can't help laughing.

"I don't know! Maybe," I say. "But I know that's not true. Any of it. I was fighting my perfectionism this whole time, and I guess it might have also been a bit of burnout? You'll see when you open your mailbox, but what I wrote for you—it was *because* I was in love."

This whole year, I've been rediscovering what love really means when you're in it. The way I fell for Neil was a study in opposites: quickly and yet agonizing, over four years and then in a single night. The getting together was the easy part, even if it felt like the steepest uphill climb at the time. The staying together is the part that books and movies and love songs tend to ignore.

Everything I wrote before we started dating made romance feel magical, monumental. But with Neil, it's not always about those huge moments. It's the tiny details, the ones that remind you the other person is caring about you, even when you're not the best at caring for yourself.

The surprise mail and *thinking of you* texts and comfort of a favorite hoodie.

"We're going to keep changing. This isn't the first time." I think back to what Miranda said. Because both of us can grow without growing apart. "Maybe we won't change at the same time—we probably won't. But we can change together. We just have to give the other person space to do it. Not to become a completely different person . . . but to grow."

"I want that. To change with you sounds like the biggest fucking honor." He reaches for my hand again, and a choked sound slips from my throat. "I'm so sorry—again—that I was unsure. The next time I need to figure something out, because I'm guessing that wasn't my last personal crisis—I want you there with me. I want to do this with you. All of it."

"We can't keep living half-lives, though," I say, because we also need to establish this. "We can choose each other while also choosing ourselves. We have our separate lives and friend groups at school, and that's okay. We can't feel guilty about any of it." He nods emphatically. "We'll still talk all the time, obviously, but we have to trust that the other person still feels the same way, and if not, we'll promise to be open about it. If we're ever feeling doubt, we'll voice it as soon as we can."

"Rowan." He curls a strand of my hair around his index finger, and I swear he has never said my name quite like this before. "Is it absurd to talk about the future when we're this young? Maybe. But when we're committed to a long-distance relationship where the distance ends after four years—three years, we're twenty-five percent there—I think we have to. I don't know how I got so fucking lucky to find you in high school, and maybe it evens out with the bad luck of us ending up in two different cities. But that doesn't matter to me. You are worth it. You're worth every train ride and care package and middle-of-the-night phone call. Even if we lived on different sides of the world, I'd upend my sleep schedule on a regular basis just so I could hear your voice. Because if I'm being entirely truthful, which is the only thing I ever want to be with you . . . I think you might be it for me."

His words settle over me, "you are worth it" and "I think you might be it for me" tucking themselves inside my heart. *God*, I've never felt like this before, not even on the last day of school. Dazed, drunk, absolutely dizzy with love. I don't know how I ever thought our epic romantic moment had passed.

Neil McNair makes every single one of them feel that way.

"What else is on that list?" I ask, trying to blink away the tears burning behind my eyes.

"I'd rather make the rest up as we go."

In one swift motion, he pulls me against his chest, his mouth landing softly on mine.

We kiss in the middle of the Common on the sunniest day of the year so far, clutching at each other like we've given up on gravity. *I think you might be it for me, too*, I tell him with every sigh against his lips.

"You're still wearing this," he says, one hand buried in the hoodie fabric. A kiss lands on my cheekbone. The tip of my nose.

"Of course. How else was I supposed to make sure you came back for me?"

When we pull away, I taste salt and realize I've started crying. I rub at my eyes, fingertips coming away streaked with black.

"My makeup is probably all over my face, isn't it?"

He steps closer, licking the pad of his thumb before gently swiping it beneath my eyes, his other fingertips delicately balanced on my cheek. It is such a small, kind gesture that it renders me speechless for a moment, and I think I might start crying again.

It's starting to seem likely that one day I'll run out of words to describe how much I love him.

"There," he says, and kisses my forehead. "There actually is one more clue, by the way." He shakes out the sheet of paper, which he shoved into his pocket while we were kissing, and makes a show of repositioning his glasses as he squints down at it. "Sorry, it's a bit risqué, and it was probably a little optimistic at the time—"

This time, I snatch the paper out of his hands. "'The place where we make passionate love the rest of the day, depending on our emotional states and general energy levels.' That's got to be the Boston Tea Party Museum, yeah? Or maybe right in the middle of Fenway Park?" A snap of my fingers. "I've got it. Up against the statue of Paul Revere."

He laughs this pure and joyous sound, his arms settling around my waist. "Lead the way."

A REVISED LIST OF NEIL MCNAIR'S FAVORITE WORDS

- desenrascar: the act of figuring things out (Portuguese)
- tîeow: to wander in a carefree way (Thai)
- firgun: the act of taking genuine and sincere pride in someone else's accomplishment (Hebrew)
- amygdala: the brain's processing center for emotions (Latin)
- collective unconscious: a part of the mind that contains universal memories and impulses (English)
- Vorfreude: the joyful anticipation that comes from imagining a future pleasure; pre-joy (German)

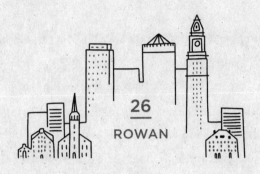

26
ROWAN

"I CAN'T BELIEVE it's really over."

Paulina and I survey what was once our room, bare beds and plain white ceilings and a distinct scent of all-purpose cleaner.

"You'll see me again in August," she says. We've decided to room together again. "Much more of me than this year, I hope." Then she grimaces. "And . . . I'll try to be a little cleaner. If you can believe it, my room at home is so much worse. With so many more penguins."

I fake a gasp. "Going to need photographic proof of that."

"As soon as I get back to Sacramento."

I take one final look at the room, this place where I studied and sobbed and slept. It was a good first home away from home, I decide. I'll miss it.

Finals went well—I didn't end the year with a perfect 4.0, which I thought might be devastating, but I got close. After the year it's been, that's more than good enough for me. Then Miranda pulled me aside after our last class and said she's thinking about taking on a research assistant in the fall for her next book. She's been focusing on teaching for a while, but she's finally ready to start writing again.

"I would love to," I said quickly, before realizing that she hadn't asked me yet.

"Great, because I was wondering if you might be interested." Then she wrapped me in a hug. "Have a wonderful summer, Rowan."

The rest of my goodbyes aren't too bittersweet, mostly because so many of them feel like beginnings, too. I submitted an article to the student magazine about long-distance relationships, which will run in their back-to-school issue, and my creative writing cohort had another Gazebo Night that left all of us in tears, stomachs aching from laughter.

I love it here, but I'm ready to go home.

Last week, I also had a long-overdue conversation with my mom. I told her Neil and I had made it through a difficult year, and that we'd emerged even more committed to this relationship.

"He's going to be in my life for a while," I said.

She waited a moment before responding. "I understand," she said. "And he's a good one—it's easy to see that. We just didn't want to see you get your heart broken. But as long as he makes you happy, we're glad to have him in our lives, too."

I assured her that he did, although there was no way I could properly describe the scope of it.

The past few weeks haven't been without their challenges, but with this renewed confidence we have in each other, we've managed to make time for phone calls and some late-night creative texting. Turns out, even if you have a natural aptitude for something, you can always get better.

Officially a psych major, Neil texted last week, and I couldn't have been more thrilled for him. *Slightly anticlimactic. Mostly paperwork. Not enough fanfare.* So I spent a solid minute sending him every celebration-related emoji on my phone.

ROWAN

first step to becoming dr. mcnair!

NEIL

Dr. McNair? That's a lot of school.

ROWAN

good thing that's your favorite thing in the world

NEIL

Well. Second favorite.

This time, when I try to peer into our future, all I see is possibility. This summer: Neil's mom's wedding, spending time with Kirby and Mara and Cyrus and Sean and Adrian, plus our families, of course. Instead of Europe, maybe a road trip down the West Coast, stopping at every independent bookstore along the way. But also, one day, an internship. A job and a career that I'm proud of. A chance to explore new countries with this person I love. Taking care of each other when we're sick, listening to each other through the easy parts and the hard parts, and everything in between.

The romantic part isn't just falling in love—I know that now. It's staying in love too.

We're going to stretch that happy ending as long as we can, even as we challenge each other and push ourselves to our limits, and then beyond that. Even as we change.

The one constant is the two of us, simply doing our best, the way that we always have.

Together.

I shut the door to my room, wheeling my suitcase into the hall just as my phone buzzes in my pocket.

NEIL

I'm about to board my flight. Love love love you. See you soon?

ROWAN

I'll be at your house in ten short hours!

I just hope seattle's ready for us.

NEIL

I think it always has been.

Epilogue

THREE YEARS LATER

HE KNOWS SHE'S out there in the crowd somewhere, but it's all a blur of violet.

Admittedly, the ceremony isn't the most thrilling. He has always been a rule-follower, though, so he tries his best to pay attention. There's an overwhelming swell of emotion in his chest amid all the pomp and circumstance, one he didn't expect, and he's grateful for it, even if endings are complicated.

When his name is called, he crosses the stage, accepts his diploma, tries not to trip over his gown. Glances toward the stands again—and *there*. He's certain he sees her now, on her feet and clapping, the sun glinting off her new short hair as she holds her hands to her mouth and yells out what must be his name. The same way he did at her graduation last week.

After he's exchanged hugs and posed for photos with everyone he's ever interacted with at NYU, plus at least a dozen he hasn't, she finds him on the field. His mom and stepdad and sister are close behind, but she gets to him first.

"Welcome to semi-adulthood," she says before throwing her

arms around his neck, kissing the space beneath his ear. Later, she'll assert that her school's commencement speaker was much more engaging than the one at his ceremony. A friendly competition, because that's something they've never quite outgrown.

At dinner, they answer about a hundred questions from his parents about their future plans, half of which they've answered already. Somehow, it's almost time for his sister to start thinking about colleges of her own, which seems outrageous because what is time.

Then, when everyone's deposited at their hotels for the night, the two of them hop the B train and make the increasingly familiar trek to Brooklyn.

The Flatbush walk-up isn't much to look at. Ivy snaking up the brick, a troublesome stair that the landlord swore he was going to get fixed before they moved in and then proceeded not to. It's their first apartment, and it is, in most basic terms, a shithole. But it's *their* shithole, with its closet-size bathroom and peeling linoleum, and that makes it perfect.

The centerpiece of the tiny living room is their overflowing bookshelf, standing proud in a sea of boxes they haven't unpacked yet.

"We might have to knock down this wall just to make room for all the books," she quips when she stumbles into a stack of Nora Roberts and quickly rights them.

"Not sure how our neighbors would feel about that."

There's a beautiful simplicity in that statement: *our* neighbors. They've only lived together for a week, since she graduated and hauled her stuff to New York, and yet the novelty of it refuses to wear off. She hopes it never does.

She drapes her cardigan over the back of a chair, docks her phone to play some music, and pats the Craigslist couch for him to come sit next to her.

Not yet.

It might be his graduation, but he has a surprise for her that he picked up from the frame shop last week, wrapped in brown paper.

She eyes it suspiciously when he digs it out from underneath their bed. "I thought we said we were going to make all decor decisions together. If this is *Star Wars* related, I might have to exercise veto power."

He swipes a hand through his hair, laughs. "Just open it."

As she tears away the paper, he watches her eyes land on the confession he wrote for her all those years ago on the last day of high school, now preserved behind glass. He blushed when the saleswoman definitely didn't try hard enough to avert her eyes, flicking over his eighteen-year-old penmanship. It's mounted alongside the piece of writing she mailed him freshman year of college, two precious artifacts of their relationship.

And now they'll get to see them every day.

"My heart is about to give out, I think," she says, dragging a fingertip along the walnut frame. His heart might be, too, seeing that expression on her face. "This is *beautiful*." She tugs him down by his tie, mouth meeting his in an urgent, dizzying kiss. They make sure the frame is safely out of reach before he slides his body on top of hers.

Monday will be her first day as a marketing assistant at a publishing house, one that's put out some of her favorite romance novels, and she'll continue to work on her own in her spare time. He'll take the next couple months off before starting grad school in the fall, the next step on his psychology journey. They finally made it to Europe last summer, a three-week backpacking trip that turned into four because they had to do just one more country. And then one more after that. They hiked the Swiss Alps, fed sheep in the Scottish Highlands, kissed on canal bridges in Amsterdam.

Even though their story that began eight years ago has now taken them across the world, the best part is when his face is the first thing she sees when she wakes up and the last thing she sees before falling asleep. The soft warmth of his gaze and the glow of his freckles, the way he loves her smile and her nose and her hair at any length—and never stops telling her.

One day, maybe he will get down on one knee and make all of this permanent. Or maybe she will; they've never cared much for traditional gender roles. Maybe it will be a day like today, attached to some major life event. Maybe it will be planned out months in advance, every detail meticulously crafted, or maybe it will be a quiet moment in bed, just the two of them, a whispered question and an emphatic, confident answer.

But tonight, they have this: the future they fought for and the promise they continue to make every single day.

A promise that started with two stuck-together pages in the back of a yearbook.

Acknowledgments

HOW CAN I wrap this up without getting emotional? These characters have been with me since 2017, and it's been the greatest gift to spend this extra time with them. When I wrote *Today Tonight Tomorrow*, I never planned on a sequel. And when it was released in the early months of the pandemic, I never imagined it would find the readership that it has. Maybe Neil has an untranslatable word in another language for this feeling, but I'm going to go with thankful beyond words. And that really only skims the surface.

I love all my characters, but Rowan and Neil have always felt different to me, holding heavier pieces of my heart than some of the others. The more time passed, the more you asked what happens after the last page. And slowly, slowly, the wheels started turning and I realized there might be more to their HFN ending on the last day of school.

My whole team at Simon & Schuster Books for Young Readers has been deeply supportive of Rowan and Neil from the beginning. Thank you to my editor, Nicole Ellul, whose enthusiasm always makes me eager to dive right in. Thank you, too, to Justin Chanda, Kendra Levin, Cassandra Fernandez, Samantha McVeigh,

Laura Eckes, Morgan York, Amanda Brenner, Sara Berko, Sarah Mondello, and Laura Bradford for helping make all of this happen.

A huge thank-you to Taryn Fagerness for getting *Today Tonight Tomorrow* into the hands of readers around the world.

To my agent, Elizabeth Bewley, and full-circle moments.

This book's epilogue would not exist without my husband, Ivan, who told me it absolutely needed one. He was right, and I can't imagine the book without it. Thank you for being the biggest fan of sequels.

Carlyn Greenwald, thank you so much for the suggestion that saved this book. Marisa Kanter and Sam Cheung, for letting me bother you about NYU, and Vanessa Kanter and Noah White, for the Emerson insight. Kelsey Rodkey, for reading the ugliest versions of my books and still telling me they're great. Doing this without any of you would be incredibly lonely.

Finally—and again—to the readers, the ones who've been there since the beginning and the ones who are only just now picking up Rowan and Neil's story. The way you've embraced these characters has quite literally changed my life. Rowan and Neil mean the world to me, and you have my immeasurable gratitude for this chance to give them a true HEA. With all of my heart, thank you.

About the Author

RACHEL LYNN SOLOMON is the *New York Times* bestselling author of *Today Tonight Tomorrow*, *The Ex Talk*, and other romantic comedies for teens and adults. Originally from Seattle, she's currently navigating expat life in Amsterdam, where she can often be found exploring the city, collecting stationery, and working up the courage to knit her first sweater. Connect with her on Instagram @rlynn_solomon or online at rachelsolomonbooks.com.

Turn the page for a sneak peek at
New York Times bestseller
See You Yesterday

"THIS HAS TO BE A MISTAKE."

I pull the extra-long twin sheets up over my ears and mash my face into the pillow. It's too early for voices. Much too early for an accusation.

As my mind unfuzzes, the reality hits me: *there's someone in my room.*

When I fell asleep last night after testing the limits of my dorm's all-you-can-eat pasta bar, which involved a stealth mission to sneak some bowls upstairs that were forbidden from leaving the dining hall, I was alone. And questioning my life choices. All those lectures about campus safety, the little red canister of pepper spray my mom made me get, and now there is a stranger in my room. Before seven a.m. On the first day of classes.

"It's not a mistake," says another voice, a bit quieter than the first, I imagine out of respect for the blanket lump that is me. "We underestimated our capacity this year, and we had to make a few last-minute changes. Most freshmen are in triples."

"And you didn't think it would be helpful for me to know that before moving in?"

That voice, the first voice—it no longer sounds like a stranger. It's familiar. Posh. Entitled. Except . . . it can't possibly belong to her. It's a voice I thought I left back in high school, along with all the teachers who heaved sighs of relief when the principal handed me my diploma. *Thank god we're done with her,* my newspaper advisor probably said at a celebratory happy hour, clinking his champagne glass with my math teacher's. *I've never been more ready to retire.*

"Let's talk out in the hall," the second person says. A moment later, the door slams, sending something crashing to the carpet.

I roll over and crack one wary eye. The whiteboard I hung on Sunday, back when I was still dreaming about the notes and doodles my future roommate and I would scribble back and forth to each other, is on the floor. A designer duffel bag has claimed the other bed. I fight a shiver—half panic, half cold. The tree blocking the window promises a lack of both heat and natural light.

Olmsted Hall is a freshmen-only dorm and the oldest on campus, scheduled for demolition next summer. "You're so lucky," the ninth-floor RA, Paige, told me when I moved in. "You're in the last group of students to ever live here." That luck oozes, sometimes even literally, from the greige walls, wobbly bookshelves, and eerie communal shower with flickering light bulbs and suspicious puddles *everywhere*. Home sweet concrete prison.

I was the first one here, and when two, three, four days passed without an appearance from Christina Dearborn of Lincoln, Nebraska, the roommate I'd been assigned, I worried there'd been a mix-up and I'd been given a single. My mom and her college room-mate are still friends, and I've always hoped the same thing would happen for me. A single would be another stroke of bad luck after several years of misfortune, though a tiny part of me wondered if maybe it was for the best. Maybe that was what the RA had meant.

The door opens, and Paige reenters with the girl who made high school hell for me.

Several thousand freshmen, and I'm going to be sleeping five feet from my sworn nemesis. The school's so huge I assumed we'd never run into each other. It's not just bad luck—it has to be some kind of cosmic joke.

"Hi, roomie," I say, forcing a smile as I sit up in bed, shoving my Big Jewish Hair out of my face and hoping it's less chaotic than it tends to be in the mornings.

Lucie Lamont, former editor in chief of the Island High School *Navigator*, levels me with an icy glare. She's pretentious and petite and terrifying, and I fully believe she could kill a man with her bare hands. "Barrett Bloom." Then she collects herself, softening her glare, as though worried how much of that conversation I over-heard. "This is . . . definitely a surprise."

It's one of the nicer things people have said about me lately.

I should be wearing something other than owl-patterned pajama shorts and the overpriced University of Washington T-shirt I bought from the campus bookstore. Medieval chain mail, maybe. An orchestra should be playing something epic and foreboding.

"Aw, Luce, I've missed you, too. It's been, what, three months?"

With one hand she tightens her grip on her matching designer suitcase, and with the other she white-knuckles her purse. Her auburn ponytail is coming loose—I can't imagine the stress my appearance has caused her, poor thing. "Three months," she echoes. "And now we're here. Together."

"Well. I'll leave you two to get acquainted!" Paige chirps. "Or—reacquainted." With that, she gives us an exaggerated wave and escapes outside. *If there's anything you need, day or night, just come knock on my door!* she said the first night when she tricked us into playing icebreaker games by making us microwaved s'mores. College is a web of lies.

I hook a thumb toward the door. "So *she's* great. Amazing mediation skills." I hope it'll make Lucie laugh. It does not.

"This is unreal." She gazes around the room, seeming about as impressed with it as I was when I moved in. Her eyes linger on the stack of magazines I shoved onto the shelf above my laptop. It's possible I didn't need to bring all of them, but I wanted my favorite articles close by. For inspiration. "I was supposed to have a single in Lamphere Hall," she says. "They totally sprung this on me. I'm going to talk to the RD later and try to sort this out."

"You might have had better luck if you moved in this weekend, when everyone was supposed to."

"I was in St. Croix. There was a tropical storm, and we couldn't get a flight back." It's wild that Lucie Lamont, heir to her parents' media company, can get away with saying these things, and yet I was the pariah of the *Navigator*.

Also wild: the fact that for two years, she and I were something like friends.

She sets her purse down on her desk, nearly knocking over one of my pasta bowls. Spinach ravioli, from the look of it.

"There's an all-you-can-eat pasta bar." I get up to collect the bowls and stack them on my side of the room. "I thought they would cut me off after five bowls, but nope, when they say 'all you can eat,' they aren't messing around."

"It smells like an Olive Garden."

"I was going for a 'when you're here, you're family' vibe."

I take back what I said about killing a man with her bare hands. I'm pretty sure Lucie Lamont could do it with just her eyes.

"I swear, I'm usually not this messy," I continue. "It's only been me for the past few days, and all the freedom must have gone to my head. I thought I was rooming with a girl from Nebraska, but then she never showed up, so . . ."

We both go silent. Every time I fantasized about college, my roommate was someone who'd end up becoming a lifelong friend. We'd go on girls' trips and yoga retreats and give toasts at each other's weddings. I'd be shocked if Lucie Lamont went to my funeral.

She drops into her plastic desk chair and starts the breathing techniques she taught the *Nav* staff. Deep inhales, long exhales. "If this is really happening, the two of us as roommates," she says, "even if it's just until they move me somewhere else, then we'll need some ground rules."

Feeling frumpy next to Lucie and her couture tracksuit, I throw on the knitted gray cardigan hanging lopsided across my own chair. Unfortunately, I think it only ups my frump factor, but at least I'm no longer shivering. I've always felt *less* next to Lucie, like when we teamed up on an article about the misogyny of our middle school's dress code for the paper we were convinced was the epitome of hard-hitting journalism. *By Lucie Lamont*, read the byline, our teacher elevating Lucie's status above my own, and in tiny type: *with Barrett Bloom*. Thirteen-year-old Lucie had been outraged on my behalf. But whatever bond had once existed between us, it was gone by the end of ninth grade.

"Fine, I'll bring back guys to hook up with only every other night, and I'll put this sock on the door so you know the room is occupied." I reach over to the closet, which is just wider than an ironing board, and toss her a pair of knee socks that say RINGMASTER OF THE SHITSHOW. Well—just one sock. The ninth-floor dryer ate one yesterday, and I'm still in mourning. "And I'll only masturbate when I'm positive you're asleep."

Lucie just blinks a few times, which could be interpreted as lack of appreciation for my shitshow sock, a visceral fear of the M word, or horror that someone would want to hook up with me. Like she didn't hear about what happened after prom last year, or laugh about it in the newsroom with the rest of the *Nav*. "Do you ever think before you speak?"

"Honestly? Not often."

"I was thinking more along the lines of keeping the room clean. I'm allergic to dust. No pasta bowls or clothes or anything on the floor." With a sandaled foot, she points underneath my desk. "No overflowing trash bins."

I bite down hard on the inside of my cheek, and when I'm quiet a moment too long, Lucie lifts her thin eyebrows.

"Jesus, Barrett, I really don't think it's too much to ask."

"Sorry. I was thinking before I spoke. Was that not the right amount of thinking? Could you maybe set a timer for me next time?"

"I'm getting a migraine," she says. "And god help me for needing to acknowledge this, but I feel like it's common courtesy not to . . . you know. Indulge in that particular brand of self-love when someone else is in the room. Sleeping or not."

"I can be pretty quiet," I offer.

Lucie looks like she might combust. It's too easy, really. "I didn't realize this was so important to you."

"It's a very normal thing to need to navigate as roommates! I'm looking out for both of us."

"Hopefully by next week, we won't be roommates anymore." She moves to her suitcase and unzips a compartment to free her laptop, then uncoils the charger and bends down to search for an outlet. Sheepishly, I show her that the sole outlets are underneath my desk, and we discover there's no way for her to type at her desk without turning the charger into a tightrope. With a groan, she returns to her suitcase. "I can only imagine what your priorities would have been as editor in chief. We're lucky we dodged that one."

With that, she unpacks a familiar wooden nameplate and sets it on her desk. EDITOR IN CHIEF, it declares. Mocking me.

It was ridiculous to think I had a chance at editor when asking people if I could interview them sometimes felt like asking if I could give them an amateur root canal.

It doesn't matter, I tell myself. Later today, I'll interview for one of the freshman reporter positions on the *Washingtonian*. No one here will care about the *Nav* or the stories I wrote, and they won't care about Lucie's nameplate, either.

"Look. I'm also not entirely enthused about this," I say. "But maybe we could put everything behind us?" I don't want to carry this into college, even if it's followed me here. Maybe we'll never be the yoga-retreat type of friends, but we don't have to be enemies. We could simply coexist.

"Sure," Lucie says, and I brighten, believing her. "We can put your attempt to sabotage our school behind us. We'll braid our hair and host parties in our room and we'll laugh when we tell people you gleefully annihilated an entire sports team and ruined Blaine's scholarship chances."

Okay, she's exaggerating. Mostly. Her ex-boyfriend Blaine, one of Island's former star tennis players, ruined his own scholarship chances. All I did was point a finger.

Besides—I'm pretty sure the Blaines of the world won in the end anyway.

"I just have one more question," I say, shoving aside the memory before it can sink its claws in me. "Is it uncomfortable to sit down?"

She looks down at the chair, at her clothes, forehead creased in confusion. "What?"

Lucie Lamont may be a bitch, but unfortunately for her, so am I.

"With that stick up your ass. Is it uncomfortable to—"

I'm still cackling when she slams the door.

ʊ ʊ ʊ

College was supposed to be a fresh start.

It's what I've been looking forward to since the acceptance email showed up in my inbox, holding out hope that a true reinvention, the kind I'd never be able to pull off in high school, was just around the corner. And despite the roommate debacle, I'm determined to love it. New year, new Barrett, better choices.

After a quick shower, during which I narrowly avoid falling in a puddle I'm only half certain is water, I put on my favorite high-waisted jeans, my knitted cardigan, and a vintage Britney Spears tee that used to be my mom's. The jeans slide easily over my wide hips and don't pinch my stomach as much as usual—this has to be a sign from the universe that I've endured enough hardship for one day. I've never been small, and I'd cry if I had to get rid of these jeans, with their exposed-button fly and buttery softness. My dark ringlets, which grow out as opposed to down, are scrunched and sulfate-free-moussed. I tried fighting them with a straightener for years to no avail, and now I must work with my BJH instead of against it. Finally, I grab my oval wire-rimmed glasses, which I fell in love with because they made me look like I wasn't from this century, and sometimes living in another century was the most appealing thing I could imagine.

It was an understatement when I told Lucie the freedom had gone to my head. Every other hour, I've been hit with this feeling that's a mix of opportunity and terror. UW is only thirty minutes from home without traffic, and though I imagined myself here for years, I didn't think I'd feel this adrift once I moved in. Since Sunday, I've been shuffling from one welcome activity to another, avoiding anyone who went to Island, waiting for college to change my life.

But here's something to be optimistic about: it doesn't seem to matter if you eat alone in the dining hall, even as I remind myself that I'm New Barrett, who's going to find some friends to laugh with over all-you-can-eat pasta and the Olmsted Eggstravaganza even if it kills her.

After breakfast, I cross through the quad, with its quaint historic buildings and cherry trees that won't bloom until spring, slackliners and skateboarders already claiming their space. This has always been my favorite spot on campus, the perfect collegiate snapshot. Past the quad is Red Square, packed with food trucks and clubs and, in one corner, a group of swing dancers. Eight in the morning seems a little early for dancing, but I give them a *you do you* tilt of my head regardless.

Then I make a fatal mistake: eye contact with a girl tabling by herself in front of Odegaard Library.

"Hi!" she calls. "We're trying to raise awareness about the Mazama pocket gopher."

I stop. "The what?"

When she grins at me, it becomes clear I've walked right into her trap. She's tall, brown hair in a topknot tied with UW ribbons: purple and gold. "The Mazama pocket gopher. They're native to Pierce and Thurston Counties and only found in Washington State. More than ninety percent of their habitat has been destroyed by commercial development."

A flyer is thrust into my hands.

"He's adorable," I say, realizing the same image is printed on her T-shirt. "That face!"

"Doesn't he deserve to eat as much grass as his little heart desires?" She taps the paper. "This is Guillermo. He could fit in the palm of your hand. We're hosting a letter-writing campaign to local government officials this afternoon at three thirty, and we'd love to see you there."

I'm annoyed by what *we'd love to see you there* does to my camaraderie-deprived soul. "Oh—sorry," I say. "It's not that I don't care about, um, pocket gophers, but I can't make it." My interview with the *Washingtonian*'s editor in chief is at four o'clock, after my last class.

When I try to hand her back the flyer, she shakes her head. "Keep it. Do some research. They need our help."

So I tuck it into my back pocket, promising her I will.

The physics building is much farther away than it looked on the campus map I have pulled up on my phone and keep sneaking glances at, even though every third person I pass is doing the same thing. It wouldn't be as bad if I were excited about the class. I've been planning to switch out—registration was a nightmare and everything filled up so quickly, so I grabbed one of the first open classes I saw—but damn it, New Barrett is a rule follower, so here I am, trudging across campus to Physics 101. Monday-Wednesday-Friday, eight thirty a.m.

My T-shirt is pasted to my back and my perfect jeans' perfect buttons are digging into my stomach by the time I spot the building. Still, I force myself to remain hopeful. This probably isn't an omen. I don't think omens are usually this sweaty.

In my pocket, my phone buzzes just as I'm walking up the front steps.

Mom: How do I love thee? Joss and I are wishing you SO MUCH LUCK today!

The text is time-stamped forty-five minutes ago, which I attribute to the campus's sketchy service, and there's a picture attached:

my mom and her girlfriend, Jocelyn, in the matching plush robes I gave them for Hanukkah last year, toasting me with mugs of coffee.

My mom's water broke in her sophomore year British Poetry class, and as a result, I was named after Elizabeth Barrett Browning, most famous for *How do I love thee? Let me count the ways.* College is where the two best things in my mom's life happened: me and the business degree that enabled her to open the stationery store that's supported us for years. She's always told me how much I'm going to love college, and I've held tight to the hope that at least one of these forty thousand people is bound to find me charming instead of unpleasant, intriguing instead of off-putting.

"I'm just so excited for you, Barrett," my mom said when she helped me move in. I wanted to cling to her skirt and let her drag me back to the car, back to Mercer Island, back to the HOW DO I LOVE THEE? cross-stitch hanging in my bedroom. Because even though I'd been lonely in high school, at least that loneliness was familiar. The unknown is always scarier, and maybe that's why it was so easy to pretend I didn't care when the entire school decided I wasn't to be trusted, after the *Navigator* story that changed everything. "You'll see. These four or five years—but please don't get pregnant—are going to be the best of your life."

God, I really hope she's right.

PHYSICS 101: WHERE EVERYTHING (AND EVERYONE) Has Potential, declares the PowerPoint. Beneath the text is an image of a duck saying "Quark!" I can appreciate a good pun, but two on one slide might be a cry for help.

The lecture hall is thick with the scent of hair products and coffee, everyone chattering away about their class schedules and the petitions they signed in Red Square. The professor is tinkering with a cluster of cables behind the podium. It's one of the larger auditoriums on campus and fits nearly three hundred students, though so far it's only a quarter full. Or three-quarters empty, but I'm trying not to be a pessimist this year.

I've never been a back-of-the-classroom person, despite how much some of my old teachers might have wished I'd been, so I climb the stairs and pause by an empty seat at the end of the fifth row, next to a tall, thin Asian guy glaring at his laptop.

"Hey," I say, still a little out of breath. "Are you saving this for anyone?"

"It's all yours," he says in a flat voice, without even looking up from his screen.

Yay, a friend.

I strip off my sweater and take out my computer, and I must make some amount of noise while doing this because the guy lets out a low hum of a sigh.

"Do you know the Wi-Fi password?" I ask.

Still no eye contact. Even the floppy collar of his plaid red flannel looks thoroughly annoyed by me. "On the board."

"Oh. Thanks."

Fortunately, I don't have any additional opportunities to bother him before the professor, a middle-aged Asian woman in a tangerine blazer with black hair cropped to her chin, switches on the podium mic. Eighty thirty on the dot. "Good morning," she says. "I'm Dr. Sumi Okamoto, and I'd like to welcome you to the spectacular world of physics."

I open a fresh Word doc and start typing. New Barrett, better Barrett, takes notes even for a class she's not sold on yet.

"I was nineteen when physics entered my life," she continues, her gaze flicking up and down the rows of the auditorium. "It was my last semester before I needed to declare a major, and I was stressed, to put it lightly. I'd never considered myself a science person. I started college entirely unsure of what I'd study, and my introductory class was life-changing. Something clicked for me in a way it hadn't in my other classes. There was poetry to physics, a beauty in learning to understand the world around me."

There's a clear sincerity in the way she speaks. The class is rapt, and I'm half compelled to stick it out.